Learning

some things happen for a
reason ...

a novel

Jane Lambert

'In this spirited extended monologue, Jane Lambert gives
us a backstage pass behind her character's angst and antics
and, with great humor and humanity, charts one woman's
journey not only towards the heights she dreams of but
into her heart as well.'
Ernest Thompson ~ *On Golden Pond*

This book is dedicated to
my mum, who believed I could write,
and to my dad, who told me to get on with it.

♥

With special love and thanks to my illustrator, Lesley Clavey-Lambert and RSL Design, to my editor, Doug Watts at JBWB for his guidance and good humour, to Kristian for his technical expertise, to my early readers, Clare Farrelly, Camilla Sacre-Dallerup, Claire Winsper, Ros Lambert, Sue Holderness, Jennie Madden and Rula Lenska, to my dad, who has been there for me through every page of this book, to my mum for being unlike Emily's, and to all my loving family for their unwavering support and encouragement in everything I do.

ACKNOWLEDGEMENTS

Grateful acknowledgement is made for permission to reprint lyrics from 'Make You Feel My Love', words and music by Bob Dylan Copyright © 1997 by Special Rider Music.

Thank you to the following for allowing me to reproduce copyrighted material:

The George Eliot Fellowship.

David Franzoni, author of *Gladiator* © 2000.

Excerpt from *Three Sisters* by Anton Chekhov, translation by Peter Carson, is reproduced by permission of Penguin Books Ltd.

The extract from *Miranda* by Peter Blackmore is used by the express permission of the publishers, Creselles Publishing Company Limited, Colwall.

Lines from *On Golden Pond* by Ernest Thomson by kind permission of Earl Graham at The Graham Agency, New York.

Author photograph: Sacre Images

CONTENTS

FOREWORD

Seventeen weeks on tour is a long time to share a dressing room with someone. But I knew Jane and I would get along just fine because we soon discovered we shared a love of chocolate — and writing. During our offstage time in *Calendar Girls* we'd tap away at our manuscripts, reading bits out loud to one another, while sipping tea — and sharing chocolate. I am so excited that Jane's novel is flying the nest and is to be shared with others. You can't help but fall in love with the calamitous Emily, who, at the age of 43, finds herself dressed as a pineapple promoting fruit juice or selling turbo steam cleaners on live TV in her quest to become an actress. For anyone who has ever considered taking a leap of faith in pursuit of personal fulfilment, *Learning To Fly* will not only inspire you, but make you laugh, cry and nod in recognition. So fasten your seat belts, reach for the tissues and the chocolate, it's going to be a bumpy ride.

Camilla Sacre-Dallerup ~ dancer, author, actress, presenter & motivational speaker.
Camilla's book, *Strictly Inspirational* is available from Amazon.

PROLOGUE

It is never too late to be what you might have been ~ George Eliot

Reasons for and against giving up the glitzy, glamorous world of flying:

Pros:
1. No more cleaning up other people's sick.
2. No more 2 a.m. wake-up calls, jet lag, swollen feet/ stomach or shrivelled-up skin.
3. No more tedious questions like, 'What's that lake/ mountain down there?' and 'Does the mile high club *really* exist?'
4. No more serving kippers and poached eggs at 4 a.m. to passengers with dog-breath and smelly socks.
5. No more risk of dying from deep vein thrombosis, malaria or yellow fever.
6. No more battles with passengers who insist that their flat-pack gazebo *will* fit into the overhead locker.
7. No more wearing a permanent smile and a name badge.
8. No danger of bumping into ex-boyfriend and his latest 'I'm-Debbie-come-fly-me'.

Cons:

1. No more fake Prada, Louis Vuitton or Gucci.
2. No more lazing by the pool in winter.
3. No more ten-hour retail therapy sessions in shopping malls the size of a small island — and getting paid for it.
4. No more posh hotel freebies (toiletries, slippers, fluffy bathrobes etc.).
5. Holidays (if any) now to be taken in Costa del Cheapo, as opposed to Barbados or Bora Bora.
6. No more horse riding around the pyramids, imagining I'm a desert queen.
7. No more ice skating in Central Park, imagining I'm Ali MacGraw in *Love Story*.
8. Having to swap my riverside apartment for a shoebox, and my Mazda convertible for a pushbike.

'Cabin crew, ten minutes to landing. Ten minutes, please,' comes the captain's olive-oil-smooth voice over the intercom. This is it. No going back. I'm past the point of no return.

The galley curtain swishes open — *it's showtime!*

I switch on my full-beam smile and enter upstage left, pushing my trolley for the very last time ...

'Anyheadsetsanyrubbishlandingcard? Anyheadsetsanyrubbishlandingcard? ...'

Have I taken leave of my senses? The notion of an actress living in a garret, sacrificing everything for the sake of her art, seemed so romantic when I gaily handed in my notice three months ago, but now I'm not so sure ...

Be positive! Just think, a couple of years from now, you could be sipping coffee with Phil and Holly on the *This Morning* sofa ...

Yes, Phil, the rumours are true ... I have been asked to appear on Strictly Come Dancing. *God only knows how I'll fit it around my filming commitments though.*

Who are you kidding? A couple of years from now, the only place you'll be appearing is the job centre, playing Woman On Income Support.

This follow-your-dreams stuff is all very well when you're in your twenties, or thirties even, but I'm a forty-year-old woman with no rich husband (or any husband for that matter) to bail me out if it all goes pear-shaped. Just as everyone around me is having a loft extension or a late baby, I'm downsizing my whole lifestyle to enter a profession that boasts a ninety-two percent unemployment rate.

Why in God's name, in this wobbly economic climate, am I putting myself through all this angst and upheaval, when I could be pushing my trolley until I'm sixty, then retire comfortably on an ample pension and one free flight a year?

Something happened, out of the blue, that catapulted me from my ordered, happy-go-lucky existence and forced me down a different road ...

'It's not your fault. It's me. I'm confused,' Nigel had said.

'I don't understand,' I said, almost choking on my Marmite soldier. 'What's brought this on? Have you met someone else?'

'No-ho!' he spluttered, averting my gaze, handsome face flushed.

'But you always said we were so perfect together ...'

'That's exactly why we have to split. It's too bloody perfect.'

'What? Don't talk nonsense ...'

'I don't expect you to understand, but it's like I've pushed a self-destruct button and there's no going back.'

'Self-destruct button? What are you talking about? Darling, you're not well. Perhaps you should get some help ...'

'Look, don't make this harder for me than it already is. It's time for us both to move on. And please don't cry, Em,' he groaned, eyes looking heavenward. 'You know how I hate it when you cry.'

I grovelled, begged him not to go, vowing I'd find myself a nine-to-five job so we could have more together time, swearing that I would never again talk during *Match of the Day* — anything as long as he stayed with me.

Firmly removing my hands from around his neck and straightening his epaulettes, he glanced at his watch, swigged the dregs of his espresso, and said blankly, 'Good Lord, is that the time? I've got to check in in an hour. We'll talk more when I get back from LA.'

'NO!' I wailed. 'You know very well that I'll be in Jeddah by then. We've got to talk about this *now*. Nigel ... Nigel ...!'

For three days I sat huddled on the sofa in semi-darkness, clutching the Minnie Mouse he'd bought me on our first trip to Disneyland, as if she were a life raft. I played Gabrielle's 'You Used to Love Me' over and over. I wondered if Gabrielle's boyfriend had dumped her without warning, leaving her heartbroken and bewildered, and the pain of it all had inspired her. If only *I* had a talent for song writing, but I don't, so I channelled *my* pain into demolishing a family-sized tin of Celebrations chocolates instead.

Cue Wendy, my best friend, my angel on earth. We formed an instant friendship on our cabin crew training course. This was cemented when she saved me from drowning during a ditching drill. (I'd stupidly lied on the application form, assuming that it didn't really matter if I couldn't swim, because if I were ever unfortunate enough to crash-land in the sea, there would surely be enough lifejackets to go round.)

'Look, hon, this has got to stop,' she said in an uncharacteristically stern tone, a look of frustration on her porcelain, freckled face. (As a redhead, Wendy has been religiously applying sunscreen since she first set foot on Middle Eastern soil as a junior hostess twenty years ago; whereas I would roast myself like a pig on a spit in my quest to look like a Californian beach babe.) 'Okay, so it's not a crime to scrub the toilet with his toothbrush, but who knows where that could lead? You've got to stop playing the victim before we have a *Fatal-Attraction* scenario on our hands.'

'Eight years, *eight years* of my life spent waiting for him to pop the question, and now he's moving out to "find himself". I think I'm entitled to be a little upset, Wendy.'

Prising Minnie out of my hands and hurling her against the wall, she straightened my shoulders and looked deep into my puffy eyes.

'I promise you that, in time, you will see you're better off without that moody, selfish, arrogant ...'

'I know you never thought he was right for me, but there is another side to him,' I said defensively. 'He can be the most caring and sweet man in the world when he wants to — and I can't bear the thought that we won't grow old together,' I sobbed, running my damp sleeve across my stinging cheeks.

'Come on now; take off that bobbly old cardie. I'm running you a Molton Brown bath, and you're going to wash your hair, put on your uniform and high heels, slap on some make-up and your best air hostess smile, d'you hear?' she said, pulling back the curtains. 'And while you're in Jeddah, I want you to seriously think about where you go from here.'

'But I want to be home when Nigel ...'

'You always said you didn't want to be pushing a trolley in your forties, and how you wished you'd had a go at acting. Well, maybe this is a sign,' she said gently, tucking a strand of greasy hair behind my ear. 'It's high time you did something for *you*. You've spent far too long fitting in with what Nigel wants.'

'It's too late to be chasing dreams,' I sniffed, shielding my eyes from the watery sunlight. 'And anyway, I just want things to go back to how they were. Where did I go wrong, Wendy? I should have made more effort. After all, he's a good-looking guy, and every time he goes to work there are gorgeous women half my age fluttering their eyelashes at him, falling at his feet. He can take his pick — and maybe he did,' I whimpered, another torrent of tears splashing onto my saggy, grey jogging bottoms.

'Get this down you.' Wendy sighed, shoving a mug of steaming tea into my hands as she frogmarched me into the bathroom. 'And don't you dare call him!' she yelled through the door.

Perhaps she was right; she usually was. She may be a big kid at heart, but when the chips are down, Wendy is the one you'd want on your flight if you were struck by lightning or appendicitis at thirty-two thousand feet.

For the last year or so, hadn't I likened myself to an aeroplane in a holding pattern, waiting until I was clear to land? Waiting for Nigel to call, waiting for Nigel to come home, waiting for Nigel to propose, waiting until Nigel felt ready to start a family?

Yes, deep down I *knew* she was right, but I was

6

scared of being on my own. Did this make me a love addict? If so, could I be cured?

Jeddah, Saudi Arabia

'*Hayyaa'ala-s-salah, hayya 'ala-l-falah* ...' came the haunting call from the mosque across the square, summoning worshippers to evening prayer. It was almost time to meet up with the crew to mosey around the souk — again. Too hot to sunbathe, room service menu exhausted, library book finished, alcohol forbidden, and no decent telly (only heavily edited re-runs of *The Good Life*, where Tom goes to kiss Barbara, and next minute it cuts to Margo shooing a goat off her herbaceous border), the gold market had become the highlight of my day.

Donning my abaya (a little black number that is a must-have for ladies in this part of the world), I scrutinised myself in the full-length mirror. No wonder Nigel was leaving me; far from looking like a mysterious, exotic, desert queen, full of eastern promise, it made me resemble a walking bin liner.

I read the fire evacuation drill on the back of the door and checked my mobile for the umpteenth time, then cast my eyes downwards, studying my toes. I know, I thought, giving them a wee wiggle, I'll paint my nails. It's amazing what a coat of Blue Ice lacquer can do to make a girl feel a little more glamorous, and less like Ugly Betty's granny.

As I rummaged in my crew bag for my nail varnish, there, stuffed in between *Hello!* and *Procedures To Be Followed in the Event of a Hijack*, was an old copy of *The Stage* (with another **DO <u>NOT</u> PHONE HIM!!** Post-it note stuck to it). Idly flicking through the pages, my eyes lit up at the headline:

DREAMS REALLY CAN COME TRUE.

Former computer programmer, Kevin Wilcox, 40, went for broke when he gave up his 50k-a-year job to become a professional opera singer. 'My advice to anyone contemplating giving up their job to follow their dream, is to go for it,' said Kevin, taking a break from rehearsals of La Traviata *at* La Scala*.*

That was my life-changing moment; an affirmation that there were other people out there — perfectly sane people, who were not in the first flush of youth either, but were taking a chance. *That's* what I'd do. I'd become an actress, and Nigel would see my name in lights as he walked along Shaftesbury Avenue, or when he sat down to watch *Holby City*, there I'd be, shooting a doe-eyed look over a green surgical mask.

'What a fool I was,' he'd tell his friends ruefully, 'to have ever let her go.' Hah!

But revenge wasn't my only motive. Faux designer bags and expensive makeovers were no longer important to me. I wanted the things that money can't buy: like self-fulfilment, like the buzz you get on opening night, stepping out on stage in front of a live audience. Appearing through the galley curtains, proclaiming that well-rehearsed line, 'Would you like chicken or beef?' just wouldn't do any more.

Inspired, I grabbed the telephone pad and pen from the bedside table, and started to scribble furiously.

1. Apply to ~~RADA/CENTRAL~~ any drama school that will have me.
2. Hand in notice.
3. Sign up with temping agencies and find part-time job.
4. Sell flat, shred Visa, store cards, cancel gym membership, and *Vogue* subscription (ouch!).

From: academy@ads.ac.uk
To: m.mouse@gmail.com
Subject: Audition

Dear Emily,
Following your recent audition, we of The Academy Drama School are pleased to offer you a place on our one-year, full-time evening course.
We look forward to meeting you again at the start of the autumn term, details of which are attached.
Sincerely,
Edward Tudor-Barnes
Principal

Whey hey! It was reckless, irresponsible and utterly mad, but I was tired of being sensible or doing things simply to please others. Ever since I'd played the undertaker in a school production of *Oliver!* I'd wanted to act. Okay, so I may be running twenty-five years late, but now nothing and no one was going to hold me back.

CHAPTER ONE
Looking for my Inner Dog

WHERE THE HELL AM I? Blinking, I prop myself up on my elbows and slowly take in the swirling, green, psychedelic wallpaper, and the assortment of quirky knick-knacks that clutter every surface. There's a collection of china figurines, including *Diana, Forever In Our Hearts.*

'This was at a high point in her short life,' Beryl, my landlady, had informed me tearfully, as she showed me the room. 'This was the moment when she took to the floor with John Travolta during her state visit to the White House.' She sighed, clutching the figurine to her ample bosom. There followed a moment of respectful silence, then pulling a hankie from her sleeve, she gave Di a little dust and returned her to her spot, next to the limited edition Smurf family, the matador, resembling a camp Action Man in white tights and cape, baby Jesus in swaddling clothes and the Eiffel Tower snow globe with built-in music box.

Oh, how I yearn for my minimalist Ikea!

My throat tightens and tears prick my eyes. Come

on now! Remember what the lady at the self-storage said: 'You're allowed access at any time,' she'd explained in a sympathetic tone of voice, as if consoling a distraught mother who'd just lost custody of her children. That's all right then, I tell myself, swallowing hard. Whenever I'm feeling low, I can pop along to the self-storage for some home-comfort therapy.

I swing my legs out of bed and Beryl's burnt-orange shag pile tickles my toes. How I miss the cool, clean feel of polished wood underfoot.

I tiptoe along the landing to the bathroom and there, lurking in the shadows, like a feline Mrs Danvers, is Shirley, Beryl's sluggish, obese, spoiled-rotten cat. Those speckled, almond-shaped eyes bore through me unflinchingly. Ever since I refused to open the back door for her and forced her through the cat-flap, I've had a chilling suspicion she's been plotting her revenge.

I enter the avocado-green bathroom and tease the mildewy, slimy, plastic shower curtain across the rusty rail. I turn the tap full on, and the shower head, about as much use as a watering can, emits a trickle that would leave your petunia bed gasping. A startled spider tries to make a break for it up the side of the bath, but slithers back down, leaving me to do a kind of naked *Riverdance* as it swirls around my feet.

What I'd give to be languishing now in my sparkling-white, Italian-tiled bathroom, complete with walk-in power shower and scented candles.

Come on, don't be such a wuss! Stay focused. Tonight's drama class will reaffirm that all this hardship is going to be worth it. It will. It *will*.

In the meantime, I have an appointment at Trusty Temps Agency. After all, I can't carry on living off the paltry proceeds from the flat. This is supposed to be my emergency money, to support me after the course, during those 'resting' periods, in between theatre and TV contracts, daahling.

'Do you have Power Point?' lisps the girly recruitment consultant, running her French-manicured nail down my brief CV.

'No.'

'Excel?'

'Excel? Yes ... I mean no.' (Lying = v. bad idea, Emily.)

'I see ... Word?'

'I think so ... I know how to send an email. And ... I can do attachments ...'

'Typing speed?'

'Not bad ... for two fingers,' I mumble.

'Which switchboards have you used?'

'Erm ... none,' I whisper, biting my bottom lip.

Uncrossing her long, slim legs, she lets out a heavy sigh, and forcing her glossy lips into a smile, says with a hint of superiority, 'I'm afraid most of our positions are for people with these skills — but we'll keep you on file.'

'Sure,' I say with a careless toss of my head, trying to look self-assured and unconcerned, whilst inside I'm feeling like a technophobic old bat.

I stuff my CV in my bag, pull on my coat and beret, then take the walk of shame from the back office, through the reception area, past all the busy, busy consultants, furiously tapping their keyboards, whilst holding terribly important conversations on the phone.

Now what? It's starting to dawn on me with scary clarity that two decades of working in a metal tube has not armed me with the necessary skills to survive in the business world. I'm a dab hand at putting out a fire, boiling an egg to perfection at altitude, or serving hot liquids in severe turbulence without spilling a drop, but what use is all that in the wired-up world of desktop, data entry and mail-merge?

How naïve to think I could just walk into another job! Oh God, what is to become of me? Am I destined for a life of Pot Noodles and Primark? What am I going to do? There's rent to pay and my Visa bill, and now drama school fees. What in God's name am I going to do?

I trudge along the rain-soaked street. I can't face returning to Knick Knack Corral just yet. I turn the corner, and there, like a safe harbour in a storm, are the twinkling lights of Starbucks beckoning me in. Yes, I know, I know I shouldn't be splashing out £3.20 on a caffeine fix, but I am in the grip of a major confidence crisis, and a large caramel cream Frappuccino is cheaper than therapy.

Sinking into a squashy sofa, I take a sip of my coffee, draw a deep breath and take out my notebook and pen.

<u>Potential Job List:</u>
1. ~~P.A./Receptionist/ Switchboard Operator?~~
2. Waitress?
3. Shop assistant?
4. Tour guide?
5. Cleaner?
6. Telesales?
7. Dog walker?
8. Market researcher?

Hmm. None of the above fills me with inspiration, but in my current state, I'd gladly don a baseball cap and serve greasy burgers from a catering van at a football stadium.

'Are your gums sore, my angel, is that why you're a grouchy girl today? Mummy make it better. Mwah,

mwah.'

My gaze is drawn to the next table, where a group of yummy mummies in Cath Kidston, accessorized with matching designer tot, sip cappuccino and cluck and coo ...

'I was just warming his milk, and I swear I heard him say "Mama". Didn't you, Toby? What a clever boy! Yes, you are. You're Mummy's special boy.'

My eyes mist over, and I am consumed by a sudden yearning to belong to that members-only club; to have a little person to dress up in spotty dungarees, to romp around the park with, and to read *Peppa Pig* to.

Next to them is a table of young, svelte businesswomen, sipping their skinny lattes.

'Let's go in there and show them what we're made of, girls. Here's to new clients!'

'New clients!' they all cheer, chinking coffee cups and giggling.

Busy people with busy lives ... children to pick up from school, meetings and post-natal classes to attend, deadlines to meet. And me? No job, no prospects, no daily routine ...

~~9. Wife and mother~~
~~10. High-powered businesswoman~~

... I'd go hungry, I'd go black and blue
I'd go crawlin' down the avenue
No, there's nothin' that I wouldn't do
To make you feel my love ... filters Adele's soulful voice through the speakers.

Well, I can either sit here crying into my coffee, or take hold of the reins, buckle down and find myself work.

I know I'm hardly a suitable candidate for *The Apprentice*, but surely there must be a vacancy

14

somewhere for a well-travelled waitress with first aid and fire-fighting skills, who can say 'Welcome to London' in six different languages?

The earlier drizzle has now turned to torrential rain, so I dive for cover under the candy-striped awning of Galbraith's The Jewellers. Row upon row of diamond rings blink at me through the glass. My chin starts to quiver and a huge tear sploshes down my cheek. Will I ever experience the thrill and romance of someone proposing on bended knee, before I reach the age of Hip-Replacement-Boyfriend? I had such high hopes when I was five, dressed in my mum's white nightie and high heels, clutching a bunch of buttercups in my grubby fingers, an old net curtain and crown of daisies on my head.

Through the blur of my tears I squint at a sign in the window:

RETAIL CONSULTANT REQUIRED
APPLY WITHIN

Before I have time to talk myself out of it, I press the buzzer ...

Miss June Cutler, manageress of Galbraith's Jewellers, leans across the gleaming glass counter and peers at me over her half-moon glasses.

'Ideally, we are looking for someone with retail experience in the jewellery trade, as many of our items are *very, very* valuable,' she whines in a Sybil-Fawlty voice.

'I may not have worked in a shop as such,' I retort, 'but I have sold duty free goods, and so I am ... *au fait* with handling money and expensive items.' (Working in the first class cabin has taught me to always have a little, posh phrase up my sleeve — preferably French — when dealing with supercilious, la-di-da people.)

'A bottle of Blue Grass eau de toilette is hardly a Rolex watch, is it?' she says, with a taut smile of her thin, aubergine lips. I feel the hairs on the back of my neck bristle.

'We didn't just sell perfume and alcohol, but luxury goods as well; like gold and silver necklaces and designer watches: Cartier, Dunhill ... and ... and...'

Bloody typical! There was a time when I could have won *Mastermind* with 'The World's Leading Designers' as my specialist subject, but just when I'm under the spotlight, the names escape me.

Miss Cutler, meanwhile, is scrutinising me as if I've just stepped off the set of some Tim Burton scary movie; then I catch sight of my reflection in the antique, gilt-framed mirror opposite, and do a double take. What the ...? I have blood-red rivulets trickling down my face. Oh my God, the heavy rain must have caused the dye from my beret to run! (£3 from Primark, what do you expect, Emily?) I pull out a length of loo paper from my pocket, and a chewing gum wrapper falls to the floor.

There's a stony silence. Here it comes, another helping of 'I'll keep you on file' — not sure I can handle two rejections in one day.

'Very well,' she says with a sigh, holding out my damp, crumpled CV, like it's a snotty hankie. 'I have been left in the lurch rather, so you can start tomorrow at nine — sharp.'

'Thank you,' I reply, vigorously shaking her hand, sending the charms on her bracelet jingling.

Giving me a final once-over, she says pointedly, 'Just one more thing — dress code here is smart.'

'Bib, bob, bab, bub, bib. Rubber baby, rubber baby, rubber baby. Mmmaaa, mmmaaay, mmmeee, mmmow, mmmooo. Laaa, laaay, leee, low, looo. Did,

16

dod, dad, dud, did ...'

To the casual passer-by peering through the window of The Academy, we must look like we're auditioning for a part in the next series of *Mr Bean*; but apparently contorting one's face grotesquely and making ridiculous sounds is how an actor prepares. Seriously.

'Taking a deep intake of breath, fill those lungs with air, like a balloon. Now pushing the diaphragm in and out, I want you to pant like a dog.'

Pant like a dog? Oh no, purleeease, no. How much more humiliation can a grown woman take? I came here to learn to be a serious, classical actress, not a clown.

'This exercise strengthens the diaphragm, loosens the facial muscles and helps your voice to develop,' says Portia, as if reading my mind.

As the *Evening Standard*'s Most Promising Newcomer of 1980 (I Googled her), Portia Howard obviously knows her stuff, but I'm still not convinced.

'No, no, no!' she says, swooping down on me, her dangly earrings tinkling like wind chimes. 'I don't want to see any movement *here*,' she says, firmly tapping my shoulders. 'It must all come from down *here*,' she continues, as she prods my diaphragm.

'Now try again. Fill those lungs ... that's it, and let out short, sharp breaths. I want to *feel* that diaphragm bouncing. There, you see, you've got it!'

I'm chuffed I've got it, but all the same, I can't help feeling I sound like a cross between a chat-line hostess and a woman in labour.

'Remember, as well as the voice, the body is an actor's tool. This next exercise is a good warm-up before an audition or performance. It's called The Wet Dog Shake. Okay, everyone, let's imagine you've just come bounding out of the sea, and now you're going to shake yourselves dry,' she says, as she drops to her knees, her long, tapered fingers splayed out in front of her on the grimy floorboards. 'Let's start from the top with the nose (she starts wiggling her nose), now the head, tongue, the shoulders (she shimmies her shoulders), legs ... come on ... bark if you wish ... go for it ... release your inner dog!'

James, Mr Respectable-Bank-Manager by day, catches my eye, and we exchange an incredulous look. Sally, the mousey, bespectacled, hitherto rather timid accountant has hurled herself into the exercise with rather more gay abandon than is necessary, tongue hanging out of the corner of her mouth, resembling not so much a shaking dog, as someone having stuck a wet hand in the toaster.

'Come on, you can do better than that!' pants Portia. 'Instead of huddling together like a pair of sniggering school kids, James, Emily, follow Sally's lead. Let yourselves go! What are you afraid of? Making fools of yourselves? If you want to be actors, you have to learn to let go of your inhibitions. I want to *see* those tails wagging. I want to *feel* that sea spray *flying* off your coat. Wag that tail. Shake, shake, shake yourselves nice and dry. Wag, wag, wag. Come on ...!'

A few nervous titters echo around the room, but then slowly, tentatively, like lemmings, we all follow Portia's lead, and our performing arts class becomes less *Fame*, and more *Geriatric Gym, The Musical*.

'See, that's not so bad, is it? Now roll onto your backs and kick those legs high in the air!' she cries, her pewter bangles clinking like rigging against a sail mast.

Is she barking mad, I wonder (excuse the pun), or is she just making fun of us? I mean, is this what *real* actors do? Somehow I can't quite picture Dame Helen kicking her legs high in the air and panting like a dog prior to a performance.

'This is ridiculous,' blurts out Poppy, whose every sentence ends with a question mark. 'Basically, I don't hold with all this horseshit.'

Her strained, cut-glass tones echo around the room as we all stare at her bug-eyed, legs suspended in mid-air.

Rising to her feet and smoothing her skinny jeans, she continues, 'Release your inner dog? What has all this pretentious rubbish got to do with being an actor? I don't believe for one moment that Keira Knightley has *ever* had to crawl around a filthy floor on all fours, pretending to be a dog, so I don't see why I should.'

'Good point, Poppy,' says Portia calmly. 'Keira has probably never done The Dog Shake, and you certainly don't have to if you don't wish. But exercises like this teach you to be more fluid in your movement, to release blockages in energy, so that you can express emotion through your body — as well as build up the stamina to cope with eight shows a week, without ... '

'Yah, but I'm basically not interested in theatre. I plan to go straight into TV and films. I don't know about the rest of you,' she says, scanning the class, perky nose in the air, 'but I want to learn about camera technique, about close-ups and continuity, and ... giving the director exactly what he wants ....'

'Whoa, whoa, whoa,' says Portia, holding up her hands. 'My class isn't about showing you a short-cut to fame and fortune — if I knew that, do you think I'd be here now?' she says with a half-laugh.

'Obviously not,' Poppy fires back. 'But *I* have no intention of ending up a fifty-something has-been, teaching drama in a damp and dreary basement for the rest of my life.'

Catching her breath and her composure, Portia says with a little, enigmatic smile, 'Good for you. But what this "fifty-something has-been" can teach you is how to bring truthfulness and honesty to your story telling. I can arm you with the right tools to *survive* in this dog-eat-dog, heart-breaking, wonderful business; talent alone is not enough. You need humility, patience, harmony ...'

With an unabashed toss of her bouncy, shampoo-commercial hair, Poppy Hope-Wyckhill collects her D&G tote bag, places her jacket carefully around her shoulders, and struts out of the grubby basement of The Academy on her patent wedge boots, in search of celebrity and riches elsewhere.

'So if there are any more of you who are here just because you want to see your faces on the big screen or the cover of *Hello!* and are not willing to commit to hard work, sacrifice, and to embracing new challenges, then this is not the place for you,' says Portia, directing her words at each and every one of us in turn. 'Don't be afraid to speak up.'

The clock ticks loudly, a distant underground train rumbles below, feet pound the floor above, as the muffled strains of some big musical number vibrate through the cracked ceiling.

According to Wikipedia, Portia has worked at The Royal Shakespeare Theatre, The National, and even been in a Merchant Ivory film. So why is she here? Is it the case that after a certain age the parts dry up? What hope is there then for me? I'm a bit ashamed to ask this, but is there an element of truth in Poppy's outburst? I too am beginning to secretly wonder what all this inner dog stuff has got to do with acting, but am scared to admit it, even to myself. There's too much at stake now to even contemplate giving up.

'Right,' says Portia enthusiastically, rummaging in

her well-worn, Mary-Poppins bag, 'before we start working on audition pieces, we're going to spend this week exploring our emotions. Acting is, after all, about drawing on your own experiences and using them truthfully, in order to bring whatever character you're portraying to life.'

Producing a small, brightly coloured ball she continues, 'This next exercise is called Fling the Feeling. As you throw the ball to the next person, I want you to call out an emotion, and express it in a way that conveys its meaning. I'll start. *Passion!*' she purrs in a husky, breathy voice, à la Joanna Lumley.

'Joy!'

'Shame!'

'Guilt!'

'Sadness!'

Shit, that's what I was going to say.

'Envy!'

'Jealousy!'

The ball's heading this way ... ooh, I can't think straight ... Oh, God, oh, God, this is so embarrassing ... what *am* I going to say?

'... PANIC!' I squeal.

'You bastard!' I mutter. 'How can you let me down like this?' As fast as I pump the air in, the faster it is released with a loud *hisssss*. I knew I should have caught the bus. Fired on my first day. Great!

I fumble in my voluminous bag for my mobile and dial Galbraith's number.

You have used all your calling credit, comes the unsympathetic, recorded voice. Heavy rain starts to pound the pavement. Shit! Right, that's it! Wielding the pump, I unleash my pent-up anger and frustration on my bike, much to the sly amusement of early

21

morning commuters, as they scuttle to the station, clutching their take-away coffee, ears wired to iPods and hands-free.

Squelching and wheezing my way up the hill, I make a mental note to a) learn how to mend a puncture and b) invest in waterproofs.

'I'm *so* sorry I'm late, Miss Cutler,' I pant. 'I would have got here quicker if I hadn't had to wheel my bike and I wanted to call you, but my mobile was out of credit and ...'

'You'd better clean yourself up,' she says, her steely gaze resting on my oil-stained hands. 'And may I remind you, Emily, you are on probation. If you are serious about working here, then you had better pull your socks up.'

Blimey, I haven't felt like this since fourth form, when I was hauled up in front of the headmistress for not wearing regulation knickers at gym.

'The stock room looks like a bomb's hit it,' she snarls. 'Health and Safety are visiting next week, so I'd appreciate it if you could tidy the place up, and ensure the fire exits are kept clear.'

'Sure,' I say in a sugary sort of way, jaw clenched.

(Another tip gleaned from years spent bowing to the whims of rude passengers: whatever verbal abuse flies your way, DO NOT rise to the bait. Respond in an overly polite manner, and it will annoy the hell out of your antagonist.)

As I chain my bike to the railing, I spy them through the dimpled glass, sitting in our favourite spot, by the open fireplace, and I smile inwardly.

My life may be starting to resemble a black comedy, but with a supporting cast like mine, I can just about deal with the fact that I've got Cruella De

Vil for a boss, and that my acting dream is fast turning into a horror movie.

With abundant hugs and vats of wine, we gaggle of five have cried, advised, sympathised and propped one another up through divorce, cancer and single parenthood, so what's a mere mid-life career crisis and a broken heart in the grand scheme of things?

'Darling!' squeals Wendy, jumping up and wrapping me in an Eternity-fragranced hug. 'We've missed you. How are you? You look ... fantastic.'

'I don't,' I snort, pulling at my fluorescent-yellow sash, suddenly conscious of my bare, rain-washed face and baggy, unflattering clothes.

'Come and sit down,' she says, patting a space on the monk's bench between her and Céline.

'*Chérie!*' says, Céline, kissing me four times, as is customary in her native Paris. She is French 1960s' Vogue personified; translucent skin, sculpted cheekbones and a natural, wide-mouthed smile (something we see little of nowadays).

'Well, how's it going?' asks Wendy eagerly, extricating my arms from my dripping wet anorak.

'Fab,' I say with forced gaiety. They both look at me searchingly. 'Well, no, actually ... awful.'

I feel someone tug my hastily tied, damp ponytail. I spin round, and there, brandishing a bottle of Sauvignon, is Rachel.

'Hey, how's our aspiring actress?' she says, stooping down to kiss me, her silky, chestnut hair tickling my cheek. 'Let's take a look at you,' she says, sloshing wine into my glass, as she studies me with her perfectly made-up eyes.

'You look more relaxed than when we last met, not long after you and Ni...'

'Ahem! To new beginnings!' Wendy says quickly, raising her glass.

'New beginnings!' we chorus, happy to be together once more.

'You're missing all the fun, you know,' says Wendy sarcastically. 'The new first class service means the darlings can now eat *whatever* they want *when* they want; one minute you're serving Chicken Chasseur to 5B, then 1E is asking you for boiled eggs and toast, whilst the group at the bar are crying out for crème de menthe frappé and canapés. Gaah!'

I pretend to wince, but the way I feel right now, I'd gladly serve a Jumbo-load of raucous, demanding passengers single-handedly every day until I'm sixty-five, if it meant having my old life back.

'Now, who's for some houmous and warm pitta bread?' says Wendy, heading for the bar.

Turning to Céline, I ask dutifully, 'How's Mike?'

'On a nine-day Sydney/Melbourne,' she says, letting out a wistful sigh. 'But he's coming straight from the airport to stay at the flat for two days when he gets back,' she adds quickly, face lighting up.

I shoot her a knowing glance over the rim of my glass.

'Don't look at me like that,' she says in that to-die-for accent of hers.

'Like what?'

'That you-are-wasting-your-time look.'

I open my mouth to speak, but close it again and swirl my wine around my glass, eyes down.

'He's leaving after Christmas ... next year,' she says, voice falling away.

'Why not this year, Céline? How many more Christmases must you wait?'

'The twins have their exams this year and it's his wife's parents' Golden Wedding next June. So, I must be patient.' She smiles weakly, fixing my gaze from under the eyebrow-brushing fringe of her sleek, ebony bob.

Mike is a classic case of how a uniform with four gold bands and a peaked cap can transform a balding, beer-bellied, unsexy, middle-aged man into a *fairly* attractive, dapper specimen — hardly Mr Darcy material, but a darn sight more pleasing on the eye than off-duty-Mike, believe me, with his high-waisted trousers and Concorde novelty socks.

'It's just that I know how important a husband and children are to you, and I worry that by the time he leaves — *if* he leaves — it will be too late.'

'*C'est la vie.*' She shrugs. 'Nothing in life is guaranteed ... *rien du tout.* You were with a single man and still it didn't work out the way you hoped.'

Tilting her head, she squeezes my hand and says softly, 'I am so sorry about Nigel.'

'Ah well, it's probably for the best,' I say half-heartedly, fighting back the tears.

Faye comes over from the far end of the table, perches on the edge of the bench, swivels round to face me and says warmly, 'Darling, it's *so* good to see you.' She brushes aside my wet fringe and plants a warm kiss on my forehead.

'How's Tariq?' I enquire, anxious for news of my beloved godson.

'He's started school and loves it,' she says, beaming, as she always does at the mention of his name.

Is it only six years ago that we sat here, in this very spot, by the fireplace, toasting Faye's new, glamorous life in Dubai? ...

'You've only known him a few months, Faye,' we'd said with a mixture of excitement and consternation. 'Are you sure you're doing the right thing?'

'I know it's a gamble. But it feels right.' She'd smiled, stroking her little bump, the huge rock on her finger catching the light from the fire. 'And now Junior's on the way, I just know it's fate. I've waited a long time for my dashing prince to come along, and I'm lucky he found me in the nick of time, before I'm faded and forty-five, and my biological clock comes to a grinding halt.'

'Ooh, it's like *Lawrence of Arabia* and *Love Actually* all rolled into one,' I'd said, swooning back into the sofa.

The 'fairytale' began one New Year's Eve in the Gulf ...

Determined not to spend yet another Hogmanay in pj's and a comfy cardie, getting slowly sozzled, whilst watching repeats of *Only Fools and Horses* — either that, or at some dire party, being groped at midnight by a total stranger with rubber legs and beery breath — we requested the same trip, packed our sparkly frocks and headed off to the sun.

So there we were, dressed to kill, huddled around the buffet table by the swimming pool, retching and spluttering into our napkins like a bunch of ladettes, having discovered the grey stuff we'd just devoured was in fact lambs' brains, when out popped a tall, swarthy, linen-suited stranger from behind the swan ice-sculpture.

'Ladies, ladies, ladies! This is a great delicacy in my country,' he'd said with mock indignation and a mischievous grin.

We didn't move or speak for several seconds, so mesmerised were we by this smouldering vision of unexpected, exotic gorgeousness — think Antonio Banderas.

'Sahir,' he'd said in a low voice, bowing slightly, then chivalrously kissing our hands in turn. His long-lashed, melted-chocolate eyes held your gaze, making you feel like you were the only woman at the party —

correction — on the planet. 'I am the owner of the hotel.' Signalling the waiter, he then called authoritatively, 'Champagne for the ladies!'

Up until that moment I had never believed in love at first sight, but as the strains of Lionel Richie's 'Hello' floated across the shimmering pool, you could almost hear Cupid's arrow whistle past and hit its targets, as surely as if Oberon himself had squeezed some magic potion in their eyes.

Backlit by the orangey-red, evening sunlight, Faye positively dazzled. The sequins in her dress and the diamond combs in her golden hair glittered and sparkled, and Sahir fell hopelessly under her spell. He propelled her to the dance floor, and that was it: the start of a glamorous, heart-fluttering, pulse-quickening Mills-&-Boon-style love affair.

Faye begged and shamelessly bribed crew scheduling with home baking and fresh produce from her mum's allotment, swapping her rostered flights for Dubai night-stops. She'd be met at the airport by a chauffeured, air-conditioned Mercedes, wined and dined at the best hotels, and showered with expensive jewellery. We lived our romantic fantasies through Faye.

Funny, isn't it, how a girl's overwhelming desire to be scooped up by a dark, brooding Mr Darcy in breeches and a white, floppy shirt, may cause her to misplace her common sense and ignore the sirens screaming in her ears; because, you see, for all his good looks and charm, this knight turned out to be a villain in disguise.

Whilst eager to embrace her new culture, Faye struggled with the language, the loneliness, the heat and the homesickness.

'Strife and sacrifice are good,' her new husband had told her coldly. 'This teaches discipline and humility.'

'But I never see you. If you're not at the hotel, you're either "on business" in Abu Dhabi or Bahrain. Then when you *are* at home, you're tired and irritable and don't have time for me and Tariq,' she'd cried, painfully aware that she sounded like the archetypal nagging wife.

'My mother and sisters, they help with the boy. What is wrong with you?' Sahir sniped at her. 'You are spoiled and ungrateful.'

She loathed the way he always referred to Tariq as 'the boy', like some fusty, Dickensian father, and she hated the way his mother and older sisters took over the childcare and the running of the house, jabbering and whispering to one another, as if she were invisible.

'Why can't it just be the three of us, Sahir?' she'd once said to him tentatively.

'In my country we look after the family. Will you see them thrown out onto the street?' he'd yelled.

'I don't mean ...'

'Enough! I will hear no more of this,' he said, gripping her arm and shaking her, those same eyes that once made her heart melt, now angry and cold.

What had happened to the bubbly, self-assured, fun-loving, golden girl? Where had she gone? Faye realised she was totally miscast in the role of the subservient, dutiful wife and daughter-in-law. There was only one thing for it: to flee her gilded cage, taking her baby chick with her.

The story of their clandestine escape in the dead of night could have been plucked straight from the pages of an edge-of-the-seat John Grisham thriller.

'Tariq is my son and he belongs here. I have contacts in high places in London. Remember this.'

Her ex-husband's threats regularly terrorise her

mind during those drifting moments before sleep seizes control — usually in some crew hotel thousands of miles away from home.

I hope with all my heart that this time my gut instinct is wrong, but although Faye has been granted custody, I have a nasty feeling we haven't seen the last of Sahir.

Nevertheless, despite a string of seriously disastrous relationships between us, we all remain silly, romantic fools, firm in the belief that Mr Right may yet appear; ETA as yet unknown. It's not as if we're expecting some Greek god to come along, but even one of the Grecian-2000 variety would do very nicely, thank you.

That is all but Rachel; she called off the search some fifteen years ago, when she married her childhood sweetheart, Dave, who is a policeman. They keep our belief in love and romance alive. Yet behind that happy, smiley exterior lurks a deep sadness, a grief, which she hides very well; we all know it's there, lying just beneath the surface, and so we are careful never to speak of it. But sometimes when she thinks no one is looking, a shadow flickers across her face, and you may momentarily catch a glimpse of the anxious, heartbroken Rachel, and then she is gone, as the mask is raised once more.

The town hall clock is chiming twelve by the time we totter out onto the pavement and giggle our nighty-nights and must-do-this-more-oftens. I jam on my cycle helmet and pedal hard, head bent against the needle-sharp rain.

An aeroplane drones overhead, its taillight blinking in between the squally clouds. I find myself gazing wistfully at it. My mood darkens in that instant.

Where is Nigel right now? In mid-air, or sleeping

in a king-size bed in some far, exotic land, a nubile, twenty-something by his side? It doesn't bear thinking about. Does he ever spare a thought for me? What would he make of my new life?

'Minnie,' he used to say (Minnie — as in Mouse — was his pet name for me on account of my stick-thin legs and big feet), 'it's too late for all that showbiz malarkey. Stay home with me and let's make a family.'

Why did he only ever say those things with several pints inside him? Had he really wanted children? Or had he been testing me, playing with my emotions? I'll never know now. What's wrong with me? Why can't I have a serious, uncomplicated relationship? Is that too much to ask?

An enormous, articulated lorry thunders past, drenching me in filthy spray. From somewhere deep inside me, an animal-like scream bursts out, piercing the cold night air.

Come on now. Pull yourself together. YOU ARE A LIBERATED, INDEPENDENT, STRONG WOMAN WITH A GOAL. YOU ARE A LIBERATED, INDEPENDENT, STRONG WOMAN WITH ... waterlogged shoes and dripping hair plastered over your eyes.

I feel anything but independent or strong, and my goal feels a world away. Have I been pitifully naïve? No matter, as it's a little late in the day for doubt and uncertainty. Like it or not, I am now travelling down a one-way street, and the big question is, does it lead to a dead-end?

CHAPTER TWO
Diamonds Are a Girl's Worst Enemy

THE BLACK, GAPING ABYSS YAWNS before her, the sharp smell of fuel burning her nostrils. She inhales deeply as she is swallowed up. Her eyes are blinded by the flickering, white lights, her ears deafened by the roar of engines above. She should never have got mixed up in this assignment. Not only was it dangerous, but doomed to failure. She should have walked away from the situation while she still had the chance and suffered the consequences. But there's no turning back now, so she focuses on the sliver of daylight in the distance. Not much further ...

Huffing and puffing, she is spewed out of the tunnel onto the relative calm of the road. She looks up. Terminal One Departures. She glances at her watch. 0610. Just enough time to make contact, hand over the diamonds and return to base. Mission accomplished.

No, sadly, I am not on the set of the latest Lynda La Plante thriller; on the contrary, I am starring in my very own drama, entitled *Payback Time*. And my crime? Smugness — displaying sheer, unadulterated smugness. You know how it is; you dare to pat yourself on the back for a job well done, and next minute, a giant Monty Python foot appears from above and squishes you into the ground. That will teach you for being so damned pleased with yourself!

Determined to win over Miss Cutler, who is on the verge of firing me on account of my poor sales record, I scrambled together an emergency marketing strategy, which happened to involve a bearded Scotsman and a one-thousand-five-hundred-pound diamond necklace ...

'I'm looking for something a teensy-weensy bit special,' the unsuspecting browser had informed me as he entered the shop. 'It's my wife's fiftieth tomorrow, and she's feeling ...' he looked around cautiously, checking he wouldn't be overheard '... *the change*,' he mouthed exaggeratedly. 'I'd like something with a wee bit of sparkle to cheer her up.'

'I see,' I whispered back discreetly. Here was my chance! Opening one of the cabinets, I said, 'How about this pastel gem-set bracelet? Notice how it shimmers with all the colours of the rainbow.' I tilted it back and forth, so the stones' reflection danced tantalisingly around the walls, like a kaleidoscope.

'I was thinking of something a bit simpler,' he said.

'Aah,' I nodded, undeterred. 'Well, in that case, how about this nine-carat gold pendant, hand-crafted in Italy?'

'Erm ...'

'Or this eighteen-carat belcher-bar necklace? Its extra length means it can be worn as a belt, a choker or a layered necklace,' I gushed, whilst demonstrating its many uses, just like I've seen those shopping channel presenters do. 'Layered jewellery is featured on all the major catwalks this season, so your wife would be up to the minute with the latest fashion.' He

32

bit his lip.

I could feel Miss Cutler's x-ray eyes burning through my head from behind the two-way mirror in the back office.

Please, God, let me make a sale.

'Let me see now ...' I said, brain racing, eyes darting wildly about. 'Aha, I know the *very thing!*' I launched into the window, swiping a fourteen-karat, white gold, diamond choker from the black velvet display stand. 'What woman wouldn't feel a million dollars wearing this?' I glanced at the clock — 5.26p.m. — just four minutes to closing time; four minutes to save myself from the dole queue.

'... and ... and Princess Diana wore the exact same style of choker when she took to the dance floor with John Travolta at The White House in the mid-eighties,' I added quickly.

He toyed with his beard.

'A high point in her short life,' I whispered sombrely.

'It's a wee bit more than I intended spending ...' he said pensively, as he peered at the price tag.

'Reaching fifty is quite a milestone,' I replied, in a kind of cool, throwaway tone, shamelessly swaying the dazzling diamonds in front of his eyes, like a hypnotist's pendulum, hope hovering.

He glanced at his watch. 5.28. Beads of perspiration glistened on his forehead.

'I'm catching the first plane back to Edinburgh in the morning, and I suppose a box of Milk Tray from the airport shop wouldn't go down very well.' He sighed, fishing out his wallet, resigned.

'Absolutely not,' I squeaked, snatching his credit card. The diamonds winked at me conspiratorially as I snapped shut the leather presentation case. Placing it under the counter, I coolly sashayed over to the cash desk, struggling to quash my overwhelming desire to do a Highland fling right there, on the shop floor.

Transaction completed, I carefully gift-wrapped the box, not forgetting the curly-wurly ribbon effect with the scissors, which I did with a dramatic flourish.

'Thank you, miss. You've been very helpful. I cannae wait to see Morag's face the morrow when I get hame.'

'I'm sure she'll be thrilled. Have a good flight back.' I smiled smugly, opening the door for him. Yesssssssss!

In buoyant mood, I waltzed around the floor with the vacuum cleaner, singing to myself as I went. Saved from the humiliation of begging for an overdraft increase — again. From now on Miss Cutler would realise I was an asset to the shop and would be devastated when I inevitably had to give up my retail career for that of a West End star.

Then all at once Henry Hoover died. I spun round, and there stood Cruella, her head shaking.

'Ah-hem! What is this, Emily?' she asked coldly, holding up one of the presentation cases.

'A jewellery box.' I shrugged.

'That is where you are wrong, Emily. This is no ordinary jewellery box,' she snarled, face blazing, the veins in her swan-like neck pulsating madly. I stared at her, puzzled.

'This is a jewellery box that contains ...' she said, milking every moment of her Wicked-Witch-of-The-West performance '... a very valuable item belonging to *your customer!*'

Opening the box, she dangled the choker in front of my eyes. OH-MY-GOD. I felt the colour drain from my face as my insides plummeted ten floors. I dropped the nozzle, realising with sinking horror that I had wrapped up the wrong box and sold nice, Scottish businessman one-thousand-five-hundred-pounds' worth of diddlysquat.

'Maybe we can trace him through his credit card? Or perhaps I could go to Heathrow tomorrow and try to ...'

My voice fell away, as judging by Miss Cutler's beetroot colouring, she was about to spontaneously combust.

So, that is how I come to be loitering around the airline check-in desks minus a ticket, a fifteen-hundred-pound diamond choker clasped tightly in my mitts.

The terminal is already abuzz with suited and booted businessmen on their way to Brussels or Belfast for a hard day's wheeling and dealing.

I scan the concourse, looking for a tall, wiry, bearded Scotsman, clutching a boarding pass for Edinburgh and a beautifully wrapped box.

Couples cling to one another, off on romantic breaks to Vienna or Athens ... Hang on a minute! My gaze rewinds to the Vienna check-in queue. Eyes narrowing, I move in for a closer look. It can't possibly be. He's ten and a half thousand miles away ... and yet ... I'd recognise that sunburnt, bald patch anywhere. (As a first class galley slave, you can spend a lot of time gazing at the back of pilots' heads, patiently waiting, steaming hot tea burning your hands, while they finish prattling on to air traffic control and punching buttons on the automatic pilot thingy.)

It *is* him, I swear. And who's that woman he's got his arm wrapped around? Swiping my shades from my pocket and pulling my cycle helmet down over my eyes, I venture nearer and take up position behind a pillar.

'Vienna? Two passengers?' says the check-in girl, switching on her Stepford-Wife smile. Taking their tickets, she taps furiously on the computer. (Ever wondered what on earth takes these people so long? Surely they only need input names and *window* or *aisle*, yet the way they hit those keys you'd think they were composing a pre-board passenger description: *balding man, medium height, bad dresser: 22A. Dowdy-looking, very likely long-suffering wife: 22B.*)

'Any chance of an upgrade?'

Oh, yes, that's our Mikey all right. The cheapskate, asking for an upgrade on his twenty-pound concessionary ticket. Bloody typical.

I glance up at the departure screen: VS3001 TO EDINBURGH CLOSING GATE 5.

Oh, Lord! In all the drama I've completely forgotten about finding Mr Beardy Man — Mr Soon-To-Be-Divorced Beardy Man if I don't get my act together pronto.

Zipping my way in between trolleys and wheelie suitcases, I race towards the security gate. Standing on tiptoes, I spy him in the distance, collecting his coat, shoes and a small gift bag from the conveyor belt.

'Boarding pass,' grunts the security man.

'Please let me through. I need to give this to that gentleman down there — it's really important,' I beg, waving the box in the direction of the long line of travellers, waiting to be prodded and processed.

'If you don't have a boarding card I can't let you through,' he says firmly, darting me a scathing glare.

'*Please.* I can't explain now, but if I don't get this to him ...'

'Stand aside,' he growls, as a queue starts to form behind me of red-eyed travellers, brandishing their boarding passes, impatient to proceed.

There's nothing else for it — filling up my lungs to maximum capacity, I push out my diaphragm and emit a rip-roaring, show-stopping 'WAIT!'

It's like someone has momentarily pressed the freeze-frame switch. All eyes swerve in my direction — all eyes but those of the one person whose attention I so desperately desire. He is now trundling along to gate five, blissfully unaware of the brewing storm about to hit north and south of the border.

Back on the road, my mind is buzzing with the thought of what I'm going to say to Miss Cutler, and more importantly, do I tell Céline that Mike is not in Oz, but on a romantic, Viennese mini break with his wife?

It's just like one of those letters on the *Woman's Weekly* problem page:

Dear Keren,
One of my best friends has been dating a married man for ten years. He keeps promising her he's going to leave. I saw him at the airport today, canoodling with his wife. He'd told my friend he couldn't see her as he was going away on business. Do I tell her and risk ruining our friendship, or do I turn a blind eye?
Yours,
Anonymous.

Do I really need an agony aunt to advise me what to do, when the answer is spelt out before me in ten-foot, flashing, neon letters? TELL HER.

'Oi! Look where you're going, willya! Bloody cyclists!' hollers an irate taxi driver, through the open window.

* * *

'I'm afraid head office has taken the matter very seriously,' gloats Miss Cutler. 'My hands are tied. I have no alternative but to let you go.'

'If you could just give me one more chance ...' I grovel, panic rising.

'If I were you, I'd go back to what you do best — serving ready meals and selling novelty goods to tourists,' she says in a condescending, I'm-telling-you-this-for-your-own-good sort of way. 'It's a tough old world out there, and jobs aren't easy to find — even for the young.' Ouch.

She presses the door-release button; I draw a deep breath and exit the shop, cycle-helmeted head held high.

I am in a kind of daze, oblivious to the pushing and jostling of hurried passers-by. This is serious; I now have no job, my meagre savings are fast disappearing, my overdraft has reached its limit, and I am barely able to cover the monthly minimum payment on my Visa card. An empty, lost feeling takes hold of me. Perhaps Miss Cutler is right; perhaps I should have stuck with my safe, familiar job and my secure life, instead of foolishly casting myself adrift without a set of oars. I've lost my way. I used to be so focused, so positive that despite all the hardships, things would work out in the end. I feel like I got six winning numbers in the lottery and now I can't find the ticket.

Grabbing a mozzarella and tomato panini, I head for the river to think.

As I chain my bike to the side of the bridge, my thoughts turn to Céline. I pull out my mobile from my bag and scroll for her number. My finger hovers over the green button. Why am I hesitating?

As one of her closest friends, it is my *duty* to tell her, but how? Taking a bite of my sandwich, I rehearse what I'm going to say:

'Céline, are you sitting down? I'm afraid I have some shocking news for you ...'

No, too dramatic.

'Céline, as much as it pains me, as one of your closest friends, I feel duty-bound to tell you ...'

Nope, too convoluted — just cut to the chase.

'Céline, Mike's not in Australia. He's in Vienna with his wife.'

The number rings once then diverts to voice-mail. A wave of relief breaks over me. I compose this text instead:

<Mike not in Oz. In Vienna with wife. So sorry. Call me. Luv E x>

I stab the SEND button and off it flies, like winged Mercury, into cyberspace — and the deed is done.

THE SCENE IS THE WELL-FURNISHED LIVING ROOM OF A SEMI-DETACHED HOUSE ON THE OUTSKIRTS OF EDINBURGH. A SWEET, HOMELY COUPLE ARE SIPPING CHAMPAGNE AND GIGGLING.

MAN: Cheers! Many happy returns, pet. (HE TAKES A BEAUTIFULLY WRAPPED BOX FROM UNDER THE CUSHION.) This is just a wee something to show you how much I love and appreciate you.

WOMAN: Ach, you shouldnae have. (DABBING HER EYES AND SMILING, SHE KISSES HIM AND OPENS THE BOX. IT IS EMPTY. SHE BURSTS INTO FLOODS OF TEARS) Is this some kinda cruel joke?

CUT TO AIRPORT. A BALDING, MIDDLE-AGED MAN AND HIS WIFE APPEAR THROUGH THE SLIDING DOORS OF THE ARRIVALS HALL. THEY ARE LAUGHING AND JOKING, PLAINLY HAPPY IN ONE ANOTHER'S COMPANY. A TALL, STRIKING FRENCH WOMAN IN AIRLINE UNIFORM APPROACHES THEM.

FRENCH WOMAN (TO THE MAN): How was Sydney?

MAN: I ... er ... what the blazes are you doing here?

FRENCH WOMAN: I could ask you the same question.
WIFE: Aren't you going to introduce us, darling?
FRENCH WOMAN PULLS REVOLVER FROM HANDBAG
AND SHOOTS ...
CUT TO A POLICE INTERVIEW ROOM. IT'S 2 A.M. DI
JACK TEMPLETON PACES THE FLOOR WHILST
SIPPING COFFEE FROM A POLYSTYRENE CUP.
A DISTRESSED WOMAN SITS AT THE TABLE, HEAD IN
HER HANDS, SOBBING.
DI TEMPLETON: Don't lie to us. Your fingerprints are
all over the necklace — and the box. As if that wasn't
bad enough, you've got the bleedin' gall not only to gift
wrap the empty box, but to do the curly-wurly ribbon
effect as well! Jeez, I've seen some callous, pre-
meditated crimes in my time, but this ...
EMILY: How many more times? I swear it wasn't
planned — please, please, you've got to believe me ...

I awake in a knot of sheets and a cold sweat, heart banging wildly in my chest. I switch on the oriental lady bedside lamp and peer at the clock — 0345. I close my eyes tight and toss and turn. I wish I could sleep, but Céline's pale, tear-stained face and reddened eyes haunt my semi-consciousness. I listen to her message again:

What you tell me, it is impossible. You have made a big mistake. Mike loves me. Why you don't accept this and be happy for me? Please ... it is for the best you don't call. Jamais. *Never.*

There's an iciness in her voice I've never heard before, and it chills me to the core. There I go again, little Miss Fix-It, sticking her nose into other people's affairs. Will I never learn? How could I have been so cruel and thoughtless? Not content with turning my own life upside down, I've gone and ruined a menopausal woman's milestone birthday (and possibly her marriage, for that matter), blown apart my friend's ten-year relationship, and tragically worse, our precious friendship to boot. Twenty years deleted with the press of a button.

I seem to be lurching from one disaster to another; I've lost my job, one of my dearest friends, and at the grand old age of forty, am sleeping in a single bed in a home I don't own, an assortment of kitsch knick-knacks and an ancient moggy who hates me for company.

AARGH! In a fit of pique, I hurl my mobile at the wall. The Smurfs scatter in all directions, Action Man topples over onto Diana, who is sent crashing onto the tiled hearth, taking the Eiffel Tower snow globe with her, which starts manically playing 'Jingle Bells'.

Horrified, I gawp at the shattered pieces.

Bzzz! Bzzz! Scrambling through the devastation, I grab my phone. New message: YES! Please, pleeease let it be Céline, telling me she forgives me and we shouldn't let a stupid man destroy our friendship ...

<We need to talk. Call me. Nigel.>

Five days. I have just five days to prepare for the most important audition of my life. I was voted off first time round, but now I've been recalled; this is my one chance to prove that whilst I may not be the youngest or most glamorous contestant, I have got what it takes; that *je ne sais quoi*, the X-factor.

'It's only dinner,' I told Wendy breezily. 'It's no big deal.'

'Please don't rush back into his arms. Promise me, hon,' she said, face darkening. 'You're just starting to resemble your old self again, and I don't want you going back to square one.'

'I give you my word. I won't do anything stupid,' I

replied, secretly wondering if forty is too old to wear white ...

I wipe the steam from my recently acquired reading glasses and peer at my face in the bathroom mirror, in all its 3-D glory. Blimey. When did that happen? Those lines. When did they appear? And those grey hairs? And oh, my God, who stuck them there? Those gorilla legs?

I scrabble in my toiletries bag for a razor: there's a squashed tube of foundation, a bottle of Tesco Value bodywash, a few crumbs of blusher and a blob of sticky lip-gloss. Is this the same woman who, not so very long ago, thought nothing of spending $90 on mascara and a makeover at Macy's?

Having rejected every outfit in my wardrobe, I end up buying a little, classic black dress from Autograph for £85. Now, before you throw your hands up in despair, I'll let you in on my shameful secret: I haven't cut the price tag off, and provided I don't spill anything on it, I give my word that I will return it to the customer services desk after D-Day.

'You look amazing,' says Nigel, unusually nervous, as he pulls out a chair for me. (Wow! He hasn't done that since 2009.)

'Thank you,' I reply frostily, as I surreptitiously shove my cycle helmet under the table. I take a dainty sip of water and pretend to study the menu. I mustn't make it too easy for him. It will take more than a curry and a compliment to win me back.

'You've been on my mind a lot lately,' he continues in a low voice, pouring me a glass of wine.

Don't say anything. Play it cool. Let him do the talking. Dilemma: do I put on my reading glasses so I can actually read the menu, or do I order blind for the sake of vanity? If I am to spend the rest of my life with him, then surely I should feel comfortable being myself. After all, this is the man who held my hair back when I had my head down a toilet after one rum punch too many on *The Jolly Roger* in Barbados; the same man who's seen me sans mascara, wearing a green face mask, a ratty towel on my head and a brace on my teeth. But maybe that's the whole point: the very reason he left; maybe he wants a wife who looks her best all the time, not one who scrubs up well only when the occasion calls for it.

'Whenever I'm in LA I can't help thinking about our trips to Disneyland, and how we used to act like a couple of crazy kids,' he continues, swallowing hard. 'And only last week, I was on the Star Ferry in Hong Kong and remembered the time your scarf blew off into the sea, and how we'd lock ourselves away in my suite and make love for hours and live on room-service. So many amazing memories. You will always mean a lot to me, don't ever forget that.'

A huge current of relief and ecstasy surges around my body. 'Oh, Nigel, I've been thinking about you too ...'

'But I'm worried about you, Em,' he says, reaching for my hand. 'I heard you jacked in the job and are studying drama and living in a rented room. Don't you think you're a little too old to be changing courses? You've got to think of the future.'

'You only get one life and when you left ...'

'But that's not my main reason for wanting to see you,' he interjects.

Stay calm. Play hard to get. Deep breaths ...

'I've something important to say ...'

'Yes?' I whisper, heart doing the quickstep.

'I thought it best to do the decent thing and tell you face to face before you hear it from someone else.'

My stomach does a backward flip. I feel the colour drain from my face. I twist the corner of the tablecloth tightly between my fingers, knees wobbling like crème caramel.

'First of all, despite what you might have heard, I want you to know that I didn't sleep with Maddie until we broke up.'

'What? Who's Maddie?' I say, sharply pulling my hand away from his.

'She's new … you … you don't know her. She … she only joined at the end of last year. Anyway, nothing happened until …'

'Whooooa! So all that stuff about self-destruct buttons and "finding yourself" was a cover-up?'

'Not exactly … no. Let me finish, please. You don't know how hard this is for me …'

'You had me believing that you were having some sort of mental breakdown, when all the time you were sleeping with some young bimbo. How could you?' I snap, throwing down my napkin, unsure of whether to fling myself on the floor or fly out of the door.

'Keep your voice down, Em, *please*,' he says through clenched teeth, nervously looking around at the other diners.

I stare at him in disbelief.

'Typical! That's all you care about; what people think of you. You are so damned self-centred! You invited me for dinner to relieve your guilt. Worried about me? Hah! Don't bother. I'll be *fine*,' I say, snatching my jacket, helmet and bag.

Grabbing my wrist, he mumbles, 'I still care about you, Em. You're like family to me … I can only move on with my life if I know you're going to be okay. Maybe in time, we could even be …'

'Oh, pur-lease, don't say it! Let go of me! What an idiot I was to even *think* of getting back with you.'

I stagger out of the restaurant into the street, finding it hard to breathe. I unchain my bike from the lamppost, hands trembling.

'Don't be like this,' comes a voice in my ear. 'At least let me give you a lift home, Em, *please.*'

'Not necessary,' I hiss, jamming on my helmet and flicking on my lights.

'There's just one more thing you should know,' he blurts out, face ghostly in the silvery beam of the streetlight. 'Maddie's pregnant.'

CHAPTER THREE
Anna Karenina Meets Mr Muscle

IT'S 5.30 A.M. I'M WEARING RUBBER GLOVES and wielding a loo brush. How did my life come to this? I left the airline so full of hope and promise, now here I am with my arm stuck down a toilet. I hate my job, I hate my life, and I hate myself for having got into this mess.

I should have carried on flying; okay, so it wouldn't have altered the fact that Nigel left me and some other woman stole the life I should have had, but at least I would have been a comfortably off singleton. Thanks to some hair-brained notion that I could become the next Meryl Streep, I am now an impoverished forty-something without a place to call home, my life packed away in bubble wrap at a warehouse off the M4.

Who needs therapy or self-help books to mend a broken heart? All you need do is follow these three easy steps: a) Give up your well-paid, secure and interesting job. b) Sell your comfortable home and move into someone's poky backroom, complete with resident psychocat. c) Forgo all luxuries and live from hand to mouth doing menial jobs.

Et voilà! You'll have so many majorly serious problems to contend with (like SURVIVAL) that being dumped by your boyfriend will seem a minor blip by comparison.

My positive side tries to persuade me that jobs like this are all good, character-building stuff. Besides, should The Rovers Return or The Queen Vic be looking for a cleaning lady, my hands-on experience may just give me the edge over actresses who've never operated a squeezy mop or emptied a Dyson.

Pah! Dream on. It's time I faced up to the fact that I'll never make it as an actress. One thing I have learned over the last few months is that acting isn't just about remembering lines and moves; you have to let go of your inhibitions, be a little bit dangerous and take the plunge. Something always holds me back; fear of making an idiot of myself, I guess, and the harder I try, the more awkward and nervous I feel.

'Stop thinking so much,' Portia keeps telling me. 'Thinking about how we sound or look makes us self-conscious, and self-consciousness is suicide for an actor.'

I shudder when I think of the huge sacrifice I've made — and for what? I squirt another dollop of Toilet Duck and scrub furiously, tears plopping into the bowl.

'G'day!'

Startled, I wheel around, toppling over onto my bucket of cleaning stuff.

'Sorry, I didn't mean to scare you,' says the tall, young stranger, crouching down and handing me my grubby J-cloth and can of Mr Muscle. His Pacific-blue eyes hold my gaze.

'I'm Dean. Night security. I must have been on patrol when you arrived.'

47

'Emily,' I sniffle, proffering a yellow, rubber-gloved hand. 'The new cleaner … in case you were wondering.'

'Well, Emily, nice to meet you,' he says, treating me to a dazzling smile. 'Maybe see you around tomorrow.' And with that he is gone.

I trudge up the steps of The Academy under the stony gaze of the comedy and tragedy masks above the door. I wonder what stories they could tell. How many hopeful, impassioned students have passed this way before? How many have become Hot Property, and how many are now scraping together a living as market researchers or living statues?

'You've had twenty-four hours to think about this, and now you're telling me that your motive, the event that's going to get those anger juices flowing, that's going to *fuel* your performances in time to come, is the fact that you had a puncture and were late for your first day at work?' says Portia, scrutinising me with a look of despair in her kohl-rimmed, piercing green eyes.

A collective snigger reverberates around the room. I must be some kind of masochist, to have spent the last ten months putting myself through this kind of torture.

I'm starting to realise that the optimist in me has been telling lies; encouraging me to keep on keeping on, because any day now I'll find the key to that secret door which leads to the actor's holy grail; that special place which separates the truly talented from the merely mediocre. But let's be realistic for once; I'm never going to find the key, am I?

My toes clench together in my jazz shoes, my face

and neck flushing the colour of a strawberry smoothie. I used to believe that drama school would teach me about making sense of Shakespeare, how to walk in a bustle and corset without keeling over, how to flirtatiously flutter a fan, and to step, ball change and sing simultaneously without getting breathless. No one warned me that you had to take part in a Jeremy-Kyle type reality show before you were allowed to pass 'GO'. If they had, I would have stuck to serving chicken and beef at thirty-two thousand feet.

'Come on, Emily, surely you can do better than that? Haven't you ever been accused of something unfairly or had your heart broken in two?'

'Sure, but ...'

'Well then, how did that make you feel?'

'I ... I ...' I murmur, shrugging my shoulders and casting my eyes downwards, wishing I could silently slither down a gap between the floorboards.

'Didn't you feel betrayed, wounded, bloody furious?' she probes.

'Of course, but ...'

'Well then, now's your opportunity to break through those emotional boundaries and tell us what's in your heart. No one's going to laugh at you. If you're serious about becoming an actor — a *good* actor — then you have to live on the edge, bare your soul. Acting is all about trust, Emily.'

'I know, *I know*,' I reply sheepishly. 'It's just that, well ... I'm not entirely comfortable with all this *touchy-feely* stuff. Please don't get me wrong,' I add quickly, desperately searching for the right words, 'I ... I'm not exactly the stiff-upper-lip type ... far from it ... I mean, I cry at *Britain's Got Talent* ... but ... well, it's just that ...'

Dammit, I've spent the last few months trying so

hard to keep the lid on my pent-up emotions, blot out the horrible, hurtful memory of Nigel and move on, so the last thing I want to do is go opening up the wound again before it's had time to heal — and certainly not in front of a bunch of virtual strangers.

'Do you want to be one of those actors who believes they've done a good job so long as they remember their lines and don't bump into the furniture?' continues Portia, tearing into me. 'Or would you rather be the type of actor who *inhabits* a role, who sets the stage alight, who can hold an audience in the palm of their hand, make them squirm in their seats, move them to tears, or cause them to laugh uncontrollably?' Her eyes are flashing now, as her amethyst ring catches the late evening sun, sending a whirlpool of lilac light around the room, like a glitter-ball.

'But isn't acting all about pretending?' I say weakly. 'Don't tell me you have to have committed murder before you're eligible to play the villain in an Agatha Christie.'

All eyes hit the floor, and an uncomfortable silence hangs in the air. I flush even harder.

'Acting is about finding the truth in imaginary circumstances,' says Portia matter-of-factly.

Maybe she's right. It might make me feel better to get it off my chest. All the same ... some things are personal. How I wish this were over. I can't carry on just staring at the floor though. It's humiliating. Got to do something ... oh well, here goes ...

'Those years we spent together, the plans we made, it all meant nothing to you, did it?' I say, quietly, haltingly. '*You* were the one who brought up marriage and children, not *me*, and then when I said I was ready, you backed away ... "I've got to find myself," you said ... what a joke! You bastard. You didn't even have the decency ... no, let me finish ... you didn't even have the decency to tell me what was *really* going on.'

All the bottled-up emotions swirling around inside me since that hideous night come flooding out, filling my words with a mixture of anger and sadness. A big tear slides halfway down my cheek, attaching itself to my nostril, and my legs turn to plasticine. I grab the corner of the chair.

'Why couldn't you have sat me down and told me the truth? That you'd fallen out of love with me and met someone else? But no ... you wanted me to think you were having some sort of mental breakdown, when all the time you were sleeping with *her*. And I was too in love to see through you ... even blamed myself. Hah! You're nothing but a coward and a liar ... Come back! Don't walk out when I'm talking to you! Why must you always bury your head in the sand? Come back ...!' I cry, my outstretched arm flopping limply by my side.

My performance is greeted by complete silence. Moments pass.

'Are you all right?' asks Portia gently, handing me a tissue.

'I'm fine, really I am,' I say, giving my nose a blow that could warn shipping. I'm not faking it; I really am all right. In fact, I'm more than all right; I'm elated, in a strange sort of way. I did it, and it feels great — liberating — like this huge, tangled mass of poisonous emotions wrapped around my heart has been hacked away and finally lost its stranglehold. I wasn't just saying those words; they came from somewhere deep inside me.

'At last! I *knew* you had it in you,' says Portia, with a note of triumph. 'Now, hold onto that emotion and file it away under *ANGER*, ready to be unleashed as and when the part calls for it,' she continues, squeezing my arm.

I rejoin the group, sitting in a circle on the floor. I suddenly feel as if everything has fallen into place. Up to this very moment I have been stumbling, muddling my way through, putting on a brave face to the world, pretending that I'm better off without Nigel. It's now rapidly, brilliantly dawning on me that I truly had been clinging to a lost cause, and I'm free at last.

My tyres hiss as I pedal along the rain-drenched road home. I freewheel down the hill, feet off the pedals, head tilted back, face cooled by the sudden downpour. I feel lighter somehow, as if at any given moment my bike and I could soar up into the black night, just like in *E.T.* I'm filled with — not sure what, but this much I do know: I am no longer afraid of being alone.

Just three weeks to the day since I left The Academy, and I have my very first audition this afternoon: for Chekhov's *Three Sisters.* Not quite the television costume drama of my dreams, rather a 'profit-share', pub-theatre production. (In other words, no pay probably.) Yet make no mistake, there will be plenty of actors vying for parts, as the venue's prime location means you might get spotted by agents and casting directors ...

'Can yew plaaay the balalaika, Protopopov? Pop, pop, pop. Komarovsky, can yew plaaay the bala-lai-kaa? Kaa, kaa, kaa. Ivan Denisovich, can yew plaaay the bala-lai-kaa? Kaa, kaa, kaa...' (No, I am not teetering on the brink of madness; this is my very own Mr Bean warm-up exercise, Russian style.) 'Vladimir Putin,

Mikhail Gorbachev, Rudolf Nureyev, samovaaar ... rrr...'

Ouch! My mascara wand drops to the floor as I flop onto the bed, one arm flailing about for the box of tissues on the dressing table. I open the weeping eye cautiously, and my gaze lands on the bank statement and Visa bill scattered on the floor. How can I even contemplate going for this audition today? What if I get the part? (Unlikely, I know, but say I do?) With daytime rehearsals and only travel expenses paid, how can I possibly survive?

Think positive! It will be good experience, and you never know who might be in the audience, and then that could lead to something ... couldn't it? Oh, bugger it! I'll go. I've always had a romantic fascination for things Russian: a snow-dusted Red Square, a horse-drawn sleigh with handsome Cossack in scarlet tunic at the helm, Anna Karenina, Dr Zhivago; I grew up wanting to be Julie Christie in a floor-length, sable coat with fur trim hat (and confess I still do).

I splash my bloodshot eye with cool water, sweep my hair up in a chignon, fasten my gran's cameo brooch to the ruffled neck of my blouse, and lace up my black, vintage-look, Primark boots. With a dramatic swish of my coat, I stride over Shirley, poised just below the top step, and glide downstairs, proclaiming, 'To Moscow, Roman Abramovich, to Moscow, and don't forget your babushka ...'

* * *

Ignoring the stench of beer and the odd peanut, I slither around the stained and grubby floor of The Red Dragon pub, going 'sssss.' I want to stand up and shout, *Could somebody please explain to me what this has got to do with Chekhov?*

'Right then, that's the end of the warm-up, and in a

few moments we'll be calling you into the room one by one, so please have your audition pieces ready,' says someone called Rocket, with dreadlocks and a clipboard.

I pace up and down, quietly practising my speech — again:

"'Sir, I desire you do me right and justice, and to bestow your pity on me; for I am a most poor woman, and a stranger, born out of your dominions, having here ... having here ...'"

Oh, God, what comes next?

'Emily Forsyth!' calls Rocket.

A queasy feeling floods my stomach. I'm ushered into a poky back room, where I'm introduced to the creative team.

'Now, Emily, what audition piece are you going to do for us?' asks Hugh, the director.

'I'd like to do Katherine ... Queen Katherine from *Henry The Eighth*.'

Casting me a sympathetic glance, he nods. 'In your own time.'

Four pairs of expectant eyes upon me, I breathe in, trying to steady my voice.

"'Sir, I desire you do me right and justice, and to bestow your pity on me; for I am a most poor woman, and a stranger, born out of your dominions, having here no judge indifferent, nor no more assurance of equal friendship and proceeding ...'"

With my audience just inches away, and crates of mixers, packets of assorted crisps and pork scratchings occupying almost every available space, it's hard to imagine I'm a sixteenth-century queen in a grand hall, begging my husband not to force me into a quickie divorce.

"'... in God's name turn me away, and let the foul'st contempt shut door upon me, and so give me up to

54

the sharps't kind of justice.'"

I lift my eyes from my kneeling position.

'Thank you,' says Hugh, breaking the long silence. 'Now we'd like you to read part of Olga's speech for us.'

The script starts to quiver as I take it from him.

'Turn to page two, beginning from the top please.'

I try to channel my nerves into capturing Olga's mood of despair.

'"Don't whistle, Masha. How can you! Every day I teach at the Gymnasium and afterwards I give lessons until evening, and so I've got a constant headache and my thoughts are those of an old woman ..."'

PSSCHH hisses a toilet from above, GERDUNG, GERDUNG go the pipes.

'"I've felt my strength and my youth draining from me every day, drop by drop. And one single thought grows stronger and stronger ..."'

I play the speech distractedly at first, but halfway through find myself relaxing into it and actually enjoying it.

Then suddenly it's over: my one and only chance to make an impression. I wonder if they'll let me do it again ...

'Thank you for coming. We'll let you know on Monday.'

Monday? That's a whole three days. But hang on! What am I fretting about? I can't afford to take the job even if they do offer it to me. So it's for the best if I don't get it. Just put it down to experience.

Monday 4 p.m.

Humph! So I'm not good enough for their play, eh? Their loss. Not for them, a *thank-you-for-my-first-break* mention when I collect my BAFTA, so bollocks to them.

Half an hour later, the *Desperate Housewives*

theme tune comes drifting across the landing into the bathroom. Jeans at half-mast, I stagger and stumble to the bedroom, and swipe my mobile from the dressing table.

'Emily, it's Hugh.'

I hold my breath for a moment.

'Oh, of course, the audition. Hi,' I say in my best I'm-a-very-busy-person voice, heart leaping into my throat.

'Good news ... we'd like you to play Olga for us. What do you say?'

My tummy does a double somersault. I open my mouth to speak, but catch myself in time. I want to grovel with gratitude and swing from the chandelier (or in this case, the wire-framed fabric light fitting with rayon fringe), but I mustn't appear too desperately keen. I count to three, then say coolly, 'I'd love to — thank you — I'd love to.'

'Great. Rehearsals start Monday. Rocket, our deputy stage manager will e-mail you all the details. Good to have you on board.'

'Thank you,' I say again, trying to maintain my composure until he rings off.

'YESSS!' I whoop, punching the air and landing with a thud.

'Emily, is that you?' calls Beryl from downstairs.

Hastily zipping up my jeans, I screech over the banister, 'Beryl, I got the job!'

'Fan-bloody-tastic, darlin'! Let me just turn *Countdown* off an' I'll crack open that bottle of Asti Spumante in the sideboard. I've been waiting since Christmas for an excuse to drink it.'

Three glasses of lukewarm Asti Spumante later, and my euphoria has turned into sickly panic. With daytime rehearsals for three weeks, how am I going to earn any money? Why didn't I think this through more carefully? *Look before you leap*. Will I never learn? My self-esteem may well have had a bit of a boost, but the same can definitely not be said for my bank balance. There has got to be a way ...

'"Masha will come to Moscow for the summer ... *aargh!* ... for the *WHOLE* summer ... Masha will come to Moscow for the whole summer ..."' I repeat, as I wind my way in between the desks, flicking my duster with one hand, balancing my script with the other.

'Hello again!'

I spin around, tripping over computer cables and a waste paper basket.

'Sorry, I've gotta stop freaking you out,' says Dean, grabbing my elbow, his piercing gaze meeting mine. My heart gives a little flutter.

'Glad to see you looking cheerier than last time we met.'

'Yes, sorry about that,' I reply, glancing at him sideways.

'Guy trouble?'

'That, and one of those where-the-hell-is-my-life-going moments.'

He looks at me blankly. He must only be in his twenties, so I guess this concept is about as alien to him as Snapchat is to me.

I glance at the clock. 'Sorry, I don't mean to be rude, but I've got to be at my next job in less than an hour, and I haven't started the vacuuming yet.'

'Sure thing. You know, we should ...'

'Sorry?' I bellow over the roar of the hoover.

He shakes his head and mouths 'goodbye'.

I pedal through the damp, chill, early morning air, chanting, 'Aleksander Ignatyevich Vershinin, Aleksey

Petrovich Fed... Fedotik.' Gaah! Why is no one in Russia called Bob Jones or Jim Smith? I glance at my watch. 7.15. 'Aleksander Ignat... Ignatyevich Vershinin, Aleksey Petrovich Fedotik ...'

My other job is at The Red Dragon, which is very handy, as we rehearse here. The only way I can afford to do the play is by taking on another early morning cleaning job. End of.

Using all the female charm I could muster, I persuaded the landlord that good beer and Sky TV alone were not enough to lure the clientele. What the place needed was a woman's touch: a splash of bleach here and a squirt of air freshener there. (That was the polite, edited version.)

Anyway, it worked. So from 7.30 a.m. I'm Mrs Overall, picking chewing gum off bar stools and replenishing paper towels. Then, fast-forward three hours, and I'm Olga Prozorov, schoolteacher and eldest sister to Masha and Irina, dreaming of marriage and Moscow.

There's even a shower I can use. The pipes gurgle and rattle a bit when I turn it on, and it splutters and drips freezing cold water, but at least I don't arrive at rehearsal smelling like a compost heap.

By the end of the week, I'm sleepwalking my routine:

04.30: Alarm goes off. Hit snooze button.
04.35: Alarm goes off. Roll out of bed.
04.45: Down a bowl of Special K.
0450: Grab bike and pedal like the clappers.
0515: Arrive at office. Clean.
0700: Leave office for pub. Clean.
0845: Shower, change, stop at Norma's Diner for tea and runny egg on toast.
1000–1800: Rehearse.
1830: Home, dinner, learn lines and go over what we

did today.

2200: Bed, in order to be up at 0430 to repeat all of the above.

In between times, I am also sending out mail-shots to agents and casting directors:

Please cover my performance as Olga in 'Three Sisters' at The Red Dragon Pub Theatre, Lady Jane Walk, Richmond. 2nd October –1st November at 7.30.

Even if only four or five turn up it will be worth it — won't it?

* * *

TONIGHT AT 7.30

THREE SISTERS
BY
ANTON CHEKHOV

I feel my stomach lurch as I glance at the sandwich board outside the pub. This is it. No more 'Sorry, what's my next line?' or 'Should I be sitting at this point?' After three weeks' rehearsal, I *think* I'm pretty solid on my lines and moves, but there is always that fear lurking somewhere in the shadows, of stepping out in front of an audience and thinking, Who am I? What the hell am I doing here? Who *are* these people?

I make my way upstairs to the cramped, communal dressing room. Where, oh where is the star on the door and the mirror with light bulbs all around it?

I am the first to arrive and bag myself a wee corner. With fourteen of us in the cast, it's going to be a tight squeeze. I lay out my make-up, hairbrush, bottle of water and lucky elephant charm (a treasured gift from the cleaner at the crew hotel in Mumbai). I then distribute my First Night cards.

One by one, the others start to drift in, and nervous, excited chatter and vocal warm-up exercises soon reverberate around the room.

There is a rap at the door and Hugh enters, pushing eighty-year-old Betty, playing Anfisa, the nanny, into the lap of Verschinin (he's the lieutenant, who's in love with Masha, my sister, but they're both married, his wife's suicidal and ... well, it's complicated).

'Break a leg, everyone. Unfortunately our audience tonight is a teensy-weensy bit thin on the ground, but please don't let that put you off. I want you to act like the place is full — which I'm sure it will be once the reviews are out.'

Another knock on the door and Rocket calls breathlessly from the other side, 'Act One beginners, please!'

As I wait in the blackness of the wings, I begin to wonder if there's anyone out there at all. No excited chatter or rustling of sweetie papers, but then comes a solitary cough, as the door at the back slams shut. The lights go down and the opening music, by some Russian composer whose name I can't remember, let alone pronounce, crackles through the speakers. I clear my dry throat, fumble my way through the leaden darkness five steps to the makeshift stage, and take up position. The music fades and the lights snap on, burning my face, blinding me with their glare. Here goes ...

'"... Andrey could be good-looking, only he's filled out a lot and it doesn't suit him ..."'

A mobile phone goes off.

'Hello ...'

'"But I've become old, I've got very thin ..."'

'It finishes around 10.30, I think ... I *hope* ...' (snigger) ...

60

"'I suppose because I lose my temper with ...'"

'Okay, darling, see you in the bar. Hmm? I'm not sure ...'

"'... the girls at the Gymnasium. Today I'm free, I'm at home, and I have no headache ...'"

'Ooh, I know ... make it a vodka and orange ... a double ... I'll need it! Byee!'

'Shh!'

"'I feel younger than yesterday ...'"

We haven't even reached the end of Act One and I am consumed by an overwhelming sense of despair. Marvellous method acting? Would it were true.

What in God's name is that guy doing? "' ... Andrey, don't go off ...'"

I don't believe it. He's getting up. KER-CHUNG! goes the seat as it flips up. EEEEEEAK! creaks the door. A shaft of light streams through from the bar.

"'He has a way of always walking off. Come here.'"

'GOAL!' comes a collective, triumphant cry from the bar, just as the door swings shut.

I guess Chelsea must have scored against Sheffield then.

We brazen it out to the interval — somehow. Acts Three and Four go a little better, and apart from the odd sneeze, our meagre audience seems to settle down. Maybe they're actually getting into it. On second thoughts, judging by the lukewarm applause as we take our curtain call, maybe they were comatose.

It wasn't meant to be like this; I didn't expect a standing ovation and flowers to be thrown at our feet, but I wasn't prepared for this: to be in a production where the actors outnumber the audience. Is this what I have sacrificed my job and everything for? This is not my dream. I had such high hopes. Things are just not panning out as I expected.

My bubble has burst already. My nails are chipped and dirty; my knees are bruised from pushing and shoving desks around the office and scrubbing stone steps at the pub. I wouldn't care had I had one reply from a casting director or agent; even a *WE REGRET TO INFORM YOU* would have been nice, courteous.

'Well done, everyone!' enthuses Hugh, giving us the thumbs-up as we trudge up the stairs. 'The drinks are on me.'

I'm about to make the excuse of having to be up at 04.30, when Susannah, who plays Masha, as if reading my mind, says, 'Come on, sis', shall we show our faces and have just one?'

'Why not?' I say flatly, forcing a smile.

'Ladies!' calls Hugh, waving us over to the bar.

'Hugh's a sweetie,' whispers Susannah. 'I've worked for him before, and not only is he a brilliant director, but he really values his cast. The theatre is his life-blood. He should be at The National — but then shouldn't we all, darling?'

Despite early success (she was plucked from drama school at the age of nineteen to play Rumpleteazer in *Cats*), Susannah tells me she has struggled since, doing the odd commercial and bit part on telly.

'The only way I get to do the juicy, classical roles is on the fringe, in productions like this, with a couple of students or maybe a pensioner or two for an audience at matinées. But who knows, one of these days, Sam Mendes may be out there scouting for new talent,' she says brightly. 'Top up?'

She's right, and I feel ashamed for harbouring snobbish thoughts about the lack of dressing room space, the non-existent set and having to cobble together our own costumes. Some of this company have great talent and experience, and despite the hardship, they remain driven and believe in themselves. They are an inspiration to me.

No, I will not give up. NEVER.

Poor Dean. I don't imagine for one moment that a long, dreary, Russian play about three miserable sisters is his cup of tea. Nevertheless, desperate for a paying public (fewer than ten in the audience and performances are now threatened with cancellation), I cajole, chivvy, then bully him into coming along — and to bring as many of his mates as he can muster.

'Okay, you win,' he says eventually, holding up his hands, mouth breaking into a wide, toothpaste-ad grin. 'I'll come. I seem to remember I saw the movie with Whoopi Goldberg when I was a kid, and I quite enjoyed it.'

I look at him quizzically. Movie? Whoopi Goldberg doing Chekhov? 'Aah,' I say, cruelly amused. 'I think you may be mixing it up with *Sister Act.*'

'Hmm,' he says pensively. 'But it's funny, right?'

'Er ... not exactly.'

His eyes bore into mine. 'All right, I'll come, and I'll bring some of the guys as well — but on one condition,' he says, folding his arms as he leans against a desk.

'And what's that?' I enquire breezily, scooshing some anti-static cleaner onto a computer screen.

'That you'll let me take you for dinner one night.'

Unaccustomed as I have become to being asked out on dates (let alone by a guy twenty years younger than me), and particularly when I'm looking like Nora Batty, I blush a shade of dark red.

'Well?' he says expectantly, fixing me with a challenging look.

'I ... but ... well ... you don't have ...' I say guardedly. 'Okay ... but no fewer than six friends,

63

agreed?'

'Yay! Gimme five!' he says.

'What? Oh ... yay!' and we slap palms. Please don't laugh.

'How old?' splutters Wendy over lunch the next day, looking at me agog.

'I told you, about twenty-seven, twenty-eight,' I reply, nonchalantly taking a bite of my ham and cheese toastie.

'You cradle snatcher, you!' says Rachel, putting down her coffee cup.

'Now listen, he was really insistent and we need an audience, so what choice do I have?' I say reverently.

'Maybe he has a fetish for rubber gloves?' says Wendy.

'Either that, or he's got an Oedipus complex,' adds Rachel.

'Hey, I take offence at that,' I say, screwing up my face. 'You're all just jealous.'

'Damn right we are,' says Wendy. 'So when are we going to meet this antipodean hunk?'

'Whoa, not so fast! He's only asked me to dinner, not to walk down the aisle with him. And I never said he was a hunk.'

'No, but I bet he is,' says Wendy, eyes twinkling mischievously, desperate for details.

'Okay, so he is tall and looks like he works out, but what has that ...?'

'I knew it!' she says, thumping her fist on the table, sloshing coffee and mineral water everywhere. 'Isn't life funny? Here we are, flying all over the globe, never meeting anyone, and you work as a cleaner at the crack of dawn, when the only people around are milkmen and all-night garage attendants, and quick as a flash — oops, excuse the pun — this gorgeous, young guy from the other side of the world sweeps you off your feet!'

'You know, when I was a teenager, I watched films like *The Airport Affair*, and read novels like *Love in the Skies* and *Captain of My Heart*,' says Faye wistfully. 'I was sold a dream of an air stewardess's life: stolen glances in the cockpit and romantic, candlelit dinners overlooking the Taj Mahal. And the reality? "Bring me another crew meal. This one's burnt".'

'Yes, and "I didn't have a starter so knock five dollars off my share of the bill",' chips in Rachel.

'The people who wrote this stuff should be sued for misrepresentation. They should tell it as it is,' says Faye, toying with the sugar. 'That you're more likely to meet your Mr Right cleaning toilets than on board a plane bound for Rio.'

'Somehow I don't think *Love in a Broom Cupboard* or *Kiss of the Cleaner* would exactly fly off the shelves,' I remark. 'Now, talking of dishy, charming pilots, which we weren't, any developments in the Mike/Céline situation?'

'Don't ask!' they groan loudly, in triplicate.

'The latest thing is, he and his wife are now moving to a bigger house with land and stables so the kids can have horses. I mean, honestly, are these the actions of a man who is about to leave home?' says Rachel, shaking her head wearily.

'Why she stays with him, I'll never know,' I say. 'Such a lovely girl, with so much to give.'

'She once said to me, "What if there is no one else out there for me?" As if, and anyway, surely being on your own is better than this constant heartache?' says Wendy.

'I guess things are never black and white. I mean he must have something, mustn't he?' I say feebly.

There is a thick silence between us as we stare into our empty coffee cups.

'Shit! Is that the time?' says Faye, gesturing for the bill, a slight wobble in her voice. 'I've to pick Tariq up from school, and I daren't risk being late.'

'Lunch is on me,' says Wendy, helping her put on her jacket. 'Now go!'

'I'll call you,' mimes Faye, cupping her phone between her ear and shoulder as she dashes out of the door.

'I'd better make a move too,' says Rachel, pulling out her purse. 'I've got to check in in three hours, and I haven't packed yet.'

'Where are you off to, Rachel?' I enquire.

'A six-day Kinshasa, and it's still the rainy season, so you can't even sit by the pool. Don't you miss it?'

'I did in the beginning, but not now. Six days of Sudoku and reading *Hello!* cover to cover would drive me insane.'

'What are your plans for the rest of the afternoon, hon?' asks Wendy eagerly. 'There's a new gallery just opened in Twickenham. Do you fancy going along to have a look?'

'Mind if I give it a miss? I've got to work on my lines — and I've promised myself a MOT this afternoon,' I say, pointing to a spot of Vesuvian proportions, smouldering on my cheek.

'Silly me, I was forgetting, you've got to look your best for your toy-boy,' she teases.

'It has nothing to do with him,' I say firmly, 'and anyway, you're a fine one, what's this I hear about you and the LA hotel fitness trainer?'

'No comment.' She winks, snatching the bill. 'My treat, girls. I insist.'

66

'Thanks, sweetie,' I say, squeezing her shoulder. 'Next time it's definitely on me.' (I've lost count of how many coffees, lunches, drinks and dinners I now owe, though Wendy reassures me that this isn't how friendship works. All the same, when I get that West End job ...)

'Off you go, Rachel,' says Wendy, tapping her PIN number into the hand-held machine. 'You know what the M25 can be like at this time of day.'

'Thanks, angel. I'll see you both at the play. Sooo excited! Break a leg, Em!' she says, grabbing her car keys and blowing a kiss.

Wendy escorts me to the rack where my bike is parked. As I lean forward to release the padlock, I flinch.

'Darling, you've got to give up this cleaning lark,' she says, rubbing my back gently. 'Surely there's something else you could do — less physically demanding and better paid.'

'I know. I promise once the run is over, I'll hang up my Marigolds for good.'

'I'm glad to hear it,' she says, sliding elegantly into her car. 'Now go home, get some rest, and oh, do something about those nails, please. I can hardly believe that this is the same Emily Forsyth who, not that long ago, was awarded a distinction for Cabin Crew Grooming.'

I peer at my distorted reflection in my bicycle bell, face like a Cabbage Patch doll, messy hair poking out from under my cycle helmet. Was that woman really me? The one who had monthly manicures, pedicures and facials? The one who was photographed for the in-flight magazine, gracefully pouring tea into a china cup, and lovingly tucking in a sleeping passenger with a tartan blanket?

I pedal through the park, my tyres making a

scrunching sound on the crisp, copper and gold autumn carpet. A startled stag bounds out of the bushes and off into the distance, a garland of ferns trailing from his battle-scarred horns. An unexpected rush of contentment floods through my veins. There's definitely something to be said for this spartan life. Sometimes, like now, it gives me a fresh view of the world. I must have driven through this park hundreds of times in my nifty little sports car. Did I ever notice things like this back then? Did I ever smell the damp undergrowth, or stop to watch the heron balancing on one leg in the rushes? Despite being flat broke, exhausted and spotty, I wouldn't swap my life now. It's a small price to pay to be allowed to act on a professional stage (albeit four wooden pallets shoved together, barely twelve feet long). No one ever said it was going to be easy. Most good actors start from the bottom, don't they? It's not as if I have dreamy aspirations of becoming the next Kristin Scott Thomas or anything; but so long as I can keep myself financially afloat, who knows what opportunities may come my way. In the meantime, I have a date with a cucumber face pack and a jar of Cutex Cuticle Cream.

'Is that the excited chatter of an audience I can hear?' says Susannah in disbelief.

'OMG! Did someone say the word *audience*?' says Ed, playing Chebutykin, sarcastically, cocking his ear.

'Darlings!' says Hugh, bursting into the dressing room, beaming expansively. 'Now don't let it throw you, but we have actually sold twenty-six tickets! I knew that review in *Time Out* would do the trick. Good luck, everyone, and oh, this is your five-minute call.'

With only forty seats in the place, that's two-thirds

full.

What a difference an audience makes; to hear reactions to what's said on stage lifts everyone's spirits and performances. Everything is heightened, and the lines ring out earnest and true.

Instead of the usual, muted interval break, the atmosphere in the dressing room tonight is lively and buzzing.

'You know the bit where I say, "Your clock is seven minutes fast"? Well, I got a reaction! Woohoo!' says Nick, playing Kulygin. 'They've actually picked up on my psychoneurosis — that I'm more concerned about the clock than the fact that my wife may be sleeping with another man. Bitch!'

'I do love you really, darling,' says Susannah, blowing him a kiss in the mirror.

'This calls for a celebration. Tea all round,' I say, flicking the kettle switch and collecting everyone's mugs.

As Act Four unfolds, we have the audience in our grasp — not one shuffle or yawn or mobile phone menace.

'"If only we knew, if only we knew!"'

The music fades. The lights go to black and there is silence. Lights up, and we join hands for the curtain call. Thunderous applause cracks the air, accompanied by cheering, whistling and stomping.

There's Dean on his feet, doing one of those shrill whistles I've always wanted to replicate, but never quite mastered (you know, the one using your index finger and thumb?).

Soon the whole audience is up on their feet. We all look at one another in astonishment, savouring the atmosphere. Dean is true to his word, and his rent-a-crowd has come up trumps.

'See the trouble I go to to get you to have dinner

with me?' he says later in the bar, handing me an enormous glass of wine. 'We really enjoyed it, didn't we, guys?'

'Aw, you're just saying that,' I say, fishing.

'Nope, but strewth, what was the big deal with Moscow? I was there in June, and I much preferred St Petersburg.'

'Darling! Well done!' A familiar, cultured voice cuts through the raucous babble, and I turn to see Portia walking towards me, arms outstretched, theatrical in her long, burgundy velvet coat and fedora.

'Is this the same woman who, not so long ago, was embarrassed to lay bare her emotions?' she says, clasping me to her. 'You shone tonight, Emily. I'm proud of you.'

'Really?' I say, secretly thrilled, but a part of me believing she's only being polite.

'*Really*. Your performance worked. You breathed life into Olga, and my heart went out to her. I wept at the end.'

'It's so nice of you to say so, but I can't help feeling I come across too whingeing, too bitter at times.'

'Not a bit of it. You got the balance just right.'

'I'm not so sure,' I say, giving a self-deprecating shrug. 'Some nights I feel my insecurity infects the audience and I lose them altogether. The more I think about it, the worse it gets.'

'If you're worrying too much about the audience, then you're not concentrating. Believe in yourself more, Emily. Remember Shakespeare's words in *Measure for Measure*? "Our doubts are traitors, and make us lose the good we oft might win by fearing to attempt".'

'I guess you're right,' I say thoughtfully. 'Anyway, why should I worry? It's hardly the West End, is it?'

'Listen, darling, I've done more plays in run-down

halls and spit-and-sawdust pubs than you've had ... airline dinners.' Her expression turns sombre as she says, 'Treat each job with professionalism, no matter if it's the stage of a pub or ... or The Palladium.'

I look deeply into her face, willing some of that God-given talent, some of those long years of hard-grafted experience to rub off on me.

'Are you up for Waltzing Matilda's karaoke bar later?' interjects Dean, resting his elbow on my shoulder.

'Sweetie, you were fab!' chorus Wendy and Faye, popping up unexpectedly behind me.

'Emily, what are you drinking?' calls Hugh from the bar.

'Portia, come and meet ...'

I turn around and she is gone.

It seems I've only just drifted off, when I am woken by Rod Stewart belting out 'Maggie May'. I open one eye. 04.30. Slamming the OFF button on the radio alarm, I raise my head from the pillow. I feel like I'm drowning in a swirling, green, psychedelic sea. I fall back, holding my head in agony. The thought of overflowing bins and disinfectant makes me want to throw up. With rehearsals over, at least I'm free from nine until the evening show, I tell myself as I stagger to the bathroom, one hand grimly holding my head, the other my stomach.

The road approaching the office is riddled with bumps and potholes, and normally I manage to avoid the majority of them, but this morning, with my eyes half shut, I cycle headlong into each and every one, rattling my bones and jarring my nerves. It's Dean's day off, thank God, otherwise seeing me look like Bride of Dracula in Marigolds, the dinner à deux would doubtless be cancelled without further ado.

Yes, okay, I admit I'm actually looking forward to it. He is rather fanciable and I am flattered to be asked out by someone younger; besides which, it will make a nice change from Lean Cuisine for One.

As I push the Dyson to and fro, gradually, agonisingly, fragments of last night seep into my fuzzy consciousness, torturing my mind. Last night I truly believed my rendition of 'Dancing Queen' was worthy of a part in *Mamma Mia!* Now, in the cold, sober light of day, it's dawning on me that I must have sounded like a wild dingo.

That night, and for the remaining ten performances, we are back to an audience of sleepy pensioners, uninterested schoolchildren and the odd drunk from the bar. We now know how it feels to have an appreciative crowd, and so the remainder of the run is an anti-climax; a bit like getting upgraded to first class once, and then having to revert to flying economy.

Dean turns up on the last night for our dinner date decked out in an ill-fitting, rumpled suit. He confesses he watched scene one then retired to the bar, so by the time the curtain comes down he's had 'a gutful of piss'.

'The table's booked for ten forty-five,' he says, planting a slobbery kiss on the back of my neck. I stare at the floor and notice his trousers barely reach his ankles, and that he's wearing a pair of shabby trainers (try to ignore this, Emily).

Pressing his hand firmly into the small of my back, he steers me towards the door. Why am I already starting to feel this was a bad idea?

The Thai, doll-like waitress, wearing turquoise silk

and an hibiscus flower, smiles graciously and leads us to a dark corner of the cram-packed restaurant.

By the time our Tom Yum Goong soup arrives, I *know* this was a mistake. I should have insisted we just go for a drink. I vaguely remember Faye telling us that night at Waltzing Matilda's that she's joined a dating agency, and that one of the golden rules is to only agree to a coffee or drink on the first date. Then if you discover you haven't got that much in common, you don't have to endure an interminable and costly meal. Why didn't this piece of professional advice register in my brain? (Probably because at the time it was otherwise engaged in Abbaville.)

'You won't believe it,' Dean says, slurping his soup noisily, 'but this little, bendable iPhone I picked up in Tokyo has voice dialling, I can switch between music tracks by twisting it, like this ... *and* I get unlimited internet.'

'Really?' I say vaguely, eyes ghoulishly transfixed by the blade of lemon grass hanging from the end of his damp chin.

'And it has a games and iMovie app,' he says, thrusting it towards my face. 'Now Mum and Dad can see my Mrs Robinson in the flesh.'

'Sorry?'

'That's what Mum and Dad call you. You know, older woman seduces younger man.'

'What?'

'I can ask it questions too, just as you would a person. Listen!' he says proudly. 'Any good bars in this area?'

This-might-answer-your-question ... squawks the virtual assistant.

God help me, how am I to survive beyond the Sou Si Gung? I sneak a look at my watch and stifle a yawn. This is *so* embarrassing.

73

'Some of my mates are going to that new nightclub in Kingston. I said we might meet them there,' he says keenly, his glassy-eyed stare glued to my breasts.

'Look, Dean, I'm really sorry, but nightclubs aren't my thing,' I mumble, covering my chest with my napkin.

'Cool. We could go somewhere quiet for a drink — just the two of us.' He lurches forward and reaches across the table for my hand, knocking over my wine and sending the basket of prawn crackers into orbit.

'It's been a long day,' I squirm. 'I don't mean to be rude, but do you mind if I give it a miss?'

His face clouds over and an awkward silence falls between us.

The evening has got to end NOW. I stand up and fish in my bag for my purse.

'Oh, my God! I just remembered, I promised to feed my landlady's cat while she's away. Poor thing will be starving. Please take this towards the meal,' I say, clumsily shoving a twenty-pound note into his hand.

'No, please, this is my treat. Look, if your landlady's away let's buy a bottle of wine and have it at yours.'

Subtlety is obviously getting me absolutely nowhere, so there's nothing else for it: Emergency Evacuation Procedure to be deployed pronto ...

'Great idea, but not tonight, eh?' I say, giving a staged yawn. 'Now I really must go. Thanks for the meal. It was lovely.'

'But what about your main course?'

I hesitate, then spying a taxi, I leg it out the door and do a death-defying dash across the road. As I jump into my getaway car, I heave a sigh of relief, not daring to look back.

I push the living room door open a fraction.

'I'm home, Beryl.'

'Nice time?'

'So-so. Glass of wine?'

'No, thanks, dear, I've got my Johnny Walker,' she says, shaking her tumbler of scotch so the ice clinks.

'Okay then, good night.'

'Good night, sweet'art.'

Flopping onto the bed, I take a huge gulp of wine, pop open some Pringles, put on my iPod, switch off the light, and close my eyes. Ah, bliss!

Mobile rings. It's Wendy.

'Hi, hon. Sorry, I didn't expect you to pick up. I was going to leave a message. Don't want to interrupt your hot date.'

'It's okay. I'm lying on the bed with ...'

'Sorry, sorry. I'll ring tomorrow.'

'... Michael Bublé and a tube of Pringles.'

'What? No Dean? What happened?'

'Aargh, don't ask. It was a disaster. I left him at the restaurant.'

'Why? Look, I know we've pulled your leg unmercifully about the age thing, but who cares? Look at Joan Collins, look at ... Samantha in *Sex and the City*.'

'It's not just that. We simply don't have anything in common — and he dribbled his soup and spilled wine everywhere.'

'Give the guy a chance, Emily. He was probably nervous, poor lamb. How sweet of him to treat you to dinner, when he probably doesn't earn much.'

'*And* he wears Bart Simpson socks.'

'So?'

'I know, I know, I'm being a heartless bitch. But he's just not for me. How do I face him again, Wendy? What do I say?'

'I say you should give him another chance. He may grow on you.'

'No way.'

'Okay then. If you're sure you don't want to see him again, just feed him the *it's-no-use-I'm-a-lesbian* lie. That usually does the trick.'

'He's made me realise that I don't actually mind being single. Ironic, isn't it? I used to be like Olga: desperate to marry, but if only the Olgas of this world could see you don't have to have a man in tow to prove to the world how special or wanted you are.'

'But what about romance, Em?'

'I've given up on romance, Wendy. It just doesn't work for me.'

'It's early days yet, hon. Never say never. Mr Darcy may be just around the corner.'

'I'd forgotten what a minefield the dating game is. All that wondering what to wear, what to say, trying to be someone you're not; I'm getting too old for all of that. Besides, the Mr Darcys of this world go for the wasp-waisted, wrinkle-free-and-ringlets type of girl. Anyway, enough of me. What about you?'

The ensuing silence is charged with emotional intensity. Wendy and I are so close on so many levels, just like the sisters we longed for as little girls, yet the door to one area of her life is firmly barred to me. Sometimes, like now, I give it a gentle push, in the hope that it may open a fraction.

'Wendy, it's been seven years. Steve wouldn't want you to spend the rest of your life alone.'

'I know, I know,' she says, a slight tremor in her voice.

Why does tragedy call on those who least deserve it?

Wendy was a supernumerary hostess on her first flight to Mombasa. Steve was a photographer and

76

painter, on an assignment for a wildlife magazine. The moment their eyes met over the crushed Coke cans and empty nut packets of Wendy's drinks trolley, they were smitten. They shared the same humour, love of sport and travel. He encouraged her to paint. She taught him to ride horses. Before long they were living together, and finally, thirteen years into their relationship, they decided to tie the knot in a private ceremony in the place where they had met. A chill still goes through me when I remember the night I got the call, telling me that Steve had drowned in a windsurfing accident. How could he have? He was a strong swimmer. There had to be some mistake. But the tidal currents can be strong and unpredictable in that part of the world, and when Wendy saw him waving to her on the shore, she had no idea he'd run into difficulty.

I flew out to support her with making the heart-rending arrangements to bring his body home. But since the funeral, she has buried her grief, packed away her palette and easel, and when not flying, immerses herself in teaching disabled children to ride, and supporting Steve's family.

In her usual, upbeat way, she says she's grateful to have known such tender, respectful, kind, all-consuming love just once in her life, as some people, even married people, don't ever experience that.

'So, what's this I hear about you and a certain fitness trainer then?' I venture.

'He's quite cute,' she says coyly. 'But he's just for fun. Not husband material, before you ask.'

'And? Are you seeing him again?'

'Uh huh.'

'When?'

'I've got a three-day LA next Thursday.'

'What's his name?'

'Randy.'

'Randy. That's very ... American. Attractive?'

'Yeees ... in a kind of Action-Man-doll way.'

'You mean he has bendy arms and legs?'

'Naturally. *And* swivelling head.'

'Chiselled cheekbones? Dimpled smile? Designer scar on his left cheek?'

'Yep.'

'Muscular torso?'

'Of course. *And* this model also comes equipped with detachable designer shades.'

'Fuzzy, GI haircut?'

'And plastic, moulded pants.'

'So, not detachable then?' I quip, choking on a Pringle.

'Absolutely not!'

Our innate sense of the of the ridiculous runs amok, until I am so deprived of oxygen that I collapse in a heap, sloshing red wine over Beryl's pink candlewick bedspread. Oops. Another item to add to the diminishing deposit list of:

1 x headless, china figurine.

1 x out-of-tune, musical snow globe.

2 x chipped Smurfs.

1 x damaged carpet (candle wax).

1 x traumatised cat (though Beryl need never know about that one).

CHAPTER FOUR
Little White Lies

OKAY, I CONFESS. I AM A COWARD. There, I've said it. But how else was I supposed to avoid the embarrassment of seeing Dean again? And depending on which way you look at it, my sudden allergy to Mr Muscle could be considered a legitimate excuse for not being able to return to work. Besides which, what hope do I have of securing an acting role with hands like bunches of gnarled carrots?

So, Job Centre, here I come! Then it hits me like a slap in the face with a wet flip-flop: I have made myself unemployed and am therefore not eligible for benefits; unless chipped nails, and an embarrassing liaison with a security guard young enough to be my son, qualify as extenuating circumstances. Oh, God, why do I never think things through?

I spend the next two weeks see-sawing between positivity and a nervous breakdown. Then a delayed train from Waterloo leads me to the paper rack at WH Smith's ...

* * *

THE STAGE
JOBS & AUDITIONS
BEATBOXERS WANTED FOR NEW CLUB
o – k ...?
LAP DANCERS
Am not that desperate. Besides, too old and too much cellulite.
ACTORS TO PHONE BUSINESS PEOPLE
Telesales? I'd rather stick a knitting needle in my head.
SHOPPING CHANNEL PRESENTERS

Flogging power tools and gadgets on the telly may not be quite the break I had in mind, but it would be experience in front of a camera, wouldn't it?

Many actors would probably pooh-pooh the idea, but women on the verge of bankruptcy cannot be choosers. It's all very well wishing to perform the classical greats, but the hard fact of the matter is that the profit-share production has made zero profit, and Kevin Spacey and Sam Mendes haven't gotten round to calling yet. So I e-mailed the channel and after a brief Skype interview, where I had to sell a Puff the Magic Dragon ornament to an imaginary audience, they offered me a trial slot.

It may not be presenting *The One Show*, but it's got to beat scrubbing toilets and other people's coffee-stained mugs, hasn't it?

And who knows, today, shopping channel presenter, tomorrow, heaving-bosomed, bonnet-wearing period-drama heroine — okay, so period-drama heroine's mum/maiden aunt.

'There's nothing else for it — lift up your dress please,' commands George, the butch, no-nonsense sound engineer, as she strides purposefully towards me, swinging a transmitter and clip-on microphone, like a lasso. Whatever possessed me to wear my tattiest knickers, the ones with the elastic showing, on today of all days?

A receiver is poked in my ear.

'Emily, can you hear me?' comes an anonymous voice.

'Yes.'

'Say something please, so I can check the sound levels.'

'Erm ... she sells seashells on the sea ...'

'No need to shout, and mind your sibilants. Now, if I speak to you whilst we're on air, whatever you do, do not acknowledge me, okay?'

'Okay.'

'Ignore the camera, and direct all your comments to Annabelle. Take your lead from her. Remember the presenter's mantra: P-R-N. Personalise, Romanticise, be Natural. Imagine you're having a chat over the garden fence. Okay? Aaand five, four, three, two, one.'

'Good afternoon, and welcome to our brand new Victorian lifestyle programme,' gushes the oh-so-glam Annabelle, switching on her glossy-lipped, Hollywood smile, bang on cue. 'Joining me today is Victorian *expert*, Emily Forsyth, who is here to talk to us about an *exciting* new range of home products, inspired by the Victorian era.' Leaning towards me with outstretched, perfectly manicured hand, she continues in her saccharine timbre, 'Hello, and welcome.'

'Hello.' I force a smile, lips sticking to my teeth, à la Wallace and Gromit.

'Now, Emily, do tell us, when did this passion for Victoriana start?'

I wrestle with my mind, which is ordering me to

tell the truth: *six days ago, when I got this job.*

'It began at school, Annabelle. I always loved History, and the Victorian era in particular has always held a special fascination for me.'

'Let's start with this beautiful little Victorian figure. But it's not just an ornament, is it, Emily? When we lift up the lady's crinoline, we see it is in fact a beautifully crafted trinket box,' she says prissily, holding the hideous thing up to camera.

I nod earnestly, thinking that it wouldn't look out of place on a shelf in Poundland.

'Yes, Annabelle, as you said, beautifully crafted — a work of art, in fact.'

'Personalise!' comes The Voice in my left ear.

'I ... I remember when I was a wee girl, my great-grandmother had one of these on her dressing table. I've lost count of the number of beads on her dress ...'

'Show us the dress in more detail,' cuts in The Voice again.

Startled, I look up and spy myself fleetingly in the monitor. I've never seen myself on screen before (apart from the time our school was on the regional news because Miss Farquahrson, our games mistress, hit the headlines for being a man).

'Don't look into the camera,' snaps The Voice.

I grab the lady in my clammy hands and indicate the beading with my trembling finger.

'Erm, notice the ... the detail, yes, *detail* on the dress,' I stammer, swallowing hard. 'Each bead is painstakingly stitched on by hand (*what the hell am I saying?*). These are called bugle beads,' I continue knowledgeably, 'and these teeny-weeny ones are seed beads, measuring just two millimetres ...'

No sooner have the words left my mouth, than several of them fall off and roll across the table and onto the studio floor. I freeze.

'Forget the beads!' barks The Voice.

Annabelle swiftly comes to the rescue, indicating the next item.

'Now, what have we here, Emily?'

'Aah, yes, the pitcher and bowl. This is my favourite piece from today's collection, and in my opinion, the best value for money.'

'Romanticise!'

'Both the, er ... jug and the bowl are made of porcelain and are ... hand-painted. Of course nowadays we would use this purely for decoration, but in early Victorian times before indoor plumbing ... erm ... yes, before indoor ...'

What in God's name is she doing?

I find myself talking to Annabelle's behind, as she crouches down on the floor, head under the table.

'Ignore Annabelle — she's off camera. Just keep talking!' orders The Voice.

With unprecedented enthusiasm I jabber, 'Notice the ... the ... scalloped, gold-reaf lim ... erm, gold-leaf rim - of the jug. This is, erm ... *complemented* by the bowl.'

'Personalise!'

'... I have one just like this on my dressing table at home. The lovely, floral design symbolises love. In the Victorian era flowers spoke a secret language ...'

Annabelle triumphantly holds up the misplaced information card, calmly resumes her seat, adjusts her skirt, flashes her gleaming smile to camera two — and proceeds to cut me off mid-flow. 'Well, that's item number 1653, the Victorian pitcher and bowl at an unbelievable price of £24.99. Ooh, I'm hearing the phone lines are very busy, so hurry to avoid disappointment. Now, Emily,' she says, moving over to the mock fireplace. 'Tell us about this charming Victorian fire-screen.'

Oh shit. Nobody mentioned anything about standing up and moving about. Guess I just follow her lead. Look relaxed, natural. No sudden, jerky movements. The camera tails me, past the fake bookcase and plastic aspidistra, to the hearth. Ignore it. Look natural. Pretend you're having a chat over the garden fence. Personalise. Romanticise. Be Natural.

'This is typical of the kind of fire-screen you would have found in the front parlour of a Victorian home. I have one just like this that hides a nasty electric heater. The design is hand-painted (*is there no end to my lies?*), and notice the stunning scroll design,' I gush, stooping to indicate this feature, whilst ever so subtly showing off my new, stick-on nails. I think I'm starting to get the hang of this now. The key is to stay calm and cool, be persuasive, yet not too pushy — none of that hard sell stuff. P-R-N, P-R-N ...

'Tell us, Emily, how is this *distressed effect* achieved?'

Straightening up, I feel a sudden twang.

'Hmm?' I say in a high-pitched tone, glued to the spot.

Annabelle is looking at me quizzically. I see her mouth moving, but her words wash over me. Yep, the inevitable has happened, and I am about to disgrace myself in front of the entire British Shopping TV nation. The transmitter, which is attached to my ancient, washed-out knickers, is now hanging by a thread, dangerously dangling somewhere around the knee area, like a bungee jumper about to plummet to the ground at any moment. Panic surges through me. I haven't a clue what Annabelle means by a *distressed effect*, but one thing I know for sure: several thousand viewers will suffer the distressed effect if the elastic snaps. Oh, shame! Oh, earth-swallow-me-up-shame! The phone lines will be jammed with complaints, and

I will be a national laughing stock. Just when I thought I'd broken into the glamorous, lucrative world of television, my career, just like my knickers, is in tatters before it's begun. Oh, God, oh, God, why am I such a calamity? Is this your idea of a practical joke? If you're listening, why can't you pick on someone else for a change? *Please.*

Annabelle is chuntering on and on, and I nod intelligently, trying to hide the fact that I am experiencing a major technical hitch. Dear Lord, when will this be over?

At last she wraps up the half hour with, 'Well, I'm afraid we've run out of time for this, our first Victorian special ... (... *and probably our last,* I almost hear her say). Coming up next is Tracey with her *Pampering for Pets Hour*. My thanks to Emily, and to you, the viewers at home for joining us. Bye for now. Byee.'

'Well done!' says Annabelle with an unconvincing smile. As she turns her attention to the crew, I seize the opportunity of hoisting up my knickers through my dress. Scary George appears out of the shadows, and I am unceremoniously unplugged. Now what? How do I make it out of the studio and along the corridor to the safety of the loo, without shedding my last scrap of dignity?

'I've got another presentation in studio three in fifteen minutes,' says Annabelle, consulting her watch. 'Would you like me to take you back to the green room?'

'*No!* I mean, I'll be — fine. Thanks,' I say in a falsely bright tone.

She looks at me expectantly. I rootle in my bag, pretending to look for my Oyster card. Please just go, *please.*

'Well,' she says, shrugging her shoulders, 'maybe

see you again some time. Don't forget to hand in your pass to security.'

'Yeah, sure,' I say, pausing mid-rummage to give her a little wave. 'And ... thank you.'

I look round and survey the scene. A couple of cameramen are winding up cables, whilst a studio assistant is setting up for *Des's DIY Show*. I seize my chance, and keeping my knees tightly together, shuffle out into the long, long, brightly lit corridor, past the photo gallery of perfectly groomed presenters, their twinkling-toothed smiles beaming down at me.

Never has the sight of the little skirted figure on the loo door been so welcome.

Phew! I've made it. Safe inside, I let the offending briefs drop and hastily chuck them in the bin.

I travel home in a shameful, knickerless state, promising myself that when that pay cheque finally arrives, it's off to M&S for me.

Should any of you be considering a career as a shopping channel presenter, here are some of Emily's handy, on-camera tips for ladies:

1. Wear trousers or a skirt; something with a *firm* waistband.
2. If you simply *must* wear that floaty little *Monsoon* number, NEW knickers with REINFORCED elastic obligatory.
3. NEVER use words like *unbreakable, shatterproof* or *sturdy* — you're asking for trouble.
4. Whatever happens (product malfunction or comet colliding with earth), KEEP TALKING!!

* * *

Over the next few weeks, I gulp, perspire, flounder, and fly by the seat of my pants through a variety of guest presentations, extolling the virtues of owning exercise bikes and Elvis commemorative plates. I tell myself to give it time, and I may yet become the next Lorraine Kelly.

But that was before the nylon, foldaway-bag fiasco, which firmly puts paid to any aspirations I may have of reporting showbiz gossip from a breakfast sofa.

It had worked so well in the bedroom mirror that morning, but of course, come the live show, it all goes horribly wrong …

'This handy, nylon bag folds away to next to nothing. Its clever three-in-one design allows the bag to *grow*, so to speak, by unzipping the compartments, like this. Ahem … like *this* …' At first I try the softly, softly approach, then yank it hard, the nylon bunching up as the zip's teeth refuse to let go. 'It has a drawstring for added security,' I say, dry-mouthed, grabbing nervously at the toggle, which promptly comes off in my hand. I stare at it, memories of my last tussle with a toggle flashing disturbingly across my mind: it was during a pre-flight safety demo, in front of a captive audience of around three hundred passengers. 'Pull the toggle as shown,' the cabin service director had announced into the microphone. Distracted by the rare sighting of an oh-so-dreamy passenger in business class, I yanked it too hard, and the jacket inflated with a loud hiss, leaving me standing in the aisle, looking like Mr Blobby.

'Do not inflate your lifejacket until you are outside the aircraft.' Cue mass, hysterical laughter.

Meanwhile, back in the studio, you can hear a bead drop. The cameraman's head rises slowly from behind the lens. The floor manager is gesticulating wildly with her clipboard, mouthing, 'Go onnnn!'

Say something, tolls a voice in my head ... *anything.* But it's of no use; my brain and mouth refuse to communicate with one another. Initially, fear spreads through me; then, all at once, another, louder voice cuts through the mental chaos, calmly saying, *Why have you allowed yourself to be sidetracked into this wow-factor world of easy payments and on-air testimonials? This is ludicrous. An actress is what you want to be, not Sir Alan Sugar's sidekick.*

I march back along the corridor, heels clacking decisively along the tiled floor, eyes focused straight ahead. I can almost hear the laughter echoing behind me from the Barbie and Ken lookalikes on the gallery wall.

*Where **did** they find her?*

She's obviously never been to a tanning studio in her life.

And those teeth! Has she never heard of veneers?

She couldn't sell hair extensions to Britney Spears even if she tried.

No, I do not belong to their world. (I sometimes wonder exactly whose world I do belong to.)

I've had enough of appearing calm when zips get stuck, buttons pop off, lids refuse to open, and garden fairy lights fuse. Despite being skint, I have to come up with a reasonable get-out plan pretty damn quick, as I'm down to demonstrate hand-held turbo steamers the day after tomorrow.

As I enter the green room, there's Prue from Production pacing up and down, one hand on her hip, the other clasping her mobile to her ear.

'What happened, Emily?' she says tetchily, snapping the phone shut and ushering me into the ladies' dressing room. My stomach clenches. 'I accept things go wrong sometimes, but we expect our presenters to carry on regardless, not freeze up.'

'You're absolutely right, Prue. In fact I've decided that ...'

'Sales were very poor, I'm afraid. The client's been on the phone already. He's not very happy, as you can well imagine.'

'Of course. I really feel that I'm not ...'

'We can't run the risk of losing valuable business in this way.'

'Quite. I'm just not cut out ...'

'I'm sorry, I know it's short notice, but I've decided to take you off the Turbo Steam Cleaner slot — in fact, I won't be assigning you to any more presentations in the future.' Voice softening, she continues, 'Many actors find they simply aren't suited to this type of work, so don't lose any sleep over it, will you?'

Oh no, Prue, I won't. In fact, had you come up for air and listened to what I had to say for just one moment, I would have told you that I'd already decided that you'd have to find someone else to promote your turbo steam cleaners, rotary choppers and electrical foot warmers because I QUIT!

I wish I could be like Faye. Whatever life throws at her, she always manages to radiate positivity. She's walking proof that yoga, chanting and candlelight meditation really do work. (I tried this once, but fell asleep and the candle dripped wax onto Beryl's shag pile, so decided not to risk it again.)

The day after my dramatic exit from the shopping channel, I invite myself over to hers for green tea, reassurance and reflexology.

'Why am I so hopeless at everything, Faye?' I snivel. 'Whatever I do, or try to do goes pear-shaped. My life's a mess. I'm in my forties, for God's sake!

What was I thinking of, giving up a perfectly good job and ...'

'Shh,' she soothes, pressing hard on the soles of my feet. 'Breathe, breathe, nice and slowly. Imagine you are breathing in white light. Shut your eyes and concentrate on the sound of the waves breaking onto the shore. Now visualise what it is you want, and repeat after me, *I am opening myself to new possibilities.*'

'I am opening myself to new possibilities.'

'Good. Now, whatever it is you want, start *believing* that it will happen. Imagine yourself in that situation, and it will have a positive effect on bringing about your heart's desire. It is possible for our thoughts to control the universe. What do you want from life, Emily? Visualise it ...'

NURSE: You do realise, don't you, that I could be dismissed from Holby for getting involved with a patient?

DISHY PATIENT: Look me in the eyes and tell me you don't feel it too? I love you, and if I make it through the operation, then I want you to promise me we'll spend the rest of our lives together.

NURSE: But if the Medical Council finds out ...

DISHY PATIENT PULLS NURSE TOWARDS HIM. THEY KISS ...

'Aunty Em! Aunty Em!'

I wake up with a start to find wide eyes, the colour of conkers, beaming down on me.

'Tariq! Get down! Mummy told you not to go in there!' scolds Faye.

'It's okay,' I say, rubbing my eyes. 'Blimey, how long have I been asleep?'

'Only an hour or so,' says Faye gently. 'You looked so peaceful and happy, I didn't want to wake you.

How do you feel?'

'All kind of ... floaty, more calm ... less like I want to crawl under a stone.'

'Good! Now Tariq and I insist you stay for tea, and he'd like you to read him *Gangsta Granny* again. He says your story telling is much better than mine as you can do all the voices.'

'Aah, nice to know someone appreciates my acting skills.'

'Then I've got a nice bottle of Sauvignon in the fridge we can crack open,' she says, popping two extra fish fingers under the grill.

Universe, whilst I am thankful for having been rescued from pending poverty, I think my visualisation may have got muddled with someone else's. At the risk of sounding ungrateful, an actress is what I have in mind, not a receptionist — albeit at a posh firm of solicitors on Richmond Green — and I am well aware that £9.50 an hour is not to be sniffed at. It's just that almost three months have now gone by, and despite chanting 'I am opening myself to new possibilities' at every available opportunity, nothing seems to be happening.

'Get me the Fowler versus Rogers file, Miss Forsyth.'

'Six coffee and biscuits, and one herbal tea for meeting room six.'

Brrr, brrr!

'Special Delivery for *Morgan Smith.* Sign and print here.'

Brrr, brrr!

'*Morgan Smith and Sons,* Emily speaking, can you hold please?'

'This needs to be couriered over to Westminster ASAP.'

'Good morning. Could one of your solicitors sign this affidavit please?'

'Miss Forsyth, I'm *still* waiting for that file.'

Aargh! Not sure how much more I can take of decrees nisi, disbursements and Latin phrases I don't understand.

It's dawning on me that if I rely solely on the Positive Thinking Method, I'll be so old I won't be able to memorise my lines, and the only part open to me in *Holby City* will be *GRANNY ON LIFE-SUPPORT MACHINE.* I must therefore combine positive thinking with positive action ...

I am becoming very skilled in the art of *SPC. It's a rather perilous exercise, and requires nerves of steel in order to execute it successfully, but to my mind, the potential reward is worth the risk. Hidden in the stationery catalogue on my desk, is a copy of *Contacts,* which is an actor's bible, containing lists of rep theatres, agents, casting directors and TV companies. I am methodically working my way through it, making as many as four SPCs per day when it's quiet; one if I'm lucky, when it's manically busy, like today.

'Hello, is that The National Theatre?' I whisper. 'I'd like to submit my details for casting of ...'

'Miss Forsyth! Get me a cab to chambers immediately!'

'... yes, that's two boxes of self-seal window envelopes, and one pack of black ring binders please,' I say, emerging from under the desk.

Removing my glasses, my eyes meet the steely gaze of the senior partner and my boss, the *gorgeous* Mr Nelson, with his yellowing shirt and matching teeth. Oh, Judge John Deed, where are you?

(*sneaky phone calls)

But nil desperandum! PT + SPC eventually leads to AUDITION! And not a profit-share production this time, but a *real* acting job: one with a weekly wage and a real stage in a real theatre, and proper dressing rooms — ooh, this is more like it.

I must endeavour to curb my excitement though, as I'm learning this inevitably leads to disappointment.

There's just one minor drawback about this audition: it's for a play about tap dancing, and I can't tap dance.

Well, that's not exactly true; I can just about manage a shuffle-ball-change, and since I'm auditioning for the part of the tall, thin, drippy one with no co-ordination, I guess it doesn't really matter — does it?

Linoleum is not the ideal surface for tap. You don't quite achieve that *42nd-Street* sound, and Beryl's kitchen floor is now covered in black scuff marks, which won't wash off. I try the top of a tea chest I find in her shed, but it's a little on the small side, and I keep falling off it, until it eventually splits.

Aha! Inspiration strikes. Why didn't I think of it before? The solution to my practice problem is staring me in the face every day at *Morgan Smith & Sons*: the expanse of highly polished marble floor in reception — and there's even a full-length mirror as well.

Between one and two we close for lunch, so the minute those doors are locked and the answer-phone button pressed, it's on with the tap shoes and iPod, and Miss Emily Forsyth, receptionist becomes Miss Roxie Hart, star of *Chicago*.

* * *

Audition Day – Your sins will find you out.

I take a deep breath as I enter the doors of the drill hall. Whatever possessed me to put *Tap Dancing: highly skilled* on my CV? Think positive, girl! Remember, like so many things in life, dancing is only ten percent skill and ninety percent confidence. I toss my head and stride purposefully ahead, following the clickety-clack sound of tap shoes on wood.

A woman of around fifty, with mad hair and hula-hoop earrings, ticks off my name and takes my picture.

As I emerge through the double doors into the rehearsal room, I find myself in a scene straight from *A Chorus Line;* swarms of intense, highly-trained hoofers in holey, faded dance gear arch their backs and touch their toes, some launching into little routines, spinning like tops, arms outstretched, oblivious to everyone around them. You can almost taste the adrenaline, the passion, the hope, the rivalry. I catch sight of myself in the full-length mirror opposite, all startled and skinny-legged, like a prize turkey. Well, I can either: a) Tap discreetly out of the door to the dressing room, grab my stuff and run out into the safety and anonymity of the street. b) Feign an injury if it all becomes too embarrassing — on second thoughts, perhaps not, as this could backfire and may culminate in my being whisked off to A&E. c) Pull my stomach in, stick out my chest, paste on a pair of jazz hands and a cheesy grin.

I'm here now and will probably never see these people again, so plump for option 'c'.

Neville, the spray-tanned, chief choreographer glides into the room, like a ship in full sail.

'Right, everybody, can I have a bit of hush please? Thank you. I'm going to split you into two groups. Group A will work with me and group B with Trixy here.' (She of the big hair and earrings.)

'We're going to take you through a short and simple routine, which you'll perform to Peter, the director and the rest of the choreography team. Those selected for the next stage will then be asked to read from the script. Any questions? Good.'

I am seconded to Neville's group with about twenty others, many of whom know one another.

'Darling! Mwah, mwah. How *are* you? What have you been doing since *Les Mis*?'

'Touring in *Joseph - again*.'

'I couldn't face another six months of *Hairspray*, so I've been resting, having some *me* time.'

'Mmm, I know what you mean. I was getting to the stage in *Phantom* where I was sleepwalking the routines.'

It's at this point I feel the panic start to bubble inside me.

'Now pay attention!' commands Neville, clapping his hands and striking a dramatic pose. 'Watch carefully please. Okay, Julian, from the top,' he says, nodding in the direction of the pianist.

'Shuffle, hop, step, tap, sliiide, sliiide, kick, turn, cramp roll, shuffle, hop ...'

Simple routine, eh?

'Right now, I'll do it once more, but this time I want you all to shadow me, so form a line behind me. Thank you, Julian. And five, six, seven, eight ... shuffle, hop, step, tap, sliiide, sliiide ...'

All too quickly it becomes a blur, as my brain staunchly refuses to co-operate with my body. Shuffle, hop, step, tap, kick, step, no, slide, shuffle, no, turn ... aargh!

'Everyone got it?'

At the risk of appearing completely clueless, I clear my throat and tentatively put my hand up, but then the door bursts open and the other group clatter in noisily, practising their little kicks and turns. I detest their serene confidence, their smugness.

I raise my hand once more, but yet again I am upstaged: this time by the arrival of the panel. As they take their seats behind the trestle table, the only sounds to be heard are the shuffling of CVs and photographs, accompanied by the glug-glug of mineral water being poured. Eventually they look up at us grim-faced, as much as if to say, *Well, go on then, entertain us.*

'Okey-dokey, everyone ready?' calls Neville enthusiastically, flicking his silk scarf over his shoulder and flinging his arms wide.

'We'll have Group A first, please. Now remember, try to look as if you're enjoying it, and don't forget to give it some *razzmatazz!*'

I reluctantly drag myself to my feet, then shuffle along the back row until I am safely tucked behind a tall, willowy creature, who doubtless knows what she's doing.

'And when you're ready, Julian, from the top, thank you!'

'And five, six, seven eight ...'

It only takes a couple of bars of 'Steppin' Out with My Baby', before I'm a step behind, and why, oh why do I keep on turning the opposite way to everyone else? Gotta stop looking in the mirror ... oops ... now I've collided with the girl to my left. I duck, narrowly missing an extended arm, belonging to the *Phantom* dancer in full spin before me. She darts me an icy glare. I now have a stitch in my side and have absolutely no idea what my feet are doing.

Julian ends the piece with a Liberace flourish, and we make way for Group B, who perform the routine with assured ease.

We stand about nervously as the panel scribble notes, then huddle together, whispering and pointing.

I fix my awkward gaze on a frantic bluebottle, buzzing about the windowpane, desperately seeking an escape route.

'First of all, I'd like to thank everyone for coming,' booms the director. 'It's a difficult decision and I wish we could take you all ...'

Come off it, Peter, let's be honest, don't you mean all but the red-faced, toe-tied, middle-aged clodhopper in the back row? I am amongst those called for elimination. Well, there's a surprise.

'Thank you very much for coming ... blah, blah, blah ...'

Oh *God*, get me out of here NOW.

I don't hang around for the group-hugging, kissing and sympathetic exchange of words, opting instead to trip out of the door to the changing room as fast as my shiny new tap shoes will carry me.

Never have the busy streets felt so safe and welcoming. I walk around a bit, savouring my anonymity. I am in desperate need of a shot of sisterhood to restore my sanity, so dial Wendy's number. It rings out several times. Please pick up. *Please.*

'Hello,' comes a woozily husky voice at the other end.

'Thank God you're there! I've *got* to see you. I feel like I've just been through the fast-spin cycle of the washing machine. I went to that stupid tap audition. I should never have gone. It was horrible. I wanted the earth to swallow me up. I was the only one who hadn't been in *Hairspray* or *Les Mis* ... please say you'll meet me for a drink, *please,*' I plead, my words tumbling over one another.

SILENCE.

'Sorry, sorry, you only got back from Singapore this morning, didn't you?' I say, slapping my forehead. 'What an idiot ... I'll hang up now and ...'

'Sweetie, calm down,' says Wendy, stifling a yawn, 'I'll see what the others are up to and let's meet at The Vineyard at say ... seven? No, no, make it six-thirty.'

'Perfect. It won't be a late night. I promise.'

The prospect of a girlie night immediately lifts my feelings of gloom and despondency. Two hours to kill. Persuade myself that after being subjected to such cringe-making humiliation, I deserve that sparkly top I've had my eye on in *Monsoon* sale, and don't feel too guilty about indulging in a Big Mac and double fries either.

Le cœur a ses raisons que la raison ne connaît pas
~ Blaise Pascal.

I scan the dimly lit bar and spy Céline in the corner, staring into her glass of wine. My stomach plunges. We haven't seen or spoken to one another for months: not since I sent her THE TEXT. Oh no, she's seen me. God, this is awful. What was Wendy thinking of, inviting her? She's all too aware of the situation, my having recounted every detail to her many times over in an attempt to ease my conscience.

'Céline,' I whisper, gently touching her shoulder.

She summons a weak smile and I kiss her tentatively on both cheeks. 'I've missed you.'

She pats the seat next to her and pours me a glass of wine. I hug her tightly. She stiffens.

'I am *so* sorry,' I say a trifle uneasily. 'Can you ever forgive me? I had no right to interfere. I don't blame you for being upset with me, but I honestly thought I was being a dutiful friend; all I could think of was how I wished someone had been there to warn *me* about *Nigel's* indiscretions. But if you and Mike are happy, then that's all that matters ...'

'*C'est fini*,' she mutters.

'I mean, for crying out loud, what gives *me* of all people, the right to preach about ... what did you just say?'

'Eet's feeneeshed.'

'What? You and Mike?'

'*Oui.*'

'For good?'

'*Toujours.*'

'Darling, at last you've come to your senses ... sorry, sorry, there I go again. I should learn to keep quiet,' I say, carefully setting down my glass. 'I know you're hurting, Céline, but I promise, in time you'll see it was for the best.'

'Eleven years of my life, Emily, and where did it get me? Do you know, my parents never knew he was married? I hadn't the courage to tell them that their only daughter, their good Catholic girl, was having an affair with a married man with children. All the deceit — awful.'

A huge tear rolls down her cheek and splashes into her wineglass. I resist the temptation of churning out any more of those well-meaning, but intensely irritating break-up clichés, opting instead to rummage around in my bag for a tissue.

'I bet you fifty pounds that within the year you'll be with someone else ... maybe married ... maybe even pregnant!'

'Oof!' she says, shrugging her slender shoulders in her typically Gallic way. She scrutinises herself in her compact mirror and runs the tissue carefully under her lower lashes.

'Fifty pounds is a fortune to me nowadays, I'll have

you know; it's the equivalent of around a whole day's temping, so my instinct must be pretty damn strong. A deal?'

'*D'accord!*' She smiles, lifting her glass to me.

'Just think, Céline, no more creeping around hotel corridors.'

'*Mon Dieu*, don't remind me,' she groans.

'Well, how was I to know you and Mike were an item? I thought I was doing you a favour, offering to take your "laundry" bag down to the concierge. Had I known it contained your toothbrush and Ann Summers négligée, all set for a night of steamy passion with the captain ...'

'*Oui*, but when I said I wanted to take it myself, why you did not listen? You are so stubborn,' she says, wagging her finger at me.

We dissolve into giggles as our minds flash back over a decade, to the unladylike tug of war that took place by the ice machine at The Wyndham Hotel in Houston; a war from which I eventually emerged victorious.

'Order this girl a pint of whatever it is you're drinking, my darlings. Lord knows, she needs cheering up,' says Rachel, kissing each of us in turn and chucking her bag and coat on a chair.

'What's happened, Wendy?' I ask, pouring the dregs of the bottle and summoning the waiter to bring us another.

'That bastard, Randy!' she says, voice controlled yet angry. 'I swapped my ten-day South America for a three-day LA so we could go flying over the Grand Canyon, and now I haven't heard a dickey-bird from him in almost two weeks. He hasn't returned any of my calls. The trip's on Friday, and I don't know if we're still going or not.'

'Maybe he'll surprise you by turning up at the

airport to meet you,' I say, trying to sound positive.

'I doubt it. He was a bit cool last time we spoke. He's probably spinning at the gym with some Jennifer Anniston lookalike as we speak. If he doesn't want to see me any more, why doesn't he just tell me? I mean, I know these things are awkward, but he hasn't even had the courage to dump me by text.'

'To be frank, I could never picture you as a Wisteria-Lane wife, hon, and anyway, that tan of his is *definitely* sprayed on,' says Rachel, attempting to lift her spirits. 'How vain is that?'

'Hmm. His bathroom cabinet was better stocked than Boots and Superdrug put together,' says Wendy with the hint of a smile. 'And if I'm totally honest, the chest waxing did bother me a bit too.'

'Oh, why can't love be like in the movies?' I say longingly. 'You don't know just how lucky you are, Rachel — to have met and married the man of your dreams so early on.'

'Well, I wouldn't go as far as to say he's "the man of my dreams". Don't get me wrong. He's a good man — *so* understanding and supportive of me, especially during the treatment. I do love him — most of the time. But I can't help looking around and asking myself, *is this it?* I've only ever had one boyfriend, and occasionally I find myself wondering how life would have panned out if I hadn't settled down so young.'

'Aah. Now, when we are *young,* we assume that there will be plenty of people out there in this big, wide world with whom we'll connect — and I mean *truly* connect,' says Faye, topping up our glasses. 'But we ladies who — for want of a better phrase, *have been round the block a few times* — no, let me finish — we can tell you that it doesn't happen very often — and in some cases, never.'

'True,' says Wendy wistfully.

'We're so busy proving to the world how capable and independent we are, that we can overlook the very thing that could bring us lasting happiness,' continues Faye.

'But perhaps we all expect too much from life,' says Céline. *'La vie est compliquée.'*

'If life were easy it would be boring and we wouldn't grow and develop,' I chip in.

'I'm not saying I'm dissatisfied,' says Rachel. 'I just can't help wondering what would have happened if I'd taken a different path.'

'This is all my fault,' I say. 'I should never have lent you *Eat Pray Love.'*

Who moved the coat stand? I grapple with it for a few frantic moments, before it crashes to the floor. Shirley blinks at me in disgust and scampers up the stairs. Why am I so weak-willed? I should know the score by now:

1-2 glasses of wine = happy/magnanimous.

3 = maudlin thoughts/slurred speech.

4 + = uncontrolled behaviour, verging on the silly.

Thank God Beryl's away. She and her sister are on a *Finding Nessie* coach trip to Inverness. For some strange reason she thinks me a lady and scrupulously well behaved.

On the way upstairs I notice my phone glowing in the darkness.

New Message: Hi, this is Ruby from Roaming Theatre. Thanks for your details. We'd like to see you for the role of Mummy Bear on Tuesday at eleven at St Mary's Church Hall, Whitechapel. Please bring along a speech and a song.

I came across the ad in last week's *Stage* below ...

POLE DANCERS WANTED IN JAPAN.

LOOKING FOR MUMMY BEAR TO JOIN DADDY AND BABY ON GOLDILOCKS TOUR.

I stagger into bed muttering in a gruff voice, 'Who's been sleeping in my bed?' Answer = no one for ages. But it's dawning on me I really don't care. Having a man in my life is not the most important thing any more. Don't get me wrong; it would be nice, but only if it were someone *really* special. I'm not worried about the tick, tick-tocking of my biological clock either. Despite having no home to call my own, no man in my life and no regular income, I am more content and at peace with the world than ever before. (4+ glasses of vino also brings out my soppy and philosophical side.)

I arrive at the office the following morning to be met with the news that there was a break-in last night. They are confident they will catch the culprits though, as security is going to examine the CCTV film footage. *CCTV?* I let out a stifled scream, no doubt giving the impression that I am in some way connected to the crime. No, this is worse; with mounting horror it is dawning on me that my tap routines have been captured on film. If only I could get hold of the tapes and destroy them. But I am not living in the world of James Bond movies. There's only one thing for it: clinch the Mummy Bear contract and get the hell out.

I got the job. Thank you, God! I am to spend the next two months in a furry suit and papier-mâché head, touring schools, community centres and retirement homes in a transit van. Hardly the RSC, daahling, but it's a paid job, and you never know, Trevor Nunn could be visiting an aged aunt in a retirement home in Billingham, and I could be just the sort of actress he's looking to cast in his next production. Anything is possible. One thing is certain: I am definitely not going to further my career stuck behind the reception desk of a fusty solicitors' office, am I? So, Dagenham, Whitechapel, Blackpool, Southport, Stoke and all points north, here I come!

Day 39 (17 to go)

I have decided The Goldilocks Experience is going to be excellent after-dinner conversation-filler in the future, but for now I am going to skim over this rather grim episode. Suffice to say, the production's rubbish, I'm rubbish, and not only that, as of today, my position of favourite auntie is on rocky ground, having traumatised not only Tariq, but his entire class too. The little innocents were subjected to the shocking sight of Mummy Bear being decapitated during 'Heads, Shoulders, Knees and Toes'. It was a disaster waiting to happen: I'd warned the wardrobe department in week one that my head was loose, after Daddy Bear knocked it during the finale, sending it spinning around 180 degrees. With my eyeholes facing the back, I couldn't see a thing. I'd tried to manoeuvre myself offstage, but in the end Baby Bear had to come to my rescue and guide me into the wings. But would they listen?

My flea-infested, furry costume now feels damp and stinks to high heaven, every bone in my body aches, and my face is covered in pimples, as a result of being shoved inside a helmet of paper and glue for three hours a day. I wouldn't mind, were our artistic efforts appreciated. It's bad enough trying to give it your all over the din of noisy, excited schoolchildren, but you'd think senior citizens would know how to behave; not a bit of it. If you're not battling against the high-pitched whistle of hearing aids, it's hecklers that are the problem. In a retirement home in Southport one old boy stood up, waved his walking stick, and shouted 'Bloody rubbish!' as he tottered out. Still, I shouldn't complain. Has it not all been worth it? We have, after all, been discovered: by one Harry Logan, who came to see the show in Blackpool, and has offered us a summer season as red coats at *Harry's Happy Holiday Camp*. Oh, Trevor, Trevor, wherefore art thou, Trevor?

CHAPTER FIVE
Highland Fling

'IT'S A QUARTER TO, DEARIE! I'll have your poached eggs on the table in half an 'oor,' comes Mrs McKechnie's lilting voice from the other side of the bedroom door.

Time is indeed a great healer; not so long ago, the mere mention of the dreaded PEs was enough to make my stomach heave. Why? Because pre-prepared poached eggs turn a funny, greenish colour and stink like, well ... 'nuff said. Could it be something to do with the altitude? Should I ever be lucky enough to meet Professor Brian Cox, I intend putting this theory to him (provided I don't lose the ability to speak). Anyway, according to my calculations, I must have served around ninety thousand of the revolting things during my ten-year flying career. Mrs M's freshly cooked full Scottish, though, is a world away from those breakfasts from hell, and just what's required for a day chauffeuring the rich and famous at the Scottish Open.

Okay, so acting work it ain't, but after eight weeks of scratchy faux fur and sleeping in a clapped-out van with shot suspension, the lure of a designer uniform, brand new Insignia Country Tourer (with sumptuous leather upholstery), *and* free accommodation at the four-star Glenfoyle Hotel, proved irresistible to this luxury-starved, would-be thesp.

'Ooh, how exciting!' Wendy had exclaimed, a hint of envy in her voice. 'You might get swept off your feet by some gorgeous, rich golfer.'

'Yes, I can picture him now,' I said wryly, 'charging across the golf course astride his buggy, sporting plus fours and a diamond-patterned sweater.'

As I descend the creaky, tartan-carpeted stairs in time to the piped accordion muzak, I am met by girlish laughter coming from the dining room. There are five of us from down south staying here, and we meet every morning at breakfast, when we exchange stories of the previous day's escapades.

'Come on, Emily, we're dying to hear about the gorgeous Pierre. We're sooo jealous. Did he whisk you off your feet?' asks ex-model Suzy, pouring me a cup of coffee.

'You could say that,' I grimace, swallowing a grapefruit segment whole ...

'You have heard of Pierre Dubois?' Judy, the transport coordinator had asked me.

I looked at her vacantly.

'Formula One World Champion 1986?'

'I'm not really into motor racing,' I replied, scrunching my nose.

'No matter,' she trilled, writing his name with a marker pen in big letters across a welcome board. 'He'll meet you at the hospitality tent. He's catching the eighteen forty-five to Nice, so plenty of time. Some girls have all the luck.'

'*Enchanté*,' Pierre said, lightly kissing my hand.

Hmm. So that's what Judy had meant. I wondered if he was single ... a man like that ... handsome, charming, famous, rich, French ... bound to be taken ... but then again, he could have tired of the young, gorgeous Côte d'Azur set and be on the lookout for a more mature, meaningful relationship with a middle-aged woman from Côte de Glasgow, couldn't he? The headline flashed before me ...

PIERRE DUBOIS FINDS LOVE
AMONGST THE HEATHER WITH ACTRESS

My Mills-&-Boon moment was then shattered by the revving of the engine.

'Get een, *chérie*,' bellowed Pierre from the driver's window. *Mon Dieu*, he cannot be serious, I thought. But *sacre bleu*, he was.

'*On y va!*' He grinned, leaning across and opening the passenger door.

'Erm, much as I would feel honoured to be driven by ...'

'*Tout de suite!*'

What was I to do? If I didn't act quickly, I was going to be left by the roadside, my brand new twenty-five-thousand-pounds' worth of entrusted Insignia Country Tourer about to disappear into a puff of Scottish mist. So I jumped into the passenger seat beside him. BIG MISTAKE.

Before I had time to strap myself in, we launched into a rollercoaster ride that brought back horrible memories of the time I threw up over a total stranger on the Tower of Terror at Disneyland.

Blithely ignoring the SLOW DOWN! CATTLE/ DEER/ ELDERLY PEOPLE CROSSING signs, Pierre zipped in between vegetable carts, tractors and tour coaches, jumping every red light along the way. I gripped onto the dashboard for grim death, slamming my foot on the imaginary brake. My instinct was to shriek '*Au secours!*' yet at the same time I didn't want to make a fool of myself. Then unusually, my practical side took over, and from the depths of my memory, popped up some of those all-important, survival strategies drummed into us in cabin crew training:

How to Survive a Ditching. NO
How to Survive in the Desert. NO
How to Survive in the Arctic. NO.
(Even if I'd had them, what good would barley sugars and a flare do me anyhow?)
What to Do in a Hijacking Situation. BINGO!
    1.   *Do not antagonise your hijacker*
    2.   *Appear to agree to his terms*
    3.   *Above all, DO NOT PANIC*
'AAAAAAAAAAAAAAH!'

'Don't worry, *chérie*, you are safe with me,' Pierre teased, smothering my hand with kisses.

'Shiiit!!! Please keep both hands on the steering wheel, *pleeease!!*' I squeaked.

CORRECTION: change that headline to ...

PIERRE DUBOIS AND DRIVER
IN 120 MPH COLLISION
WITH COMBINE HARVESTER

'Nevertheless, I'm still insanely jealous,' says Suzy, wiping her mascara-lined cheeks with her napkin.

'Believe me, being driven at breakneck speed by a tanked-up ex-racing driver — good-looking charmer or no — is not my idea of a romantic encounter,' I reply indignantly.

'Yes, but did you find out if he's single?' she continues, her baby-blues boring into me expectantly over the rim of her cup.

'Somehow, I didn't get round to asking. I had one thing on my mind at that moment, and one thing only: STAYING ALIVE. Anyway, girls, since I am alive, I'd just like to say how lovely it was meeting you all,' I say gloomily.

'What do you mean?' they chorus.

'We'll see you tonight at The Tam O'Shanter for the ceilidh, won't we?'

I bury my head in my hands. 'Judy wants to see me. I think I can safely say that I am about to be fired. My bag's packed and I've ordered a taxi.'

'Surely not?'

'Don't you see? Letting an inebriated, uninsured client take the wheel is a sackable, not to mention criminal offence,' I say.

'But nothing happened.'

'That's not the point.'

'Look, maybe you're overreacting. We'll keep a seat for you tonight, okay?' says Suzy, attempting a reassuring smile.

'Sweet of you, but I suspect I'll be back in London by then,' I say, toying with my watchstrap, struggling to keep the tears at bay.

I sit in the car outside the transport portakabin, trying to muster up the courage to go in. Another perfectly good job and much needed source of income about to evaporate. What will the bank say? They only agreed to temporarily increase my overdraft because I was able to prove to them that I had a well paid job to go to.

Why does stuff like this never happen to other people? This is the woman who got a police caution for driving too slowly on the M4, for God's sake. Nigel used to say the Mazda was wasted on me. I'm like a disaster magnet. If there's a cock-up to be made, then you can guarantee I'll be at the centre of it. Oh well, here goes ...

'Come in!' calls Judy.

'You asked to see me?' I mumble.

'I think you know what this is about, Emily,' says Judy gravely, crossing her arms as she leans against the desk.

I nod, eyes glued to the carpet tiles.

'We've had over twenty complaints from farmers, lollypop men and coach drivers, all reporting a lunatic in one of our courtesy cars, terrorising the community. Can you explain?'

'I wasn't driving,' I say, swallowing hard.

'You — weren't — driving,' repeats Judy, eyes narrowing.

'No.'

'Then would you like to tell me who was?'

As I recount the sorry tale for the second time, one corner of her mouth starts to curl up slightly.

When I'm done, she shakes her head, consults her laptop and says deadpan, 'I had you down to pick up Lewis Hamilton this morning but ....'

'No way,' I gasp, reeling.

'Just a joke,' she says, a smile playing across her lips. 'But can I trust you with three shopaholic golfers' wives?'

'I'm not fired?' I whisper disbelievingly.

'Just don't let it happen again,' she warns.

I draw up outside The Links Hotel, where I am greeted by a trio of Ivana Trump lookalikes — all big hair, gleaming teeth and Armani.

'Good morning!' they chorus as they teeter into the back. The air is immediately heavy with an exotic mix of expensive perfume.

'I'm Shelby, this is Charlene and Brianna.'

'Hi. I'm Emily,' I say, turning the key in the ignition.

Consulting a leaflet she no doubt picked up in the hotel lobby, Shelby leans forward and says, 'First of all, we'd like to visit this place where Macbeth was crowned — Scone Palace, right?'

'And maybe some shopping in *Edinburrow*?'

'And I'd like to look for the Loch Ness monster.'

'And we gotta go to the Queen's place ... er ... Balmoral, right? Is she on vacation there right now?'

They look crestfallen when I explain we'll be lucky if we manage to tick two of the boxes on their bucket list.

'But Scotland looks real small on the map,' they say in a disbelieving tone. As I twist the rear-view mirror, I register the look of dissatisfaction in their faces.

Oh dear, things are not getting off to a very good start.

By the time we reach Scone (via various bijou antique shops), it's nearly noon, and I make a mental note to keep a careful eye on the time, as whatever happens, we mustn't be late for the sponsors' dinner at seven-thirty.

For the last twenty-four hours, the ancient little town of St Andrews has been besieged by an army of broadcasting vans and helicopters, lighting rigs, cameras, press, florists, and caterers — all in preparation for tonight's glittering event.

I stride ahead to the red sandstone, ivy-clad walls of Scone Palace, followed by my trio of Trumps, gingerly picking their way through the gravel on their vertiginous heels.

PALACE CLOSED FOR MAINTENANCE

Damn! What now?

There's only one thing for it: I'll have to put those

improvisation skills I perfected at drama school (not) into practice and devise my very own tour. I cast my mind back some twenty-five years, to when I played SECOND WITCH/GENTLEWOMAN in a fifth-form production of *Macbeth*. I'm not altogether sure if what the Bard wrote was historical fact, or if he invented the whole thing. No matter, as long as they enjoy the day, who cares if the truth gets a little distorted? After all, if The Reduced Shakespeare Company can get away with it, why shouldn't I?

'Welcome, ladies, to Scone Palace, crowning place of Scottish kings, including Robert the Bruce and the tragic Macbeth, as immortalised in Shakespeare's play.'

Striking a kind of Richard-the-Third-meets-The-Hunchback-of-Notre-Dame pose, I cackle, "'When shall we three meet again, in thunder, lightning or in rain? When the hurly-burly's done, when the battle's lost and won.'"

The ladies gawp at me with a mixture of bewilderment and fear.

'It was a stormy day — a bit like today, in fact — and Macbeth was out taking a stroll on a gorse-filled moor, when he stumbled across three witches, who chanted, "All hail, Macbeth, King of Scotland!"

'Macbeth replied, "What are youse talkin' aboot you stuppit wummin?", but before he could say 'Johnny Walker', they disappeared into the *swirrrrling* mist.

'He returned to the palace, and in this very doorway here, stood Lady M, her arms folded, face like thunder.

'"Where have youse bin?"

'"Sorry, ma wee pet, but I bumped into three witches, and you'll never guess what they told me?"

'"This had better be good," said Lady M, rolling her

113

eyes.

'"They predicted that I'm going to be king someday soon."

'"Och, away with you!" she exclaimed mockingly. But the seed was sown and King Duncan was invited over on the pretext of dinner.

'"Come away in, Your Majesty. Lovely to see you! We've got haggis, neeps and champit tatties for your supper — ooh, and a bottle of Glenmorangie — I hear it's your favourite."

'Later the same evening, when they were in the kitchen preparing the coffees, Lady M handed her husband the kitchen knife and said, "Now's your chance ... go on!"

'"He's an auld man, dear ... I cannae *murrrder* him," whined Macbeth.

'"Don't be such a wuss! Are you a man or a moose?" hissed Lady M. "You do want to be king, don't you?"

'Macbeth nodded meekly.

'"Well, go on then!" she said, flicking his legs with the tea towel.

'Macbeth reluctantly did the deed, and did become king, but was haunted by Duncan's ghost — and the ghosts of a few others he bumped off along the way, including Banquo and someone called MacDuff.

'Then Lady Macbeth started showing signs of madness, sleepwalking and constantly washing her hands, moaning, "Out, damn'd spot!"

'One fateful night, she threw herself off that tower just above us and fell to her death. She landed right here, where we are standing now.'

There is a chorus of 'Gee!' and 'Omigosh!' as smartphones are whisked out of designer bags and pointed at the sacred place in the gravel.

'Such a pity the palace is closed today,' I say,

114

secretly surprised and impressed at my impromptu performance, 'as in the Long Gallery you may see ...'

My voice fades away, as I'm suddenly aware of someone standing in the arched doorway behind me. A dour-faced, beefy-looking man studies me menacingly, arms folded across his chest, kilt swishing in the breeze. I wonder how long he's been standing there ... 'Erm,' I murmur sheepishly, rocking back on my heels, 'scones and tea anyone?'

I peel back the sleeve of my jacket, hardly daring to look at my watch. Oh, ladies, how could you? It is now half past four, and we arranged to meet thirty minutes ago. I have been ordered around St Andrew Square numerous times by a particularly mean traffic warden, who was not in the least bit impressed that I am chauffeuring the wives of *celebrity* golfers.

Finally, one by one, my ladies spill out unsteadily through Jenners' revolving door onto the street, clutching their glossy carrier bags.

Okay, so it could be argued that as one of the UK's oldest department stores, Jenners may be of minor historical interest, but it's hardly in the same league as Edinburgh Castle, The Scott Monument, Holyrood Palace or The Grassmarket, is it? Like it or not, this shopaholic threesome are going to learn that there is more to this fine city than tartan, whisky and designer labels.

'Now, before we head back, ladies, we've just time to visit the statue of Greyfriars Bobby, a famous, and much loved wee dog,' I say, twisting my neck as I attempt to reverse the Insignia into a space more befitting a Smart car. Brianna shoots me a weary smile, while Shelby nudges Charlene wide-eyed, as much as if to say, *Omigod, is she gonna start barking now?*

Arm in arm, my reluctant tourists clatter down the cobblestones of Candlemaker Row, towards the granite drinking fountain, upon which sits the scruffy, bronze Skye Terrier.

'This statue commemorates the loyalty of a watch dog called Bobby, who sat by his master's grave in the Greyfriars kirkyard for fourteen years,' I enthuse. '*Fourteen!* The church gardener made him a shelter under a stone slab next to the grave.'

They look at me, glazed.

'Every day, at one o'clock, when the canon sounded from Edinburgh Castle — as it still does today ...' Charlene yawns ' ... Bobby would make his way to the coffee house in Greyfriars Place, where the owner would feed him.' Shelby is studying her nails.

'If you'd like to follow me, ladies, we can see the actual graveyard where Bobby and his master are buried.'

'Hey, girls, look at that darlin' li'l gift shop,' squeals Charlene. And with that, just like the three witches, they disappear into thin air.

No, *please* no, we haven't time for this.

I glance at my watch for the umpteenth time. Just as I'm about to burst into the shop and drag them out by their hair extensions, they re-emerge and we head off.

I wipe the condensation from the windscreen with my sleeve and peer at the stream of bright red brake lights ahead, blurred in the teeming rain. Shifting uncomfortably in my seat, I watch the numbers on the digital clock go round: 17:55 CLICK, 17:56 CLICK. They seem to gather speed as the clicking gets louder. I can feel the panic welling inside me. In ninety minutes we have to travel some forty-five miles, and my ladies have to be pampered and preened in preparation for the piping-in of the haggis; and they don't strike me as the ready-in-a-jiffy type. The windscreen wipers swish back and forth. What am I to do? Dial 999 and request a police escort? Not a good idea, Emily. After yesterday's dramatic events, best to lie low where the Fife constabulary is concerned

I study them in the rear-view mirror, laughing and preening as they compare one another's Pringle and Prada, and spray one another with Highland Heather and Dolce & Gabbana, blissfully unaware of the mounting crisis.

A few more torturous minutes go by before the line of traffic slowly surges forward across The Forth Road Bridge.

We arrive at the hotel with the petrol gauge on red and twenty minutes to spare.

'Thanks, honey,' says Shelby, pressing a one pound coin into my clammy hand as she passes her copious bags to the doorman. 'Have a nice evening!'

Nerves in tatters, I shut my eyes, lower my head onto the steering wheel and heave a sigh of relief. It's over. Now all I have to do is run a bath, pull on my jammies, order a takeaway, grab a quarter bottle of wine from the mini bar, and point the remote at the telly for the concluding part of the *Taggart* repeat. Last night's episode ended with DS Jackie Reed in a deserted multi-storey car park. It's late, and just as she's about to drive off, a man in a balaclava pops up and holding a gun to her head, says, 'Don't scream. Just do what I tell you ...'

I was almost certain that voice belonged to Ed from *Three Sisters,* but the end credits rolled by so fast I couldn't catch the actor's name. Tonight I'll sit closer to the telly and won't blink, or maybe he'll be unmasked and then I'll know for sure.

But just as I draw up outside The Glenfoyle, I

remember the ceilidh. Oh, God. That's the last thing I need. After the day I've had, I'm liable to bite someone's head off or burst into tears if someone so much as steps on my big toe.

Pull yourself together, girl. You promised you'd go, and it would be impolite not to show up. Besides which, cooked breakfasts and sitting in a car all day are starting to take their toll on your waistline, and a couple of hours of manically throwing yourself around a dance floor will give you some much needed exercise. But I hate exercise. Come on, The Tam O'Shanter's only a five-minute walk round the corner; at least then you'll have shown your face and you can be back home in time for the end credits.

The moment I open the door, Mrs McKechnie pops out of her private sitting room.

'All right, dearie? You're awfy late the night. Can I fix you a wee bit o' tea?'

'No, thanks, Mrs McKechnie, I've got to fly, I'm going ...'

'Och, you cannae go out without something tae eat.'

'No, really, I ...'

'I think the others are away oot already.'

'Yes, and I'm late,' I say pointedly, as I sidle up the stairs.

'Tell you what — I'll leave out some cheese and crackers and a wee slice of Dundee cake for your supper. My Ewan loved that cake. No wonder he was sae fat,' she says, chuckling.

I've reached the grandfather clock — only a few more steps and I'm home and dry.

'I still go to visit his sister, Aggie, on Arran. She's on her own tae. We were thinking of going to Spain next spring, but she's worried her feet'll puff up wi' the flight.'

118

I've made it to the landing.

'It's an awfy shame, but she cannae walk that well noo.'

The phone rings.

'Och, I bet that's her. We're *telepathetic*.'

THANK YOU, AGGIE!

Sucking in a deep breath and my stomach, I enter the swing doors of The Tam O'Shanter pub. I duck and dive my way past the maze of whirling revellers, in search of Suzy et al.

'Yoo hoo, Emily! We're over here!'

I weave my way over to the large table, where The Glenfoyle Gang plus the local mob are seated. There's Shonah, farmer's wife and sister of Duncan, landlord of The Tam O'Shanter, Alasdair, driving instructor and part-time pipe band leader, Ruth, primary school teacher and Scottish country dancing amateur champion, and Iain, fisherman and potter.

Before I've a chance to sit down, Ruth drags us all up to the dance floor to join in with Drops of Brandy. Admittedly I did a bit of Scottish country dancing at school, but being tall, had always to take the role of the man, so a fat lot of good that is to me now. Ruth and the locals do their level best to steer us in the right direction, but we are hopeless, like dodgem cars, colliding with one another and causing multiple pile-ups. I've got a stitch in my side, but just when you think it's all over, that diddley-diddley music has a nasty habit of going round and round and round again and again — and again.

Finally it stops, and we stagger back to our table, gasping for air.

'Everyone enjoying themselves?' comes a sexy Scottish burr behind me.

I swivel round on my barstool and my heart does

the Eightsome Reel.

'Oh, everyone, this is Duncan, my bro',' says Shonah breezily.

'Please take your partners for The Gay Gordons!' announces the caller.

Duncan holds out his hand to me and says, 'May I have the pleasure?'

'Charmed, I'm sure,' I pant in a silly, Scarlett-O'Hara tone of voice. Where the hell did that come from?

Though not as manic as the last reel, there's a twirly bit in the Gay Gordons, and by the end, I'm starting to feel dizzy and sick.

'Are you okay?' asks Duncan, his left hand resting on my waist, shifting my pulse rate up yet another gear. 'Would you like to sit down?'

'I'm fine,' I wheeze, flicking a rogue strand of hair from my sticky forehead.

Why don't I just tell him the truth? *Well, no, actually, I've got an excruciating pain in my chest, I'm seeing stars and may well collapse in a heap at any moment.* But no, I opt instead to be relentlessly pushed and pulled and flung hither and thither until I am rendered a gibbering wreck. I have no control over my legs and am minus one shoe, and yet weirdly, I could ceilidh all night.

The Duke of Perth, Strip the Willow, The Dashing White Sergeant, Drops of Brandy all merge into one, and suddenly it's 12.30 and we're all joining hands in a swirling, stamping circle. '"O ye'll tak the high road and I'll tak the low road ..."'

Reunited with my shoe, I bid everyone goodnight. Out on the street, I can hear my heart pounding in my ears. Barefoot, I head for The Glenfoyle via the West Sands, stopping for a moment to marvel at the low-hanging, milk-bottle-top moon. I close my eyes, breathe in the cool, pure air and listen to the gentle, rhythmic lapping of the waves. I dip my throbbing feet in the freezing water and gaze up at the stars. My eyes swim as memories of Nigel and I sitting on warm, exotic beaches, sipping Pina Colada in the small hours, flood my mind.

'Look, Minnie, there's Orion, and to his right, can you see, The Bear?'

'Where?'

He'd take my hand and guide it towards the diamond-filled sky.

'There!'

'Emily!'

I spin round, startled. There's Duncan, breathless, his auburn hair glinting in the silvery light.

'You left this behind,' he says, holding out my bag.

'Oh, my God, how stupid of me. Thank you,' I say, quickly wiping my tear-streaked cheeks with the back of my hand.

'I was thinking ...' he says. 'It's my night off tomorrow. There's a wonderful wee fish restaurant along the coast here. Perhaps you'd like to join me for dinner?'

I open my mouth to speak, unsure of what I'm going to say, memories of my last dinner date flooding back in glorious technicolour. Maybe I'm just not ready yet.

'Well, I ...'

'Here's my number,' he says, whipping out a business card from his wallet. 'Call me tomorrow ... if you want to ... when you're back from your travels. Now, can I walk you home?'

'No, I'm fine, really, but thanks for the offer,' I say, taking the card from him, but all the while keeping a formal distance.

'Good night.'

Those kippers don't smell too good this morning, and the accordionist sounds like he's on speed. Thank God, after yesterday's marathon, I haven't got too far to go today. My mission is to collect a VIP from his private jet, which is due to land at the RAF base, some twelve miles away.

'Sit in your vehicle and wait for the officers in the escort car,' commands the tall, uniformed guard at the barbed wire perimeter gate, as he hands me my security pass. Ten minutes go by. My eyes feel heavy and my head is thumping. My chin sinks involuntarily onto my chest ...

I am woken by a flashing, amber light, and the officer rapping sharply on the window.

'Proceed!' he yells, arm whirling like a windmill. I crunch the gear into first, the barrier lifts, and no sooner am I through, than the escort car roars off into the distance, past an aircraft hangar — and out of sight.

I am now driving down the middle of the runway without the foggiest idea where I'm headed. My heart is pounding, and I let out a stifled scream as a low-flying Tornado roars overhead. It's just like a scene from a James Bond movie. Any minute now a man dangling from a helicopter will shower the car with gunfire.

I glance to my right, and there in the distance, is a small, sleek, twin-engined jet with the escort car parked alongside it, light rotating, hazard lights blinking. As I draw up, the door is lowered and a veteran golfer I've seen on the telly, promoting luxury Spanish apartments, emerges. I step out of the car (taking the ignition keys with me this time) and flash him my sweetest smile, swiftly followed by an icy glare thrown in the direction of Starsky and Hutch.

The minute that legendary bottom touches the

back seat, I slam my foot on the accelerator, determined to keep up this time.

The security barrier is raised, and we are back on the main road. Relief washes over me. I'm so tired I can't conjure up any polite conversation, but in any case, my passenger is preoccupied with his laptop and making calls to his personal assistant.

'What time is my radio interview, Monica? Right, order the car for nine, and oh, call Sean's office and tell them I can fit in a round tomorrow.'

My ears prick up. Sean? Sean? Does he mean Scottish Sean? *The* Sean? Surely not? Yesh, Mish Monneypenny, I think it musht be.

'So, will you be playing any golf during your visit?' I ask airily, hoping he may drop a few clues.

'Hmm?' he says, sliding his Ray-Bans down his nose.

'I was just wondering if you are going to play golf while you're here?'

I am suddenly aware of how idiotic that sounds with his bag of clubs in the boot.

'I'm playing in the Pro-Am on Thursday,' he says distractedly, stabbing the keypad on his phone.

The midday sun is beating through the windscreen, squeezing all the oxygen out of the car. A sign flashes past my drooping eyes — St Andrews 8 miles.

'Mind if I open my window?' I ask.

'Sure, go ahead.'

I fumble for the switch, and the back window flies open, sending his papers into a flurry.

'Oh, God, I'm *so* sorry,' I say, pulling over to the side of the road. I dive out of the car and flail about on the hard shoulder, in a desperate attempt to retrieve them all.

'Please, just drive!' he yells from the window,

running his fingers through his thinning hair. 'I have an appointment in twenty minutes.'

Guess I've blown my chances of an introduction to Mr Connery then.

Mr Grumpy safely dispatched, I aim for the beach. I kick off my heels, the salt water cooling my blistered feet. A plane drones overhead. I picture the scene inside that metal tube: the trolley, laden with meals and drinks, emerging from the galley, queues forming for the loo, call bells ringing.

I lower my gaze and look out to sea. I may have no career to speak of and be living from hand to mouth, but I am changed; happy to be standing barefoot in the shifting sand.

I return to The Glenfoyle and quietly shut the door to avoid being accosted by Mrs McKechnie. I tiptoe over to the hall table.

Dear Emily,
You left your mobile in the dining room. It kept ringing so I answered it. Please phone Saline? (foreign lady) ASAP.
Mrs M.
P.S. Have left your phone on top of the clean towels in your room.
P.P.S. Would you like poached eggs again for breakfast – or how about kippers for a change?

'Hi, Duncan. It's Emily. Remember me? The clodhopper at the ceilidh?'

'Of course I remember you. Are you up for dinner tonight? I made a reservation just in case.'

'Look, I'm really sorry, but my friend's flight has been diverted, and she's got an unscheduled night-stop, so she's getting the train over ...'

'So, I'll just have to take you both out,' he says.

'No, really ...'

'Or better still, I'll give my pal Drew a call and we'll make it a foursome. We'll pick you up around eight at The Burns Hotel, okay? Cheery-bye!'

'But Duncan ... hello?'

Slosh some ylang-ylang oil into a hot bath and languish there. I open one eye, to meet the button-eyed stare of the knitted poodle loo roll cover sitting on the cistern. Don't look at me like that. He was so insistent. I had no choice. It would have been impolite to refuse — and anyway, it could be just what Céline needs right now to lift her spirits. But what if his friend is arrogant or boring as hell — or married?

I blow away the foam from my downy legs. Good God, girl, you should be ashamed. You're getting lazy. Just because you sleep alone now, doesn't mean you should let standards slide. I stretch a dripping arm across for my toiletry bag, and ferret to the bottom in search of my Ladyshave. An ancient, squashed sachet of passion fruit face-pack finds its way to the surface.

Flicking the razor back and forth, my taut face cracks into a wide grin. A tiny bit of me that's been lying dormant for almost two years may now be starting to wake up at last.

I hear the quietly thrumming motor of a taxi below. I look at the bedside clock. Towel drying my hair with one hand, whilst pulling on my tights with the other, I hop over to the window. It's Céline. Uh oh. She is destined to be subjected to a blow-by-blow account of Mrs M's daily movements if I don't scarper — and I do not refer to the latter's busy schedule.

I throw on my carefully planned outfit, hastily twiddle my hair into a messy bun, apply some lippy and a smidge of mascara, pull on my boots, pop a Smint in my mouth, grab my pashmina and bag, and launch myself out of the bedroom and down the stairs like a rocket.

'I get this pain at night. The doctor says it's trapped wind, but I'm no so sure. I should go back to see him, but they're always sae busy. Still, I don't complain. Och, Emily, there you are.'

'Céline!' I say, hugging her tight.

'What a nightmare!' she says, rolling her huge eyes. 'Everyone complaining. I say to one passenger, "*Alors, monsieur,* you would prefer to fly with just three engines instead of four?" That bloody well shut him up.'

'How I miss the darlings ... not.' I say, looking at my watch.

'Is it normal for your stomach to swell up when you fly?' pipes up Mrs M. 'I only ask because ...'

'Lord, look at the time!' I interject. 'Come on, Céline, we're going to be late,' I say, pushing her out of the door. 'See you at breakfast, Mrs M.'

'Kippers or poached eggs?'

'Kippers please,' I reply. 'Just for a change.'

Linking arms, we walk along the shore road towards The Burns Hotel.

'Perfect! We've got ten minutes for a quick G and T and a chat before our escorts arrive. I want to hear *all* the gossip,' I say, bubbling over with anticipation. 'Go!'

'You dumped Mike's car in his swimming pool?' I say, pushing open the door of the hotel reception and ushering her into the lounge.

'*Oui* — and the keys,' she says as casually as if she's just told me she shredded a couple of his shirts. '*After* I drive all over his precious garden.'

'You're kidding! Did anyone see you?' I say, eyes wide, hardly daring to believe what Céline has just told me.

'Good evening, ladies!' says Duncan, sauntering over from the bar. Damn. They're early. Just when we're almost at the climax of her story. I make a mental note to probe her further when the men are out of earshot. Talking about exes on a first date is a definite no-no, besides which, I don't want them thinking she's some kind of neurotic, bunny-boiling garden/car-wrecker.

'This is Drew,' says Duncan, indicating the Guy Ritchie lookalike on the barstool.

'Hi,' says his friend, getting up, then boldly kissing us on both cheeks. Bollocks to you, Mike! Revenge is sweet, they say; I say there's nothing like being taken out for dinner by two braw Scotsmen to help mend a broken heart.

Ladies, I have good news! The age of chivalry is NOT dead. I can report first-hand that this ancient practice is still being carried out in the Kingdom of Fife.

Pulling Out Of Chair √

Buying Of Drinks √

Listening skills √

Helping On With Coat/Pashmina √

A Land Rover whisks us away to Crail, a small fishing village along the coast.

As we turn off the main road, we are tossed around on the back seat like pinballs, until Drew eventually parks up on a remote, steep, grassy bank.

'It's a short walk from here,' he says, pointing to a row of twinkling lights, high up on the cliff's edge. They each open a door for us (√), and we are led along a twisty, narrow pathway. Had I known a pre-dinner hike was on the menu, I would never have

127

worn my new, kitten-heel boots with pointy toes. I stumble and stagger up the hill, battling to prevent my gypsy skirt from billowing up over my head.

Céline, on the other hand, is dressed perfectly for the occasion, in a classically tailored trouser suit with flat pumps. She strides elegantly ahead, as if on the catwalk, flanked by our two hosts, her well-cut bob swishing back and forth.

Duncan turns and waits for me to catch up. 'Are you okay? Do you want to take my arm?' he asks, like I'm some old granny trying to cross the road.

'No, I'm fine, you go on ahead,' I say brightly, my pashmina flying across my mouth and nose.

I look up, and coming into view at last, is a stone built, whitewashed cottage, with tiny, leaded windows. A wrought iron sign bearing the name Maggie's Fish Restaurant in weatherworn lettering swings back and forth, squeaking in the blustery wind. The heavy, wooden door creaks open and it's like we've stepped back in time; there's a fireplace big enough to sit in, a young lass, perched on a beer barrel, plays a reel on the fiddle, lobster pots hang from the beams, candles glow from wax-covered bottles, and the smell of fresh fish, mixed with smouldering, damp wood, hovers in the air.

Duncan and Drew pull our chairs out for us to sit down (√) and order a bottle of wine.

'So, ladies, how did you two meet?' asks Drew, while we wait for menus.

'On our cabin crew training course,' I say, nervously twiddling my napkin and glancing at Céline.

'Did you ever experience any emergency situations?' he asks eagerly.

''fraid not. But lots of hilarious ones, didn't we, Céline?'

'Well …?' says Duncan, filling our glasses, his voice enthusiastic.

'Don't get us started, please, we could be here all night,' I say.

'Go on,' they implore, sounding genuinely interested. Oh well, they did ask …

We are in our element now, and our initial awkwardness gives way to uninhibited, frivolous banter.

Before we know it, Maggie's coming over with the dessert menu. I drag Céline off to the ladies for a nose-powdering expedition.

'Well?' I say to her excitedly, as I close the door.

'You have a little piece of broccoli in between your teeth, *chérie*.'

'Never mind about that,' I say, glancing in the mirror, horrified at my Edward-Scissorhands hair. 'So, what about Drew?'

'*Pas mal*,' she shrugs, giving nothing away.

'*Pas mal? Pas mal!* You are joking. He's *gorgeous*, and he can't take his eyes off you,' I say, pulling my comb through my tangled mop.

She blushes madly and smiles. I haven't seen that beautiful smile for so long. I've grown so accustomed to seeing her looking strained and on the brink of tears.

'Come on,' I say, baring my teeth, checking in the mirror for any more bits of vegetation. 'Our knickerbocker glories will be melting.'

'Okay, guys, now it's your turn to speak,' I say, sinking my long spoon into gooey chocolate and whipped cream. 'How did you two become friends?'

'At school,' Duncan replies, pouring the coffees. 'More than thirty years ago now — I can hardly believe it. We used to go fishing and camping together in the holidays. We were inseparable.'

129

'Aye,' says Drew. 'Then when I was in my twenties, I went out to South America to work for The Forestry Commission. Since coming back, I've been running the Laird's estate out at Brig o'Muckhart. Whenever I'm in need of a dram and a blether, I call in on my old pal here,' he says, draping his arm fondly over Duncan's shoulder.

Céline's starry gaze falls to her watch. '*Mon Dieu!*' she groans. 'It is almost ten. The last train leaves at ten forty-four.'

Duncan signals for the bill, and he and Drew fish out their wallets.

'Shall we go Dutch?' I ask, reaching under the table for my bag.

'Och, away with you, it's our pleasure,' says Drew, putting his bank card on the table.

'Absolutely! What kind of a man invites a lady to dinner, and then expects her to pay?' snorts Duncan.

Most of the men I've dated, I think.

Generosity: check √

'Who is it?'

One eye focuses on the luminous numbers of the digital clock: 02:10.

'Emily, *c'est moi*, Céline.'

I sit bolt upright. 'Oh, my God, Céline, what's happened?' I babble, my mind racing. I should have made sure she caught the last train instead of allowing her to disappear with a man we only met once. I can picture her at the other end of the line, battered and bruised, waiting at A&E for me to pick her up.

'I can't sleep,' she says, with breathless excitement. 'I had a wonderful evening, and when I come back from Chicago, I'm going to Breeg ... Breeg ... *merde*! ... to visit Drew on the estate!'

'You call me in the middle of the night to tell me this?' I tease, beaming at her down the phone.

Like a pair of giggly teenagers, we dissect every bit of the evening, and by the time we say goodnight, the grandfather clock is clanging three, and I've demolished six shortbread fingers and a Bacardi Breezer from the mini bar. Wish I hadn't ordered kippers for breakfast.

'The Japanese have been knocked out of the tournament,' announces Judy, scanning her list. 'Emily, you're next out. Their names are Mr Takahashi, Yamamoto and Nakamura, plus entourage and luggage. They're booked on the seventeen-ten to Heathrow,' she continues, tapping the keys of her laptop. 'They'll be waiting for you in the reception of The Golf Hotel.'

They say something good comes of everything, and as Judy throws me the keys of the twelve-seater, Vauxhall Vivaro, I give thanks to Goldilocks and the Three Bears for having taught me to drive a minibus.

'*Konichiwa!*' I say with a slight bow of the head, as I open the boot for the caddies to load up.

'*Konichiwa!*' they chorus as they all climb aboard, nodding madly, like a brood of hens.

'Lovely day for flying,' I yell, as if they're stone deaf, my arms flapping about, giving my best aeroplane improv.

'Aaah!' More and more nodding.

Smiling at them in the rear-view mirror, I tighten my fingers around the leather-trim steering wheel, rev the engine, release the handbrake, and head out along the coastal road to the airport.

The sea glimmers like tinsel in the brilliant, afternoon sun. A wispy vapour trail sweeps across the cloudless, forget-me-not blue sky, while The

Proclaimers belt out 'Letter from America' through the airwaves.

Céline must now be five hours into her flight; lunch service over, pushing the duty free trolley through the cabin, flogging Hermès scarves and giant Toblerone.

A sparkle of excitement flashes through me as I imagine her and Drew together, in matching tweed, hand in hand, roaming the heather-filled hills of the estate, stopping to admire a proud stag running along a craggy ravine, Drew putting out his hand to touch her face, parting her fringe and kissing her gently on the forehead. She so deserves to be happy. She makes no secret of the fact that she wants to be married and have a baby, and maybe, just maybe he could be THE ONE. There's a selfish reason too behind my wanting this to work: for almost a year I've been examining my conscience; blaming, tormenting myself with thoughts of *what if?* What if I hadn't interfered by blowing the whistle on Mike? Maybe he would have been true to his word and left his wife and family, and maybe he and Céline would have lived in wedded bliss. Doubtful, I know, but there's this niggle in the back of my mind ... now if this blossoms into romance, I can forgive myself at last. But then what if Drew turns out to be a no-good Celtic cad? She gives her heart so easily, and if he breaks it I'll ...

'*Tomatte! Tomatte!*' comes an urgent cry from the back.

Swerving off the road onto the grass verge, I screech to a halt. What in God's name ...?

The doors are flung open, and my passengers all scramble out, over a prickly hedge and into a field. A dozen or so shaggy cows stop mid-chomp, curious at this sudden, human invasion.

For goodness sake, I mutter to myself sniffily,

you'd think they'd have gone at the hotel.

'*Kochi! Kochi!*' they call, beckoning me over and wildly waving cameras at me.

Flicking on the hazard lights, I reluctantly clamber down, hoist up my skirt and heave myself over the hedge, snagging my new-on-today tights, dammit. The camera is thrust into my hands, amid more vehement head-nodding.

Feet sinking into a cowpat, I look through the lens, and as I depress the shutter, I bite back a smile, and ask myself just how I come to be standing in a soggy field, pinched between a herd of hairy Highland coos and a group of goofy-grinned golfers from Japan.

Nose pressed against the porthole, I watch the lights become a blur as the 737 hurtles down the runway. I am thrust back into my seat as we lumber up into the air, then circle, climbing ever higher. The airport buildings quickly give way to steel-grey sea, then all at once we emerge above the clouds, leaving the drab, drizzly world behind. The aeroplane shudders as the landing gear grinds back into the fuselage. The sun glitters on the wing. I close my eyes. There is a chorus of CLICK, CLICK, CLICK as the FASTEN SEATBELT sign is extinguished, PSCCHHHH from the water boiler in the galley, directly behind me, KERCHINK, KERCHINK go the tongs, smashing the congealed ice cubes apart ...

I tumble into semi-consciousness, as the events of the last ten days merge and are played out in my head — walks on the beach, the golf, the ceilidh, Céline and Drew. Ooh, could this be the start of something? I know it's early days, but I have a good feeling about it. And Duncan? Will I hear from him again, or was he just a Highland fling? We exchanged numbers, but I won't call him. If he calls me, that's fine, but I won't be checking my mobile every day, hoping for a voice-mail or text. Nope, I am no longer a needy, clingy woman, dependent on a man for my happiness; Nigel put paid to that, and that's no bad thing.

'Ladies and gentlemen, we shall shortly be arriving at London Stansted ... '

My tummy starts to wobble; I am entering no man's land once more.

No job, no prospects, what will become of you? And remember - you're not getting any younger, whispers Mrs Negative in my ear.

Pay no attention to her, says Mrs Positive. *Yes, you may be travelling along a rocky road, but you must carry on with your journey and deal with the consequences. Be strong. Your lucky break could be waiting just around the corner.*

God, I hope you're right, Mrs P.

CHAPTER SIX
What's My Cue?

'"A GLASS OF SALT WATER, PLEASE."'

My fellow passenger darts me a sly, sideways glance and shuffles uncomfortably in his seat.

'Branworth station. Branworth station, next stop,' cuts in the guard's muffled voice over the tannoy. I put *Miranda* away with the other nine scripts — the other nine, untouched, UNLEARNED scripts.

After weeks of phoning, e-mailing, sending entire rainforests of letters/CVs, and generally stalking regional theatre companies, I've got a three-month contract as an Acting ASM (assistant to the stage management team/actor/general dogsbody) in the Regency seaside resort of Branworth on the north west coast. My reward at the end of the season will be the much coveted Equity union card — a little plastic card that is my proof that I am a proper professional, and which gives actors discount on everything from theatre tickets to hair removal.

I swing my rucksack onto my back and feel a twinge.

I wonder if I'm capable of learning nine parts in

almost as many weeks, when I have difficulty memorising my PIN number.

The Jeremy Hart Repertory Company is one of the few left of its kind. Nowadays most actors have the luxury of three weeks of rehearsal; not so here, with a new play to learn every week. The audiences are made up of the local community and regulars, who plan their holidays around the play season. Many of the actors have appeared here year after year and have a huge local fan base.

When I'm not required to rehearse, I have to hunt for props, help paint the set, assist the wardrobe department, beg shops and restaurants to display our posters, and keep tea, coffee, milk and biscuit supplies replenished.

'Three pound sixty, duck,' says the taxi driver, as we draw up outside Gloria's Hollywood Apartments — reputedly the best theatrical digs in town.

I push a fiver into his hand. 'Keep the change,' I say distractedly, looking upwards.

'I'll look for your name in lights!' he calls, peeping his horn as he pulls away from the kerb.

I press the buzzer. A figure descends through the frosted glass, and I am face to face with a lady sporting a dated beehive, tight, velour top, leopard skin, stretchy ski pants and black satin slippers with fluffy feathers.

'You must be Emily. I'm Gloria. Come in, love, and I'll show you your apartment,' she says, beckoning me inside. 'You're in the Betty Davis Studio,' she announces proudly, as she bustles up the flock-wallpapered stairway in a vapour of 4711 cologne and nicotine, gold pendants jingling. Framed, black and white, signed photographs of Gloria with various celebs cram every square inch — there's Ken Dodd,

Lily Savage, Su Pollard, and that nervous woman from *Keeping up Appearances,* who was always spilling her tea.

'Would you like a cuppa?' she asks.

'Mmm, yes, please,' I reply, dropping my rucksack to the floor. She disappears in a swish of bamboo curtain, through to the galley kitchen.

'How about a Gypsy Cream as well?' she calls. 'You must be starving after your journey.'

'That'd be great.'

I take in my surroundings; the living room-cum-bedroom is spotlessly clean, with a standard lamp, crushed velveteen settee and sheepskin rug. There's a giant television in one corner and a single bed in the other, covered in a paisley-patterned eiderdown. The walls are artexed, giving them that rough, seventies, faux-farmhouse effect. Off the corridor is the burgundy bathroom suite, with matching, twisted-loop pedestal mat and loo seat cover.

'You know, I always fancied being an actress myself,' says Gloria, handing me my tea and biscuit. 'When my mother died and left me the house, I decided to convert it and take in theatricals. They've all stayed here: the Roley-Poleys, Hinge and Bracket, Canon and Ball, the Krankies, Dottie Wayne, Joe Pasquale … and last week I had the cast of *Saturday Night Fever.* If you could pay me on a Friday, please — and I prefer cash. Oh, and don't forget to sign my visitors' book before you leave. Don't hesitate to knock if you need anything,' she says handing me my key, then clip-clopping down the stairs.

After unpacking, I wander down to the beach, and out to the end of the deserted pier. I look out at the heaving ocean and draw a deep breath. So, this is the life I've dreamed of — the life of a jobbing actress — how will it pan out? What will the rest of the cast be like? Might Duncan surprise me by turning up at the stage door one night?

I head back towards the shore, buffeted along by the strong wind, whipped up from the sea. As I draw closer, I notice the lights are on in the chippy. I order a haddock supper, which I devour with greasy fingers on a bench in a draughty, graffiti-covered shelter.

With the light now starting to fade, I find my way to the little repertory theatre.

SEE TWO PLAYS IN ONE WEEK! boasts the poster pasted outside. And there's my name in tiny print at the bottom of the cast list. No backing out now. I look down the long list of performances, and the scary thought of those thousands of lines hastens me back to Gloria's for an early night.

Heart racing, I climb the stairs to the rehearsal studio. I pause momentarily as I turn the door handle and suck in a deep breath. The room is full of actors talking in loud, confident voices, laughing, squealing, hugging and air kissing one another.

'Darling! How *wonderful* to see you again — can't believe it's a year ...'

'Been working, much?'

'Oh, this and that — a bit of voice-over work and one episode of *The Street.*'

'I hardly recognised you — the botox takes years off you ...'

'... I'm not complaining though — that soup commercial will pay my mortgage for the next six months ...'

The door opens and Jeremy, the director, whom I recognise from the audition, appears, followed by his creative team.

'Good morning, everyone, and welcome to The Civic Theatre for this, our fortieth anniversary season. Gather round,' he says, indicating the circle of chairs. 'Now, for the benefit of those who haven't been here before, to my left is Babs, who's in charge of wardrobe, Lesley, set designer, Ellis, lighting, Richard, sound, Mark, stage manager, and his second-in-command, Abi, DSM.' (Deputy stage manager.)

'Hi!' says Abi, who is crouched on the floor, marking the layout of the set with white tape.

Jeremy looks anxiously at the door, then his watch. 'Well, we'd better get started. Let's go round the room and everyone introduce themselves please. Then tell us the name of the character you'll be playing in our opening production.'

The door flies open and a well-preserved actress I vaguely recognise from an eighties' sitcom sweeps into the room, a long, red PVC raincoat draped around her shoulders, clutching what looks like a meerkat with hair extensions.

'So sorry I'm late, Jeremy darling. You know how I *hate* early mornings.'

'Margo darling!' gushes Jeremy, leaping to his feet and kissing her on both cheeks. 'Let me grab you a pew.'

Scooping up a chair, he announces, 'Ladies and gentlemen, she doesn't need introducing, but put your hands together please, and give a warm welcome to our leading lady, Margo Dalziel!'

Margo smiles graciously, gives a regal wave and says, 'Aren't you forgetting someone, darling? This is Phoebe, everyone,' she says, proudly holding up a scrawny paw. 'You see, she's saying "hello,"' she gushes, smothering the meerkat in kisses.

'Right, let's crack on, folks,' booms Jeremy over-brightly, eyes studying the ceiling. 'Here are your rehearsal schedules. Please take one and pass them on ...'

Wednesday a.m.
Read-through
Coffee and character discussion
Block Act One (i.e. note down stage directions)
Lunch
Wednesday p.m.
Start running Act One
Tea and question/answer session
Continue running Act One
Thursday a.m.
Start blocking Act Two
Coffee and costume fittings
Continue blocking Act Two
Lunch
Thursday p.m.
Start running Act Two
Tea and question/answer session
Continue running Act Two
Friday a.m.
Stagger-through of Act One (without scripts)
Shit!
Stagger-through of Act Two (without scripts)
Shiiiit!
Saturday a.m.
Director's notes
Run-through of play
Director's notes
Sunday
Day off (is he having a laugh?)
Monday a.m.
ASM to collect final props and dress the set
Lunch
Monday p.m.
Technical rehearsal on stage
Tuesday a.m.
Full dress rehearsal

140

Director's notes
Tuesday 19:30
1st performance
Director's notes

I know I'm a newbie to the luvvy life, and I am perfectly prepared to earn my thespian wings by working my socks off, but I can't help feeling a tad panic-stricken when I realise that after our first opening night, we will have to start the whole process over again the very next morning for the following production; only this time we'll also be performing the play we rehearsed last week every night, with matinées on Thursdays and Saturdays, which dramatically cuts down on rehearsal, prop-finding, line-learning time.

After every final performance, I have to pack away all the props, help 'strike' (take down) the set and put up the new one. The opening day of a new play it's my job to dress the new set, which involves hanging curtains, pictures, laying rugs, filling shelves with books, ornaments etc. in time for the full dress rehearsal at 2:30, followed by yet more director's notes, and another first night.

At the risk of appearing unreasonable, when exactly am I to learn my lines and stage directions, let alone eat, sleep, wash my smalls? I raise my hand gingerly.

'And so to our first play, *Miranda*,' says Jeremy, pulling a file from his bag. 'Emily, our latest recruit, is to play our mischievous mermaid.'

Jeremy motions for me to stand up. All eyes swivel in my direction. I slowly lower my arm, tugging at my recently chopped hair, wishing it would magically grow back.

It's obvious what they are all thinking, and I want

to say, *I know, I know I'm at least twenty years too old for the part, but is it **my** fault their first choice got a last-minute offer to play Liesl in* The Sound of Music *tour?*

'This isn't *Phantom of the Opera,*' grumbles Babs at my wardrobe fitting. 'We simply don't have the budget for wigs.'

A long, blonde wig is eventually found scrunched up in a Tesco carrier bag from a 2001 production of *Les Liaisons Dangereuses,* and after a gentle soak in some Dreft, it is grudgingly met with Babs' approval.

My very first scene is with Charles, the chauffeur, who has to carry me on stage and around the room, whilst I marvel at the furnishings and paintings.

According to the script, Charles is *broad and tough looking*, so don't ask me why five-foot-five Vincent Crumb has been cast in this role. Vince is as camp as the Rio Carnival and skinny as a rake. I may not be Victoria Beckham, but the way he wobbles and wheezes as he carts me around, makes me feel less like a delicate mermaid, and more like a beached whale.

'We haven't time to spend on this now, so please can you work on this scene in your own time?' says Jeremy, clutching his forehead. 'Right, moving on ...'

Like Sir Ian and Dame Judi, I used to bemoan the demise of weekly repertory, where fledgling actors like me could learn their 'craft' (to use theatre-speak). Why, oh why is this wonderful institution being allowed to disappear? This will kill British theatre, I thought. But that was before the reality of fly-by-the-seat-of-your-pants rep kicked in ...

* * *

Miranda — Opening Night

'Everyone got their personal props?' calls Abi, standing in the doorway, scanning her clipboard.

'I've lost a glove!'

'Anyone got any hairspray?'

'Can you call Babs? A button's just come off my jacket.'

'Has anyone seen my cigarette holder?'

Excited chatter from the auditorium blares through the speakers. Every seat sold. I feel sick.

During the dress rehearsal this afternoon I 'dried' three times, and my wig got caught in the zip of my tail during a quick scene change.

I close my eyes and inhale deeply, just like Faye taught me to, in an attempt to steady my frazzled nerves. I breathe in the sweet perfume of the two bouquets of flowers on my dressing table: freesias from Mum and Dad, and pink roses from Duncan. I glance at the card: *Break a leg. D.* Pretty neutral, noncommittal. Not even *x.* But the fact he sent flowers is a good sign, isn't it? He could have just sent a card or a 'good luck' text — or nothing at all.

'Act One beginners, please.'

I'm not on for nine pages, but set off early to allow myself time to waddle down to prompt corner in my fishtail. I also need to have a practice-run in the wheelchair, which only materialised half an hour ago.

I scoot up and down the backstage area, heart going da-dum-da-dum-da-dum.

'We have clearance,' announces Mark, giving the thumbs-up. 'Break a leg, everyone!'

The lights go down, and the curtain goes up on Act One, Scene One.

'Fade music. Cue telephone … go!' whispers Abi into her mic.

Limbering up stage left is Betty, the maid, played

by Tamara, an actress fresh out of drama school. The green cue light is illuminated, and with a little skip and a jump, she takes to the stage.

Ten minutes! Ten minutes of our precious rehearsal time was spent discussing 'motive' and which room Betty's in when the telephone rings.

'As it's late afternoon, I feel she's in the kitchen putting away the tea things, or maybe preparing the vegetables for dinner. Which scenario do you prefer, Jeremy?' she'd said. 'I could even be wiping my hands on my apron as I enter.'

My jaw had tightened. Yeah, yeah, whatever, sweetheart. This is weekly rep, remember, not the bloody National Theatre. Just get on with it. How I wish Jeremy would put her in her place.

Despite being the youngest member of the company, Tamara doesn't have to carry out ASM duties. She's the daughter of the well-known playwright and director, Maurice de Fresnes, and is therefore leap-frogging her way up the theatrical ladder. She's deigned to join our company for the one play before she begins rehearsals for the Regent's Park open air summer season — not that I'm jealous.

'I know, *I know* she can be rather tricky,' Jeremy had said, taking me aside on one particularly bad rehearsal day. 'But what you have to remember is that she was in an award-winning, short film at last year's Lithuanian Film Festival. And like it or not, we are lucky to have her as she's being mooted as the next Carey Mulligan.'

So, this is her licence to get away with murder; she's either having a tantrum, on the verge of tears, doing incessant warm-ups, or prancing about, practising her red-carpet smile.

Vince swigs water from one of the bottles on the props table, his eyes darting about nervously.

The green light comes on. Knees bent, he scoops me up into his bony arms, and we veer onto the shaky set of the doctor's Bloomsbury flat.

Under the glare of the lights, it's as if I am watching someone who looks and sounds like me moving around the stage and saying the lines.

"'Am I heavy?'"

"'No, Miss ... quite the contrary.'"

"'You look so very strong.'"

"'Do I, Miss?'"

"'What wonderful muscles!'" (Snigger from the stalls.)

"'I do a bit of amateur boxing, Miss,'" groans Vince as he chucks me onto the sofa, one page early, which means I have no alternative but to cut my line, 'Carry me round the room, will you, Charles?'

Civic Theatre stalwart, Vanessa Morrell, playing Clare, the doctor's wife, swans on upstage right, saying, "'You can put Miss Trewella down, Cha...'" and glowers in my direction.

I am dumped in the offstage darkness after my first scene, and fumble my way to the quick-change area, where Babs is standing by with my long dress and pearls, in preparation for Act Two, Scene One.

'Breathe in,' she commands through a mouthful of safety pins, yanking the waistband of the tail tighter around my midriff.

Meanwhile, Rocky Balboa is pacing up and down stage right, in preparation for round two ...

If adrenaline gives a person the superhuman strength to lift a car, then please God, can it not do the same for Vince?

"'Ah, here she is. Put Miss Trewella on the settee, Charles.'" And my prayer is answered.

Our first-night nerves gradually vanish as Doctor Theatre works his magic, shifting the action up a gear, giving the lines punchiness and pace.

We are now just one scene away from the interval, and my favourite bit of the whole play, where I have the stage all to myself — the pivotal moment, where the audience realises for the first time that Miranda is not an invalid after all ...

I flop into the wheelchair; Babs fusses with the ribbon of my négligée, and the jewelled clasp in my hair, then tucks the tartan blanket tightly around my legs and under my feet, so the tail doesn't poke out.

Margo, playing the nurse (looking for all the world like Barbara Windsor in *Carry On Doctor*), pushes me on stage.

"'Why did you never get married, Nurse Cary?'"

"'I never wanted to,'" she replies, her gin-infused breath wafting over me.

"'Don't you find men attractive?'"

"'No ... nor they me ... which makes it easier.'"

'I'd take you out any night of the week, sweetheart!' comes a voice from the gods. Several guffaws echo around the auditorium.

Coquettishly batting her false eyelashes, Margo cries, 'See you in the bar afterwards, darling!' which prompts several wolf-whistles.

"'I love men.'" I yell this line, determined to get us back on track. Margo thumps the back of the chair and eventually says, 'Well, well ...' This is not in the script, and therefore slightly worrying. She then proceeds to cut the next page of dialogue.

The lights slowly fade and the set is bathed in greeny-blue light. Thunder rolls, lightning flashes, the rain lashes against the windowpanes and the haunting wisps of 'Fingal's Cave' by Mendelssohn drift through the air. Cellos and bassoons gather momentum; Miranda, trance-like, removes her négligée (bit of a barney with Jeremy and Babs about this stage direction, due to my refusal to bare my assets to an audience of elderly holidaymakers — or any holidaymakers for that matter. Two large shells, strategically super-glued to flesh-coloured, strapless bra save the day). She lets down her flowing locks and flicks her scaly tail high into the air. Lightning, thunder, gasps from the audience, curtains, wild applause. This is what is *supposed* to happen ...

"'Good night. Turn on the wireless, will you; and switch off the lights as you go out.'"

"'See you in the morning.'"

"'Don't forget my scallops.'"

"'There are just as good fish in the sea as ever... Good night.'"

MIRANDA MANIPULATES HER CHAIR OVER TO THE FRENCH WINDOW.

Why won't the bloody thing move?

MIRANDA MANIPULATES HER CHAIR OVER TO THE FRENCH WINDOW.

I push the wheels with all my might, but ... NOTHING. I lean forward ... if I could just reach the door handle ... oops ... nearly. The chair rocks back and forth. Nervous whispers come from the auditorium.

'Release the brake!' hisses Abi from the wings. Aha! How stupid of me. I grab the lever and flick it to the down position; the chair starts to roll backwards on the raked stage, towards the orchestra pit. The audience holds its collective breath as I push the wheels forward with all my might and hurtle towards the French windows, crashing into the small table, with the goldfish bowl on it.

MIRANDA LOOSENS HER HAIR SO THAT IT CASCADES DOWN OVER HER SHOULDERS.

My trembling hand, now slippy with sweat, can't get the hair clip to undo. I tug at it, and the wig moves precariously to the side, so decide to abandon that bit of business.

I'm trapped, unable to move, the négligée and blanket now tangled up in the wheels.

Please bring the tabs in and end the agony. Pleeeease.

The curtains come in slowly, jerkily, and our first night audience is left at the interval, doubtless believing that *Miranda* is a horror story, with the central character bearing a scary resemblance to Norman Bates' mother in *Psycho*.

Thank the Lord I haven't a part in next week's play — but then at the dress rehearsal, Jeremy drops a bombshell:

'Darling,' he says in a low voice as he places a suspiciously reassuring arm round my shoulders. 'We have a bit of a — situation on our hands ...'

'What kind of a — "situation"?' I ask tentatively.

'It's nothing to worry about ...'

Why do I get the feeling he's lying?

'Our sister theatre in Blackpool is having serious technical problems with some new sound equipment. The producer's having a hissy fit and is demanding that Richard be there tomorrow for the opening night, and — well, our budget doesn't stretch to a free-lance sound engineer, soooo, as the only spare member of the stage management team, the duty falls to you, my sweet.'

My stomach plummets like a drop tower. He CANNOT be serious.

'Oh, Jeremy, please let's get one thing straight,' I say with pleading eyes. 'I may be a dab hand at splashing a bit of paint around, or knocking a couple of bits of wood together, or finding props for you, but operating a sound desk? I can't even operate my DVD player properly.'

'You'll be *fine,*' he says with feigned conviction. 'You can shadow Richard tonight, and the systems here are all manual, not a computer in sight, so you see, you'll be fine, trust me. Okay, everyone, let's start from where we left off — the top of Act Two, please!'

I now know what ASM *really* stands for: A Stupid Mug.

***Ahoy there!* A Farce** (What an understatement.)
Here I am in a tiny, hot, soundproof box at the back of the auditorium. It's airless, rank with sweat (where's a Jo Malone scented candle when you need one?) and has a deck of dials and switches that reminds me of the cockpit of a 747.

The door opens and Mark's head peers round.

'Good luck!' he says, giving me the thumbs-up.

'House lights, down. Cue music ... go!' crackles Abi's voice through my headphones (or 'cans', as the techies call them). My quivering finger depresses the switch, and the theme music from *Desert Island Discs* swells the theatre.

'Fade music. Sound cue one ... go!' cuts in Abi's voice again. The tinny sound of rolling waves and the screech of gulls sifts through the speakers, setting the scene. Phew. I wind the reel-to-reel tape to the next red marker. There are several pages of dialogue before my next cue, so daring to relax a little, I take a swig of water and look down onto the set and my, dare I say, *impressive* handiwork. The balsa wood palm trees look surprisingly realistic (as long as no one leans against them), although my last-minute brainwave of dressing the stage with real coconuts (2 for 1 at Morrisons) is proving to be a bit of a safety hazard.

The play is a three-hander, and as the only female

in the cast, Margo is in her element, playing a *femme fatale*, shipwrecked on a desert island with her husband and her lover. This week she is wearing a skimpy, low-cut, raggedy tunic, held together with angel breath. Her character is supposed to be in her twenties, but I'm learning that being top of the bill here has its perks — other than financial — one of them being you get to choose your own parts and costumes.

'Cue music ... go!' calls Abi. 'Well done, Emily, you made it to the interval. Fifteen minutes, please.'

Blimey, maybe I'm not such a technophobe after all. Who knows, if this acting lark doesn't work out, a career as a sound engineer might not be beyond the realms of possibility.

There is a knock at the door and Ellis enters, carrying a mug of tea and a Kit Kat.

'Hey, well done, you! Richard had better watch out — we have a budding sound engineer in our midst.'

'Please don't tempt fate.' I smile through my slug of tea.

'Just do exactly what you did in the first half and you're home and dry.' He winks reassuringly, shutting the door behind him.

The three bells ring out.

'Ladies and gentlemen, please take your seats as this evening's performance of *Ahoy There!* will continue in two minutes. Two minutes please.'

Only three more sound cues to go until we reach the end of the play. Whey hey! I can almost taste that glass of chilled Sauvignon waiting for me at the bar.

'"Rupert, I think I can see something in the distance. Could it be ... could it be a ship?"'

I slowly wind the tape forward manually, in preparation for the ship's siren, two pages of

150

dialogue hence. Hmm. Strange. Can't see the marker. Rewind the tape using the switch this time, and look again. No red marker. Maybe I didn't wind it on far enough. I press the fast-forward switch. Whirr. Nothing. I press rewind. Whirr. Nothing.

I've found a red marker on the tape but which sound effect is it?

'Cue ship's siren ... go!' instructs Abi. Heart knocking against my chest, I depress the switch, keeping everything crossed ... and the screech of monkeys echoes around the auditorium.

"'Rupert, Geoffrey, it **is** a ship!'"

"'We have one flare left, thank God. I'll just go and set it alight. They are bound to see us,'" says Rupert, exiting stage right.

The budget and fire regulations won't allow for pyrotechnics, so Rupert has to exit stage right, cover his face in soot as the flare sound effect is being played, then reappear on stage. Terror floods through my veins. It's like watching a train about to crash in slow motion, and not be able to do a thing about it.

'Cue flare ... go!' says Abi, the tiniest hint of exasperation in her usually super-cool voice.

Nothing.

'Cue flare ... go!'

Nothing.

'What was that noise?' ad-libs Margo, cupping her hand to her ear.

'What noise?'

'I think I heard the flare.'

'Flare?'

'The-one-Rupert-set-alight-just-now-over-yonder,' she says loudly, with a dramatic gesture.

Rupert eventually stumbles back onto the stage, mouthing something into the wings. The three actors look at one another with fear in their eyes.

When will this end? After what seems an age, they start jumping up and down half-heartedly, calling, "'Ahoy there!'"

'Cue ship's siren ... go!'

Silence.

Monday night's punters are party to the rarely performed, alternative ending of *Ahoy There*, where the threesome is marooned forever. And the face blackening? Well, that has some deep, symbolic meaning, which I haven't quite worked out as yet.

Week Four: *Murder on the Tenth Floor.* A Thriller

This week I'm murdered in the first half of the play, thank God. A few lines at the beginning, followed by twenty-five minutes' dead acting, until the interval. During the break, I have to change into my 'blacks' and take up the stage management duty of chief lift operator.

The play is set in a multi-storey office block. The 'lift' is a wooden, sliding door, painted silver. I have to squeeze in behind the scenery wall before the start of the second half, and wait for the red cue light to turn green. At Detective Inspector Lord and Sergeant Cooper's entrance, the light comes on, and I pull the string attached to the top of the door as smoothly as I can. Then I'm stuck there until they exit, almost at the end of the play.

'The door must positively gliiide, Emily,' Jeremy had said. That's all well and good, but he's not the one squashed in there with practically no room to manoeuvre, let alone breathe.

The play is completely sold out — nothing like a good, juicy who-dunnit to pull in the bored holidaymakers from their B&Bs on a dull, drizzly night in Branworth.

"'Stay right where you are!'" orders Vince, as this

week's villain, Jack Spencer. He flicks on the torch and trains the beam onto my face. "'I'm afraid you know too much,'" he continues, pulling a gun from the inside pocket of his overcoat.

"'Don't be a fool, Jack. The police won't buy your story. But I can help you ...'"

Vince pulls the trigger. I know the routine now: grab the corner of the desk, clutch chest with other hand, squeeze blood capsule, fall to knees, open mouth slightly as if to speak, glazed look, fall on my side, back to the audience (so they don't see me breathing), and remember what Jeremy said: 'Don't over-act, darling — remember, less is more.'

But hang on, where's the bang? The trigger clicks again. Nothing. Vince shoots me one of his customary, boggle-eyed, Frank-Spencer looks. I half expect him to twitch his shoulders and utter an 'Hmm, Betty.'

No good relying on him to get us out of this. He spouts his lines verbatim, but as I discovered in *Miranda*, throw the unexpected at him, and he clams up.

A mega-dose of adrenalin rushes around my body, and I find myself backing away, ad-libbing like mad.

'You won't get away with this, you know. No, you won't. No, siree! The police will be here soon. There's no way out — unless you'd care to try the window. But the windows are double-glazed, so you won't be able to break them ... even with a chair... nope ... no way ...'

My back is now pressed against the 'lift' door, blood trickling through my fingers onto my shirt, for no apparent reason. Vince is rooted to the spot, doubtless petrified of what I may say or do next. There's only one thing for it ...

In a last ditch attempt to rescue the situation, I feign prising the door open and fall in backwards, as if into the lift shaft (a black masking curtain). I then spin around once (less is more), crying 'Aaaaaaaaaaah!'

Abi looks at me flabbergasted from prompt corner, as I snatch one of the cast iron stage weights and drop it to the floor with a thud, signifying my sticky end.

A good bit of improv, I think, until it dawns on me horribly as the plot unravels, that all references to the shooting (of which there are many) have now to be changed on the hoof, and the two local am-dram enthusiasts, cast in the non-speaking roles of ambulance men, don't get to come on stage at all.

Week Six: Another Op'nin', Another Wig

Strike a match within three feet of my head, and I will combust. Yet despite the half can of hairspray and ton of kirby-grips, my mangy hairpiece keeps falling off.

'Could we do away with the hairpiece altogether, Babs?' I beg, as she spears my head again.

'You're supposed to be a nineteen-year-old virgin bride, Emily, and without it ...' she says, casting a critical eye over me, 'well, I'm afraid there's no nice way of putting this, you — you look more like the bride's mother.'

'Well, what about my *Miranda* wig?'

Judging by Babs' reaction, you'd think I had just suggested wearing my birthday suit and a pair of Doc Martens.

'I beg your pardon? Did you say your *Miranda* wig?'

I nod, smiling weakly.

'You can't possibly wear that wig! Our regulars would recognise you right away from two weeks ago. No, you have to look completely different. There!' she says, standing back and studying my reflection. 'As long as you don't move your head around too much, it'll stay put, and on matinée days you'll have to keep it on in between shows.'

It was bound to happen sooner or later — and tonight it does ...

"'Oh, Archie, you do love me, don't you?'"

"'Of course I do, Shirl. You're the only girl for me.'"

"'Oh, Archie!'"

"'Oh, Shirl!'"

Archie takes me in his arms and spins me around. As I come in to land, I notice a blonde, ferret-like thing sitting on his shoulder.

"'I can't — wait — until — we're — married, darling,'" I squeak. I know I have another line, but my concentration is broken. Unaware, Archie/Vince looks at me intently through his Coke-bottle spectacles, eyes hugely magnified, drops of perspiration glistening in the furrows of his terrified brow. I can't think what to say. Remember what they drummed into us at drama school? If your concentration goes, stop and momentarily focus your attention on something very familiar to you, and this will jog your memory ...

'Oscar Charlie, got a pick-up from Station Road ...'

We look at one another gormlessly.

'Oscar Charlie, are you in the vicinity?'

I bite down hard on my lip, fighting a laugh. The Branworth taxi service is mysteriously filtering through the speakers! I ad-lib my way to the end of the scene, but try as I might to retain a sense of professionalism and carry on regardless, my dialogue is expelled in short, sharp bursts, like machine gun fire. The curtains come in, and we all fall about the floor like naughty school kids; the first of many bouts of 'corpsing', as it's called.

Week Eight: *Salad Days*

No part to learn, no technical responsibilities, just a million props to find, including four of those old-type mobile hairdryers; you know, the ones on castors, with giant hoods?

Have been into almost every hairdresser in Branworth. They are all very trendy places with staff of an average age of twenty-three. With their brightly coloured hair, body piercings, tattoos, funky clothes and waif-like figures, I feel about ninety-five next to them.

'Do you have any old hairdryers I could borrow for a play?' I yell over blaring rap music. 'You know the old-fashioned type with a hood ... and wheels ...'

My request is usually met with blank looks or mild amusement. I chicken out from asking them to display our poster and flyers. I get the feeling that neither they nor their cool clientele are likely to want to spend their Saturday night watching Timothy and Jane dancing and singing 'Oh, Look At Me!', accompanied by Minnie, the magic piano.

Footsore and hairdryerless, I start to wend my way back to the theatre, wondering if it may be at all possible to adapt the whole thing to the present day. Problem is, we're back in that *frightfully* nice world where *gay* means happy, and people go to *marvellous* parties and drink *lashings* of beer, and say things like *gosh* and *he's a thoroughly decent chap*.

I'm ravenous, and an illuminated Fish 'n' Chips sign lures me up a little side street. As I'm waiting in the queue deciding whether or not to have mushy peas, reflected in the mirror, I spy a board outside the pebbledash house opposite ...

HAIR BY MADGE
SHAMPOO & SET HALF-PRICE
FOR PENSIONERS WEDNESDAYS

Now that looks just the kind of place ...

'Yes, love?' says the lady behind the counter, fish slice at the ready.

'Sorry, gotta go,' I say, flying out of the door. Forget jumbo sausages and mushy peas, there's more pressing business at hand.

'If you can manage to get them downstairs, then you're welcome to borrow them,' says Madge, opening the stock room door. 'Can I leave you to it?' she says, consulting her watch. 'My lady's colour should have come off five minutes ago.'

'Sure, thank you, and here's the poster, and oh, I'll drop off the tickets for Thursday night's show tomorrow morning.'

Isn't life weird? Not so long ago, I was pushing a trolley through a metal tube, and now here I am, proudly propelling a dusty old hairdryer with wonky wheels through a shopping precinct. Oh, the glamour!

Week Eleven: *Round & Round The Rectory* (aka *Another Cringeworthy Farce*)

'No, no, no, Emily! You pop up from behind the sofa *after* the telephone rings, not *before*,' booms Jeremy's voice from the darkness of the dress circle. 'Now let's go back to the top of the scene from the bishop's entrance.'

In an ideal world we would have rehearsed this for three weeks, ensuring that the slick co-ordination of lines and moves is imprinted on the brain. But in this drama production line, you've barely time to erase the previous character and plot from your memory before you're twenty years younger than last night, and are speaking in a West Country accent as opposed to 'Received Pronunciation' (or 'RP', as it is called in Thespian Land). The art of ad-libbing is a must here, to be pulled out of the hat whenever the playwright's words elude you.

So, to the play itself: vicar, vicar's wife, bishop, gardener and ditsy maid (more typecasting). Lots of diving under beds, popping in and out of cupboards and toe-curling double-entendres like, 'Ooh, put that away before somebody else sees it!'

No unruly wig this week, thank God, just a maid's cap and an Eliza-Doolittle accent.

"'Good evening, bishop. May I take your mitre?'"

"'Thank you, Edith. Is the vicar at home?'"

"'Yes, your 'oliness. He's in the library and is expecting you.'"

BISHOP EXITS UPSTAGE RIGHT.

"'Edith! Edith!'" *(FROM OFFSTAGE.)*

"'Lawks, that's Bill, the gardener!'"

I bob down behind the sofa.

Silence.

'Hold it! Emily! Emily!' calls Jeremy tersely.

'Yes?' I say, peering dubiously over the top.

'Is there a problem?'

I stand up, shielding my eyes from the glaring lights. 'No. You told me not to appear until the telephone rings.'

'That's right, but Richard's cue for the telephone ring is your line, "He must have seen me come back from town", is it not?'

'Sorry, I ... I was concentrating on when to appear and clean forgot my line. Sorry,' I mumble sheepishly.

'Okay, everyone, let's go back to the top of the scene once more, thank you!'

Last night I dreamt I was naked on stage, it was my turn to speak, and I had absolutely no idea what play I was in. I will never pull this together by tomorrow night. There is nothing else for it: forget all that terribly useful stuff Portia drummed into us about Stanislavsky. There simply isn't time to explore the inner self. The only technique I'm interested in is survival, and if that means strategically placing bits of the script under the bed, behind the sofa and in the cupboard, then so be it.

HOW TO SURVIVE WEEKLY REP
by
Emily Forsyth.

This actors' manual is to be my project whilst waiting for my next job. The headings so far are:

Chapter 1

Emergency Stage Evacuation
(procedures to be followed when you have absolutely no idea what your next line is).

Chapter 2

Violent Convulsions (aka 'corpsing').

Chapter 3

How to Survive Farce
(after not enough rehearsal and avoid having a nervous breakdown).

I will have to amend chapter three, as the procedures are not watertight, as I discovered tonight — to my cost ...

Act Two, and I am within touching distance of the finish line. A couple of pages of dialogue, in which to catch my breath after my leap over the back of the sofa, swiftly followed by energetic dive into the cupboard, to avoid being found by the vicar and his young (ahem) wife. Vince is playing the role of Reverend Pritchard and Margo, Mrs P.

So here I am, crouched down in my usual spot, having a quick slurp of my water and a sneaky look at my script, in preparation for my final scene. My ears prick up as I hear Margo deliver my cue line — two pages early.

Before I have time to shift my brain into gear, the cupboard door is flung open and I am revealed, like a rabbit caught in the headlights. In one hand I am clutching my script, and a bottle of Evian in the other; but worse than this, my skirt is hitched up over my knees and my nasty pop-sock secret is out. I rise slowly, staring into the black void, frantically scanning my memory for my line — nothing. My improvisation skills too let me down, as I find myself saying, 'I'll just pop upstairs ma'am and see if her ladyship requires anything.'

'Her — *ladyship?*' enquires Margo, eyes wide, a slight tremor in her voice.

'Yes, her ladyship, your mother, who has been upstairs, bed-ridden these ten years since,' I reply, tripping up the stairs. 'God love 'er.'

'But *we* require you to pour the tea,' says Margo firmly, grabbing the hem of my skirt through the spindles. '*Nowww.*'

'Begging your par-don, ma'am,' I continue, wrenching myself free, 'but I shan't be a moment.' And I disappear out of sight, onto 'the landing'.

'Pssst! Abi!' I hiss, waving my arms in the direction of prompt corner.

Abi looks up, removes her cans and says in a loud whisper, 'What are you doing up there? Get back on stage.'

'What's my line?' I mouth exaggeratedly.

'What?'

'What's — my — line?'

'How should I know?' she replies, frantically flicking through her script. 'You're in a different play to the rest of us.'

Part of me is tempted to climb down the backstage scaffolding and retreat to my dressing room, leaving my fellow actors to it. After all, this is Margo's fault for skipping two pages of dialogue in the first place. But then Portia's words ring out in my head: 'Acting is all about teamwork and being a supportive company member.'

With this in mind, I come to Vince and Margo's rescue by hysterically screaming an improvised exit line: 'Lawks! Sir, Madam, come upstairs right away! Her ladyship is ... DEAD!'

They scuttle upstairs and we huddle together on the tiny 'landing' until Abi has no alternative but to bring the curtain down.

I emerge from the stage door and thread my way through the hordes of eager autograph hunters waiting for Margo. Someone taps me gently on the shoulder.

'Excuse me, please will you sign our programme?'

I turn forty-five degrees and promptly burst into tears, as Wendy and Céline, arms outstretched, shroud me in a triple hug.

'Hey, don't cry,' says Wendy, wiping my cheeks with her thumb. 'It was supposed to be a *nice* surprise.'

'Oh, it *is*, believe me,' I blub, my Poundland mascara smudging the collar of Céline's white Chanel blazer. 'It's just the relief of seeing your familiar faces. It's all been too Mr Bean for words. I've aged about twenty years in the last few weeks.'

'Rubbish. You have lost weight, though,' says Wendy, laying a gentle hand on my arm.

'You were so *h*ilarious as the maid,' chips in Céline. (She has this charming way of emphasising the 'h' of English words.)

I flinch. 'I never believed those people who said the stress some actors experience during performance is the equivalent of a small car crash — until tonight. Tonight, let me tell you, I felt like I was in a multiple pile-up on the M25. Anyway, it's over. For now. So, come on,' I say, slotting my arms through theirs. 'Let me buy us all a drink. I'm afraid there are no decent wine bars in this town, just The Lobster Pot. Their house white isn't bad.'

'I know a place overlooking the sea that stays open all night, where we can drink champagne from crystal flutes, and eat smoked salmon by candlelight,' says Wendy.

I look at her, puzzled.

'Ta-raa!' She beams as she produces a cool box from behind her back. 'Come on. We reserved a bench on the prom.'

'Ahem! I'd like to propose a toast,' I announce, rising unsteadily to my sandy feet, the bubbles in my glass fizzing. 'Be we in Branworth or Bermuda, may our friendship last forever!'

As Céline raises her arm, the flame from a tea-light catches something glittering on her left hand. Squinting at it, I say cautiously, 'Céline, is that what I think it is?'

She lowers her long, sweeping lashes.

'What, you and ...?'

Her million-euro smile speaks for itself.

'Oh, my God. No way! You mean ... Drew?'

She nods her head vigorously. There is a lengthy pause. Then we all start screeching and hugging, jumping around in a circle, doing a kind of demented dance.

'Refill, girls!' says Wendy, popping another cork.

'Come on,' I say, wiping away more tears. 'Fill me in on *all* the details, please. *When* did he propose? Have you set a date yet? *Where* did he propose? Did he get down on bended knee? Have your parents met him? Does Mike know?'

Céline laughs and covers my mouth with her hand. '*Lentement, chérie!*'

Taking a deep breath she says, '*Alors,* when I return from Scotland ...'

And so we sip champagne and talk girl-talk into the wee, small hours, just like old times — well, almost. The only difference is, we're not sitting on a king-size bed, having room service in The Dallas Marriott, but picnicking on a chilly beach in a northern seaside town by moonlight.

I gaze up at the stars and give private thanks to the universe, God, or whoever is responsible for letting me off the hook. The guilt that has been relentlessly stalking me since Céline and Mike's break-up has been served a restraining order, and I am no longer its prisoner.

CHAPTER SEVEN
The Hills Are Alive

AS MY TRAIN GATHERS SPEED, I swear I can feel my head becoming steadily lighter.

Closing my eyes, I unleash the thousands of lines, cues, stage directions and quick scene changes of the last twelve weeks, allowing them to flow out of my brain, through the window, and into the ether.

I am hurtling towards the Lake District, to spend a few days fell-walking with Duncan. I'm not a particularly sporty person, but I've kind of led him to believe I am. Well, you know how it is when you first meet someone and you want to make an impression? You find yourself saying things like, 'What a coincidence! I *adore* abseiling too.' (Then, when you find yourself dangling from a precipice, you wonder whatever possessed you to say such a thing, with total disregard of the possible consequences.)

'We are now approaching Oxenholme station. Oxenholme station, the next stop.'

I draw a steadying breath, as if I'm about to step out on stage; only this time there's no script, no direction. We've stayed in touch by phone, text messaging and the odd card, but I've known him for such a short time, and now we are to spend four whole days in one another's company. What will we talk about? What about the sleeping arrangements? It's one thing discovering I am no sportswoman, but since having my hair chopped, I resemble Rod Stewart first thing in the morning; and what about my nocturnal teeth grinding? (Alleged.)

The train slows to a halt, and my insides do a loop-the-loop as I catch sight of him on the platform, scanning the long line of carriages, a bunch of flowers clutched tightly in his hand. *Chill. Don't appear too keen. Chill.*

As I step down, I look around, pretending I haven't yet noticed him.

'Emily?' Those gravelly, Celtic tones send a shiver down my spine. I turn around, heart racing.

'It *is* you! I hardly recognised you. What have you done to your hair?'

'Hi,' I say coolly, pulling at my crop self-consciously. Oh dear, he doesn't like it. He goes to peck me on the cheek and our heads bash together. I giggle nervously, like a silly schoolgirl.

'The car's this way,' he says, shoving the flowers awkwardly into my hand, and taking my rucksack in exchange.

We make superficial chit-chat until we reach The Forest Hill Hotel, a converted, seventeenth-century mansion, set in beautifully landscaped gardens.

'Mr MacIntyre! Good to have you with us again,' says the man behind the oak wood reception desk, firmly shaking Duncan's hand.

'You're looking well, Max,' says Duncan, patting him on the back. 'I see the conservatory's finished at last. It's looking good.'

Hmm, obviously not the first time he's been here

165

then. I find myself pondering if this is where he always brings his current muse. I make a mental note to play hard to get and not allow the breathtaking scenery, fresh air and *vin de la maison* to go to my head.

'Let me show you to your room.' Max gives a genteel smile as he takes my bag. 'I've put you in The Sycamore Suite.'

He holds open the studded, panelled door and gestures for me to enter. While he and Duncan chat on the threshold, I absorb my surroundings: very olde-worlde, dominated by a wonderfully opulent, four-poster bed and huge fireplace. There's a chaise longue in rich fabric and lots of scatter cushions in country house colours. I feel like the new Mrs De Winter in *Rebecca.*

There's a tiled wash stand in the corner, complete with pitcher and bowl (none of your £24.99-shopping-channel tat, but the real McCoy), and dried lavender and a sampler hanging on the wall: *Catharine Alexander. Born in the Year of our Lord 1692.*

I peek in the bathroom, which has one of those traditional, roll top, cast iron baths with clawed feet. My radar homes in on the abundance of miniature bottles of bubble bath, shampoo, cleanser, toner and moisturiser; and not the usual cheapo stuff either — the the Molton Brown range, no less (my favourite) — all there for the swiping. There are even His and Her slippers with *FHH* stitched in green and gold thread. I wonder if you're allowed to keep those. I mean, it wouldn't be very hygienic to pass them on from one guest to another, would it? You could end up with verrucas or athlete's foot. Oh, and as for the fluffy, white, monogrammed, towelling bathrobes hanging on the back of the door ... don't you dare even think about it, Emily Forsyth. That would be downright dishonest and not worth the risk of being rumbled.

I wander back into the bedroom, take a rosy apple from the pewter fruit dish, and unhook the crooked, latticed window. I look out across the manicured lawn to the velvety hills beyond, dotted with grazing sheep, like balls of cotton wool. Not a rambler in sight, and the only sounds, a rushing stream, a bleating chorus and distant birdsong.

'Dinner will be served at eight,' says Max. 'I'll go down to the cellar and bring up a bottle of your favourite claret.' He exits, pulling the door to.

'Do you like it?' asks Duncan, putting his arms around my waist, his rough chin brushing my ear.

'It's lovely,' I say breathlessly, desperately trying to keep my raging emotions in check, as he plants a gentle kiss on the nape of my neck. *Stay cool, Emily.*

'And *you're* lovely too,' he whispers, turning me to face him, ruffling my hair and kissing me again, urgently, hungrily — this time on the forehead, then the lips. My half-eaten apple drops to the floor. Oh, to hell with it! I am no pure, du Maurier heroine; I am Emily Forsyth, aged almost forty-three, and I haven't been kissed for longer than I care to remember.

Oh, dauphinoise potatoes, mangetout, beef filet in a red wine jus, how I have missed you! I have been trapped in a world of frozen ready meals for far too long, and after tonight's dining experience, I never want to go back there.

'The last roll to mop that up with?' asks Duncan, passing me the bread basket, the other hand attempting to stifle a cheeky snigger.

How I wish I were one of those fortunate people who lose their appetite when in love, but alas, *l'amour* makes me famished; and I even find room for homemade sticky toffee pudding with custard *and* ice cream to finish — and scoff Duncan's chocolate mints with my coffee, as well as my own.

'Now, lassie, we have to be up early if we're to reach the summit of Pike o' Blisco by lunchtime,' calls Duncan from the bedroom.

'No problem,' I reply through a mouthful of toothpaste. I undo the top button of my new pyjamas, then hastily do it up again. Giving myself the final once-over in the bathroom mirror, I enter the bedroom, to find Duncan sprawled out on the bed, poring over a map.

'We'll make a brief stop here, at Brown Howe for coffee, then we should reach the top by midday,' he says, indicating a tiny, blurred speck with his thumbnail. 'That's the easy bit. The route is then full of ups and downs, and is fairly hard going in places. Do you reckon you're up to it?'

'Me? Absolutely!'

'Then we'll aim for Great Knott. We should gain around five hundred metres in under two miles.'

'Lovely,' I say, eyelids sagging. The room is now starting to spin. (Sambuca after half a bottle of wine was maybe not such a great idea after all.) If I could just rest my head for a moment ... Please God, don't let me snore or dribble on the broderie anglaise pillowcases ...

I awake next morning with the bright September sun on my face, the white muslin curtains swelling like sails in the breeze. I sit up in bed, rub my eyes awake, and peer in disgust at the panda-eyed, spiky-haired hooker in the wardrobe mirror. How the hell did she get in here? Someone should call security.

Duncan appears from the shower, wrapped in a towel, looking scrumptious and smelling fresh and minty clean. Holding out the bathrobe he says, 'Come on, Porcupine Head, breakfast in twenty minutes.'

We exit the back garden via the squeaky gate, over a rickety, planked bridge, and across a gurgling stream. A pheasant darts out of the hedgerow, frantically flapping its wings, then soars upwards, coming to land on a tangle of boulders, high above us.

The springy grass soon gives way to rough and rocky terrain. As the path begins to rise up steeply, I start to feel as if I'm wearing a corset, the laces being pulled tighter with every step I take. Duncan, meanwhile, is zigzagging his way up like a mountain goat.

I knew I should have broken in my brand new walking boots before today. I already have a nasty blister on each heel. That will teach me to lie about belonging to a hill-walking club.

My head bobs up over the craggy ridge, where I find Duncan perched on a cushion of lilac heather. He's locked in a world of his own, eyes narrowed, ranging over the distant mountains. My heavy breathing wakes him from his reverie and he smiles.

'Coffee?' he says, hauling me up, then opening his rucksack and placing two plastic beakers and a thermos on a makeshift table of flat stone.

Strange, isn't it, how a smell or a taste can turn back the years, evoking memories of long ago? As I sit there sipping my coffee, I am a teenager again, travelling with Mum and Dad in our campervan from Ayr to Inverness to see Granny and Granddad. We'd stop by the roadside, traffic whizzing by, and out would come the deckchairs, tartan rug, sandwiches and thermos flask. Yes, there's definitely something special about coffee from a thermos; it tastes of long car journeys, picnics and summer camp.

'Wow! Look at that!' says Duncan, passing me his binoculars.

'What? Where?' I say, scanning the landscape, unsure of what I'm supposed to be focusing on.

He crouches down behind me and guides the binoculars towards Scafell mountain range, their summits poking through the band of hovering mist. 'There!'

'Oh, Duncan!' I cry, the wind stealing my voice away. 'They look like islands in the sky.'

'You haven't seen anything yet. Just wait until we reach Crinkle Crags. The views from up there are sensational,' he says, sliding his brawny arms through the straps of his rucksack. 'You okay to continue?'

'You bet!' I say with what I hope sounds like eagerness, as I hobble in his wake.

I have gasped in awe at the Rockies, the Himalayas and the Grand Canyon, but through a tiny porthole at thirty-two thousand feet, they seemed unreal: remote, unattainable, aloof, inanimate. These mountains leap out at you, inviting you to reach out and touch their rough, rugged edges, to explore their rock faces and scree gullies, to dip your throbbing feet in their icy, tumbling waters, shelter in their shadowy crevasses, be bewitched by their unusual, brooding shapes, daunted by their noble magnificence. They are very much alive, their colours and moods constantly changing with the elements.

'Close your eyes,' orders Duncan, leading me by the hand along a grassy, undulating path. 'Now open,' he says, placing his hands on my shoulders and turning me around.

Forget the sun rising over Hong Kong Harbour, the

Manhattan skyline from The Empire State, or the thunder of the mighty Niagara Falls; there is nowhere on earth that I would rather be than here, atop Crinkle Crags, overlooking Bowfell and the Langdale Pikes, like felt cut-outs against a painted sky. I am drunk with fresh air and wonderment, possessed by a mad desire to run in the grass without any shoes, à la Julie Andrews. So, what's a blister or ten when you're madly in love?

As we pass through the iron gates and up the hotel driveway, lined with blood-red rhododendron bushes, I stop, turn and give one long, last respectful look at the Langdale Pikes; strong, magisterial, graceful and wise.

Duncan lightly kisses the top of my head. 'Impressive, aren't they?'

I want to tell him that this has been the best of times, that I have never heard such sweet silence or felt such inner peace, that I'm so happy it hurts, that I never want to leave, that I think he's amazing, and …

'Race you to the room!' he calls, sprinting through the car park.

Surrounded by honeysuckle-scented candles, I languish in the deep bath, intoxicated by the sweet, jasmine-fragranced vapour rising from the steaming water. I feel like I'm floating in a flower-filled, English summer garden.

I have noticed myself getting stronger over these few, short days, and with that physical strength has come a mental strength, the like of which I haven't felt since pre-Nigel.

'Emily! You still in there?' calls Duncan, rapping sharply at the door. 'Your pina colada's going warm, and we've been called in to dinner.'

'Just coming!' I say, causing a tidal wave to crash over the flagstone floor. I grope for the snowdrop-white towel, its fibres like a long, thick lawn. I wrap it around me, savouring its sumptuous fluffiness.

I limp into the stone-walled dining room, bravely smiling through my pain at the other residents who bid me, 'Good evening'. Duncan, in pale blue shirt and black waistcoat, rises and waves to me from the far corner. 'You look gorgeous,' he says, running his hand lightly down my spine as he removes my pashmina. 'Fresh air suits you.'

'I'm starving,' I reply, gleaming at him, instantly wishing I'd simply said 'thank you.'

The moment I sit down on the carved chair, I slip off my strappy heels and wiggle my throbbing toes.

As he pours me a glass of wine, I peer at the faded tapestry suspended from a black, wrought iron, fleur-de-lis rail next to our table. He tells me an army of local women wove this by hand some four hundred years ago, and that it represents the people and the community of the village. On closer inspection (with the aid of my glasses; yes, I now wear them with pride, my new mantra being *what you see is what you get*) I am able to decipher the hotel (formerly the manor house), the church, the higgledy-piggledy farmers' cottages, surrounded by a tumult of peaks; Crinkle Crags, Bowfell and Pike o' Blisco; the very same ones I've scrambled and clawed my way up, and slipped and slithered down. They may be responsible for my aching limbs, calloused heels and black toenail, yet they have stirred something in my soul. I wonder if this is the same 'something' that motivated those local women long ago, that inspired Wordsworth to write poetry, and that has given me the appetite of a hungry hippo.

Dinner over, we take a stroll in the late, rosy pink

172

sunshine (me, sans shoes). We pass the tiered fountain, sparkling water spouting from a chubby cherub's mouth, on into the peaceful sanctuary of the verdant, aromatic herb garden, filled with rosemary, sage, thyme, chives, basil and parsley. The lavender bends and sways under the weight of the droning bees. The fragrance is soothingly hypnotic. The heavily laden fruit trees, watched over by the moss-coated statue of the goddess, Pomona, cast mystical shadows on the lawn.

I give a little shiver. Duncan gently places his jacket around me. I lay my head on his shoulder. Sliding his hand around my waist, he leads me inside.

By the fading glow of candle and firelight, he undresses me slowly. He laces his fingers through mine. Our breathing becomes faster, his mouth feverishly covering me with kisses.

'God, Emily, I want you,' he whispers, scooping me up and throwing me onto the four-poster, which makes a peculiar *boing* sound. I resist the temptation to laugh, and closing my eyes, let out a small gasp. Farewell, feminism! I am being swept away by a tsunami of emotions, like those heroines in Barbara Cartland novels — and I am relishing every single moment of it.

My eyes flicker open, and I peer at the clock. Where did the last ninety-six hours go? This morning we will go our separate ways: he north to Fife, and I south, to London. What happens now? The subject of another meeting has not been broached. Hardly daring to breathe, I study his sleeping face; the small scar above his top lip (the result of an altercation with the neighbouring farmer's Alsatian when he was five), his lightly freckled, slightly bent nose (broken at rugby as a teenager), his thick hair, flaming copper in the

173

morning sun's rays. What is going on in that head of his? He's gallant, affectionate, but what does he *really* think of me? Will he suggest another rendezvous, or will it simply be a peck on the cheek and cheery-bye? I haven't a clue how he feels, and all too soon breakfast will be over, bags packed, and the train will carry me far from him. I have to know.

'Good morning, Spike,' he croaks, pulling me towards him and nuzzling me with his stubbly chin. (Spike is his pet name for me now — a term of endearment, I guess. All the same, I would have much preferred something less canine and more feminine: e.g. Princess or Gorgeous.)

'Hey, what's up? You look so far away,' he says, squinting at me with his bad-boy grin.

'I ... I ... oh, nothing,' I lie.

'Come on, spit it out,' he coaxes, tilting my face to his.

Oh well, here goes ... Swallowing hard, I search those steely-blue — or are they grey? — unreadable eyes.

'I was just wondering if ... if we ... oh, it doesn't matter. Forget it.'

A huge tear slithers down my face, dammit, and my nose starts to run. I hastily turn my head away. I know I'm meant to be keeping my distance, but I'm too old to be playing games. What I really want to say is that I think I've fallen in love with him, does he feel the same way, or am I just another notch on the Forest Hill four-poster? If that's the case, I'd rather know now before I get in any deeper.

Feeling so pathetic makes me cross. So much for my new-found, inner strength, eh? Get a grip, woman! Don't spoil things by getting all serious on him.

'Think I'll have porridge for breakfast,' I sniff, summoning a faint smile as I head for the bathroom.

The moment my train starts to glide forward, Duncan turns and walks away briskly, without a backward glance. I slowly lower my arm and stare out of the window, through a fog of tears. I wasn't expecting a scene from *Brief Encounter,* but he could have at least waited a few more seconds until we were out of view. It's as if the door has been slammed shut and I am left out in the cold, wondering if it will ever be opened again.

The mauve and green hills flicker through my reflection. Only hours ago I was up on Scafell, the wind in my hair, the happiest woman alive. Now I feel empty and sad, and to be honest, rather lost. I am bound for my rented room at Beryl's, no job, no prospects, and the man I love hundreds of miles away. But how can this be real love after such a short time? It happens: look at Céline and Drew ...

Will I ever see him again? 'I'll call you,' he said. I feel used. Dammit. Here I go again. I have been serenely self-sufficient for ages now, and one little, romantic fling throws everything into chaos, exposing my needy, insecure side.

Maybe it really is time to put stability back into my life. I should forget my dream, wake up and behave like any normal middle-aged woman, by getting a proper job with a pension scheme and Christmas bonus. Yes, I may well be forced to do a u-turn. But not yet.

'Tickets, please.'

I pull down my rucksack and there, protruding from the flap, is a small package, wrapped in brown paper. I rip it open: *Fellwalking with Wainwright.* On the flyer is a dedication ...

To my wee Spike.
There are many more hills for us to climb. Dx

I hug the book to me, grinning girlishly. How fickle my emotions are! A few scribbled words, and doubt and insecurity are transformed into optimism and joy in an instant.

I lean back into the headrest, shut my eyes, and slip into a dreamy, cinematic state, reliving every walk, every meal, every waking moment of the last four, wonderful, love-drenched days; I am once more at the summit of Crinkle Crags, looking out over Great Langdale, head nestled in Duncan's chest; cut to that day it rained, when we dunked soggy digestives in our tea and he had to cut me out of my cagoule hood when I pulled the drawstring too tight (me and toggles just don't get on); pan over to Red Tarn lake, where I *finally* learned to swim (hallelujah!) ... A faint ringing permeates the scene, becoming persistently louder. I awake with a jolt, realising it's my mobile. I dive into my bag, painfully aware of several sets of scornful eyes upon me. (I'm in the Quiet Coach.)

'Hello,' I whisper.

'Emily? It's Dolly from *Peach Promotions*. Got an assignment for you starting Tuesday. Pop into the agency tomorrow around ten, and I'll give you all the details, darling.'

There! Doesn't something always turn up? What does she have in mind, I wonder? In-store cheese sampling? Demonstrating the latest in dust-busting gizmos? As long as it doesn't involve wearing a furry costume, I really don't care.

CHAPTER EIGHT
Pattie Pineapple and Pino Pinuccio

I SCRUTINISE THE GIANT CUSTARD BLOB staring back at me in the full-length mirror and give a little start. I am wearing green tights with matching pixie boots, a yellow, hooped tunic with latticework design, complemented by a green tuft strapped to my head.

My latest role is as Pattie Pineapple — yep, a pineapple — please don't laugh — promoting a new type of fruit yogurt drink. I am in my forties, for God's sake. What the hell am I doing? I'm a joke. Other women my age are wearing business suits, attending video conferences and ordering their Ocado shop on their iPad.

The changing room curtains swish open.

'Perfect fit,' says Sadie, the wardrobe supervisor at *Peach Promotions*, looking me up and down. 'Could have been made for you.'

'Gee, thanks,' I say, the half-smile on my face disintegrating into a look of disgust.

Waterloo Station. Next Morning.
I take up position on the concourse, waiting for battle

to commence. I peer up at the clock. 7.05. I lower my gaze and wave to the orange and the strawberry, loitering by Lush. There's an apple reading a newspaper by WH Smith, and I realise things could have been much, much worse, as I spy the one in the banana costume pacing up and down outside Accessorize.

God, I hope no one I know passes by.

The station is starting to fill up now. I pick up my tray of Caribbean Crush from the tropical-coloured stand and brace myself.

'Good morning! I'm Pattie Pineapple. Would you like to taste a glass of Caribbean Crush to set you up for the day? It has all the vitamins you need ...'

As the rush hour gains momentum, the gentle flow of sedate travellers turns into an ugly stampede. As fast as I can replenish my tray, the samples are snatched by a sea of greedy, clamouring commuters, sprinting full-pelt for ready-to-depart trains.

I soon abandon my carefully-learned spiel, realising I might just as well be saying,

Would you like to taste a glass of extra strong laxative? Guaranteed to make you go ten times a day.

The bulbous design of the costume makes you rather unsteady, so when I'm struck by a briefcase at high speed, I topple over, my green-clad legs flailing in the air, Caribbean Crush all over the concourse. I squeeze my eyes tightly shut and prepare to be trampled to death. What a way to go, dressed as a piece of fruit. I'd always had something a little more glamorous in mind.

'Here, hold on to me,' comes a deep, cultured voice at my side. My eyes focus on a pair of shiny, black, lace-up, city-slicker shoes, attached to pinstriped legs. The stranger slides his strong hands under my armpits, and I sag against him, knees buckling.

178

Slowly, steadily, I am raised from the ground, like a sunken ship.

'Are you okay?' he says, coming round to face me, firmly gripping my shoulders.

My eyes lock into his cobalt blue gaze, heart going pitter-patter, knees about to give way again.

No, I think I may faint. Please take me home with you.

THE TALL, DARK STRANGER SCOOPS PATTIE PINEAPPLE UP IN HIS ARMS AND WHISKS HER AWAY ON THE 0810 TO ASCOT.

'Yes, I'm fine, thank you,' I mumble, coming to my senses, nails digging into my palms in acute embarrassment.

'Take care.' He smiles, handing me my sticky tray. I blush the colour of Caribbean Crush.

'Thank you, I will. This isn't my normal job ... I don't usually go around ...'

'Gotta dash,' he says, stealing a sideways glance at the departure board.

' ... dressed like this. Bye.'

Pattie Pineapple is the catalyst; the moment I hit rock bottom and decide to take charge of the mess that is my life ...

I invest in new publicity photographs, a showreel, a voice demo and the latest edition of *Contacts*. I make calls and send e-mails every day. Replies are rare and mostly negative:

Dear Emily,
Thank you for your recent enquiry. We regret to inform you we are now fully cast.
(So why, only two days ago, did you suggest I submit my details?)

179

Dear Emily,
We acknowledge receipt of your CV and photograph, but have decided to use a cast we have worked with before. We will keep you on file.

Dear Emily,
Thank you for sending us your details. We are currently looking for actors who can sing, have ballroom dancing skills and play the cello.

Dear Emily,
Thank you for your interest in our production of 'The Glass Menagerie', but we are looking to cast television 'names' only. We will keep you on file.

Dear Emily,
The parts as yet uncast are: 1) Jaz: overweight and vertically challenged. 2) Maria: a beautiful actress with striking Latin looks (think Penelope Cruz) who is a highly skilled tightrope walker.

Not one to let constant rejection deter me, I remain optimistic and with dogged determination, continue in my quest for a job, firm in the belief that by the law of averages, something will turn up sooner or later — and eventually it does.

One of the seventy or so agents I have contacted invites me to his office to discuss the possibility of taking me on his books. This is unusual; agents normally won't consider you unless they are able to see you perform, and by that I mean a part in an actual play or TV episode, not giving your Lady Macbeth in his office. That said, it's nigh on impossible to find a job without an agent. However, this one has a vacancy for someone of my age range and type. When he asked me about my most recent work, I omitted, somewhat wisely, I think, to mention the role of Pattie Pineapple.

I press the buzzer of Lionel Butler Personal Management.

'Fourth floor,' comes an anonymous voice from the intercom grille, as the door clicks open. The lift has a piece of paper sellotaped to it, with OUT OF ORDER scribbled across.

I climb the dark, winding staircase. The paintwork is peeling, and the well-worn carpet looks like it could do with a good douse of Shake 'n' Vac.

I press the bell, and 'Somewhere Over The Rainbow' rings out. How camp is that!

The door is eventually opened with a flourish by a man of about seventy, with a shock of silver hair, wearing a lilac shirt and pale pink, polka dot cravat. The great man himself, I presume. He mouths 'Come in,' and waves me inside as he continues his phone conversation.

'Versatile? Absolutely! *And* he has his own dame's costumes and wigs. Grreat! He'll be with you at eleven tomorrow, okay? *Ciao!*' Without pausing for breath he continues, 'You must be Emily. Lionel. Sorry for the mess, darling.' The phone rings again.

'Ooh, it's all go here today,' he says apologetically, as he skips into the office. 'Grab a pew. Won't be a tick.'

I squeeze myself onto the creaky Chesterfield sofa, in between a pile of papers and a huge, slumbering cat. The walls are covered in theatrical posters and photographs, including one of a dark-haired, youthful Lionel in a line-up, shaking hands with the Queen.

'Apologies, darling,' he says, bustling back into the room. 'I have six pantomime dames to find before Friday. *Six!* Please come this way.'

The office is small and chaotic, and our conversation is constantly interrupted by the phone ringing or the whirring of the ancient fax machine.

'Now, I've got your details here ... somewhere,' he says, hunting through the towering stacks of letters, photographs and copies of *The Stage*.

'Puck, get down!' he says, shooing another cat off the printer.

'Aha, here it is!' he says, waving a piece of crumpled paper. He reaches for his glasses, attached to a gold chain around his neck, and scans my CV.

Chewing my bottom lip, I wait a couple of agonising minutes for the verdict, hopes and dreams fluttering.

'Well, considering you've had no agent or contacts in the business, you've certainly kept yourself busy, haven't you? I like that ... shows determination and staying power,' he says, picking up a pen. 'Tell you what, I'll take you on for a trial period of six months, and then we'll take it from there. How does that sound?'

I have to make a superhuman effort not to pin him to the photocopier and smother him in kisses.

'Ten percent commission on theatre, fifteen on TV and commercials, seventeen on films ...' (My God, I should be so lucky.) 'Oh, and I insist on sole representation. Sign here, and ... here.'

He hands me my copy of the contract and says, 'Well now, let's get you out to work, daughter!'

I glide down that grubby staircase, imagining a sea of flashing camera lights popping, and a swarm of journalists thrusting microphones at me, calling out,

Can you confirm, Miss Forsyth, you're signed up to play Samantha's sister in the next Sex and the City *movie?*

Miss Forsyth, any truth in the rumour you're dating

your co-star?

Okay, okay, so it's not some plush office in the West End of town, and he may not be the crème de la crème of agents, but who knows, maybe, just maybe, my life is about to change.

Lionel, I love you! I've been on his books for barely two days, and he's got me *two* auditions: one for a pasta sauce commercial and another to understudy on a Number One Tour ...

In a blind panic, I accost one unsuspecting passer-by after another.

'Please can you direct me to Alpha Advertising in Dean Street?'

'Sorry. No live here.'

'Ich bin auf Urlaub.'

'Scusi? I no speak English.'

'Ooof - sais pas.'

God, is no one actually from this town?

In desperation, I dive through a beaded curtain, into a dimly lit lap-dancing club. A drag queen, wearing a pointy, Madonna bra and rolling a joint, says in a tough-as-boots voice, 'Yeah, it's a couple of blocks away.' Taking me by the hand, he/she leads me back out onto the rain-drenched, Soho street. 'Turn right, and it's the second turning on your left.'

'I'm here for the *Pinocchio* ... no, the erm ... the tomato sauce commercial casting,' I pant, a puddle forming around my feet.

The receptionist scrutinises me with her oh-I'm-so-bored expression, and mumbles through her Angelina pout, 'Fill in this form and take a seat.'

'Where's the ladies?'

'Emily Forsyth and Ninian Moncrieff!' calls a shrill

voice from the corridor.

A middle-aged, Bertie-Wooster type in cords, checked shirt and squeaky, Church's brogues places *The Times* under his arm, scrapes a comb through his slicked-back, greying hair, and swaggers over to the young woman with headphones slung around her neck.

'Emily Fors...!'

'Just coming!' I cry, nervously unbuttoning my dripping wet mac.

The studio door slams shut. At the far end is a long, leather sofa, crammed with young, trendy, advertising executives, sipping their take-away Starbucks.

'This is Ninian and Emily,' says the woman with the headphones.

'Okay, you've read the blurb,' says a man with a goatee beard and small crucifix dangling from his left ear. I'm about to explain I haven't yet had the opportunity to read the blurb, on account of being late, due to signal failure on the District Line (again), and then getting lost, and not being able to run very fast in my new wedge shoes, but he ploughs on without pausing for breath.

'Now ... Emma ...'

'Actually, it's Emily.'

'Let's have you first. Stand on the white cross please, and when you're given the nod, say your name and agent's name to camera. Just leave your things on the floor. Okay?'

Dilemma: do I just give my details deadpan, or do I smile and say it with feeling, thereby conveying my warm, sincere personality and versatile acting talent? Never having been for a commercial casting, I don't know the protocol.

'When you're ready please.'

I plump for a bit of both — not too serious, not too gushing.

Ninian opts for the cool, I-do-these-all-the-time approach.

'Thank you,' says Goatee, leaping up. 'Now, just to recap — the scene is a small, intimate Italian restaurant. If you'd like to sit down here, please,' he says, propelling us over to a metal table and chairs. 'In front of you is a plate of pasta cooked in *Pino Pinuccio* sauce. I'm afraid it's cold, but I assure you it was freshly cooked this morning. Now, I want a bit of improvised chit-chat to begin with, and then as you start to eat, you, Emma, go into wild raptures at the taste,' he says, clicking his fingers whilst simultaneously stamping his foot, like he's about to launch into a paso doble. 'You, hubby, on the other hand, carry on eating, oblivious to the stares and sniggers from the other diners. Okay?' he says, clapping his hands, then leaping backwards onto the arm of the sofa, long legs swinging back and forth.

'Camera rolling ... and ... action!'

Looking around me at the stark, white walls, I say in a thin voice, 'I'm so glad you brought us here for our anniversary, darling. What a lovely surprise.' Ninian looks at me expressionless.

I poke the oily pasta with my fork, and as it reaches my mouth, I say, 'Mmm, this pasta is really delicious.'

Goatee jumps up, tugging at his beard, crucifix swinging wildly back and forth.

'No, no, no! We want a bit of va-va-voom! Let us feel our mouths salivating, let us *taste* that pasta sauce, let us be *swept* along with the sheer enjoyment, the *passion* ... think *When Harry Met Sally*, think ... think ... *orgasmic*!'

He flops back down, eyes twirling in annoyance.

Ninian sighs and fires me a withering look. I've a good mind to chuck the bowl of pasta over his perfectly coiffed head. I know he isn't supposed to say anything, but God almighty, it's like sitting opposite a tailor's dummy.

I wonder if he works much; perhaps *MORTUARY CORPSE* is his speciality, and he has a string of enviable TV credits to his name: *Silent Witness, Law & Order, Casualty, Holby City, Midsomer Murders, Lewis;* the possibilities are endless.

'Now let's try it again, please,' hisses Goatee, chewing gum furiously as he glances at his watch. I glimpse the panel: a stony-faced woman with half-shaved hair yawns, a young guy sporting a topknot and grungy jeans waggles his sneaker-clad foot, while the cool rock chick in denim skirt and cowboy boots plays with her iPhone.

Okay, you arty-farty advertisers, you want va-va-voom? I'll give you va-va-voom!

Two thousand pounds may be a drop in the ocean to Ninian Moncrieff, but to me it's a fortune. And that cheque with my name on it is just within my grasp. All that stands between it and me is a few moments of humiliating myself in front of a bunch of strangers. That's not so bad, is it?

I close my eyes, take a deep intake of breath and fling my head back, diving into a frenzied attack on the mound of pasta, stuffing it into my mouth with both hands, covering my face with *Pino Pinuccio* sauce, panting and moaning.

'Mmm. More ... more ... Yes, yes, YESSSS!'

Ninian looks at me, open-mouthed, eyes wide.

'Thank you!' booms Goatee eventually, jumping to his feet. 'Well, what can I say? Meg Ryan, eat your heart out! We'll be in touch.'

Ninian scarpers, doubtless terrified he may end up

having to escort me back to the tube. I am left to pick up my bag, coat and last morsel of dignity in stunned silence. I fumble in my pocket. Where's a tissue when you need one? Head held high, I exit, leaving behind a blob of pasta sauce on the door handle.

I enter the crowded waiting area, woefully aware of the other candidates' eyes boring through me as they pretend to read their scripts.

I clear my throat. 'Where's the loo?' I ask the receptionist.

'Second door on the left,' she mumbles, without lifting her eyes from her *Heat* magazine.

Dammit, it's engaged, so I about-turn and make a break for it, leaving behind a trail of bloody devastation.

The sleek, silver limousine with tinted windows rolls up outside the five-star Bel Ombrage Hotel in Piccadilly. The green-uniformed doorman bounds down the shiny, black-and-white-tiled steps to greet the new arrivals. Seizing my chance, I scuttle through the buzzing atrium, across the vast, glossy marble floor, past the immaculate receptionist, and into the vanity room to repair my face and composure. No damp roller-towel here, or those fierce, noisy blow-driers that blast out stale air; a pile of fluffy, white hand towels nestles in a scrolled iron wall basket, an array of luxurious toiletries stands in a military row along the frosted-glass shelf, and an enormous glass vase full of white lilies sits on a granite-topped table, as Vivaldi's 'Four Seasons' tinkles through the floral-scented air.

The blood-red water swirls down the plughole as I scrub the encrusted tomato sauce from my face and hands. After pampering myself with cleanser, toner, moisturiser, and eau de toilette, I haven't the bare-faced gall to just sneak out, and besides, am in dire need of cheering up, so grab myself a window seat in the Palm Room and order a cream tea. God, these frightful auditions are costing me a fortune.

Okay, so I may not be the new face of *Pino Pinuccio,* and I may have kissed goodbye to a couple of grand, but maybe a stint as an understudy on tour is what fate has in store for me now.

I snuggle down into the leather sofa and richly textured cushions, pull *Forbidden Love* from my rucksack, and turn to Act One, teeth sinking into my jam-and-clotted-cream-covered scone.

Am going to Wendy's for supper tonight — please God, it's not pasta.

CHAPTER NINE
Be Careful What You Wish For
At my signal unleash hell ~ Gladiator

I AM BEGINNING TO WORRY. There's a dark side to my character emerging that I didn't know was there.

When I first got the understudy job I was naturally over the moon, but as the weeks go by, I'm becoming a teensy-weensy bit frustrated. I know the part now, and whilst I may not have starred in my own TV series or graced the cover of celebrity mags, dare I say it, I think I could play the role just as well. Day after day, week after week, the waiting, the hoping ...

Wishing someone to be struck down with laryngitis or mild tummy bug is one thing, but willing someone's foot to get trapped in a revolving set is something else entirely. Evil. I'm horrified that I'm capable of such a thought.

I trudge through the stage door, idly kicking the snow from my boots, the latest copy of *Hello!* and a bag of Jelly Babies clutched in my woolly mitts.

'Evening, Arthur. Dressing room ten, please.'

'Reckon you'll no be havin' much time for readin' the night, doll,' he wheezes, glancing at my magazine as he hands me the key.

'Mmm?' I say, signing in, mind elsewhere.

'It's no' for me to say,' he says, hoisting a shaggy eyebrow.

I slowly start to climb the spiral staircase, calling in at the greenroom on the way for a brew.

'Company manager's been looking for you,' grunts one of the lighting guys from behind his *Nuts* magazine.

'Right. Thanks,' I say breezily, spilling milk everywhere, my stomach dropping ten floors. Surely not? I mean I saw Amanda barely two hours ago. I watched her performance from the darkness of the stage-right wings and she was on fine form, giving her 'I-love-you-but-we-must-part' speech.

It was at that point that I'd decided to make a break for it. Technically, I'm not supposed to leave the building until the curtain comes down, but I've religiously watched and mouthed every performance from the wings of Brighton's Theatre Royal, to this, our final stop, The Dukes in Edinburgh. With just five minutes of the matinée left, what could possibly happen to her?

Mistake no. 1: leaving theatre early.

Mistake no. 2: gorging on All-You-Can-Eat buffet.

Mistake no. 3: succumbing to large glass of house red.

Mistake no. 4: ordering garlic bread.

Mistake no. 5: forgetting to switch on mobile phone.

Mistake no. 6: arriving five minutes late for 'the half'.

Mistake no. 7: accepting this job.

'... so, the silly cow's been whisked off to A&E to have it x-rayed. You know what this means?' says Simon, our company manager, running his hand nervously through his mop of unruly hair.

I feel a stab of guilt. My visualisation powers have taken on a telekinetic life of their own, like in some

Stephen King horror film.

I hadn't intended anything serious to happen. Just a minor ailment; something to lay her low for a week, say, allowing Lionel sufficient time to arrange invitations and tickets for casting directors and producers.

I swallow hard and force my lips into a weak smile. There is an expectant silence. This is the stuff of Hollywood musicals: the leading actress is taken ill, and the understudy has to take over at short notice.

I can do it. I've been practising for months, says the heroine, with an assured toss of her pretty head. *Bravo! More! A star is born!* This is the moment I have waited for, *longed* for all these weeks, these seventy-two performances, so why do I now have this overwhelming desire to flee the theatre and catch the first National Express coach out of town? Well, apart from my all-consuming guilt, the auditorium will be packed to the rafters with legions of excited fans waiting to see Amanda Butterfield and her co-star, Rick Romano, give their highly acclaimed, headline-grabbing performances as star-crossed lovers, Constance and Enrique. The fact that their on-stage passion has spilled over into reality has fuelled the public's imagination. The House-Full sign is now a permanent fixture on the pavement, while armies of eager punters camp outside in all weathers, hoping for returns.

Exquisite pairing!
The chemistry between Romano and Butterfield
is electric. Beg, steal or borrow a ticket!
~ The Billingham Gazette.
This romantic duo sets the stage alight.
You'd be mad to miss it!
~ The Yorkshire Evening Post.

'You up for it?' Simon asks, knowing full well it doesn't matter whether I'm 'up for it' or not. Why else have I been travelling up and down the country, getting paid £500 per week plus touring allowance? So I may sit in my dressing room, stuffing my face with Hobnobs and tea whilst reading trashy magazines, or to be allowed to finally finish reading *Doctor Zhivago*, which I started back in 2010?

Nah — if it's all the same to you, Simon, I'd rather give it a miss.

'Of cour-hourse!' I reply, with a loud laugh, verging on hysteria.

'Knock 'em dead, girl!' he says with more enthusiasm than he feels, I suspect.

I feel my bottom lip trembling. Oh, my God. This is it. I'm trapped. There's no way out. Stay calm. Deep breaths. STAY CALM. I AM IN CONTROL. I AM A PROFESSIONAL ACTRESS. I CAN DO THIS. I AM IN CONTROL.

'Miss Forsyth to dressing room two *immediately*,' cuts in the wardrobe mistress's calm but commanding voice over the tannoy. I float downstairs in a daze.

'Arms up!' instructs Doris with a sympathetic smile, as she unravels an eighteen-inch corset. Before you can say 'Mr Darcy', I am stripped of my jumper and jeans and unceremoniously wrapped up like a pound of sausages. She yanks the laces tight. I gasp for air, secretly cursing the waitress for having persuaded me to have the banoffee pie with whipped cream to finish.

'This is your five minute call,' crackles the stage manager's voice through the speaker, barely audible over the excited laughter and chatter of the unsuspecting audience. 'Five minutes please.'

The show relay is switched off abruptly, and the

only sound is Rick gargling in the dressing room next door. I stare at the stranger with big hair and heaving bosom looking back at me. God, I'm scared. My startled gaze falls on a bottle of Bach's Rescue Remedy, sitting amongst Amanda's numerous cards, flowers, make-up brushes and other leading lady paraphernalia. *Directions: Squeeze 4 drops onto the tongue.* Bugger that. This is an emergency. Unscrewing the top, I swig the lot, in a desperate attempt to stop my knees knocking together and my teeth from chattering.

I toy with my mobile. To phone, or not to phone? Why not? I'm in need of some moral support, and the evening rush won't have started yet. Why am I hesitating? He's my boyfriend, isn't he? It's no big deal. Why shouldn't I call?

'Duncan? Hi! It's Emily.'

'Uh huh. What erm … what can I do for you?' he says haltingly.

'I just wanted you to know I'm on!'

'Sorry?'

'In five minutes I'm on! Amanda had an accident and I'm on!'

Silence.

'Duncan?'

'I'm pleased for you, really I am,' he mumbles. 'Now's not a good time — but good luck. Okay? Speak to you later. Good luck.'

He hangs up and I sit there, staring at my mobile, heart sinking to the tips of my sharply pointed, excruciatingly uncomfortable, brocade shoes. Come on, girl. Pull yourself together. You're a professional, aren't you? The success of tonight's show sits squarely on your shoulders. Are you going to let a mere man come between you and your possible moment of triumph? And just think, thirty minutes from now, you will realise your girly ambition of snogging Rick Romano IN THE FLESH! (That is if we get that far; if they don't have to bring the curtain down after the first scene because of all the booing and heckling.)

'Ladies and gentlemen, this is your Act One beginners' call. Miss Forsyth and Mr Romano. Act One beginners, please.'

Oh my God, just hearing my name mentioned in the same breath as his sends a wave of electricity around my body.

Other cast members pop their heads round the door.

'Good luck!'

'Break a leg!'

'You'll be *fine!*'

Will I?

With lines swirling around my head, and pizza, pasta, Waldorf salad, red wine and Rescue Remedy sloshing around my stomach, I lumber towards the stage area, one hand clutching reams of heavy, burgundy velvet, the other the wall. I now know how Mary Queen of Scots must have felt as she made her way to the gallows. I can almost hear the solitary drum beat accompanying my every step.

As I take up position at the stage-right wings, I let out an almighty burp, the lace of my corset straining to the max. Rick gives me an encouraging thumbs-up from the dimness of prompt corner, opposite. I have only ever rehearsed with the other understudy, and wonder if he actually even knows my name. Until this moment he's probably been thinking I'm one of his many crazed, adoring fans, following the show religiously from Woking to Aberdeen.

Little does he know that some twenty-five years ago, as the object of my teenage passion, his life-sized poster adorned my wall, smiling out at me, encouraging me through my A-levels, comforting me when my pet rabbit died, and when Blair Galloway dumped me for Miss Young Farmer 1988.

His hair is flecked with grey now, and he may be sporting a paunch in place of a six-pack, but there's still something effortlessly magnetic and wildly attractive about him. His come-to-bed eyes are bluer than the sky, his seductive smile makes your legs wobble, and that mellifluous voice would make the football results sound like *Fifty Shades of Grey*. The moment I have dreamed of for a quarter of a century has finally arrived, and I'm so overfed and petrified I could vomit, and my breath reeks of garlic. I swipe an extra strong mint from my newly acquired cleavage, and crunch it fiercely.

'We have clearance!' hisses the stage manager. Oh, my God, what's my first line? Breathe, breathe, you can do this. You are ready. She sells seashells on the seashore, she ... what is my first line? Help! I can't remember! It's too late to rush round to prompt corner. Why the hell didn't I bring my script down with me? The lights are going down. Betty bought a bit of butter ... the stage manager's stepping out in front of the curtains ...

The excited chitter-chatter gives way to a deathly hush.

'Ladies and gentlemen, may I have your attention please. Due to the indisposition of Miss Amanda Butterfield, the role of Constance at this evening's performance will be played by Miss Emily Forsyth.'

A gargantuan groan reverberates around the auditorium. I feel like the booby prize in a raffle. I can almost hear them tutting and spluttering on their Mint Imperials, saying things like, 'Never heard of 'er.'

'Has she been on the telly?'

'Bloody cheek! These tickets cost a fortune ...'

The lights dim and an eerie silence descends. I leave the security of the wings and venture out onto the vast stage. The curtain rises. Someone coughs. Any minute now they are going to start jeering, baying for my blood. All at once I am drowning in a sea of white light. I feel like a prisoner of war caught climbing the perimeter fence, exposed by the stark beam of a searchlight. *Hände hoch!* Sweat trickles down my spine. I step forward, push out my diaphragm, open my mouth to speak and — nothing comes out. *Get a grip!* a voice in my head tells me. My brain is scrambling for the words. *You do know it.*

I can't stand here like something from Madame Tussauds, so out of sheer desperation, am about to throw myself on the floor and burst into floods of tears, hoping Rick will take it as a sign to come on early, when the lines tumble out in the nick of time.

The next two hours are a blur. It's as if I'm on automatic pilot, drifting through a fog, the dialogue and moves appearing out of nowhere ...

Then all at once I am standing centre stage, hand in hand with Rick as we take our final bow. It's over. I've done it, and I didn't muck up my lines or belch or bump into the furniture.

I close the dressing room door firmly and lean against it, heaving a mighty sigh of relief. Alone at last! I feel giddy and ravenous. I unpin the heavy, Antoinette wig, kick off Amanda's two-sizes-too-small shoes, and rip open the bag of Jelly Babies. Those little, red, black and green faces smile back at me sweetly as I devour them greedily. There's a knock at the door. Thank God! That will be Doris coming to unlace me.

'Yesh!' I call, through a mass of congealed strawberry, orange and lime jelly.

'Well done, baby!' drawls Rick, bursting into the room, frilly shirt unbuttoned to the waist, a bottle of bubbly and two glasses clutched in his strong, manly hands.

Whoa! I blink several times, jaw scraping the floor. I need a reality check here. Standing before me is the demigod, Rick Romano; a man adored by millions of women the world over, inviting *me* to drink champagne with him. And here am I, with what resembles a pair of tights on my head, mouth so crammed full of Jelly Babies I'm unable to string two words together.

'Tank yub,' I drool, flashing him a gummy smile.

Amanda now recovered (it was just a slight sprain), I am demoted to understudy for the final four performances. To be honest, I don't mind. Whilst it was all terribly exciting, I made a pact with God that night — if he allowed me to get through to the end without messing it up for everyone and making a complete numpty of myself in front of one thousand, three hundred and fifty people, I would be happy with my lot and never ever harbour nasty thoughts about a leading lady again (or anyone for that matter).

On a high after the final performance, and full of Christmas spirit and mulled wine, I've just booked a cab to take me to St Andrews, some fifty miles away. I must be crazy, blowing a chunk of my final pay cheque on this alcohol-fuelled whim, but it will be worth it, just to see the look of surprise on Duncan's face.

I was secretly hoping he might suggest flying out to Spain to meet Mum and Dad over the holiday. Am I letting the sisterhood down by wishing to have a man by my side over Christmas? I can't bear the prospect of those pitying glances from Mum's well-meaning pals. I can almost hear them now, saying things like, 'What a shame. They made such a nice couple.'

'She'd have made a lovely mother.'

'Didn't he run off with someone younger?'

'Well, you know what these pilots are like … girl in every port.'

And worse still, what about The Leery Beast (aka Giles)? He lives in the apartment next door and believes he's the George Clooney of the Costa del Sol. He reeks of Brut, dyes his hair jet-black, and his teeth are more Tippex-ed than Simon Cowell's. Oh, and his salsa moves have to be seen to be believed. Mum has tried to pair him off with one of her divorced and desperate yoga pals, but at sixty-eight, he's naturally looking for someone in their thirties/forties.

'Merry Christmas!' calls the driver as he pulls away from The Tam O'Shanter in a spray of slush. There's a light on upstairs. Good. He's still up. I scrabble in my rucksack for the sprig of mistletoe I pinched from the theatre bar.

Leaning in the doorway, I push the bell, heart thumping in my chest.

Come on, Duncan, it's freezing out here! I pull my beanie hat further down and hopping from one foot to the other, ring the bell again, long and hard this time. The stairway lights up eventually, and Duncan's six-foot-two frame looms through the stained glass. The door opens.

'Happy Christmas!' I beam, holding the mistletoe over my head, lips puckered. Moments pass. I open my eyes and meet Duncan's stony gaze.

'Well, aren't you going to give me a kiss and invite me in?' I giggle girlishly.

'Why didn't you let me know you were coming?' he mumbles.

'I wanted to surprise you,' I reply lamely.

'Who is it, darling?' comes a breathy, female voice from the top of the stairs. My stomach dives into freefall.

'Erm, it's a bit difficult ... ' he stammers, not daring to look me in the eye.

My mind goes numb and my heart wedges itself in my throat.

'It was stupid of me to come. I ... I ...'

Dropping the mistletoe, I hoist my bag onto my back and retreat into the darkness, my vision blurred by snowflakes and tears.

'Emily! Come back. Let me explain ...'

I scurry as fast as the ice and my bulging rucksack will allow, pursued by a dressing-gowned, barelegged Duncan.

'Please, please ... let me explain ...'

I stop and turn, darting him a pained look. 'No need!' I snap through my foggy breath, body trembling with cold and shock. 'I thought you were different. Go back to your girlfriend. She must be wondering where you are.'

'Och, Emily, please don't be like this ... it's not what you think ...'

I push him away and he skids on the ice. With glacial dignity, I stride off into the bitter night, no idea where I'm headed.

It wasn't meant to be like this; it's 1.30 in the morning, it's snowing, I don't know where I'm going to sleep, and the man I thought was my boyfriend is a two-timing cheat. Betrayed. Again. What a terrible start to Christmas. I feel my bottom lip start to wobble; then the last image of Duncan flashes across my mind — flat on his back, pale knees planted on either side of him, and a little bit of me smiles. Real men don't wear slippers.

'Cooee, Poppet! Over here!'

I trawl the sea of expectant faces and drivers' meet-and-greet boards. There, in the midst of them all, are Mum and Dad; Mum waving excitedly, Dad towering over her, subdued as always. They look older, more frail, and I swear Mum has shrunk.

They had often talked of retiring early to the sun, and when Dad suffered a heart attack due to the stresses and strains of running a road haulage business, they were spurred into action before it was too late.

Nowadays Dad spends most of his time on the golf course, while Mum fills her days with yoga, Spanish language and cookery classes.

'Oh, I have good news for you, darling,' chirrups Mum, turning to me as we pootle along the coastal road towards Denia. 'According to Lydia, Giles has found himself a lady friend at last, so should be on his best behaviour at the Christmas party. She's called Crystal — or is it Charity, Brian?'

Dad shrugs his shoulders. 'Anyway, it's one of those footballers'-wives type names. We've not met her yet. I can't imagine what she'll be like.'

'I can't *wait*.' I smile, relief washing over me. In my current mood, this year might well have been the year I finally snapped, were The Leery Beast to pinch my bottom or make his usual quips about mile high club membership.

'And while we're on the subject of relationships,' she says cagily, 'any word from Nigel?'

'No, Mum.' I let out a heavy sigh, eyes boring into the back of the driver's seat, throat constricting.

'Such a shame. I really liked Nigel. We both did, didn't we, Brian?'

I meet Dad's gaze in the rear-view mirror. He shakes his head wearily, runs his hand through his non-existent hair, and winks at me.

'I don't know what's wrong with men these days,' she continues. 'But darling, you know, you've got to make the best of yourself. When you were flying you never went out without make-up and you wore such pretty, feminine things. Now, whenever I see you, you're in jeans and your hair makes you look like a man. I used to love it when you swept it up in a chignon; very Grace Kelly. Now, well now, you look like — Joan of Arc's mother.'

'I've changed, Mum. Designer labels, high heels and manicures aren't me any more. I don't need those things to make me feel good.' (Why do I always feel this need to defend myself?)

'I know, poppet, but without a proper job, you need to set about finding a man to look after you. Your father and I won't be around forever, and you're not getting any younger,' she says in an anguished tone.

'I don't need a man to look after me,' I say through gritted teeth, staring out of the window. What is it about Christmas? I can cope with my failed relationships/career, lack of money and other disappointments the rest of the year, but because it's Christmas everything seems heightened. While most people my age are defrosting the family-sized turkey, baking mince pies, icing the fruit cake and welcoming the kids back from uni, I'm sitting in the back of my mum and dad's car behaving like a sulky teenager. To add insult to injury, tucked in my rucksack is my seasonal round–robin letter from my American school friend, proudly telling me that she and her husband have just celebrated their twenty-first wedding anniversary with a romantic trip to Cape Cod and are still very much in love, that Brad and Candy got top grades in their exams, Brad has already been offered a job at Citibank, whilst Candy's taking a year off to do voluntary work in Honduras. Stapled to it is a photo of the family around the Christmas tree, wearing identical smiles and festive jumpers.

Oh dear, I'm turning into a bitter, curmudgeonly harpy, aren't I?

The Christmas Party:
'I've put you in charge of canapés, poppet,' says Mum, hastily removing her apron, then thrusting two oval, silver platters at me as she trots over to the door. 'And Brian, I'm relying on you to keep people's drinks topped up, and oh, put some party music on — no brass bands or country and western though — some Julio Iglesias would be perfect.'

Before long the champagne corks are popping, crackers are being snapped, and guests are grooving in paper hats to Elvis's version of 'Here Comes Santa Claus.'

Back in cabin crew mode, I glide in between the guests.

'Vol au vent, Lydia?' I say, tapping Mum's posh yoga teacher on the shoulder.

'Emily! So lovely you made it home this year. Your mother told me about Nigel. Men, eh? Always on the lookout for a younger model. But we middle-aged girls must never give up hope, must we?' She winks, her overly tanned face stretching into a sympathetic smile. 'Aah, you must be Chantelle,' she says, making a beeline for the bleached blonde sporting a cropped top and skirt the size of a Kleenex tissue.

We middle-aged girls? Excuse me! Lydia has to be

sixty-five if she's a day.

My nostrils quiver as the unmistakable whiff of Brut drifts disconcertingly by, evoking memories of Christmases past. 'Well, hello!' says Giles in his customary, Leslie Phillips-ding-dong way, waving his beer glass unsteadily with one hand, whilst surreptitiously pinching my bottom with the other. 'Great to see you, old girl! Been on the telly yet? One of these days, eh? Better get your autograph now before you're rich and famous, what?' He guffaws, spraying my face with *San Miguel*.

'Absolutely!' I say, forcing a laugh.

'Well, go on, what do you think of my gorgeous lady? Isn't she something?'

'Yes, she's quite ...'

He leans towards me, voice lowering to a confiding whisper. 'And you won't mind me telling you that the sex is ...'

'Breaded sprout anyone?' I say, beating a hasty retreat with the veggie platter.

'Thanks,' says Chantelle, attempting to scoop up a sprout between her bejewelled, acrylic talons.

'Here, let me help you.' I smile, passing her one in a napkin. 'I'm Emily, by the way.'

'Oh, yeah, Giles told me about you,' she says, ejecting bits of almond through her botoxed lips. 'You're trying to be an actress, right?'

'That's one way of putting it,' I say in an apologetic tone.

'Chantelle was just telling me Giles bought her *two* Christmas presents, the lucky girl,' cuts in Lydia eagerly. 'But she hasn't told me yet what they are.'

'Well ... you're lookin' at 'em,' says Chantelle, proudly sticking out her DDs. 'I'd wanted a boob job for ages but couldn't afford it, and Giles said he'd be happy to pay for the op.' (I bet he was, love. *Ding-*

dong!) 'He's a real diamond.'

'How very ... *sweet*,' says Lydia, nonchalantly playing with her string of pearls, trying to look and sound as if it's perfectly normal to find a pair of silicone implants in one's Christmas stocking.

'Another vol au vent, Lydia?' I ask, filling the sudden silence.

'Lovely,' she says super-brightly. 'I *adore* Julio Iglesias, don't you?'

'Come on, you two,' I say, collecting the last of the glasses. 'It's gone midnight and you both look exhausted. Why don't you go to bed and I'll finish clearing up?'

My parents exchange a knowing glance.

'Sit down, love,' says Dad tentatively. 'We need to have a little chat.'

'What is it?' I say, panic rising. 'You're not ill again, are you?'

'No, no, love. Nothing like that. It's just ...' He shuffles awkwardly in his chair.

'Your father and I are worried about your future,' interjects Mum.

'Why?'

'Why? Because you may be over forty, but you're still our little girl, our one and only, and we want you to be happy.'

'But I *am* happy.'

'You can't live like this at your age. It's all right when you're young, living from hand to mouth, but not now ... especially now that ... '

'What? Now that I'm on the shelf, you mean?' I say in a half-jokey way.

'Why you gave up flying and your lovely little flat, I'll never know.'

'Because life's short, because I wanted new

204

experiences and don't want to look back when I'm old and think I wish I'd tried that, because ... because ... ' My argument is starting to sound hollow, even to my ears. 'So, what you're saying is I should just throw in the towel?'

'No, of course not, but if you got a steady job you could do amateur dramatics in your spare time. Then you'd have the best of both worlds, wouldn't you?'

'Oh, Mum,' I groan.

'You're capable of so much more. You could have gone to university and studied languages. You were always good at languages, wasn't she, Brian? You could have worked for the Foreign Office or the United Nations even.'

'Come on, Brenda,' says Dad, getting up and gently guiding her to the door. 'That's enough. Let's go to bed. You've said your piece. It's Christmas. Don't spoil it.'

'We just want you to be happy, love,' says Dad, lightly kissing my forehead.

I pour myself the last of the port, switch on the telly and snuggle up on the sofa in the soft glow of the Christmas tree lights; but even James Stewart in *It's a Wonderful Life* can't quell this growing sense of unease stirring inside me. Because you see, deep down, I know they're right.

1ˢᵗ January – A new start? Call me - please - D x

Huh! I flip the card over. A man in full Highland dress smirks at me from under his Glengarry hat. I grab the letter opener from the rack and stab him in the sporran.

'You know what men are like,' says Wendy over our traditional, post-Christmas debriefing. 'The thing with that woman was probably just a meaningless fling. Some guys don't have to be in love to have sex.'

I shake my head and take another big slurp of wine.

'*Exactement.* To them it is like having a pint or ... *rosbif* and Yorkshire pudding,' says Céline, all innocence, topping up our glasses. I find myself smiling through my tears.

'Come on, be reasonable,' coaxes Rachel, twirling a long string of spaghetti. 'If he didn't want you back, why send you cards and text messages every other day? He's *crazy* about you.'

I feel a fleeting pang as she says this. 'Not good enough. I can't trust him,' I retort, piercing a baby plum tomato with my fork. 'I want an honest, committed relationship. Is that too much to ask? Or does it only happen in books and films? I promised myself after Nigel I wouldn't give my heart so easily, and the first man to come into my life ... I was too open, too willing,' I say, extending my glass for another refill.

'Our problem is, darling, we're living in the Jane-Austen world,' says Faye. 'The older I get, the more I realise Mr Darcy is not going to emerge from the lake and carry me off. Maybe we have to lower our expectations a little, otherwise we're going to end up popping microwaved meals for one, and paying single room supplements for ever more.'

'Perhaps I *am* living in the past, but I refuse to *make do.* If that means being alone for the rest of my life, then so be it. I refuse ... abso ... abso-lute... I will *not* be anyone's Yorkshire pudding,' I say, slipping sideways off my chair.

Our scars make us know that our past was for real.
~ Jane Austen, Pride and Prejudice

CHAPTER TEN
Tinker, Tailor, Spinster, Spy

'RIGHT, THAT'S YOU DONE,' says Senga from make-up, snapping the can of hairspray shut and removing the towel from around my shoulders. 'Now pop along next door and see Bruce in wardrobe.'

My bloodshot peepers blink several times under the harsh glare of the high-watt bulbs. No girl should ever have to subject her face to foundation and blusher before sunup. Not that I'm complaining — quite the opposite. Call it positive thinking, cosmic ordering, heaven-sent or just bloody good timing; a bit part on telly is just what the doctor ordered after another false start in the boyfriend department.

Bruce runs his stubby finger down the call sheet and ticks off my name.

'Now, er ... Emily, I see Miss MacFarlane as your typical, nineteen forties' village spinster — disappointed by love, bitter, repressed, dowdy, frumpy ...'

Yep, okay, Bruce, we get the picture. Loud and clear.

'She's definitely a tweeds and brogues sort of woman,' he continues, whipping the tape measure from his neck, and swiftly wrapping it around me. He bustles over to a rail of rather drab-looking garments and flicks through them, eventually pulling out a muddy-brown, herringbone-tweed suit.

'Try this on for size,' he says, pulling back the dressing room curtain.

I look at my reflection in the mirror. It's scary. I look like the sort of woman who lectures at the WI and knits toilet roll covers in her spare time. Bruce's arm bursts through, brandishing a suspender belt, a pair of seamed stockings and clompy, vintage shoes.

'Sorry, dear, we've no size sevens — you'll have to try and squeeze into these, I'm afraid.'

I yank the curtain open.

'Give us a twirl,' says Bruce, hands on hips, giving me the once-over with his beady eyes. He plonks a battered felt hat firmly on my head. '*Voilà*! Frumpy spinster personified! The bus will meet you outside,' he says, resuming his ironing.

I am ON LOCATION! I have always wanted to say that. It sounds so glamorous and exciting, doesn't it? I wipe the condensation from the minibus window with my moth-eaten glove, revealing a rather dreich car park, teeming with hordes of people, huddled round a mobile caff, sipping steaming liquid from polystyrene cups.

A figure in a bright orange kagoul taps on the door and a hooded face peers round.

'Hi, I'm Jules, the third assistant,' she says breathlessly. 'We're running a bit behind schedule because of the rain, but we'll try not to keep you waiting too long. Help yourself to breakfast.'

'Round up the extras for the bicycle scene,' cackles her walkie-talkie, and she disappears.

My nervous nausea of earlier has now turned into pangs of hunger, so I make a beeline for the breakfast queue.

Mmm. My taste buds tingle as the succulent bacon rashers sizzle in the pan. The chef thickly butters the soft, floury bap and slaps the bacon inside, adding a squirt of tomato ketchup, before pressing the top down with his palm. I reach up, like a kid in a sweet shop, and take it from him with both hands. I bite into it, and some of the melted butter, mixed with bacon fat, oozes down my chin. I am in paradise.

'Emily, come with me,' says Jules, suddenly reappearing at my side. 'I'd like you to meet Oona, who plays Elspeth. You're doing your scene with her, yeah?'

'Fine,' I say, spitting crumbs everywhere. Jules strides off towards a huge trailer, and I teeter after her in my size five-and-a-halfs, cramming in the rest of my bacon roll as I strive to avoid the puddles.

We climb the steps and Jules knocks on the door.

'Come away in, dear,' comes a familiar voice from inside.

'Oona, this is Emily, who's playing Miss MacFarlane,' says Jules.

'It's an honour,' I say, wiping my greasy fingers on my skirt and dropping a little curtsey. Aargh. Why in God's name did I just do that? She's not the Queen. But then Oona is a legend in Scotland; she's been in *Doon Place* since it began in the seventies, and is the only original member of the cast.

Her character has been through two husbands, has four children, seven grandchildren, survived a war and a chip pan fire.

'You look frozen, dearie,' she says warmly. 'Let's have a wee cuppa and run our lines until they're ready for us.'

Jules' radio bursts into life again.

'I'll pop back when we've finished setting up,' she

says.

Oona may look like your typical, sweet, old granny. But take away the grey wig and padding, and behind that Mrs-Doubtfire exterior, is a glamorous, go-getting sixty-something, who drives a Lamborghini, has a toy-boy husband, and is signed up to do the next series of *Strictly Come Dancing.*

'Just ignore the camera, dear, and if you fluff your lines, so what? You can do it again. If you survived weekly rep, then this'll be a doddle, so it will.'

A make-up girl bustles in to re-do us and tuts as her eyes are drawn to a blob of ketchup on my cream blouse.

'Okay, we're ready,' pants Jules, popping her head through the window of the trailer.

'Emily, my darling, can you hear me?' booms Rob, the director, through a megaphone at the bottom of the hill.

I give him the thumbs-up. 'Good. Now, on *action!* I want you to cycle like you're a woman on a mission — you're bursting to tell Elspeth that you've just seen the village tart coming out of Tam MacLeod's house. Stop outside number nineteen, which is where the washing line is, okay? You then deliver your first line over the hedge. Clear?'

'Cool,' I casually cry, as if I'm an old hand at this, stomach churning noisily, like a cement mixer.

'Quiet, please! Cameras rolling ... sound running ... aaand ... *action!*'

I swiftly pull my hat down so it's secure, firmly grip the handlebars, take a deep breath, and I'm off.

'CUT!' roars Rob over the high-pitched squeal of brakes.

One of the crew runs over and hurriedly applies some WD40. He pushes the bike back up the hill, while I totter behind, aware of several sets of eyes upon me, impatiently waiting to start the scene again. I'm tempted to shout out, *I'm not normally this slow at walking, but they didn't have any shoes to fit me,* but decide against it, as that would sound whingeing and pathetic. I tell myself to just get on with it, and mount the bike again.

'Quiet, please! Cameras rolling ... sound running ... aaand ... CUT! Plane overhead!'

I abort take-off in the nick of time, saving myself from another embarrassing uphill stagger.

We roll again, and as I rattle downhill, I rehearse my first line quickly in my head:

Morning, Elspeth. I was on my way from the kirk, when I saw Jeannie MacLeod coming ... aargh! *... I was on my way from the kirk, when I saw Jeannie **Frazer** coming out of Tam MacLeod's house ... Morning, Elspeth ...* I apply the brakes, but slither past number nineteen, eventually coming to a halt outside number twenty-seven.

'Cut!'

Someone pokes about the brakes with a spanner, as the technical crew prepare for another take. A make-up lady appears from nowhere and attacks me with a powder puff, tucks in some stray hair, and readjusts my hat.

'Right, can we crack on, folks? I'd like to get this done before the rain comes!' yells Rob, twitching with impatience as he glances up at the storm clouds gathering in the distance.

Huffing and puffing, I mount the bike again. Surely this time ...

'Quiet, please! Cameras rolling ... sound running ... aaand ACTION!'

Morning, Elspeth. I was on my way from the kirk when I saw Jeannie Frazer coming out of Tam

211

MacLeod's house. Morning, Elspeth. I was on my waaaaaay ...

I'm applying the brakes, but nothing's happening. I fly past a bewildered Elspeth and her line of washing, and am now freewheeling at dangerously high speed, heading for the huge light reflectors, lamps, crew and extras at the end of the street. I swing my leg out and drag my foot along the ground, in an attempt to slow myself down, but end up parting company with the bike, falling flat on my face, tweed skirt over my head, stocking tops showing.

'CUTTT!'

I lift my grazed chin, just in time to see Rob smacking his forehead, throwing down his headphones and storming off the set.

Concerned crew and make-up ladies swarm round.

'I'm fine, really I am,' I lie, forcing myself to my feet, mortified by all the fuss, stockings and pride in shreds. My knees and chin are stinging like mad, and I'm on the brink of tears — more from embarrassment than pain. I am whisked away, cleaned up and brought a cup of hot, sweet tea.

'If you feel up to it, we'd like to try the scene again as the light's starting to fade,' says Jules with a sympathetic smile. 'And don't worry, we've tested the brakes and they're fine now.'

Poised for take-off, I shut my eyes for a moment, then take a deep breath. My chin is on fire, and my feet are throbbing, but goddammit, I will not be beaten by a wonky, old bone-shaker ...

As Rob looks through the lens, a hush descends over the smoking chimneys and plastic cobbles of Doon Place.

'Yep, yep, not bad ... check the gate ... okay, everyone, thank you. It's a wrap!'

Last week Scottish soap star, this week undercover agent ...

CHARACTER BRIEF:
Wealthy, middle-aged woman in make-up rut.
TRUE IDENTITY:
Emily Forsyth, actress-in-waiting,
temporarily working as mystery shopper.
LOCATIONS:
Various posh department stores.

Decked out in my Primark suit, and clutching my briefcase, containing personal details, photographs, store maps and an M&S sandwich, I enter the doors of Harrods, into The White Hall, and straight on.

Having helped myself to a sneaky spritz of Issey Miyake, I then scoot off in search of my first contender for The Mademoiselle Morette Cosmetics Consultant Award: Trudie Harper, aged twenty-nine, been at Harrods for five years, has trained in customer care, colour matching and application techniques.

My mission is to give honest feedback on her customer service skills. I'm idly toying with a pot of facial soufflé, when up she pops from behind the counter.

'Good morning! May I help you?' She smiles, displaying an array of perfect teeth.

I take a deep breath. 'Yes, you can actually. I'm in need of some expert advice ...'

'Time for your break, Trudie,' says an older assistant with stiff hair and Dame-Edna specs. 'I'll look after the lady for you.'

Damn.

'Coooee!' I call, standing on tiptoes and waving to my imaginary husband in the distance. 'What? This minute?' Turning to the assistant, I say with an exasperated sigh, 'Men! He can't even choose his own socks without my say-so.' And I make a bee-line for men's underwear and ties.

'How may I help you, Madam?' says a well-dressed young man, pouncing on me out of nowhere.

'Just … browsing,' I reply, and jump on the escalator, to the first floor. As I approach the top, there they are, rising up like a phoenix, perched on a pillar, swathed in duck-egg blue silk — totally impractical, doubtless ruinously expensive, amazing, irresistible, must-have shoes by Kurt Geiger — just the thing for Céline and Drew's wedding.

I glimpse the price tag. Don't even go there, Emily. I run my finger wistfully along the elegant heel and across the stylish, pointed toe. I slip my foot into one. It fits like a glove. I try the other. Perfect. Parading up and down the shop floor, I imagine the scene at the wedding …

DUNCAN: I've been watching you all through the ceremony. Couldn't take my eyes off you. You look amazing. What a fool I was! There'll never be anyone else like you.
EMILY: Look, Duncan, I'm here with someone else. He's the jealous type and won't be very happy if he finds me talking to another man. (SHE CROSSES HER LEGS SEDUCTIVELY, HER KURT GEIGER SHOES EMPHASISING HER TRIM ANKLES. DUNCAN DESIRES HER MADLY. ENTER GEORGE CLOONEY)
GEORGE: There you are, darling. (HE KISSES HER AND PLACES HIS ARM AROUND HER TINY WAIST) I've been looking everywhere for you.
EMILY: I think we've said all there is to say, Duncan.

'Would you like those, Madam?'

'Mmm?'

'The shoes ... are they what you're looking for?'

Oh, what the hell, I can always save money by hiring a hat and buying the dress from a charity shop, can't I?

'Yes, I'll take them,' I say quickly, before my sensible and boring alter ego takes control of the situation.

I return to the counter, and play *MIDDLE-AGED WOMAN IN MAKE-UP RUT* so convincingly, that Trudie ends up giving me a complete facial. As for her customer service skills, I am walking proof that they are impeccable, since I am persuaded that the cure for attracting the wrong men is contained in a tub of Anti-Sagging Day Cream.

Mystery Shopper Daily Payment: £75.00
Kurt Geiger Shoes: £110.00
Anti-Sagging Day Cream: £28.00
Today's profit: -£63.00

CHAPTER ELEVEN
matchmakerqueen.com

I AM SUCH A TYPICAL LIBRAN: I do not refer to my good taste, charm and diplomacy, but to my indecisiveness, or in this case, my wanting to make the right choice, so that with one look, Duncan will rue the day he cheated on me. So, do I wear the Audrey-Hepburn picture hat to the wedding, or the fascinator with lilac ostrich feathers? I can't decide, and now the taxi's waiting to take me to the airport and I'm still in a quandary. Plump for the Audrey Hepburn look, as though less dramatic, it looks more sophisticated and goes better with my pixie crop and clutch bag (free gift with the anti-sagging day cream). I shove the hat in the box, grab my suit bag and hurry downstairs.

'Bye, sweet'art,' says Beryl, holding the door open and planting a raspberry-pink kiss on my cheek. 'You have a great time and don't give that bloody bastard another thought, d'you hear? Bleedin' men, they're all the same.' (Beryl's husband ran off in 1989 with a lady who worked in Snappy Snaps.)

'I promise,' I reply, climbing into the cab.

'Don't forget to bring me back some wedding cake,' she calls, waving.

'Em! Over here!' resounds Wendy's voice from a corner of Heathrow's Caffè Italia. I fetch a cappuccino and join them.

'Ooh, this is going to be just like old times,' says Rachel. 'I know I shouldn't say it, but when Dave told me he couldn't make it 'cause he's on nights, I had to stop myself from jiving around the kitchen.'

'Rachel!' we chorus with disdain.

'Well, weddings aren't his scene, and I can't imagine he'd enjoy three days of steam baths, manicures and female chat, can you?' she retorts, taking a bite of her blueberry muffin.

'Actually, I've *so* been looking forward to having some guilt-free, girly time too,' admits Faye with a smile. 'I adore Tariq, but I long to have a lie-in and a serious conversation about something other than Transformers and Spongebob Squarepants.'

'And *I'm* dying to soak in a spider-free bath and stretch out in a double bed with crisp, white, cotton sheets,' I say, letting out a long sigh.

'This is the final call for passengers travelling to Edinburgh. Please proceed to gate five, and have your boarding cards ready for inspection.'

The gravel crackles and spits as the taxi crunches to a halt at the end of the long, tree-lined driveway, leading to Abermorie Castle in Perthshire. There, in the arched doorway, stands the beautiful bride-to-be. She gives a whoop of joy as she bounds down the stone steps, two at a time.

'*Enfin, mes amies!*' she squeals, flinging her arms around us.

A scrubbed and spotty youth with ginger,

Brylcreemed hair, wearing a two-sizes-too-big tartan jacket, greets us with *'Ceud Mile Fàilte'* (a hundred thousand welcomes). He loads our suit bags, vanity cases and hatboxes onto a trolley and directs us to reception, where we are allocated our rooms.

'Meet you downstairs in the spa in half an hour for a treatment and a swim,' calls Céline excitedly.

My room is entered via a stone turret staircase. I turn the key, the door creaks open, and as I step inside, I travel back in time, landing somewhere resembling Anne Boleyn's bedchamber; the walls are upholstered in rich red brocade, the canopied bed is opulently draped in velvet, and the gilded ceiling is adorned with thistles and bagpipe-playing angels. I run my fingers along the bookcase and a secret door clicks open, leading to a chapel-like bathroom. I half expect Damian Lewis to pop his head round the door and say, *Mistress Emily, will you do me the honour of joining me in the next dance?* If only ...

Flinging open the French windows, I step out onto the balcony. The rear of the castle stands dramatically on the cliff's edge, with panoramic views out across the sea to a small, distant island. I lean over the balustrade, the crashing waves below spraying my face with salt water. I shut my eyes and inhale the sweet smell of seaweed, the sun's rays filling me with warmth and positive energy. Sure, it's going to be a bit tricky over the next couple of days with Duncan here too, and how will it feel to see another woman on his arm, which, inevitably, there will be? But I am made of stronger stuff. Why should I let the lying toad spoil the magic of this place and the joy of the occasion? After all, I am the Matchmaker Queen, and I fully intend to bask in the glory of my success. Maybe I should consider setting up a dating agency as a sideline? Problem is, I know plenty of lovely, single ladies, but where are all the handsome, dashing men? Oh dear, I'm back in the realms of Jane Austen again.

I glance at my watch; I'd better hurry and get changed. My Thalaso Seaweed Wrap awaits (sounds like something you'd find in the sandwich chiller at Pret A Manger).

Wedding Day

From under my large-brimmed hat, I scan the church in search of him. There he is, seated in pew number one, flanked by Drew and a woman sporting a fascinator in peacock blue, perfectly placed on her curtain of sleek, glossy, black hair. From the back, she looks like an exotic tropical bird, and I suddenly feel thirty years out of date, with my borrowed hat and Oxfam dress with shoulder pads, à la *Dynasty*.

Is she Duncan's plus one, I wonder? As if reading my innermost thoughts, she runs her fingers tenderly through his hair, then sinks her head onto his shoulder. I wince. Is she the same woman from that awful, snowy night in St Andrews, or another conquest? Having only ever seen her from the waist down, it's hard to tell; sure I'd recognise that Felicity-Kendalesque voice, though. I crane my neck, but with the harpist plucking away just inches from me, I'm unable to hear. But why should I care? He's history. Whoever his wedding date may be, she's welcome to that two-timing cheat.

'Psst, Em!' Wendy pokes me in the ribs and turns her head ninety degrees. There, in the flower-framed doorway, stands Céline, a vision of ivory silk-organza dreaminess, her distinguished and visibly proud papa by her side. The bells fall silent; someone coughs, a baby gurgles, then a holy hush descends over the congregation. We all rise as a lone piper, playing

219

'Highland Cathedral', leads the procession to the altar. Tears of joy prickle my eyelids as I glance over at Drew, eagerly awaiting his bride; uncomplicated, baggage-free, kind, generous, nature-loving Drew, who couldn't give a damn about designer labels and flashy cars, and has had the same mobile phone for ten years. I close my eyes and offer up quiet thanks to the angels that Céline is finally free of those life-ending feelings of heartache and loneliness, and is to be cherished by a good, decent man — and one who has the physique to carry off a kilt.

Whilst the thing with Duncan has bruised my heart and my pride, I draw comfort from the fact that something good has come out of our meeting, and I see now why he came into my life. It's not yet time for me to meet my Mr Right. I've sacrificed a lot to follow my dream, and a husband would lead me along a different path, and I can't quite trust myself to not fall into my usual trap of losing sight of who I am, by putting my hopes and desires to one side and focusing on my partner's needs. Now I've come this far, there's no going back. All the same, I can't help wondering if it's going to happen before I'm too old to wear a long, dreamy dress and flowers in my hair; or might it not happen at all? Am I destined ever to be Miss Emily Forsyth, Spinster of this Parish — just like Miss MacFarlane in *Doon Place*? After all, there is such a thing as typecasting. But then is being a singleton such a terrible fate?

As we emerge from the ancient country church, the romantic skirl of the bagpipes floats through the heather-scented air. We circulate as the photographer runs around like a frantic sheepdog, rounding up his unruly flock.

'*Je vooodray la famille de la bride, s'il vous plate!*' he yells in his schoolboy-French.

From the corner of my eye, I spy Duncan, his back to me, talking and laughing animatedly. He cuts a dash, dammit, in his tailored black jacket with Celtic buttons and Black Watch kilt. Then I recall the last time I saw those bare legs; splayed out in the snow, sporting a fine pair of tweed slippers, and I crack a small, private grin. He's turning around. Uh oh. He's coming over. There's nowhere to hide. My heart skips a beat. What am I going to say to him? Stay dignified and calm and aloof. You are an ice queen.

'*Les amis de la bride*, please. Friends of the bride! *Toot sweet!*' calls the photographer.

I hurry over to where the others are gathering and flash my sexiest smile.

Later, back at the castle (there's posh for you), I am placed next to Céline's Aunt Geneviève for the wedding breakfast. With her petite figure, *haute couture* suit and Jackie O sunglasses sweeping back her waved bob, she exudes French glamour, poise and style. She looks like she's just stepped off the set of one of those classic French films like *The Umbrellas of Cherbourg.* It comes as no surprise that she has had three husbands and is on the lookout for *numéro quatre.*

She has an engaging way of speaking half-French, half-English.

'*Alors*, Emilee, are you married?' she says, tilting her pretty head as she takes a dainty bite of her smoked salmon canapé.

'No,' I reply, *my* canapé collapsing, a blob of caviar landing on my shoe.

She dabs the corners of her mouth with a lace hankie, then sprays Miss Dior on her slim wrists.

'I guess I just never met the right man,' I continue, feeling for some bizarre reason that I must excuse my

221

marital state.

She gives a winsome smile and snaps shut her Mui Mui bag.

'Aah, *chérie*, men are *très difficile*, *mais la vie* would be boring without them, *n'est-ce pas*? Take *un peu* advice from me — don't always let him know what you are thinking,' she says. '*Gardez un petit peu de vous-même pour vous-même. Le mystère est une bonne chose*,' she purrs, sipping her Dom Pérignon.

Geneviève looks to me like one of those very fortunate women who always look cool and glamorous, whether pulling a Louis Vuitton suitcase or a wheelie bin. I've met this species before on night flights; they'd wake up after their three-hour crew rest, with not a hair out of place, lip-gloss intact, fragrant and uncreased. I, on the other hand, would emerge from my bunk looking like I'd just done a double shift at KFC. What is their secret? Is it something you're born with? The Glamour Gene? I bet Geneviève doesn't possess baggy jogging bottoms or threadbare knickers for everyday.

She is an inspiration to me. Maybe I too can become a classic *femme à la mode*. I make a mental note to clear out my wardrobe on my return, and to get up half an hour earlier every day to lavish more care and attention on my appearance. *Le mystère* will be my mantra from now on, and I make a solemn vow never to enter the doors of Primark again.

I feel a hand on my shoulder. I spin round and glance up from under my hat to meet Duncan's gaze.

'Forgive me for interrupting, ladies,' he says, leaning forward. 'Emily, I need to talk to you. *Please.*'

I feel myself flushing. I am powerless to speak. Geneviève raises her gracefully arched eyebrows, then shoots me an impish grin. Taking me firmly by the elbow, Duncan steers me out onto the terrace.

'How are you?' he asks guardedly.

'Fine.'

'Acting going well?'

'Uh huh.'

The man talking to me now is not my friend, my lover, but a stranger. It feels odd to be standing at arm's length like this, making artificial chit-chat, when I long to tumble into his arms, for us to go back to how we were in the Lakes; so relaxed and natural with one another. I'm bursting to tell him all about my first telly job: the thrill of meeting Oona, I want to laugh with him about falling off my bike in front of all the other actors and crew, and does he know what a Winnebago is? But I catch my tongue in time and cast my eyes downwards, staring at the sundial.

'I've missed you,' he says, reaching for my hand.

Wrenching it free, I turn away from him and look out to sea. I'm shaking inside, partly from suppressed anger, partly deep hurt.

'Look, I'll cut to the chase — I messed up, I admit,' he says with a flippant shrug. 'I kind of understand why you're upset, but if I could just explain ...'

'What is there to explain, Duncan?' I say, cutting him off abruptly, my voice unsteady.

'Please, just hear me out ... Kate's an old flame ... we finished years ago. That awful night before Christmas when you turned up, well ... I know how it must have looked, but it wasn't like that. I was depressed, missing you, and she called round. We had a few too many drinks, and one thing led to another ...'

'Spare me the details, *please*,' I snarl.

'Let me finish,' he continues, gently cupping my chin. 'She's made me realise how much you mean to me. Och, come on, Spike, what we had was so special, wasn't it?' He pulls me towards him, eyes drinking me in from top to bottom. He removes my hat and rumples my hair. 'You look beautiful, by the way.'

I blush and my knees go weak. He takes my hand and lifts it to his lips. I feel the warmth of his breath on my fingers.

Hang on a minute! Where the hell has my brain gone? He can't just gloss over the whole incident. Getting drunk and 'one thing leading to another' just isn't good enough — and what about Fascinator Woman?

Averting his gaze, I snatch back my hat and toy with the brim.

'If you think I'm falling for that, then ... then ...' I say, fumbling for the right words. Dammit! I have waited so long for this very opportunity; to deliver the speech I've rehearsed over and over in my head: something about honesty, about trust, with a bit about betrayal thrown in for good measure. Now the long awaited moment has finally arrived, and what happens? My lines evaporate, and I find myself focusing on the greasy spot on my left shoe.

'Excuse me for barging in, but all afternoon I've been dying to ask — were you on the telly last week, in *Doon Place*?'

I veer round and find myself face to face with an older (but equally handsome) version of Drew.

'Er ... yes,' I reply, rather taken aback.

'I wasn't sure if it was you. You look totally different. But may I say how much I enjoyed your performance. My wife and I are avid followers — we rarely miss an episode.'

'How kind of you to say so,' I say, trying with all my might to contain my delight and sound modest, as if I'm forever being approached by appreciative fans.

'Apologies for the interruption, Duncan,' he says, patting him on the shoulder. 'I'll leave you two to your conversation.'

'Oh, we're done, aren't we?' I say pointedly.

'Well, in that case, will you join me in the next dance?' says Mr McCallum, dipping his head and offering his arm.

'I'd be delighted,' I say triumphantly, and flounce off through the French windows. Woohoo! I positively *hurrrl* myself into that jig like a woman possessed.

His timing was perfect. Having failed to ensnare a wedding date, being recognised from the telly is the next best demonstration of *I'm doing fine without you.* This is a marvellous piece of one-upmanship, and couldn't have worked better had I orchestrated the whole thing myself. I know I shouldn't gloat, but I really do feel the Goddess of Revenge is smiling down on me today.

CHAPTER TWELVE
Veni, Vidi, Velcro

I SPREAD AN EXTRA DOLLOP OF NUTELLA on my toast to cheer myself up.

The letterbox snaps open and shut — bank statement (I'll save that for when I'm in a more positive mood) and a mail order catalogue for Beryl.

No work for almost three weeks now. I'm getting into bad habits: slobbing around, going to bed late, getting up at lunch time, and horror of horrors, am hooked on *Loose Women*, frequently shouting at the telly when one of them says something outrageous.

I pop another piece of bread in the toaster, and flick through Beryl's *Bloom & Beazley* catalogue.

Ladies! Tired of looking sloppy chez vous?
Uh huh.
Look no further!
This 100% polyester housecoat is a must
for every fashionable lady's wardrobe.
And it has a three quarter button front for easy dressing!

* * *

So much for becoming a *femme à la mode*: if I don't act soon, I may well end up an unemployed, middle-aged, reality TV addict in a synthetic housecoat.

Who on earth wears these things? Not the Genevièves of this world, that's for sure.

Then it hits me — okay, so I'm no Kate Moss, but maybe I could model for the older woman, like in this catalogue? I turn to the back page, and before I have time to talk myself out of it, I dial the number and put on my matronly Lady-Bracknell voice ...

'Have you any actual modelling experience?' asks the PA.

'Yars ... I've ... modelled for an exotic brand of fruit juice,' I say, swallowing hard. '*And* I was pencilled in for a TV commercial for pasta sauce, but unfortunately I was already signed up to do a play with *Rick Romano* — awful, isn't it, how one's commitments clash?'

'Rick Romano?'

Good, I knew that would impress her.

'Good grief! Is he still alive? Do you have a portfolio?'

'Erm ... not exactly ...'

'One moment, please. I'll just pop you on hold while I have a word with Lady Beazley.'

As I am serenaded down the phone by 'Magic Moments', I flick through the pages of the catalogue, eyes widening ... da, da, da, da, daa, da, da, da, da, daa, da, da, da, da, da, daa. *Mag-ic, mom-ents,* stain resistant nighties. *Mag-ic, mom-ents,* polyester cardies. Da, da, da, da, daa, da, da, da, da, daa ... what the hell are interlock pantees?? Cos-y, sli-ppers, fluffy, knitted bed socks ...

'Lady Beazley can see you on Thursday at three.'

'Really? Super. Thank you. See you at ...' Click.

As I replace the receiver, I catch sight of my

reflection in the mirror; hair like a she-devil and a blob of Nutella on my faded, shapeless Minnie Mouse T-shirt.

Stand aside, Kate and Claudia! Make way for Emily, Polyester Pin-Up!

So here I am, standing in front of my open wardrobe. What to wear? I rifle through every item, tossing the rejects on the floor: nope, too young, nope, too casual, nope, not old-school enough, nope, nope, nope. All I am left with is an overly tight black pencil skirt (was I really once a size 10?), white shirt, silk scarf and my crew court shoes.

There's one problem that screams out at me as I scrutinise my reflection: it's one thing sounding like a silver surfer, but it's quite another to look the part; and I don't. Funny, I've spent the last five years covering up my grey, and for the last three days, I've been willing it to miraculously sprout in clumps. But not one of the little buggers has made an appearance — not a single one.

I did spend twenty-five minutes in Boots, toying with a box of Wella Fresh Silver hair dye, but just as it was my turn to pay, I bottled out, and put it back on the shelf.

I haven't worn heels for ages, so have been practising my Bloom & Beazley Walk, with the help of an etiquette manual I found in a charity shop: *head high, shoulders relaxed, chest/buttocks out (but not too much), knees and feet close together.*

Har do you do, Lady Beazley ... or may I call you Penelope? Yars, without a doubt, Lady Penelope, I am the pahfect person to model your interlock pantees with ribbed legs. Hobbies? My hobbies are flahr arranging, needlepoint and cookeray ...

I snap shut the clasp of my pearl necklace, poke

the matching studs in my ears, and pop on my glasses to round off the mature, no-nonsense image. As I unlatch the door, I double-check my appearance in the hall mirror. Jeez, I look like Dustin Hoffman in *Tootsie*.

I tug the bell-pull. A distant jangling resounds from inside Bloom & Beazley HQ, swiftly followed by the sound of thin heels on tiled flooring.

The door is opened by a tall, angular woman in a panelled tweed skirt and Peter Pan collared blouse, a mother-of-pearl brooch fastened at the neck, hair swept up in a tight chignon.

She peers at me through her checked, Burberry glasses.

'May I help you?' she says in a clipped, superior tone.

'Good afternoon. Emily Forsyth? I have an appointment to see Mrs Beaz...'

'I'll tell *Lady* Beazley you're here,' she interjects, a disapproving look flitting across her face. 'Take a seat,' she commands, indicating a row of gilt, red-cushioned chairs as she disappears in a rustle of petticoat.

I fold my coat neatly and place it on my lap. I cross my legs, then uncross them, then cross them at the ankles. I look around me at the framed front covers, resembling old dressmaking patterns. Oh, yes, the Bloom & Beazley Woman is definitely in need of a major overhaul.

'Lady Beazley will see you now,' echoes a voice from the landing.

I mince up the stairs, determined to sustain an image of class and sophistication.

I enter the room, step in front of the door, reverse one step, gently pushing it behind me, adjust my skirt again and clear my throat. From across the vast expanse of Chinese carpet, Lady B swivels round in her leather chair to face me.

'Ah, Miss Forsyth,' she says with a courteous smile, rising from behind her highly polished, ornate desk.

'Please call me Emily,' I say, clasping her hand in mine.

'Very nice to meet you, Emily. Did you find us all right?' she says, gesturing for me to sit down.

'Yes, thank you,' I reply, positioning myself directly in front of the chair. 'My godson's school is just across the way,' I continue, reversing towards the chair (slowly), feeling it with my leg (gently), then lowering myself onto the front of the seat (elegantly). 'I know the area well.'

While she looks through my hastily put together 'portfolio', I slide back onto the seat a little more and tuck one foot behind the other.

The room is octagonal, painted Wedgwood blue with walk in bay windows and ornate cornicing.

'Have you no publicity shots of the fruit drink advertising campaign?' she enquires, peering at me over her gold-rimmed bifocals.

'Erm, no ...' I reply, pulling at my earring, face flushing, as a vision of a giant pineapple with spindly legs pops into my head.

'Hmm. As much as I like the pictures of you in the in-flight magazines, they're hardly recent, are they?'

'No ... no,' I say in a low whisper.

I gaze out of the window onto the street below. Children in red and black uniforms spill out onto the cobbled courtyard, like an army of ladybirds. Groups of mothers, some hanging out of the windows of their four-by-fours, others with pushchairs and dogs in tow, wait at the school gates, chatting and laughing. A black Mercedes with tinted windows glides to a stop opposite the school. A tall, tanned, dark-suited man in aviator shades steps out, like a character from *Men In Black*. I narrow my eyes and lean closer to the window. *Can it be?*

'To be honest, you're considerably younger than our regular models, but as it happens, we are on the lookout for a fresh face to promote our summer collection. We want to get away from the nursing-home look and inject an altogether more exotic, fun-loving theme to the brochure.'

Of course it isn't. What would he be doing here? Anyway, it's years since you last clapped eyes on him.

'I'm thinking couples on cruise ships, walking hand in hand along white, sandy beaches ...'

And your eyesight is getting worse, remember. Only last week you embarrassed yourself by waving to a total stranger, mistaking him for Mr Khan. (He's the newsagent.)

'With the right lighting and make-up, you *could* be the new face of Bloom & Beazley.'

The Mercedes pulls away. *What if it is him though? Stop this nonsense at once. You and your overactive imagination. Remember that poor sod on the Tripoli? It never occurred to you he might simply have been a nervous flier. No, not dramatic enough for you, was it? Sweaty brow, shallow breathing spelt TERRORIST to you. You're lucky he didn't sue you — and the airline. So stop this NOW before you get yourself into deep water — again.*

'Would you mind walking up and down for me?'

'Sorry?'

'Just to give me an idea of how you'll measure up next to our male models.'

Sliding forward to the edge of my seat (keeping knees together and back straight), I rise (gracefully), and parade up and down, feeling like I'm some mongrel pooch, competing for Best in Show at Crufts.

'Super. My assistant will contact you with the arrangements,' says Lady B, looking at her watch and pushing the dog-eared *Flying High* magazines back across the table.

'Welcome aboard!' She snaps shut her laptop and rises.

'Splendid!' I say, extending my hand (confidently, but not roughly) and smiling (in a refined manner).

As I walk cautiously along the hallway, carrying a steaming hot Le Creuset casserole of Faye's signature chilli con carne, raucous laughter ricochets off the walls.

'Come on, what's the joke?' I say, placing the pot on the coffee table.

'Did she *really* say "with the right lighting and make-up"?' says Rachel, collapsing into giggles.

'Hey, it's okay for you globetrotters. I'm longing for some sun, and if that means wearing crimpolene and dyeing my hair silver for a few days, then it's a small price to pay for a free holiday.' This prompts more sniggers.

'You do know that one day, when you're famous, this *Life on the Ocean Waves* catalogue will come back to haunt you,' teases Wendy, holding out the plates.

'I wonder where you'll be going, love,' chips in Faye's mum excitedly.

'I don't know the details yet, Margie. She just said something about couples strolling along white, sandy beaches, hand in hand,' I say dreamily, lobbing chilli onto a plate. 'Her PA's going to call next week with the schedule.'

'Bet it's somewhere like Miami or the Bahamas. That's usually where the wrinklies go,' says Rachel.

'Do you mind?' I say, chucking my napkin at her.

'The big question is, who will you be paired up with?' says Faye clasping her hands together, all starry-eyed. 'Mmm, some Richard Gere lookalike maybe?'

'I don't care if it's the Elephant Man, just as long as I get to bask in the sunshine,' I reply.

Later on, when the others have left, Margie's in the bath, and it's just Faye and me in the kitchen drying the dishes, the desire to tell her creeps up on me; but tell her what exactly? That I saw some dark-haired bloke outside Tariq's school? The odds are slim and why worry her unnecessarily? But what if it turns out to be him and I didn't say anything?

As I go to put away the casserole dish, there, taped to the cupboard door, is a smudged drawing of MUMMY with scribbled, straw-like hair, crimson, butterfly-lips and huge, turquoise eyes with spidery lashes.

'Oh, Em, can you put away the rest of the soured cream please?' says Faye, brushing aside a strand of hair with her soapy hand.

'Sure,' I say, turning towards the fridge. 'Faye?'

'Yes, sweetie?'

'I may be wrong, but ...' I stop mid-sentence, hand on the door, as a photo of Tariq, grinning his gappy smile, surrounded by Goldilocks and the three bears, beams out at me from amongst the fridge magnets, post-it notes, spelling test, coupons and swimming lesson reminder.

'You all right, my love?' says Faye, removing her rubber gloves and giving my arm an affectionate squeeze. 'You look a bit far away.'

Our eyes meet. I look away swiftly. 'It's nothing ... '

233

The following month I spend three days on deck, looking out to sea, the ocean breeze teasing my stiff, smoky-coloured wig. I model a variety of acrylic dresses with easy access velcro fastenings and leather-look belts, blanket-style wraps, white polyester cardigans and slip-on, slip-free, peep-toe sandals. No Richard Gere by my side, but Victor, a silver-haired, seventy-something lothario in wrinkle-resistant, cotton twill, whose idea of wowing the ladies is to wink theatrically and whistle 'Danny Boy', which causes his false teeth to make a strange, clicking sound.

Oh, and in case you're wondering ... the Caribbean cruise? A freezing cold photographic studio in Billericay, with a deck on castors, a wind machine and a sparkling Pacific Ocean backdrop. Kate and Leo, eat your heart out.

CHAPTER THIRTEEN
The Italian Job

WITH LIONEL INCOMMUNICADO for several weeks now, and the small matter of next week's rent money and £80 minimum Visa payment to find, I have decided that today is the day I will find a job. *Any job.*

I turn right, scanning the parade of shops as I go — heaps of possibilities: there's the bakery, the off-licence, the newsagents, the cut-price bargain store, chemist, the kebab shop — on second thoughts, maybe not; with his small, razor-sharp teeth, bloodshot eyes and black, greased-back hair, there's something of the Hannibal Lecters about the man behind the counter.

Then I notice the dry cleaners, which has been closed for months, now boasts a green, white and red awning with *Il Moulino* and a windmill emblazoned across it.

I peer through the window, and spying someone inside, tap on the door. It is opened by a small man with a weatherworn face and crinkly-kind eyes, a stripey apron accentuating his barrel-like girth.

'*Sì?*'

'*Buongiorno*! Do you have any vacancies for waiting staff?'

'Do you have experience?' he asks in his thick accent. I nod.

'*Prego*,' he smiles, raising his heavy eyebrows and beckoning me inside.

I am immediately transported to some little corner of Italy. The spine-tingling tones of Pavarotti percolate through the coffee-filled air. The rustic furniture is covered with red and white gingham tablecloths, and behind the bar sits one of those old, 1950s' Gaggia espresso machines.

'Coffee?' Luigi asks, tipping beans into the grinder.

'Mmm, please.' I smile, squinting at a sepia photograph of a little urchin boy standing next to an old windmill.

'Do they have windmills in Italy?' I ask.

'*Sì*,' he replies. 'No many. This windmill, it is in Sicily. *Allora*, you want to work in my restaurant ...'

One cappuccino later, I've got a job starting tomorrow. Luigi prefers to employ native Italians, but I manage to persuade him by promising to learn a little of the language (at least enough to enable me to pronounce the names of the dishes correctly, like *tall*iatelli and not *tagl*iatelli, which caused Luigi to crack up when he asked me to read the menu aloud).
I believed my waitressing days were well behind me, but needs must; it's either this or the dole queue.

On the way home, determined to stick to my word, I call in at the library and take out *Instant Italian*. In the absence of stage, TV or film offers, learning a new language will focus my mind on something other than wondering why Lionel never calls.

Tonight is the first preview night of Il Moulino, ahead of the opening later in the month. Luigi introduces me to Rosalba, his daughter, a soprano singer, who's helping out her father in between classes and auditions. With her jet-black hair, flashing eyes and hour-glass figure, she was born to play Carmen. (Sound like I'm some opera buff, don't I? But I'm only familiar with *Carmen* and *Madam Butterfly*: the former, because in 1982, I was dragged along to see my Aunty Ailsa perform the title role in Glenderran Amateur Operatic Society's production — that's how she met my Uncle Jim — and the latter, because *Miss Saigon*, which is based on the Puccini opera, used to be my favourite musical; I saw the original touring production twelve times, because back then I worked as a Saturday usherette at The Gaiety Theatre, and developed a major crush on the guy playing Chris, the American GI.)

'Come with me, *cara*, I show you the kitchen,' Rosalba says, sweeping through the double doors, hips swaying like a pendulum.

She and the chef exchange some words in Italian, then with sleight of hand, he tosses fresh herbs and brightly coloured peppers from a giant, sizzling pan, high into the air, like a conjurer, performing his very own brand of magic.

'Bravo!' I cry, and immediately wish I hadn't. He grunts something tetchy under his breath and angrily sloshes more red wine into the sauce. Not a good start.

'Don't mind Sergio,' says Rosalba over the hiss. 'He just likes everyone to know he's the *capo* — the boss. And this ... is Nonna Maria,' she says fondly. A bird-like lady all in black sits on a stool in the corner, long ribbons of potato peel falling from her knife into a huge, dented, aluminium pot on the floor. Her face creases into a wrinkle-etched smile. '*Ciao.*'

Luigi enters, and they all start babbling at once, their voices becoming louder and higher, their gestures more vehement. There's soon enough passion and melodrama unfolding to rival any opera, and I half expect a brawl to break out amongst the colanders and carving knives. Every word is fuelled with passion and sounds to me like the Italian equivalent of *Eh, whaddayamean, you sonofabitch? Showa soma respect. Youworka for this family now — forget Don Cannelloni.*

'What was all that about?' I ask Rosalba as we head back to the dining room.

'*Allora*, my father,' she says with a careless shrug of her shoulders, 'he just wanna know why Sergio put cannelloni on the specials menu again. *Benvenuti!*' she calls, breaking away as six more customers materialise through the door.

The bell rings furiously. '*Via la quattro! Adesso!*'

I spin around full circle and then back again. Rosalba's busy taking coats and Luigi is deep in conversation with a customer. Oh, well, I can't hang around looking like a nun at an Ann Summers party, so taking a deep breath, I head towards the kitchen. Sergio darts me a surly glare and nods towards the counter. I scoop up the two plates of steaming minestrone soup, then pirouette back out through the swing doors.

As I approach table four, the lady in the group is in mid-conversation, gesticulating wildly. I stand there patiently waiting for her to finish, but I'm invisible. Fingers now burning, I attempt to navigate my way around and aim for the empty space in front of her. But just as the plate is about to make contact with its target, she waves her arms again, the plate smashes to the floor, the warm roll shoots across the table, and hot, minestrone soup flies everywhere: over her, me, the tablecloth, the wall. '*Scusi*,' I say, grabbing her napkin, frantically plucking cubes of celery and carrot from her doubtless designer suit.

I feel every pair of diner's eyes drilling through me. A concerned Luigi emerges from behind the bar.

'*Mamma mia, va bene?*'

I feel like skulking off amid the mayhem, never to return. I thought this waitressing lark would be a piece of cake, but I'm discovering that negotiating one's way around the arms of gesticulating Italians is much trickier than coping with clear-air turbulence.

The final customers gone, and the tables cleared, Nonna Maria shuffles in from the kitchen, bearing a huge casserole dish, and beckons for me to sit down. Luigi opens a bottle of red wine, and Rosalba places a basket of warm bread on the table.

Sergio sits scowling in the corner, long legs crossed, chewing on a cocktail stick.

'*Mangia, mangia!* Eat!' says Nonna Maria, nodding to me as she drizzles olive oil onto the bread; and more and more food keeps appearing.

Rosalba explains that Nonna Maria used to make the main dish every Sunday for the family when Luigi was a little boy living in Naples. It is the best lamb I have ever tasted. She translated the recipe for me, and here it is:

Agnello All'Albertone (*serves 4*)
250g leg of lamb
1 tin chopped tomatoes
2 cloves garlic
rosemary
chilli
2 tablespoons olive oil

250g ricotta cheese
500g fusilli pasta
½ onion
a little Parmesan cheese
fry onion, garlic and chilli in olive oil
cut lamb into thin strips, add rosemary and chopped tomatoes
simmer slowly for 2 hours (do not allow to become too dry)
boil pasta
place portions of ricotta cheese on plates
pour a mixture of pasta and lamb over ricotta cheese
add a little sauce and a sprinkle of parmesan cheese

Since that unfortunate mishap with the minestrone, I have ditched my tentative Englishness and adopted a more confident, Latin approach when serving our many vociferous, gesticulating, Italian customers. It can best be described as a kind of simplified cha-cha-cha (minus the hip action) and goes like this: plates in hand, approach the table, step forward, step back, step forward, side-together-side, side-together-side, aaand put the plates down, turn, step forward and back to the kitchen.

When the mood takes him, the ice-cold Sergio is starting to thaw a little and manages to crack the odd smile. To be honest, he's becoming a tad *too* friendly these days. There's an outdoor, walk-in fridge, and when I go to fetch the butter and the ice he sometimes creeps up behind me and kisses the back of my neck. His breath reeks of garlic and nicotine.

'Reeeelax, *cucciolo,*' (puppy dog — eek!) he says, massaging my shoulders. 'You are verrrrry tense.' I've learned a few choice words like *basta!* (enough!) and *finiscila!* (bog off!), which I deploy with as much firmness as I can muster, but it doesn't make the slightest bit of difference, even when accompanied by emphatic sign language; in fact my attempt at acting Italian encourages Sergio to tease me even more. What can I do? He's married to Valentina, Luigi's youngest daughter, so I can hardly go running to him, can I? I have to deal with this on my own. I don't want the situation to be blown out of proportion. No, definitely best to keep this under wraps. Godfather-like blood feuds to be avoided at all costs.

My favourite time is when the last customer has left — my cue to flip over the *CHIUSO*/CLOSED sign. Luigi calls, *'A cena!'* and we gather around the table.

For Italians, dinner is the most important part of the day. They linger over each course, discussing everything from the perfect bolognese sauce to Berlusconi and the latest *scandalo*.

Here's another of Nonna Maria's recipes for you: *Pasta al Forno.*

The pasta she uses is called *Ziti.* It's long and thick, and she breaks it into pieces, but it's hard to pin her down to exact amounts. When I asked her *'Quanto?'* ('How much?') she shrugged her shoulders and said, *'Eh, poco'* ('A little') or *'Eh, no molto'* ('Not much').

Make the tomato sauce using olive oil, a tin of plum tomatoes and fresh basil. Simmer for 3-4 hours. The meat balls are made from minced beef, bread soaked in egg yolk, parmesan cheese, parsley, salt and pepper.

When the sauce is ready, boil the water for the pasta and cook for 11 minutes. Layer peas, ricotta cheese, mozzarella, meat balls, tomato sauce. Bake in the oven for 30 minutes.

Italians eat this as a middle course, but even I find it enough as a main dish.

* * *

Coordinating the schedules of four hosties and one waitress is tricky, especially now that one of our group has swapped her Hermès for Hunters and commutes from Fife.

But tonight's the night the coven will meet for post-wedding discussion, so I've reserved a table for five at Il Moulino.

I arrive early, and Luigi shows me to my favourite table by the window, where there is a bottle of Prosecco chilling.

'For the beautiful *signore,*' he says, lighting a candle, and laying out menus.

The door swings open and a hush falls, several heads turning to sneak a look at the tanned, jaw-droppingly gorgeous creature gliding into the restaurant. (A sharp contrast to my luminous entrance minutes before, in my stylish high-vis vest, bike helmet light flashing.)

'*La belle mariée!*' ('The beautiful bride!') I shriek, jumping up.

'*Mon petit choux!*' ('My little cabbage!') cries Céline, clutching me to her tightly.

The French may be reputed to be the most romantic nation in the world, but this modern day Parisian has her head screwed on, where independence and financial security are concerned. She's holding on to her little London flat as her bolt-hole, or *jardin secret*, as she calls it: her very own private place, which ties in with Geneviève's *mystère* philosophy, I guess. In her usual, no-frills way, Céline told Drew that whilst she had every intention of making the marriage work, they should not be blinded by this *coup de foudre* (thunderbolt) and recommended they draw up a prenup, to which he agreed, without any hoo-ha whatsoever.

I'd never heard of a prenup until Catherine Zeta

Jones married Michael Douglas. I remember thinking, Oh, Catherine, you silly girl! Count yourself lucky, and don't put the dampers on it before it's begun. Now I think she's one savvy lady. If I am ever asked to relinquish my role of Spinster, I fully intend following her lead (the cheating clause being of particular importance in my case). Anyway, back to romance ...

'Well, how was the honeymoon?' I ask eagerly, pouring a glass of bubbly.

'Hello, darlings!' We turn to find Rachel, Wendy and Faye all dressed up to the nines. Rosalba sashays over to take their coats.

'*Buona sera*,' says Luigi, serving three more glasses of Prosecco.

We pore over the wedding photos during dinner and dissect the day, moment by moment.

I feel a slight pang as my eyes skim over the ones of Duncan, smiling that devilish smile of his, but the conversation is tactfully steered away from him. I decide once and for all that he belongs on the rubbish pile. But let's not focus on the negative.

I find it hard to believe that the woman in the pictures and sitting before me now is the same sad, lone figure I came across in the wine bar, little more than a year ago. She is a reminder that when you hit rock bottom the only way is up. I heave an inner sigh of relief. It turned out for the best — this time. I ran a risk and it all came good — *this time*. But I make myself a solemn vow: in future, should any of my friends choose to get involved with a married, cross-dressing, alcoholic, pot-smoking womaniser, then that's their business, and I MUST NOT INTERFERE.

'Come on, Céline, drink up — you've hardly touched your champers,' says Wendy, opening another bottle. 'You haven't gone tee-total on us, have you?'

'Kind of,' she says, biting her bottom lip. We all stop eating mid-chomp, looking at her with bush baby eyes, all thinking the same thing, but hardly daring to ask.

'You're not, are you?' says Wendy, breaking the silence.

'Eight weeks.' She nods gleefully, smoothing her stomach with her hand.

We squeal uncontrollably, pouncing on her like a pack of hyenas, smothering her in hugs and kisses, and taking it in turns to stroke her tummy (this behaviour attracts some odd looks from the other diners).

'My God, talk about quick work!' exclaims Faye.

'We are surprised it happened so quickly. We decide to try early, because now I have forty-three years. Is old, *n'est-ce pas*?'

'At last! Another baby for us aunties to fuss over,' says Wendy excitedly.

'Let's plan a Baby Shower like they do in ...' I say, my voice falling away.

All at once our excitement levels have plummeted, our thoughts switching simultaneously to Rachel and how she must be feeling right now; thrilled to bits too for her friend, of course, but again reminded of the breast cancer and chemotherapy that have virtually robbed her and Dave of their parenthood dream.

'I too have news!' pipes up Faye over the zabaglione, lifting the mood.

'Well, come on, don't keep us in suspense,' says Wendy.

'You're giving up flying?' I say, hazarding a guess.

'I'm seeing someone,' she blurts out excitedly, eyes sparkling.

'From the agency?' I say.

'Nope.'

244

'Not that Mr-Smoothie first officer on our Chicago night-stop?' asks Rachel, making a face as she flicks away a tear.

'Nothing to do with flying.'

'How old is he?'

'What's his name?'

'Is he single?'

'Sure he's not gay?'

'Is he tall, short?'

'Does he have hair?'

'Own teeth?'

'Girls, *please!*' says Faye waving her spoon for us to stop.

'He's about six foot one, forty-five, divorced, an architect, has two adorable little girls, he's called Gordon, and he's ... lovely. Enough information?'

'Where did you meet him?' I ask eagerly.

'He's a new student at my yoga class.'

By the time Luigi arrives with the cappuccinos and sambucas, we have extracted enough information about poor unsuspecting Gordon to compile a character profile that would satisfy the MI5.

Our laughter echoes around the room, and I'm suddenly aware that we're the last remaining customers.

Glancing at the clock, then nodding over to Luigi with a smile, I say, 'Girls, I hate to be a party-pooper, but it's late and the family have to eat.'

'*Merde!*' exclaims Céline. 'I have to check in in five hours.'

Luigi fetches our coats, and one by one, we kiss him on both cheeks as we file out.

'*Arrivederci, belle signore!*' he calls to us, waving.

'*Buona notte!*' we reply, laughing noisily, as we skitter down the street, arm in arm.

'*A domani!*' I cry, swerving to avoid a lamppost.

I peer at the clock. 0330. I'm exhausted, but don't want to go to sleep. I replay the evening in my head. It's impossible for me not to revel in my latest success. These matchmaking skills of mine are now a force to be reckoned with: A BABY. Whey hey! Okay, so for me life may not be so exciting. After all, my acting career has hardly taken off; as for romance, well nothing happening on that front either, but tonight has shown me yet again that things can change in an instant. We just have to keep on keeping on and eventually we will turn a corner. Of course I'd love to be playing some juicy role in the West End instead of waiting tables six days a week, but hey, looking on the positive side, just a short time ago I only knew the odd Italian word. Now I can string a sentence together, and my culinary skills have improved way beyond spaghetti hoops on toast.

Rachel then cuts through my thoughts; it's one thing being childless because, like me, you never met the right man (call me old fashioned, but I only wanted a baby if it came complete with a hands-on dad), but to have found your Mr Right early on, to both want a family, to have so much to offer a child, and then because of some cruel twist of fate, to be denied that life-enhancing opportunity, seems to me to be so unfair. But whoever said life is fair?

'Nothing but panto castings at the moment, darling. Call me in the New Year.'

'Lionel, I accept my thigh-slapping, Dandini days are now in the dim and distant past, but couldn't I play the Good Fairy?'

'Television names only, my darling,' comes the curt reply at this suggestion.

'But what about *Doon* ...?'

'A cough and a spit hardly constitute a *television name*, I'm afraid,' he replies reprovingly.

'No?'

'No. Sorry, darling. Now if there's nothing else, I've got to dash. The other phone's ringing. Stay in touch.'

Sometimes I hate this bloody, fickle business. It gives everything to some and zilch to others. The weeks are ticking by, and whilst I accept that doing other jobs is part of being an actor, my talent for positive thinking is beginning to wane. I'm starting to wonder how long I should give it: another year, five? Or will the business give up on me first?

OPERA CABARET
JOIN US AT IL MOULINO FOR WINE,
SONG & HOME-COOKED, TRADITIONAL FOOD.
A TASTE OF THE WARM SOUTH BROUGHT TO
TEDDINGTON.

Luigi beams. '*Perfetto!*' he says, smoothing the local newspaper out on the table. '*Allora,* is everything ready for tomorrow? Sergio, I need your final shopping list by the end of tonight, *d'accordo?*' Sergio loosens the collar of his chef's jacket and gives a bad-tempered shrug.

'Rosalba, the piano tuner will arrive at five o'clock. Have you made a final decision about the songs?'

'*Sì, babo.*' She sighs, her long, curling lashes almost touching her eyebrows as she looks up to the ceiling.

Rosalba and her fiancé, Luke, a dentist (they met and fell in love three years ago, when he serenaded her during painful root canal treatment), have been rehearsing tirelessly at the community centre, putting together an eclectic programme of popular Italian songs and various arias from well-known operas; nothing too high-brow, just something to

247

complement the Italian dining experience, and to hopefully set Il Moulino apart from the many other, well established restaurants in Teddington. If this goes well, it could also provide the duo with the ideal platform to showcase their musical talents.

'*Allora,*' says Luigi, rising, 'the flowers and wine will arrive in the morning. If there are no questions, then let's get back to work. We have a full restaurant this evening, and a reservation at ten for twelve businessmen, so meeting over.'

I've decided it's pointless griping about my situation any longer: frown lines are ageing, and besides, no one's listening. Instead, starting tonight, I'm going to treat my waiting on tables as one long tutorial in character observation ...

With this in mind, later that evening, I approach the table of twelve businessmen with a spring in my step and my best smiley face.

'Excuse me, sir, are you ready to order?'

The gentleman swivels round to face me, and my smile turns to a look of horror. My pad and pen fall to the floor. He bends down to pick them up, ensnaring me with his chilling gaze.

'I'll have the tricolore salad, followed by the lasagne,' he says eventually, that low, heavily accented voice that once sounded so exotic, so sexy, so charming, now turning my blood cold.

As I take the menu from him, my hand is shaking.

A numbing weight is pressing down on me; it's clear what I have to do now and the thought fills me with dread. But what choice do I have?

After I've delivered the order to the kitchen, I dash to the cloakroom, mind in a spin, grab my mobile from my coat, snatch my glasses from my head, and with shaky fingers, scroll for Faye's number. Come

248

on, come on, pick up ... *please.*

'Hello?'

'Oh hi, Margie,' I say, putting on my best calm and breezy voice. 'Is Faye at home?'

'I'm sorry, dear, but she's away on a Dallas night-stop. She lands first thing in the morning. Any message?'

'Excuse me, miss. Is the gents this way?'

'Emily? You there?'

'No, no message, thanks,' I say, slowly turning to face him, those dispassionate eyes piercing through me.

He leans towards me, rests his hand on the wall behind, his shirt sleeve brushing my cheek, the heavy, musky scent of his aftershave rendering me nauseous. I pull away, sinking into a squashy pile of coats. I feel like I'm being sucked into quicksand, heart fluttering like a trapped bird. He puts his mouth to my ear, and hisses, 'Hear this ... tell Faye you have seen me, and you will regret it. Understand?'

'How dare you threaten me,' I say, glasses sliding down my nose, betrayed by the fear creeping into my voice.

The kitchen bell rings angrily. He shoots me a deadly wink as he turns away.

Trying to breathe evenly, I straighten my skirt, smooth my hair and tell myself to keep my anxiety under control and act normally.

Sergio makes a tutting sound as I enter the kitchen and waves his hand at the two starters. '*Vai!* Go!'

This is all I need. What exactly is his problem? One minute he's being overly friendly, the next he can't stand the sight of me. Thank God this is the last order. I should be out of here by twelve-thirty. I'll go straight home and try and get a decent night's sleep. It's imperative I unscramble my thoughts and

249

emotions before I go running round to Faye's first thing in the morning.

'*Vai!*'

I think I prefer Sergio the Sleazy to Sergio the Surly; in fact neither would be preferable. Things would be so much better were he not around.

Grabbing a knife from the wall, he starts furiously chopping up parsley.

'*Vaiii!*'

Okay! I'm going, I'm going.

Blinking back hot tears, I pick up the starters and am just sailing through the doors, when he lets out a blood-curdling howl. My plates smash to the floor, sending tomatoes, mozzarella, avocado and basil hurtling through the air. I spin round to see thick liquid, the colour of claret spurting from his hand, splashing the white-tiled walls. A waxy, grey hue floods his skin; his strangely wide eyes roll back as he drops to the floor like a stone.

'Luigi!' I scream. Oh God, oh God, what's the first aid procedure? Something about elevation? Is that right? Grabbing two vegetable crates from under the sink, I remove his blood-splattered clogs and raise his legs.

'*Che cosa?*' says Luigi, appearing through the door. '*Madonna mia!*' he exclaims, raising his hands, horror sweeping across his face.

'*Ambulanza! Pronto!*' I cry, a stab of panic piercing through me.

Now what? Control the bleeding, yes, control the bleeding — but how? Nonna Maria appears at my side with a clean tea towel and kneels by Sergio, mumbling in Italian, tugging at her crucifix. I grab his slippy, blood-soaked hand and my stomach lurches as I see his lifeless, fleshy fingers dangling like broken twigs. I feel sick and giddy. Please God, this is not a good time for me to pass out. I bind them tightly and raise his arm above his head, pushing his hand hard against my chest. Blood trickles through my fingers, dripping onto my crisp, white shirt. I must keep my cool, practical head on until the ambulance arrives.

'Maria, ice! Erm ... *gelato*?' (No, no, that's ice cream) '*Glace!*' She looks at me, bewildered. No, that's French. '*Ghiaccio?* Yes, *Ghiaccio!* ' (Knew it began with 'g'.)

Sergio's eyes flicker open and he twists his head sideways, moaning like a wounded animal. The sound chills me. I gently squeeze his other hand and we hold one another's upside-down gaze. The pain in his expression slices through me. I want to tell him he's going to be okay, but can't think of the right words. '*Ambulanza* — here pronto. Tutto bene. Tutto bene.'

I look towards the door. Where *are* they?

'*Dio mio!*' cries Rosalba, appearing at my side, face blanched with shock.

'Rosalba, we must keep him warm. Get his coat.'

Where the hell are they? Please hurry, *please.*

A siren screams, and like a scene from *ER*, two paramedics burst through the swing doors wheeling a stretcher.

'We've got you, mate,' says one of them, opening his medical bag as he kneels down beside Sergio, then taking his pulse. 'I'm just going to give you some morphine to relieve the pain and steady that racing heart of yours, okay?' I look away as the needle is produced. I feel Sergio's body judder.

'You can let go now,' says his colleague, laying a reassuring hand on my shoulder. 'All right, Phil? One, two, three. There we go.'

I stagger to my feet and look down at Sergio's face, now obscured by an oxygen mask. '*Tutto bene,*' I whisper, as he is whisked out to the waiting ambulance. '*Tutto bene.*'

I just stand there, staring at my blood-drenched shirt and hands. There's a swimming sensation in my head as my legs buckle beneath me and I slump down onto the floor.

Next morning
Faye stands in the doorway in her crumpled uniform, looking at me ashen-faced. 'Are you sure it was him?' she whispers, so as not to wake anyone.

'Oh, yes,' I say emphatically. 'He spoke to me — told me not to tell you he's in the country, or else.'

'What? He threatened you?' she says, giving an involuntary shudder. 'Would you be willing to testify to that in court?'

'Of course I would,' I say with a reassuring smile. 'But let's not jump the gun, eh? Maybe he's simply here on business ...'

'Then why doesn't he just call me and make a proper arrangement to see Tariq, like he's supposed to?' she says, throwing me a disbelieving look. 'Why the secrecy?'

'Look, I'm really sorry,' I say, squeezing her hand, 'but I've got to go. It's the opening night and we're really behind. We don't even have a chef at the moment.'

'What? Not more melodrama?' says Faye, rubbing her eyes.

'You could say that,' I reply. 'Ring if you need me, promise?'

'Of course. After I've dropped Tariq off, I'll speak with the headmistress and then call my lawyer,' she says, trance-like. 'Oh God, Em — just when he's getting settled at school. I knew something like this would happen. Why can't he just leave us alone?' she

252

says, her eyes full of angry tears. 'What if he ...'

'It'll be fine, sweetie,' I say. 'Try to stay calm.'

'Em — thank you,' she murmurs. 'You look exhausted, by the way. Try and get some rest, darling,' she says, quietly closing the door, then sliding the chain across.

I jog past the bins and piled-up garden furniture, entering the restaurant through the kitchen, where Nonna Maria is by the sink, chopping onions, humming and crying at the same time.

'*Ciao*, Maria,' I pant, removing my earphones and kissing her on both cheeks.

'Any news from the hospital? Er ... *notizie da Sergio?*' These three little words unleash a torrent of Italian, of which '*aeroporto*' and '*ospitale*' are the only vocabulary I understand. I just do my customary nodding routine, interspersed with the odd '*sì*' or '*no*', then escape to the dining room with a '*mi scusi*' the moment I'm able to get a word in edgeways. It's empty and silent. I put on some *Madam Butterfly* to soothe my frayed nerves. Grabbing a stiffly starched tablecloth from the pile, I start laying up.

A retro flower power van mounts the pavement. A woman in dungarees jumps out.

'Let me give you a hand,' I say, propping the door open. Back and forth we go, until all the floral arrangements are inside.

'Twenty individual centrepieces, three large,' she says, handing me the consignment note and a pen. 'Hope it all goes well.'

'Wine order for Il Moulino,' comes a voice behind me.

'Ah, yes, that's us,' I reply, chewing on a fingernail as the delivery man negotiates his trolley around the obstacle course of rosemary, white freesias and red roses.

'Twelve cases of Valpolicella, Chianti, Lacryma Christi, Verdicchio, Pino Grigio, and Prosecco,' he says, unloading. I begin to check the boxes off against his inventory, but with so much else to do, I abandon this task and just pray that nothing's missing.

Help! Where is everyone? I can't do this on my own. The evening hasn't even begun and I have this horrible sense of foreboding. I feel panic rising inside me, mixed with guilt that I backed out of telling Faye that I thought I'd spotted Sahir weeks ago, and guilt about Sergio's accident. Just moments before, hadn't I wished him gone? Next minute, bam. He was lying on the floor in a pool of blood. An eerie sensation ripples through my body. Maybe I really do have telekinetic powers.

'That's your lot. Sign here please,' says the delivery man, thrusting his clipboard into my hand. 'When's the party?'

'Tonight, believe it or not,' I reply, rolling my eyes.

His eyebrows shoot up and he gives a low whistle.'I'd get the white in the chiller as soon as you can.'

'Sure,' I say with a hint of sarcasm, scooping up a handful of cutlery. Now, will that be *before* I've laid up twenty tables, folded eighty napkins into birds of paradise, put fresh towels in the loos, sliced up the lemons, polished the wine glasses and cutlery and filled the butter dishes?

'Good luck!' he says cheerily, shutting the door behind him.

I flop into a chair, surveying the war zone: boxes of wine, flowers, glasses, tablecloths, bread baskets, bunting, cutlery everywhere. I feel exhausted and emotionally drained, and have absolutely no idea how I'm going to get through the day, let alone the opening night. With the local press, not to mention

Michelin and Egon Ronay representatives invited, the future of Il Moulino is riding on the success of this one night. It's going to take an Oscar-worthy performance to pull this off. I haul myself to my feet, turn up the volume of the CD player and resume laying up.

Only three more tables to go. This is my favourite bit of *Madam Butterfly*: the finale, where Cio-Cio San reads the inscription on her father's knife: 'Who Cannot Live with Honour Must Die with Honour.' She stabs herself just as that two-timing, naval love-rat, Pinkerton is heard calling out her name.

Cutlery in hand, I allow my eyes to close for a moment and breathe deeply. That feels so good. The notes flow through me, as I surrender to the flood of heart-rending, dramatic, sorrowful emotion ...

'"*Con onor muore, chi non puo sebar vita, con onor amore, addio, addio! Piccolo amor! Va, gioca, giocaaaaaah!*"'

'Emileeee!'

'Aaaah!'

'This is my nephew, Francesco,' says Luigi, switching off the music. 'He will be in charge of the kitchen until Sergio returns.'

'Zio Luigi, you tell me in the car she is British, but she can sing like an Italian,' says the dark stranger, brimming with amusement.

'*Piacere*,' I say, flushing to the roots of my unwashed hair as we shake hands.

'You dropped this,' he says, bending down and handing me a knife.

'*Grazie*,' I say in a low voice, averting his gaze, sorely tempted to do a Madam Butterfly and die with honour then and there.

Back at Beryl's, I take a shower, hoping it will pep me up, but everytime I close my eyes, I see those blood-spattered tiles and the haunted look in Sergio's eyes, merging with Sahir's dark, menacing look. I shudder as his words play over and over in my head: 'You will regret it.' God, it sounds like a line from *CSI*. But this isn't a TV drama. This is real life — my life — and I don't mind admitting I'm scared.

Forty-five minutes later, I'm running back to the restaurant. As I swing round the corner, Luke's molasses-coated, tenor voice floats and soars down the grey, mizzly street to meet me, bathing the kebab shop, the chemist, the cut-price bargain store and the bakery in warm, Italian tones. Close your eyes, and you can almost imagine you're on a gondola, gliding down the canals of Venice ...

'*'O sole mio sta 'nfronte a te! O sole, o sole mio, sta 'nfronte a te! Sta 'nfronte a te! '*'

BEEP! Stand well clear. Vehicle reversing. BEEP! Stand well clear. Vehicle reversing. BEEP!

'Are you bleedin' deaf or summat? Get out the bloody way!' On second thoughts, maybe not.

I lay out the assortment of antipastos: artichoke hearts, anchovies, red and yellow peppers, various roasted veggies and olives (bought early this morning by Francesco in the market of his home town).

As the crowd starts trickling in, I take coats and serve drinks while Luigi mingles with the guests. Once they've settled in with appetizers and wine, he taps a glass with a knife and the lively chatter dies down, a sea of expectant faces turning to meet his.

'*Benvenuti, miei amici!*' Pointing to the old sepia photograph behind the bar, he recounts in halting English, how as a small boy, he had a fascination for windmills; he would spend his summer holidays at his grandparents' in Sicily, and play in the disused windmill next door. He believed its spinning blades were wings. He'd sit inside the tower and fly to far off lands, encountering giants and mystical creatures along the way. But as soon as the church clock struck six, he would race home in time to wash his hands, comb his hair and lay the table for Nonna, for he knew if he were late, there would be no supper, and a day without Nonna's cooking was like a day without play.

'*Allora, basta!* Enough!' he says, wiping his moist brow. A warm smile and a look of unmistakable pride spread across his face as he announces, 'Now I go back to the kitchen, and I leave you with my beautiful daughter, Rosalba, and my future son-in-law, Lucio Pavarotti!'

Spontaneous laughter and applause break out, swiftly followed by a series of oohs and aahs as Rosalba, in a sizzling red, floor-length, off-the-shoulder gown slinks down the stairs, through the tightly packed tables, followed by Luke, in crisp, white, wing-collared shirt sans tie and dark waistcoat, his thick, golden hair (more beach boy than dentist) sleek and shiny. The clapping dies down as he takes his place at the piano, opens the lid, straightens his back and flexes his fingers. (Blimey, he can perform root canal on me any day of the week.) Rosalba's diamante earrings sway gently back and forth, catching the light. He nods his head towards her, and with a toss of her tumbling ebony tresses, the words '"*O Mio Babbino Caro ...* "' spill from her sumptuous, painted mouth.

I haven't a clue what the lyrics mean, but I assume it's about yet another tragic, heartbroken heroine about to die either through murder or suicide.

(Rosalba tells me later it's about a spoiled brat of a daughter who wants a ring, and is threatening to throw her toys into the River Arno because her dad won't give in to her.)

Throughout the night I zigzag in between the tables, topping up red and white wine, sneaking a little sip for myself when no one's looking.

I know it's mean of me, considering Sergio's lying in hospital minus a finger, but with Francesco in charge, the kitchen is a different place. The interaction between us is easy and humorous, flirtatious even, and the food's just as good — no, *better*. And the positive vibe flows out into the dining room.

You never know what mood Sergio is going to be in, and if you don't understand him right away, he either mumbles something you just know is derogatory, or raises his voice and waves his arms about. (I have him to thank for my extensive knowledge of Italian expletives.) Next minute he's teasing you, calling you his *cucciolo*.

Then I remember the look of fear in his eyes less than twenty-four hours ago, and despite everything, I can't help feeling sorry for him. Beneath that fierce Italian bravado, he can be just as vulnerable and scared as the rest of us.

The kitchen now closed, I pour myself another glass of Valpolicella and pop a stuffed zucchini flower into my mouth — whole.

'I am serious about what I say before,' shouts Francesco, straining to be heard above the enthusiastic clapping and singing of *Funiculì, Funiculà*. 'About teaching you Italian.' His warm breath tickles my ear.

'Great!' I say, hand covering my mouth to avoid

258

showering him with bits of batter.

'*Allora*, tomorrow at … Costa Coffee? Two o'clock, *sì*?'

I give a cool nod, keeping my eyes on the stage, but biting back a hamster-like grin as I sway in time to the music.

'*Sogni d'oro!*' (golden dreams) he says, swinging his jacket over his shoulder. From the corner of my eye I watch his tall, broad shouldered frame weaving swiftly through the revelling crowd and out of the door.

It's gone two before the last few customers are persuaded to leave and past four by the time the tables are cleared and re-set, chairs stacked, floor swept, dishwasher loaded and tips divvied up.

As I unpadlock my bicycle, my hands are shaking, and my heart is beating in time to the mambo. Here I go again, reading too much into a simple, friendly gesture. Francesco has merely asked me for a coffee to coach me in Italian, and my insides are acting as if it's a proper date.

How do they do it, I wonder, Italian women? They are so understatedly chic, with their designer jeans and well co-ordinated accessories. Why, oh why am I having this conversation with myself at 5 a.m., I think, as I flick through my mishmash of a wardrobe? Gok Wan would have a field day. There's nothing else for it; I'll just have to make do with little sleep and dash into town and buy a new outfit. Now hold your horses. What the hell is happening to me? This is ridiculous. I can't afford to blow half a week's wages on new clothes, semi-date with attractive Italian, or no.

I arrive at Costa's a cool, yet not impolite, five minutes late. Francesco is already there, perched on a high stool, sipping espresso and reading the Italian newspaper, *Corriere della Sera.*

The chef's garb of white jacket and checked trousers has been replaced by faded Armani jeans and a pale blue, collarless shirt, with a navy cashmere jumper casually draped around his shoulders.

'Buongiorno, principessa!' he says rising and pulling out a seat. 'Cappuccino?'

'Mmm, please,' I say launching myself up onto the stool. I peer at the book lying on the table and rummage in my bag for my glasses — *Italian for Beginners.*

I shoot him a specky-four-eyes grin. He winks at me and disappears to the counter.

Page 1
Verbs
avere — to have
ho — I have
hai — you have
ha — he, she, it has
abbiamo — we have
avete — you (pl.) have
hanno — they have
ho una bicicletta — I have a bicycle

Francesco puts down my coffee. As we talk, I dare to study his face close-up; aquiline nose, square jaw, deep-set eyes, teeth slightly out of kilter, dark, wavy hair, tinged with grey; not handsome, in a smooth, Pierce-Brosnan way, but more of a Sean-Bean type — rugged, raw yet charming; the type of man who'd protect you in a street brawl, who too would look good in swashbuckling uniform ...

'*Allora ...*'

'What? Oh ...' I flip the book open again. '*Ho una bicicletta.*'

He shakes his head and fighting back a smirk, says, 'No, no, no. The "h" is silent — like "o". *O una bicicletta.*'

I slurp my cappuccino and repeat, '*O una bicicletta.*'

He fires me a bemused look over the rim of his coffee cup.

'What?' I say awkwardly.

He indicates my mouth. Is he making fun of me?

'*O - UNA - BICICLETTA,*' I repeat, louder this time.

He smiles, leans across the table, and gently wipes cappuccino froth from my top lip. His gaze is unflinching. My heart speeds up.

'*O una bicicletta,*' I say hurriedly, blushing madly.

'*Bravissimo!*' he exclaims, high-fiving me.

And so two afternoons a week I buy Francesco coffee and he teaches me Italian.

If I get stuck and break into English, he puts on his serious face and says, '*Non è permesso.*'

I'm discovering that often, by adding the letter 'o' or 'a' to the end of an English word, you can create the Italian: e.g. 'sense' = *senso,* 'minute' = *minuto,* 'romance' = *romanza.*

I don't ever remember language learning being so much fun. But back when I was a gawky, pigtailed schoolgirl, my Modern Language teacher was a short, dour-faced Glaswegian, sporting shabby clothes and halitosis. And now? Now my heart flips over at the sight of my teacher's smile, the tilt of his head as he listens patiently to my attempts at grammar, sentence construction and pronunciation, the way he says '*E-milee*' and calls me his '*piccola studenta*' in that make-your-knees-go-weak accent of his.

Isn't life strange? It seems to me the moment you stop wanting something badly, it comes and bites you on the bottom ...

'I hope you're sitting down, darling,' gushes Lionel in a rare phone call some three weeks later. 'The Rieger Theatre in Vienna is casting for its autumn production, *On Golden Pond,* and Gerhard Rieger *himself* wants to audition you tomorrow in London for the role of Chelsea!'

Had I been the recipient of this news a month ago, I'd be jumping up and down and swinging round the lampposts at the prospect of not only working in a proper theatre for three months, but the famous *Rieger Theatre* in VIENNA — so how come I feel kind of negative all of a sudden? Surely nothing to do with my Italian teacher? No-ho! Of course not! That's silly ... I mean, we're just friends ... aren't we? After all, our conversations haven't gone much beyond buying stamps at the *tabaccheria* or booking a *camera singola* at the *albergo*, so I can hardly call this a *romanza* ... can I?

Anyway, don't know why I'm getting in such a tizzy. They see loads of people, so I probably won't get it anyway.

Three days later, am in the newsagents deciding which lottery numbers to choose this week, when my mobile springs into life. As usual, it's worked its way to the bottom of my cavernous bag, and not until my purse, a half-eaten tube of extra strong mints, my mini Italian dictionary, a Tampax, a bottle of water, keys, my Oyster card, a scrunched up tissue, lip-gloss and satsuma are spewed all over the floor, am I able to answer it.

'Emily, darling, it's Lionel,' he says in a singsong voice I've never heard before. 'Terrific news — you got the job!'

He begins to rattle off the terms of the offer: 'Rehearsals start Tuesday in Vienna, you fly out Monday from Heathrow, you'll be met at the airport by the company manager, and you'll be staying at ... Emily, are you still there?'

'Sorry, what was that?' I say, voice drying up.

'Look, have I called at a bad time?' he continues. 'Ring me back, or better still, I'll e-mail you the details, then you'll have it all in writing. Okay? Well done!'

I remain crouched on the floor, motionless, staring at my phone. I hadn't bargained for this. Meeting Francesco has thrown everything into utter chaos. This is insane, because I hardly know him, but I DON'T WANT TO GO. But do I have a choice? If I turn it down, Lionel will understandably throw a wobbler and refuse to represent me ever again, and Francesco will realise the depth of my feelings and it will be *'Ciao, ciao bambina'* as he boards the first flight back to Napoli.

I slowly gather up my belongings and leave Mr Khan's shop, thoughts of winning the lottery now far from my mind.

Crisis talks to discuss the Vienna Situation:
'Of course you must go,' says Rachel, slamming down her wineglass and throwing back her head. 'Think of all the actors who'd give their right arm to be in your position.'

'I know, I know. But I really feel there's a growing, unspoken connection between us, and I don't think it's all in my mind ...'

'Look, hon,' says Wendy gently. 'I'm the last one to

want to burst your romantic bubble, but let's be realistic — this ... Giuseppe or Mario, or whatever his name is, may well have a wife or girlfriend back home in old Napoli. I mean, he's not so much as held your hand or kissed you, let alone proclaimed his undying love for you, has he?'

'No,' I reluctantly concede.

'It isn't forever,' says Céline, shrugging her shoulders dismissively. 'Three months.'

'Precisely,' chips in Faye. 'And if he is single and not gay, and does fancy you, he'll jolly well have to wait. Besides, we're already planning a long weekend in Vienna, aren't we, girls?'

'All the sacrifices you've made,' says Wendy. 'You've come this far. Please don't let go of your dream the moment a Mr Maybe comes on the scene.'

'Do you want to be a waitress for the rest of your life?' says Rachel despairingly. 'Is that why you ditched your job, your flat, your car, your whole ordered and secure life?'

She's right; they're all right, but what if ...?

Wendy holds her glass high. 'A toast! To our darling Emily. You've waited a long time for an opportunity like this. Congratulations, good luck and ... go for it, girl!'

I look at their ecstatic, expectant faces. I'd be letting them down too if I don't go. They've been there for me through every crappy temping job, every angst-ridden audition, every tearful rejection, every nerve-wracked performance and turbulent relationship along the way, firm in the belief that a breakthrough was just around the corner. At last, here comes the longed for pay-off, and instead of grabbing it with both hands, I'm secretly contemplating jumping ship and sacrificing everything I've worked for. And why? Because of a man I hardly know, who isn't even my boyfriend? Because my desire to be in a relationship is greater than my desire to be an actress? Where has my ambition, my drive, my self-belief gone? It's pathetic. Have I learned nothing in the last five years?

'And don't you dare go waltzing off into the mountains with Captain von Trapp either, or it's the nunnery for you, *Fraulein*!' says Rachel in a fake threatening tone.

CHIUSO/CLOSED. As I turn over the door sign for the last time, a feeling of melancholy swells my heart.

'*A cena!*' calls Luigi. Francesco slips into the empty space beside me on the banquette. There are a couple of bottles of Prosecco chilling in an ice bucket by the side, and a little pile of gifts by my place: a box of my favourite *Baci Perugina* chocolates, a copy of the Zucchero CD we play in the restaurant, and a notebook in which Maria has written several of her recipes.

'*Mille grazie, a voi tutti,*' I say, swallowing hard, looking at them all through a sudden mist. They have become like family to me.

Luigi leans across the table and pinches my cheek.

'It is not goodbye, cara, just *arrivederci*. There is always a job here for our *piccola inglese.*'

I race through the rain to the bicycle rack, tears slipping down my face.

I'm searching in my bag for my padlock key, when I hear footsteps behind me. My heart clangs in my chest. Blood pounds in my ears. The wind rattles a dustbin lid, a fox screams in the distance. I find the key at last, but my trembling hand inserts it upside down. The footsteps are getting closer. Oh my God, it's him. Sahir. *YOU WILL REGRET IT.* I should have known better than to mess with his sort; but I didn't have a choice, did I? Just when we'd allowed ourselves to hope he'd disappeared, just when I'm starting to get my life back on track. Now I'm to be struck down in my prime. Will Francesco be racked with grief, I wonder? *Mamma mia! Mia cara E-milee! Mia piccola studenta!* And oh God, how embarrassing to be found dead wearing a cycle helmet.

A dark figure emerges from the shadows.

'*Dio mio*, Francesco, it's you! I thought you were ...'

'*Chi?*'

'It doesn't matter.'

'So, *domani,* I take you to the *aeroporto*, sì?'

'That's really kind of you, but I've booked a taxi, and anyway, my suitcase will never fit on your Vespa.'

'*Imbecille!*' My eyes are drawn to the dimple on his left cheek. 'I borrow Zio Luigi's car.'

'Aha.' I am suddenly aware of my soaking wet hair, plastered to my head, and runny mascara, sliding down my cheeks, à la Alice Cooper. 'Well, in that case, *mille grazie.*' I nod, trying to sound cool, whilst quashing the surge of joy I feel at his offer.

'You say your flight is at three. *Allora*, I see you at around twelve-thirty, *d'accordo?*'

He kisses me lightly on the cheek, whispers '*sogni d'oro,*' and disappears into the black night.

Nonna Maria's recipes, inspired by family life in Naples:

Rigatoni alla Leonardo da Vinci (serves 4)
½ kg rigatoni pasta
packet of bacon
mushrooms

1 tin chopped tomatoes
2 bay leaves
olive oil
a little cream
splash of vodka
fry chopped onion in olive oil
add bacon and mushrooms
add tin chopped tomatoes and bay leaves
simmer for 40 minutes
cook pasta
add cream and vodka
pour sauce over cooked pasta

Pollo Cacciatore *(serves 4)*
1 dozen chicken thighs/legs
mixed peppers
potatoes
carrots
1 courgette
1 onion
fresh rosemary
fresh oregano
fresh tomatoes
olive oil
white wine
place all ingredients in a casserole dish
marinade in white wine and a little olive oil for 2 hours
place casserole dish in oven
cook at medium temperature for 1 hour

Polpette di Melenzane *(serves 4)*
2 aubergines
2 egg yolks
parmesan cheese

fresh parsley
fresh basil
fresh oregano
seasoning
olive oil
vegetable oil
stale French bread
natural yogurt
dice aubergines
fry in olive oil with oregano
allow to cool
soak bread in a little water
blend bread and aubergines together
add 2 egg yolks, grated parmesan, parsley, salt, pepper and basil
knead into hamburger shapes
fry in hot vegetable oil
serve with natural yogurt and fresh side salad

♥

Arancini di Riso *(serves 4)*
2 large eggs
2 cups arborio rice
grated parmigiano
250g minced beef (if vegetarian, substitute meat with mushrooms and 1 cup freshly boiled peas)
1½ cups dry, Italian-style breadcrumbs
2oz mozzarella, diced into ½ inch cubes
1 clove garlic
½ onion
2 tbs tomato paste
seasoning
olive oil
vegetable oil
splash red wine
slice onion, press garlic and sauté in olive oil

brown the mince and add a little red wine.

cook rice

pour oil into large pan to a depth of about 3" and heat at medium heat

beat eggs, cooked rice, cooked mince and ½ cup breadcrumbs to medium bowl

using about 2tbs. of mix for each ball, form into 1¾" diameter balls

Insert 1 cube of mozzarella into centre of balls

roll balls in breadcrumbs

add rice balls to hot oil and cook until brown and heat through, turning as required for about 4 mins.

using a slotted spoon, transfer to kitchen towel to drain, then season

leave for 2 mins.

serve hot

Buon Appetito!

Gaah! This is hopeless.

I close my eyes and focus on my breathing: exhale through the mouth, inhale through the nose, counting to four, hold breath, counting to seven ... *you are breathing in white light, waves are gently lapping the shore,* exhale through the mouth...

I stare at the poly-tiled ceiling, then back at the clock — 0245.

I try counting sheep: one, two, three months is a helluva long time, four, five, will Francesco still be here when I get back? Six, seven, I wonder how long it will take until Sergio gets the all-clear? Eight, nine, maybe Francesco will stay on as a kind of sous chef, ten, eleven, what will the cast be like? Twelve, thirteen, *God*, three months with a group of people

I've never met ...

I untangle myself from the duvet, switch on the bedside light and stagger out of bed. Clicking open my suitcase, I rifle through the contents, taking several items out, then promptly put them, plus a few more back in again; in case it snows, it rains, there's a heat wave or monsoon. With all this global warming, you just never know.

I pick up my pristine script from the bedside table. *On Golden Pond by Ernest Thompson.* Taking a yellow highlighter pen from my bag, I flick through the crisp pages and score through Chelsea's lines ...

'Emily, darlin', it's ten-thirty.' Beryl shuffles in, sloshes down a cup of her customary, American Tan-coloured tea on top of my shiny, new script, and draws back the curtains. 'I've cooked you a full English. Just going to fry the eggs and pop the toast in.'

I rub my eyes and take a slurp of tea. The room looks like Primark at six o'clock on a Saturday: jeans, tops, boots, belts, skirts, underwear, hangers strewn all over the floor. I scramble out of bed and into the shower. I let the water run, hoping it will turn warm, but true to form, the temperature oscillates between bearably cold and arctic.

There is much I will miss about lodging with Beryl: her late-night chip butties, our Ealing Comedy film nights, her tales of growing up in the East End, but her shower will not feature on that list. Neither will Shirley, who during my time here, has succeeded in spilling a bottle of red nail varnish over my Kindle, ruining the cashmere jumper Mum bought me for Christmas, chewing the wire of my hair straighteners and shredding my yoga mat.

I study Francesco as he queues up for our coffees at Heathrow; when I'm far from him I want to be able to recall the way his thick, greying hair curls up at the ends as it brushes his collar, how he talks with his whole body: the shrug of his athletic shoulders, the vibrant gestures of his strong, long-fingered, olive-skinned hands.

He turns around and I drag my gaze away from him, pretending to study my boarding card.

'*Allora*, I have something for you,' he says, putting down the tray and reaching into his bag. I blink at him several times, trying to keep my simmering emotions from boiling over. A package is slid across the table. My hands close around it and I give it a shake. Not a love token then; its thickness and weight speak to me of grammar, verbs and more study.

'*Aprirlo!* Open!' he says, throwing me one of his delicious, roguish grins. How I wish I could capture that now familiar expression and put it safely away in my pocket, to sustain me over the next twelve, long weeks. Even if I have no place in his heart or mind, I'm allowed to dream, aren't I?

'*Aprirlo!*'

I peer at the title, then forage in my bag for my glasses. '*Italia Oggi.* Italy, Italy ... no, don't tell me, Italy ... Today?'

'*Esatto!*'

'Hmm. Don't you think I'll be busy enough, learning lines and brushing up on my German?' I say, trying to make light of my disappointment.

'The final call for passengers travelling to Vienna with British Airways. Please make your way to gate three.'

Swept along in the moment, I boldly fling my arms around him and plant a huge kiss on his cheek. His eyes rest on mine, triggering violent tummy wobbles.

271

'I will miss my *piccola studenta*, but maybe I come to Vienna one weekend, sì?' he says, locking my hands in a firm clasp.

'Definitely,' I gasp, longing for him to say more, to take me in his arms …

'*Vai! Vai!*'

'Yes, yes … plane to catch … bye, I mean, *arrivederci*,' I say in a silly, cod-Italian voice and stride off towards Departures.

'*Cara!*' he calls after me.

'Yes,' I say, turning around, heart quickening.

'Your *glassees*,' he says, hand outstretched, the corners of his mouth twitching.

CHAPTER FOURTEEN
Lost in Chelsea

DID THE PILOT TAKE A WRONG TURNING and land somewhere in darkest Siberia? This isn't Vienna — the Strauss and coffee house Vienna of my dreams. The one with cobbled streets, horse-drawn carriages and *Sachertorte.*

I give the rock-hard pillow a punch, wipe the condensation from my bedroom window with my pyjama sleeve, and peer out through the teeming rain at the red brick industrial estate opposite.

I know, I know, this student hostel is a temporary arrangement, and I know I'm ten miles out of the city centre, but I can't help feeling a trifle let down. In fact, what the hell am I doing here? Given half a chance, I would gladly pack my belongings and be on the first plane back to London.

Two weeks later
My eyes flicker open, and I focus my stare on the chandelier suspended from the cracked, wedding cake ceiling. I reach out, tracing my fingers along the crocheted mat, feeling for my watch. I peer at the

hands: eight fifty-five. I pull on a woolly sweater over my pyjamas, pad across the tiled floor and open the flaky shutters. I step through the beam of autumn sunlight, out onto the balcony and soak up the sounds of the bustling Rudolfstrasse below: the rumbling tram, car horns, the shouts from the market stall holders, the putt-putt of scooters and the clinging of bicycle bells. I lean over the wrought iron railing, and the trailing geraniums (valiantly still flowering) brush my bare feet. Faye would be proud of me. Without wishing to sound like one of those New Age freaks, I am starting to live more and more in the moment these days (since 18th October to be precise, when I moved out of Colditz and into apartment thirteen, thirty-two Rudlofstrasse, home of Frau Anna Schildberger, retired nurse, now theatrical landlady).

The church clock, around the corner in Ringstrasse, chimes nine, reminding me that I've had my daily dose of I-am-one-with-the-universe, and to get my arse into gear if I'm to squeeze in my caffeine fix by rehearsal at ten-thirty.

I am now the proud owner of one of those sit-up-and-beg bikes, complete with wicker basket, which I picked up for just forty euros among the second-hand clothes, ornaments, paintings and general junk at the flea market.

Vienna is great for cyclists, there being plenty of cycle paths and places to park. As someone who regularly runs the gauntlet of the A316 to Richmond and beyond, this city is a dream.

I slot my bike into the rack outside my favourite coffee shop, Kaffeehaus Vancl. According to my guidebook, this has been a meeting place for poets, writers and artists for centuries. It's rather shabby, but full of bohemian character, with its marble-topped tables, creaky wooden chairs, faded drapes and ornate, gilt mirror. The atmosphere is warm and theatrical; *gemütlich,* as the natives say.

'*Guten morgen, Fraulein,*' says the waiter in tuxedo and bow tie, scraping a chair across the floor. '*Bitte sehr?*' Without waiting for my order, he says, '*Kaffee mit Schlagobers und zwei Buchteln, bitte*,' mimicking my Anglo-Viennese accent. I hold this waiter solely responsible for my growing jam-filled bun addiction.

I run my hands across the cool, mottled table and wonder who else has sat here, learning lines, sketching, penning novellas and music, and did they too dunk their pastries in their coffee, or did the art of dunking not evolve until modern times?

With sticky fingers, I pull the script from my bag and scan my lines for the section we're working on today. It's a scene between Ethel (my mother) and me. Chelsea is a dream of a part to play: complex, at odds with her father, and unlucky in love (unlimited resource of experience to draw upon there then). There are some great emotional moments; something I can really get my teeth into. I think I can safely say my days of stumbling about the stage sporting a dodgy wig and an even dodgier accent, grappling for my next line, are now firmly in the dim and distant past.

Ethel is played by Mags, the only other female member of the cast.

We hit it off right from the moment we met in the departure lounge that day at Heathrow ...

'Snap!'

My head bobbed up. Sitting across from me was an elegant woman of about seventy, silver-grey hair piled up on top of her head, an identical green script clutched in her hand.

'My daughter, I presume?' she ventured, leaning

forward.

I hesitated momentarily, and then it dawned on me. 'Ethel, how nice to meet you,' I said, shaking her hand with an enthusiastic grip.

By the time our plane touched down, we'd crammed two lifetimes into those two short hours. A retired French teacher and keen amateur actress, she'd turned professional after years of caring for her husband.

'Dementia has stolen him from me,' she said candidly. 'When he finally had to go into a home, I decided I needed to make a new life for myself. I feel guilty because he's still alive and I'm carrying on as if he's dead,' she continued wistfully. 'But most of the time he doesn't even know who I am.'

I didn't know how to respond; what words could possibly be of comfort? 'Things will get better' would sound hollow and insincere; but then the stewardess asked if we'd like another drink from the bar, and a mischievous smile stretched across Mags' face as she said, 'Oh, I think we could manage one more, don't you?'

Norman, my father, is played by theatre veteran, Oliver. With his CAA (Concert Artistes' Club) tie, highly polished shoes and trilby (which is raised whenever a lady enters the room), he is the archetypal, courtly English gent. We love to hear his stories of the good old days, touring the classics to exotic places with the Sir Donald Wolfit Company. I swear those rich, sonorous tones could be heard over the Rolls Royce engines of a 747.

Not the same can be said, I'm afraid, for top of the bill, Alan Hastings, who has been cast in the role of my fiancé, Bill Ray. Alan has spent the last twenty-five years playing psychiatrist, Doctor Chris Lane in the crime drama, *Mind Games*, which has catapulted him into stardom.

This is his first foray into stage acting, and I can see why the producers chose him: he's suave, sophisticated (if a little arrogant), and has earned a huge following of die-hard fans (mainly female and gay), who are willing to travel in their droves to see him, so is a huge box office draw. There's just one small problem: he mumbles. This type of method acting is all very well if you're Marlon Brando in *The Godfather,* where an understated look, a grunt or a whisper is all that's required to subtly communicate emotions to an audience of one: i.e. the camera lens, but not in a one-thousand-seat auditorium.

But no matter, for there are always queues of adoring autograph hunters at the stage door every night, pens, programmes and cameras at the ready.

Alan is chauffeured between the Hotel Sacher and the theatre every day (I can't begin to imagine how many euros *he* earns a week), and is always jawing on about lunching at The Ivy with Michael Caine or golfing with Hugh Grant.

I imagine this must all be very galling for Oliver, who's a wonderful stage actor, with a list of notable credits to his name, yet walks to the theatre every day, and is staying in a three-star Gasthaus. When I once asked him about his feelings on the subject, he simply said, 'Acting is not a contest, Emily. I'm proud of the work I've done, and am not interested in keeping score. "When envy breeds unkind division: there comes the ruin, there begins confusion." *Henry The Sixth, Part One.'*

(How I would love to have Oliver's ability to quote Shakespeare at the drop of a hat — and to have the grace to think more kindly of Alan.)

But try as I might, there's absolutely no chemistry between us, which is unfortunate, as we're supposed to be madly in love.

Mags tells me it's a good test of my acting skills, and recalls how she once had a similar problem, playing a sadist lesbian in *The Killing of Sister George.* The only way she could pull it off was to totally immerse herself in the thoughts and emotions of the character. (I suppose I should give thanks for small mercies: at least Alan's a man.)

What was it Portia said?

'Acting is about finding the truth in imaginary circumstances.'

Note to self: MUST TRY HARDER TO FANCY ~~ALAN~~ BILL RAY.

After all, if Mags and Jason can do it, why not me? Jason plays Charlie, the mailman. Charlie's known Chelsea since they were kids, and still has unrequited feelings for her. He's gay (Jason, that is, not Charlie), but those soul-searching eyes regard me with such adoration on stage, that an unspoken frisson has developed between us. (Oh dear, I'm falling for the wrong guy.)

I wish Jason were around more, as his presence immediately fills the air with fun and laughter. (He reminds me of many of my gay steward colleagues, who, through their razor-sharp wit and charm, would turn a ten-hour flight packed full of delayed, grumpy passengers into an on-board party.) But Jason has a boyfriend, Matthias, who lives in Vienna, and so he scoots off every night after the show.

This is not the first time I've found myself falling for a gay man. Is it because they generally have good taste, impeccable manners, dress well, smell nice, and have a great sense of humour? Or is there something fundamentally wrong with me? Why do I always desire the things I can't have?

The role of Billy Ray Junior, Bill Ray's teenage son,

is shared between two young teenagers, who attend the American International Theatre School here, and play the role in rotation.

The scenes between crotchety octogenarian Norman and thirteen-year-old Billy Ray are a master class in fine acting. The arrival of the young man at Golden Pond pulls the world-weary Norman from the quicksand of his melancholy, their fishing trips and man-to-man talks reviving the old man's zest for life. The powerful bond played out in their scenes together makes my heart hurt.

It gets me thinking about family and growing old — how we all need a little sunshine in our lives; just because you're done with work or raising children, this doesn't mean you've passed your sell-by date and are happy to spend the rest of your life in solitary confinement, with only the telly for company. Every human being needs to feel useful and wanted. I don't imagine Oliver is still treading the boards purely through financial necessity, and as for Mags, this contract is the key to her sanity.

After two weeks in a church hall, today we are to rehearse on stage for the first time.

'Ladies and gentlemen of the *On Golden Pond* Company, please make your way down to the auditorium to walk the set,' the deputy stage manager instructs over the tannoy.

We enter through the swing doors and stop dead in our tracks. I feel the hairs on the back of my neck bristle. The cables and ladders have disappeared, and the hollow, cavernous stage of a fortnight ago has now morphed into Ethel and Norman Thayer's rustic, lakefront house in Maine, New England.

The audio engineers are hunched over a huge

mixing desk in the middle of the stalls, the lighting guys are working overhead, and day turns to night in an instant, the lake shimmering in the moonlight beyond the screen door. The eerie sound of the loons echoes around the auditorium. Mags and Oliver slip quietly unprompted into character.

"'Shh. Norman, the loons. They're calling. Oh, why is it so dark?'"

"'Because the sun went down.'"

"'I wish I could see them. Yoo hoo! Looooooons! Loony looo-oooons!'"

"'I don't think you should do that in front of Chelsea's companion.'"

Gerhard, our director, sits at the front of the stage, calling instructions to the crew. We settle silently into the plush, red velvet seats until they are ready for us.

Opening night
'*Guten Abend,* Olaf,' I say to the stage doorman as I tick off my name and eagerly check my pigeonhole for post.

'*Guten Abend, Fraulein,*' he says, summoning me back to the desk with the crook of his finger. He disappears momentarily to the small office at the back and re-emerges with a huge bouquet of crimson roses. '*Für Sie,*' he says, thrusting them towards me, amused by my astounded expression.

'*Danke,*' I say, barely able to contain my soaring joy, whilst silently castigating myself for assuming Francesco would forget my opening night.

As I make my way up the stairs, Oliver's vocal warm-up exercises sweep down the corridor to meet me. 'What a to-do to die today at a minute or two to two. A thing distinctly hard to say, but harder still to do ...'

The theatre manager, in full penguin suit, gives me

a fleeting nod as he rushes past, squawking into his walkie-talkie.

'*Entschuldigung!* Sorry!' calls out the wardrobe mistress, narrowly avoiding me as she clatters down the stairs, the mailman's costume slung over her shoulder.

The deputy stage manager's voice echoes through the tannoy: 'Ladies and gentlemen of the *On Golden Pond* Company, the house is now open. Please do not cross the stage.'

I open the door to dressing room number three, which Mags and I share. She's already there in her paisley silk dressing gown, applying her make-up.

'Wow! Are those flowers from your Italian *amore*?' she asks, a girlish glint in her eye. 'How romantic!'

'I think so ...' I say, secretly hoping, as I rip open the card.

> *Buona fortuna.*
> *Mille grazie ~ Sergio.*

Mags looks at me expectantly in the make-up mirror, mascara wand suspended mid-stroke. 'Well, am I right?'

I shake my head, letting out a gutted sigh.

'Ladies and gentlemen, this is your half-hour call,' cuts in the deputy stage manager's voice again. 'Thirty minutes, please.'

A ripple of excitement mixed with sheer terror courses through my veins.

As I flick my powder brush to and fro, my thoughts drift again to Francesco. I wonder what he's doing at this very moment. Concocting one of his delicious sauces, no doubt, whilst singing along to Zucchero or Renato Zero ...

'Break a leg, my darling,' whispers Mags, pressing

her cheek against mine.

'God, have I missed the beginners' call?' I say, coming back down to planet earth.

'No. Don't panic. I like to get down there early to check my props — and I have a daft little ritual I need to perform in the wings before every opening night,' she says confidingly. 'It's too silly for words, so don't ask. See you down there. Let's knock 'em dead!'

A little jitter creeps back into my tummy. This is it. Two scenes, and I'm on. All the rehearsal and anxiety of the last three weeks, wondering if it would all come together in time, has culminated in this moment, and I'm thinking about Francesco and his pasta sauces. I give myself a severe ticking off, and take one last look at my lines, in an attempt to block him out and discipline my thoughts.

From the moment I make my first entrance, my nerves vanish as the magic takes hold, and I get lost in Chelsea; one moment a grown woman in complete control of her life, the next, a little girl, insecure and desperate for parental approval.

As we take our final curtain call, Mags squeezes my hand tightly. I look out into the packed auditorium through blurred eyes. In that instant I am reminded why actors struggle, do mind-numbing day jobs and sacrifice the material things of life; it is for this. Pooh, pooh to all that psychobabble about us suffering from some sort of narcissistic personality disorder. All I know is, nothing else has ever given me the same buzz, joy and satisfaction, or feeling of camaraderie. It beats inputting data or flogging pet potty patches and drawer organisers to shopping channel addicts any day. At last I am where I belong, doing the job I love most; I am one of the lucky eight percent of actors in paid employment, and to prove it, blu-tacked to the dressing room mirror (with light bulbs all around it!) is the invitation to my first proper opening night party ...

The Management of The Rieger Theatre, Vienna invite the cast & crew of On Golden Pond to first-night drinks in the Haydn Bar

'*Fraulein?*' says the waiter, clicking his heels as he tops up my glass of Sekt for the second time.

I give myself an imaginary pinch; I am in Vienna. I AM AN ACTRESS, WHO IS SIPPING CHAMPAGNE AT AN AFTER-SHOW PARTY IN VIENNA. I want to hold on to this feeling and keep it safe in a bottle. Then next time I'm scraping some customer's left-over spag bol into the bin and having a severe case of what's-to-become-of-me blues, I'll uncork it, close my eyes, and inhale deeply. With just one whiff, my flagging spirits will be instantly revived, and I'll be back on track.

'Congratulations!' says a deeply familiar, über-smooth voice.

I veer round and find myself eyeball to eyeball with — NIGEL.

'Oh my God, what are you doing here?' I say, covering my mouth with my hand, heart hitting the floor.

'Hey, I didn't expect you to exactly fling your arms around me, but ...'

'Sorry, it's just I didn't expect ...' I whisper, my voice disintegrating.

Why did I just come over all fluttery and apologise? This is the callous bastard who, in five minutes flat, sabotaged my whole life plan of moving to the country, having two kids (we'd even chosen names), a red setter and a vegetable garden.

'Minnie, you were fab-u-lous. Didn't know you had

it in you. Short hair suits you, by the way,' he says, his hand running down my cheek. 'It makes you look much younger. You should have had it cut years ago.' Excuse me? Is this not the same man who warned me never to cut my hair or he'd leave me? His thumb strokes my bottom lip as he holds me with his wolfish stare for longer than is comfortable. That old familiar scent of Paco Rabanne swirls around my head, awakening the past uninvited.

'God, the loos here are a bit funny, babe,' simpers a long-legged, lissom creature, bouncing over in an eye-popping, figure-hugging frocklet.

'Ah, darling, this is Emily. Emily, Natasha,' says Nigel, not looking me in the eye.

'*Natasha*?' I say, raising a quizzical eyebrow. 'Sorry, I thought ...'

'Natasha,' he says firmly.

'Hi,' she says with a coltish toss of her glossy, strawberry blonde mane.

'We loved the show, didn't we, Nige?' she continues, resting her head territorially on his shoulder. *NIGE*? He hates to be called *Nige*.

'So,' I say after an awkward pause, 'what brings you to Vienna?'

'Tasha had a night-stop and I thought I'd come along for the ride.'

'What a coincidence,' I say wanly.

'Actually, it wasn't ... a coincidence,' he says, turning to 'Tasha' with a half-smile.

'I did a two-day Houston with Wendy last week. She told me you were performing here, and then when Tasha discovered she had a night-stop, I ... *we* thought we'd surprise you.'

'We fancy getting married in Vienna, don't we, babe?' says Natasha in her little-girl-lost voice. 'It's *so* romantic. I saw the most gorgeous ring in a jeweller's

284

near the opera house, but Nige says he can get something *much* bigger in Hong Kong.'

I take a huge gulp of champagne and avert my eyes, determined not to give anything away. Eight years we were together, *eight years* of tomorrows, of 'Be patient', 'Don't let's rush into this' — eight years of empty promises. How did she manage it? Where did I go wrong? And what became of whatshername ... the bimbo he left me for ... Maddie? Did she end up on the reject pile too? Did she have their baby?

'Tasha used to be in show business — kind of, didn't you, kitten?' says Nigel, swiftly shifting the subject.

'Really?' I say flatly.

'Yeah, a model — I was with *Models One*,' she purrs. 'I could have gone into acting as I know lots of directors an' stuff, but I like this job for now. Maybe when I'm older, like you, and we've had a couple of kids, I might do it for a while.'

My jaw drops. *When I'm older, like you*? The bloody nerve! Something inside me snaps. That's it. How dare they waltz in here and invade my lovely opening night? All at once I see Nigel in a different light and realise he no longer has a hold over me. I think I'm *finally* done with loving him. He may have movie-star looks, but to the new me, they now only accentuate his air of self-obsession.

'Emily, my darling, the cars are outside to take us to the restaurant,' calls Mags from the other end of the bar.

'Well, it was nice meeting you,' I say, switching on my haughty-yet-friendly voice. 'Hope the wedding and everything is all that you wish for.'

With that, I about turn, and with a theatrical swish of my pashmina, I head for the door.

Out on the street, I slip into one of the waiting

taxis and exhale deeply. Instead of being swallowed up by sorrow, I feel strangely relieved. Everything has suddenly fallen into place. When Nigel left me, I had to convince myself that it was all for the best. Now I *know* for sure. What an idiot I was. All those wasted nights spent waiting for him to call from LA, pretending to myself that he'd been delayed or couldn't get a signal. Were he to tell me now he'd made the biggest mistake of his life, I wouldn't be tempted to take him back — not for all the diamond rings in Hong Kong. I think I can safely say those dark days are well and truly over, and that chapter of my life is now shut away in the past. I may open it again from time to time, but only to reflect on those giddy days when I was someone else. I tut inwardly as I recall how secretly upset I was when Nigel bought me an exercise bike for my fortieth. He'd casually informed me that he was doing me a favour, as he'd noticed I was getting a bit flabby around the waist. I'd felt instantly ashamed and unattractive. Now I've actually grown fond of my flabby bits, crow's feet, and the wee freckles that have started to appear on the backs of my hands — because they are part of me. To misquote Whitney: 'Learning to love your cellulite. It is the greatest love of all.'

No more regret, bitterness or resentment. In fact, I feel grateful; thanks to Nigel's betrayal, I'm following a path I would never have had the courage to take. I like my life now, with all its risk and uncertainty. It's given me an inner freedom. What if he hadn't dumped me? How would my future have panned out then? Would we have married, had children, been happy? Life is so full of what-ifs; just like when Gwyneth Paltrow misses that tube train in *Sliding Doors.*

'Come on, you old poop!' calls Mags, emerging

through the stage door giggling, arm in arm with Oliver, his gait a little unsteady, trilby pulled down over his eyes.

She shoves him into the front seat, then plonks down next to me and says, 'Lord, Emily, who was that *divine* man in the bar?'

'Him? Oh, no one of any importance,' I say, flashing her a huge, self-satisfied grin as we are whisked off into the Vienna night. (And this time I truly believe it.)

My footsteps echo down the empty street under the pewter moon, my shadow flickering along the cracked walls of Rudolfstrasse. I raise the collar of my trench coat and am reminded of those old films noirs, where spies silently disappear through enormous, heavy wood doors of once-grandiose buildings. The only things missing from the picture are the dark glasses and headscarf (and spies in thriller movies do not get drunk and waste five minutes fumbling for their keys).

I stagger through the shadowy entrance, up the long, winding staircase to the third floor and tiptoe into the apartment, quietly closing the door behind me.

I kick off my shoes and the bed groans as I flop onto it. My mobile bleeps and the little screen lights up greeny-blue. One new message: *Tonight, I think about you many times, cara. Sogni d'oro. Francesco* ☺

I curl up and slip into a smiley, alcohol-induced coma, clasping my phone tightly to me.

I awake with a tongue reminiscent of Beryl's shag pile and a body like the Tin Man from Oz. I will never drink Sekt mixed with apricot Schnapps again. In fact, I will never drink alcohol again. EVER. I pull the quilt over my head and snuggle further down, but then the irresistible aroma of freshly ground coffee and home baking wafts under the door, luring me along the corridor and into the kitchen.

'*Guten morgen, liebling!*' Anna smiles, her face and apron daubed with flour.

'*Kaffee?*' she says, picking up the coffee pot, a knowing, maternal look in her great, grey eyes.

I clamber onto the kitchen stool, wrap my hands around the warm, comforting mug and watch in fascination as she rolls and stretches dough over the expanse of her kitchen table.

'My *Mutti* used to say a good *Apfelstrudel* pastry should be so thin that you can read a newspaper through it,' she says, wiping her hands and producing a letter from the cluttered dresser.

I instantly recognise the yellow, Florentine envelope and the spidery handwriting. Francesco is a man of contradiction; someone who has his finger on the pulse of politics, literature, world music, films, fashion and sport, yet still writes letters and refuses to be lured by social media or fast food. Texting is as far as he's prepared to venture into the push-of-a-button, click-of-a-mouse, ping-of-a-microwave, selfie world. I think of him as my Mediterranean Mr Darcy — minus the disagreeableness.

Anna's Apfelstrudel recipe:
Pastry:
300 grams bread flour
pinch of salt
2 eggs
30ml vegetable oil
200ml tepid water
Filling:
buttered breadcrumbs

cinnamon
150 grams raisins
1 kg baking apples: cored, peeled and cut into pieces
lemon juice
shot of rum
Knead flour, salt, oil and water into medium-firm dough. Divide into three small loaves, brush each loaf with melted butter and allow to sit for 1 hour.
Peel, core and slice apples. Mix in granulated sugar, raisins, grated lemon peel, lemon juice, rum and cinnamon.
Roll the dough loaves with a rolling pin, then stretch rolled dough on a strudel sheet with the backs of your hands.
Coat ⅔ of the dough sheet with buttered breadcrumbs, spread apple filling over remaining third of the dough.
Tear off edges, shape strudel into roll by lifting strudel sheet.
Place strudel on a buttered baking sheet and bake at 190 degrees for 60-90 minutes until golden brown.
Tip: After baking, immediately brush with hot butter. Delicious with custard or vanilla ice cream – or why not both?

♥

'What are you doing Sunday evening?' asks Mags one night in the dressing room.

'Hmm, let me see now ... nothing,' I reply, plucking a *white* hair from my left eyebrow. 'Gotcha!'

'Good, because we, my darling, are going to the opera.'

'Opera? Blimey, isn't it awfully expensive?'

'I don't consider four euros expensive, do you?'

'Four euros! You're kidding me.'

'You don't have dodgy knees, do you?'

'What?'

'Varicose veins?'

'Nope.'

'Suffer from vertigo?'

'No. Why?'

'Good. Then you won't mind standing up in the gods for three hours.'

'*Three hours*?'

'That's nothing. Olly and I saw *Tristan and Isolde* last Sunday. Four hours thirty. But it's worth it, believe me. Oh, and dress up. Everyone in Vienna dresses up for the opera — and bring a scarf to mark your place on the lean rail.'

'What, like reserving your sunbed with a beach towel?' I say, screwing up my nose.

'Now, Emily, darling, don't be a snob. And wear comfy shoes.'

Sunday: waiting for Mags

I am having yet another pinch-me moment: I am standing before the snow-sprinkled opera house, devouring a *Wienerwurst* (the Rolls Royce of hotdogs), two tickets for *Tosca* in my pocket. Life doesn't get much better than this.

As I wipe the ketchup from around my mouth, a mature, well-dressed couple scurry past, hand in hand, laughing. Her scarf falls to the ground. He runs back, picks it up, places it around her neck and kisses her lightly on the forehead. I sense the tenderness of this moment and feel a spike of envy. Let me re-phrase the above statement: life would be perfect if Francesco were here. I don't mean I miss him in a needy, hurting way, because I'm different to the woman I was before: the one who had to be in a relationship at any price in order to feel whole. No, the reason I think about him so much has nothing to do with loneliness or sex (although I wouldn't say no); it has more to do with the fact that I miss his friendship, and the fact that he actually *enhances* my life.

Looking back, I realise that since I was sixteen, I've always had a boyfriend in tow. These relationships would usually end in dramatic circumstances, but then it would only be a matter of weeks until I found myself swallowed up by the next one. I now know it takes time to find a quality relationship with someone you are *truly* compatible with, and while we all have to compromise, moulding yourself into what your partner wants you to be is not the right way. No, I hardly dare admit it, but at last, here's a man who asks nothing of me — except perhaps to work harder at my Italian, but then only because *I want* to learn. How I love to wrap my tongue around its rich, beautiful, passionate sounds; they make me feel alive, sensual and joyous. But hand on heart, my efforts have nothing to do with some underlying desire to make Francesco like me more.

That said, I must be honest here and admit I do sometimes wonder if he thinks of me merely as his '*piccola studenta*' (becoming less *piccola* by the day, incidentally). At the airport, when he took my hands and looked deep into my eyes, there was a sense of tenderness, of intimacy; or did I misread the signs? Is my imagination up to its old tricks again? Did he mean what he said about visiting one weekend? Whilst I don't *need* Francesco as some sort of passport to happiness, I can't think of anyone better to share those special, pinch-me moments with. It's as simple as that.

From my corner vantage point, high up in the gallery, like a marksman, but armed with a pair of opera glasses, I scan the red, gold and ivory horseshoe-shaped auditorium.

Two fifty-something, classy ladies, dripping with expensive jewellery are chatting in the stalls aisle. From their body language, I imagine the English translation of their exchange to go something like this:

1st LADY: Mwah, mwah, daahling. How super to see you.

2nd LADY: Likewise. You look fabulous. Designer?

1st LADY: Naturally.

SWOONSOMELY HANDSOME YOUNG MAN APPROACHES 1st LADY.

YOUNG MAN: There you are, sweetheart. (KISSES HER) We'd better take our seats. Please excuse us.

2nd LADY: Of course. (THROUGH GRITTED TEETH) Bitch.

PAN TO ORCHESTRA PIT ...

BASSOONIST: I told him, how would you like it, to be stuck under the stage every night behind the tuba?

VIOLINIST: Honestly, mate, it's no better where I'm sitting. You get the full force of the sopranos from the front.

SWING TO A BOX ...

GRUMPY MAN: Don't start. I didn't bloody well want to come in the first place. You know how I hate the opera.

PO-FACED WOMAN: Oh really? That's funny. Because a little bird told me you were here last week with your PA — and you looked as if you were having a whale of a time ...

Mags taps my arm lightly with the programme, folded back at the synopsis page. I pop on my glasses, but only get as far as *Rome. 1800. Inside the church of Saint Andrea della Valle ...* before we are plunged into darkness. The chit-chat fades as the conductor appears in the spotlight, bowing to thunderous

292

applause. He turns to face his orchestra, nods and raises his arms. The string section hold their bows at the ready, poised, waiting for the baton to be lowered, like a starting pistol at the beginning of a race.

All at once the opening bars of the overture are released into the air, and the heavy, red velvet curtains swish open.

Because we are so far away from the action, and because my Italian is not yet up to comprehending the convoluted plots of opera (people in opera never do day-to-day things, like ask for directions or buy stamps, do they?), I haven't a clue what's going on most of the time. I suspect the lady with the high voice and big chest must be Tosca. She and Mario, her artist boyfriend, seem to have a bit of an up and down relationship, if the constant appeasing (him) and pushing away (her) is anything to go by. Her diva-like strutting and petulant tossing of her black, pre-Raphaelite hair, and the way she keeps jabbing her finger at his painting of a beautiful blonde woman, tells me she's the jealous type (it's only a painting, love), but then again, maybe Mario has a wandering eye, in which case, I'm totally on her side.

When the action takes place upstage and our view is completely obscured, I close my eyes and allow the music to swim through me; otherwise my poor sightlines are more than compensated by the very nice rear view of the conductor, who though not tall, is rather cute in that Al Pacino-esque way, with his black floppy hair, which flicks back and forth as his whole body communicates the subtle moods of the music to his players.

By the time the first interval arrives, I am transfixed, totally lost in the story (my version of the story at any rate), oblivious to the discomfort of leaning against a railing for over an hour. The safety curtain descends and the lights come up.

'I have a little treat for us,' whispers Mags, nudging me. 'Ta daa!' She produces two quarter-bottles of Sekt and two plastic champagne flutes from her bag and proceeds to pop them open and pour while I keep a watch out for the hawk-eyed ushers.

Armed with drinks and a dose of schoolgirl daring, we descend the winding stairs and join the rich and the beautiful in the *Schwind* Foyer. Here, it is the Viennese custom for the audience to promenade among the paintings and busts of famous composers, whilst unashamedly eyeing one another up and down, checking out who's wearing what and who's with whom. This all sounds horribly pretentious, but believe me, if you're there, in the midst of it, you can't help but be mesmerised by the sheer elegance, the opulence, the self-assuredness, the *Devil-Wears-Prada*-ishness of it all; glamorous, expensive-smelling ladies in designer dresses with perfect tresses and heels as high as skyscrapers, distinguished, well-bred gentlemen with slicked-back hair, tailored jackets draped squarely across their shoulders, clutching Gucci man bags.

Do any of them suspect that there are a couple of impostors in their midst, I wonder? I half expect the Posh Police to burst through the doors, prise my plastic glass of supermarket champagne out of my hand, drag me by the collar of my flea-market dress and throw me out onto the street, where I belong.

'So, you were here last Sunday?' I say to Mags, tearing my gaze away from a striking, Amazonian woman with telescopic legs, wearing a slinky LBD, leopard print turban and matching shoes.

She falls quiet for a moment. 'Olly adores the opera, like me, and I can't tell you how lovely it is to

294

be able to share things with someone again.' Lowering her eyes, she continues, 'You must think I'm awful.'

'Why?'

'Because I'm married, and am enjoying the company of another man, while my poor Easton has nothing more to look forward to than his next meal and *Judge Judy*.'

'Mags, your friendship with Oliver is nothing to be ashamed of,' I say, squeezing her hand and looking her square in the eye.

'I should be at home, taking care of my husband,' she says, her voice breaking as she looks away, pulling an embroidered hankie from her sleeve.

'You've done the best you can, but you're entitled to a life too,' I say soothingly. 'And from what you've told me, it sounds like Easton needs professional care now, which you're not qualified to give him.'

'All the same ...' The three bells ring, summoning us back to our seats. 'Come on,' she says, her taut expression relaxing. 'I bet you five euros Tosca snuffs it in the end.'

'I'm here for you if you need someone to talk to,' I say, gently touching her arm. 'I can be a good listener, as well as a good talker, you know.'

'Bless you, my darling girl. I may well take you up on your offer sometime.'

We're not quite sure what happens to Tosca, as we're too high up to see, but later, over a Maria Theresia (orange liqueur coffee), we study the programme in detail and learn that she commits suicide by throwing herself from a parapet, so Mags wins the bet.

Do women in opera ever survive?

* * *

I am woken early next morning by the persistent ringing of my mobile.

'Hello' I grunt, holding it to my crumpled face.

'Morning, poppet!' trills Mum. 'Couldn't wait to tell you — your father and I have just booked a winter Imperial cities tour to Prague, Budapest — *and* Vienna!'

'Really?' I say, propping myself up and rubbing my sleep-filled eyes. 'Brill! So you can see the play after all.'

'Ah,' she falters. 'I'm afraid we only have one night in Vienna. We leave for Prague by coach early the next day, and we're supposed to go to a Vienna Boys' Choir concert that evening — I've always wanted to see them, and it's all included — but if there's a performance of your play on Saturday afternoon, we could probably squeeze it all in, couldn't we?'

'Huh! So, The Vienna Boys' Choir takes precedence over me and my play, eh? How very dare they?' I reply, feigning offence. My former self would have been genuinely miffed by this, but the new me just thinks, that's okay. No problem. I don't want a fight. What's the point? I've been down this road too many times before. It accomplishes nothing and only leaves me feeling wretched. Mum doesn't mean to be blunt. She's just Mrs Say-It-Like-It-Is, whereas Dad is more Mr Keep-The-Peace, and Mum can't put a foot wrong where he's concerned. (Never mind trying to teach me how to knit, why on earth didn't she give me lessons in how to wrap men around my little finger?)

Still, you can't change people — particularly those hurtling towards their eighth decade. Age, or maybe my new, more frugal life is forcing me to reassess situations and my reaction to them. I think, *hope* I am becoming more tolerant, less of a control freak. I wish I had a brother, though — someone to back me up, to exchange family worries and frustrations with, to share sibling banter, childhood memories — and possibly his single friends.

'What do you say, poppet?'

'Hmm?'

'Is there a matinée on Saturday?'

'Yes. Fine,' I say brightly. 'I'll arrange two tickets, and maybe we can have an early supper afterwards. I'd like you to meet ...'

'Darling, don't tell me you've met a new man? Not an actor, is he?'

'... Mags and Oliver. They play my mum and dad.'

'Oh. I see,' she says her voice dropping. Quickly drawing a deep breath, she yammers, 'Have a guess who rang me the other day? Dorothy Devine! Greg's *still* unmarried, you know.' I pull the patchwork quilt over my head and count to ten, fighting my old instinct to snap back. She ploughs on.

'Dorothy says he's doing very well at the bank, got a lovely semi-detached house *and* a brand new company car. He hasn't dated a girl since ... well really, Dorothy and I could knock your two silly heads together ...'

Poor Mum. With Nigel now definitely out of the picture, in her mind the only way of rescuing me from pending spinsterdom or lesbianism is to try and reignite an old flame, which was extinguished for very good reason, which neither Mum nor Mrs Devine can ever be party to. I have been sworn to secrecy.

I remember the night Greg and I split up — Valentine's Day, 1999 in Pizza Express.

When he said he had 'something important' to tell me, I thought, oh my God, he's going to get down on bended knee right here, in front of everyone. How embarrassing, for you see, I'd wanted to break up with him for ages, but had allowed the situation to drift. Why? Because back then I was afraid — afraid of hurting him, afraid of being alone, afraid of change. I'd selfishly been waiting until *I* felt ready, and now I was going to be forced to confront my fears in front of a restaurant crammed full of love-sick diners.

Greg tearfully took my hand and mumbled something about having met someone at the bank — and his name was Troy. He'd tried to fight his feelings, but it was of no use. He couldn't bear this double life any longer. I almost choked on my Margherita, though looking back, should I have guessed — given his penchant for scented candles and Barbra Streisand?

Whilst a part of me was secretly relieved, liberated, a bit of me thought, *I'm* supposed to be the one doing the dumping, not him, and more to the point, I've heard of someone driving their partner to drink, but — homosexuality? If I'm totally honest, it was a crushing blow to my female pride.

'Oh, Mum. I'm sorry, I know you don't want to hear this,' I say, interrupting her mid-flow, 'but I've decided to steer well clear of men for a while.'

'I see,' she says, a surge of unspoken despair mixed with agitation crackling through the airwaves.

I'm sorely tempted to tell her about Francesco, to fill the sudden cheerless silence, to offer her a morsel of hope that her middle-aged daughter is not going to end up an old maid with whiskers and a cat. But I stop myself in time because I know from experience that I'll be bombarded with questions like, 'Could *he* be THE ONE?'

She'll get her hopes up, only to have them dashed — again. In any case, my superstitious side warns me that telling her will jinx the relationship.

Since Nigel left and I've set out on this crazy

journey, a part of me has felt selfish and guilty for the anguish I cause my ageing parents. Like Chelsea, I long to prove something to them, and now here's my big chance to demonstrate that their life-long investment has matured at last: the private school, the extra maths tuition to get me through my GCSE (failed), the piano lessons (abandoned), the summer course at etiquette academy to turn me from teenage ladette with attitude to lady (expelled) weren't all a complete waste of time and money.

I may not have turned out to be the high-flying United Nations interpreter, Supermum or Kirstie-Allsop homemaker they wanted me to be, but surely success is not necessarily a financial thing? I'm doing what makes me happy *and* getting paid for it. As a parent, surely you can't wish more for your child?

With Norman about to turn eighty and showing early signs of memory loss, the play is a reminder of my real parents' mortality and the significance of each passing day.

'They'll be here now, Mags. In their seats,' I say, glancing at my watch and continuing to pace up and down. 'Row C. I'm scared if I look down and catch their eye, I might forget my lines. In fact, a part of me wishes they weren't coming ...'

'You're going to wear out what's left of this tatty carpet,' says Mags in an unusually firm tone. 'If you carry on like this, you *will* mess it up. Forget they're there. The auditorium is the fourth wall, remember? If you're thinking about your parents sitting feet away from you, then you're not playing it for real. Chelsea will become a caricature — a phoney. I've watched you grow into her these last few weeks, and I will not allow you to lose sight of her. If your parents don't like the life you've chosen, then that's up to them. My son wasn't happy about me coming here, leaving his father behind in the care home. I visit my guilt every day, not only off stage, but on stage too.' (There's a particular scene before I come on, where Ethel sends Norman strawberry picking, but he returns early because he gets disoriented. The emotional undercurrent of fear, frustration and helplessness between them rips your heart.) 'We can use our real emotions to bring a character to life, but whatever happens, we mustn't let those emotions get out of control and overwhelm us. We get one shot at this, Emily,' she says, clasping my shoulders. 'As the old saying goes, "life is not a dress rehearsal".'

I channel all my pent-up emotion into that afternoon's performance, and am aware of a subtle shift, in that Chelsea and I connect on an even deeper level than before. Through her I am forced to confront those negative feelings of inadequacy and guilt that I still haven't gotten my life together. The scene where Ethel tells me to grow up, forget the past and move on has an added frisson of realism today, the like of which I haven't experienced before. Chelsea is teaching me about myself. All that stuff at drama school, about Stanislavsky and 'being a role' suddenly makes real sense.

'Visitors at stage door for Fraulein Forsyth,' Olaf's voice announces over the intercom. I bound down the stairs, leaping off the last three steps into Dad's arms, just as I did when I was a child.

'What can I say, love?' he says, squeezing me tight. 'We couldn't believe that was our wee girl up there, could we, Brenda?'

I turn to face Mum. Is that approval I see in her eyes — pride even?

'I don't know what to say ... I ...' she says, quickly dabbing her eyes.

'Now, that's a first,' says Dad.

'That's enough, Brian!' she says, blowing her nose then checking her appearance in the full-length mirror.

Mags and Oliver join us for a traditional supper of *Wienerschnitzel, Erdapfelsalat* (boiled potatoes and red onion marinated in oil, salt and pepper), and a local wine, from the proprietor's own vineyard in Grinzing, on the outskirts of Vienna.

This being a special occasion, I break my pre-show, zero-alcohol rule. (This regulation came into force following the Rep Season from Hell. I still have nightmares about Margo's gin-fuelled, unpredictable performances and probably will for many years to come.)

'Amazing, isn't it?' says Mum later, as their taxi pulls up outside the stage door. 'Oliver and Mags — still treading the boards at their age. And they have no intention of retiring.'

'Precisely,' I say. 'And neither do I. To find what you love to do and be paid for doing it — well, you can't get luckier than that, can you?'

'It's all very well doing what you love, but it doesn't always pay the bills,' says Mum pointedly.

I take a deep breath. 'Let's put it his way — if someone had told you when you were young, *we know how much you love nursing, but sorry, we can't possibly allow you to do it.* How would that have made you feel?'

'That's ... that's different,' says Mum.

'How different?'

'Well, for starters, I was in my twenties. You're ...'

'... middle-aged, I know. But I don't have any

responsibilities, so why not? Why shouldn't I have a shot at this before it's too late?'

'I just want you to be like other women your age ...'

'Well, I *don't,* so *haud your wheesht, mither,*' I say in my best Scots, covering her mouth with my hand, trying to lighten the mood. 'Away you go, or you'll be late for the concert.'

'Bye, smiler,' says Dad, pressing his icy cold lips to my forehead. 'I'm so proud of my wee girl.' Lowering his voice he continues, 'And though she may not say as much, your mother is too.'

'Really?' I ask, that longing for approval never far away. 'You're not just saying that to make me feel good?'

'You should have heard her during the interval, telling anyone who'd listen that that was her daughter up there. Couldn't bloody well shut her up.'

Wien Westbahnhof (Vienna West Station) — the following week

'Do not turn around,' a stern, heavily accented Eastern European warns me. 'And listen carefully to your instructions. You will be met by Smollensky under the clock at Passau station. The code word is "loon".'

'Oliver, you *Schwein*! You almost had me going then,' I say, spinning on my heels and batting him playfully with my bag.

'The Salzburg train leaves from platform six, I believe,' he says, removing his shades and consulting Gerhard's list of directions. 'We change at somewhere called ... Attnang Pucheim for Bad Aussee.'

'Isn't this exciting?' says Mags, appearing at my side with three delicious-smelling coffees. 'So sweet of Gerhard to invite us.'

Austria has more saints than you can shake a ski

302

pole at, and thanks to one of them, whose name I can't now remember, Monday is a public holiday, so Gerhard has invited us to his country house in Styria. (Alan is joining a group of his celeb friends in Kitzbűhel for a couple of days on the piste and Jason is meeting his future in-laws.)

We climb aboard (and I mean *climb.* Tight jeans a definite no-no when getting on and off Austrian trains). The whistle blows and we are on our way.

As we gather speed, the cityscape soon gives way to country hamlets, snow-laden pine trees, onion-domed churches, Babybel cows and frozen lakes. We thunder through inky-black, craggy tunnels and on, up into the mountains.

It's early evening and dark by the time the train pulls into Bad Aussee station. The squeal of brakes, the slamming of doors, footsteps crunching on tightly packed snow, the dimly lit, deserted station, the guard in peaked cap and greatcoat, all evoke a mood of winter romance. I am transported back to Zhivagoville once more. After a long absence, Yuri and I are to be reunited at last ... *Lara, my love! HE CALLS, HIS VOICE FULL OF LONGING. Yuri! I TUMBLE INTO HIS ARMS, MY WARM TEARS MELTING THE ICICLES IN HIS MOUSTACHE AS THE HAUNTING NOTES OF 'LARA'S THEME' ARE PLUCKED OUT ON THE BALALAIKA ...*

'Fritz! *Nein! Komm' her!*'

I am rudely awoken from my dreamy Russian fantasy by a crazed terrier in a tartan coat, which has launched itself at me from the darkness and is becoming a tad too friendly with my leg.

'Aaw, he's so cute,' I say, politely patting Fritz's head, but secretly wishing I could shake him off and send him spinning into the stratosphere.

'He must like you,' says Gerhard, sliding down the hood of his enormous parka and grabbing the terrier firmly by the collar. '*Willkommen* to Bad Aussee!'

Fritz and bags safely loaded behind the luggage grille, we set off in Gerhard's Jeep Cherokee for Pension Dachstein, named after the Dachstein Glacier, which towers over the little village, like an ever watchful bodyguard.

Gerhard's house is charmingly rustic: logs piled up outside, hand-painted, alpine furniture, huge, exposed beams and a green-glazed tiled stove. The fire crackles and the air is filled with the smell of damp oak, mixed with cinnamon.

We squash around the beautifully laid table. Dried herbs hang from the ceiling and beeswax candles flicker on the windowsill.

Dinner is traditional and home-cooked. We discover during the evening that Gerhard's skills are not only confined to directing and cooking: as well as drama, he tells us he studied botany at university and is in the process of patenting his herbal spa products made from alpine plant extracts. He gives each of us samples of his latest creation: bath salts made from locally mined salt and crushed pine needles. 'You are ... how does one say? My guinea pigs, *ja?*'

'If I turn up tomorrow looking like Johnny Depp, you'll know you're onto a winner,' says Oliver with a broad smile. But that's not all. This is the best bit: Gerhard is also one of Austria's leading Elvis impersonators. (I'd always thought there was something of the fifties rock 'n' roll about him.) After a few Schnapps, we persuade him to fetch his guitar (disappointingly, he refuses to don the white suit and the black, high quiff wig). We sing along to The King's hits in a mixture of German and English, and Fritz demonstrates that as well as a strong sex drive, he

304

possesses a musical ear and a sense of rhythm as he howls and prances on his back legs. But when we start singing and dancing to 'Hound Dog,' he gets overexcited again and is banished to his basket in the utility room.

The sun is coming up over the Dachstein by the time our party is over and, arm in arm, we steer one another across the road to our Pension.

My room is pleasantly warm, the embroidered sheets pristine, the mattress firm but not hard, comfortable but not squishy, and the traditional loden wool blanket as warm as a sheep (not that I've ever cuddled a sheep). I close my eyes and wait for sleep to arrive ...

Now, one of the annoying things about being the wrong side of forty is the digestion issue. I used to be able to eat/drink like a Stone Age woman without a second thought. Back then I believed Gaviscon was for windy grannies. Now it's as essential a part of my travel kit as deodorant. Only it was discovered in my hand luggage and confiscated by airport security.

Pulling on my slipper socks and Arran sweater, I stagger out onto the balcony, hand clutching my stomach. I inhale deeply, filling my lungs with freezing alpine air.

I close my eyes and imagine Francesco is beside me. I can almost smell his subtly sensuous aftershave, feel his breath in my ear, his stubble on my cheek. Without warning, a builder's burp is expelled into the sylvan silence, ricocheting across the glassy lake. I slap my hand over my mouth, looking around in shame. In that moment I am aware of muffled voices below. Eek. Did they hear?

Realising with a start that it's Oliver and Mags, I retreat into the shadows. I lie down in the half-light, like a starfish and gaze up at the painted ceiling, the dying flames from the bedroom fire throwing a pale, intermittent light onto the cows and alpine flowers, making them look as if they're dancing ... or is that the Schnapps?

I've always envied those who find their soul mate and wonder sometimes if I'll ever find mine. But I'm realising that even for those lucky ones, love can be complicated, because there's no guarantee of a Happy Ever After, is there? Forty-six years ago, Mags and Easton vowed to stay together in sickness and in health. But what if the unimaginable happens? It's one thing falling out of love and separating; you can shout and scream at an unfaithful partner, tell yourself that it's all for the best, that they weren't worthy of you anyway, but what if they get sick and can't remember who you are? You still love them, for sure, but they're no longer the same person, and the relationship you once had has gone, never to return. You can grieve for someone who's dead, but for someone who's still alive? Do you put your own life on hold, waiting for the inevitable to happen, comforted only by memories, too riven with guilt to move forward? Is it better to have loved and pay for the happiness further down the line, or is it better never to have loved at all and be spared a heart-crushing situation like theirs?

CHAPTER FIFTEEN
Il Postino

THE LATE AUTUMN SUN is slanting low through the pine trees, throwing orange light across the glassy Altaussee lake and onto the pale grey mountains. Gerhard signals for us to follow him up a twisty path to his brother's *Lokal* (bar) for some Glühwein to warm ourselves up.

'I'll join you in a minute,' I cry. 'I just want to stay here a bit longer before the light goes.' Gazing out across to the Totes Gebirge mountain range, I lift my face to the sky, drawing in the crystal clear air.

I feel an overwhelming Maria-von-Trapp moment coming on. Jamming my hands deep into my pockets I spin on the spot and am reminded of the last time I felt like this: atop Crinkle Crags with Duncan.

I feel the rough, sharp edges of a small stone and remember placing it there all those months ago, as a reminder of that magical time. I toy with it, then send it skipping across the lake.

I forgive you, Duncan, for leading me a merry jig. I pick up another pebble and throw it as far as I can across the water. This one's for you, Greg. It's okay that you dumped me for a man, and I hope you are happy now. And Mum, I know you are quick to remind me of my rapidly disappearing prime and have, on occasion, urged me to seek medical help to cure me of my 'delusional thoughts', but I understand you only want the best for me. And with this one I thee absolve, Nigel. I truly believe what you did to me was sent as a major lesson in life.

And finally, Emily, you too are acquitted of the crimes of which you have been guilty:

1. Messing up ~~sometimes~~ a lot.
2. Inability to sustain a relationship/proper career.
3. Failure to provide your parents with grandchildren and peace of mind.
4. Allowing your heart to make major decisions, instead of your head.
5. Displaying wilful behaviour, not befitting a normal, respectable, middle-aged woman.

And what about Francesco? How long will it be until I'm burning my Italian books, sobbing into my spaghetti, unable to listen to Zucchero and Puccini, swearing never to trust Italian men again?

No, this is how the old Emily would react. Here, in this spiritual place, the new Emily makes herself a solemn vow: *IF* he comes to visit, she will take things SLOWLY this time. She will not be a pushover. In the words of her relationship guru, *'Le mystère est une bonne chose.'* And if it all ends up as an Italian melodrama, she will put it down to experience and move on without a backward glance ...

I didn't think he'd actually do it — you know, book — travel eight hundred miles to see me. Why? When I got back to Vienna to find Francesco's postcard telling me of his pending visit, it immediately sent my mind in a spin.

Only last month hadn't I practically pined for him outside the opera house? Two nights ago, on the balcony, did I not smell his aftershave, feel his breath on my ear. So why aren't I yodelling from the mountain tops? What's wrong? I'M AFRAID. You see, the love affair with Francesco that exists in my head is safe. I write the plot; no complications, no conflict, a happy ending. But now his actual coming here shifts everything to a whole new plane. Will real life be as good as the fantasy?

Why couldn't I just accept our meeting for what it probably is? A brief encounter, a mild flirtation, a good laugh.

It's been two months since we last met, besides which, we haven't ever spent longer than three or four hours at a time in one another's company — and then there are always other people around (apart from our Italian lessons, when our minds are focused on verbs and vocabulary). Away from the restaurant and the coffee shop, will we have the same rapport? Will we run out of things to say? If so, three days will seem an interminably long time. I'm starting to realise how very little I know about him.

What would Geneviève do in this situation? What's happening to me? I'm falling apart at the seams.

'Don't you dare put him off,' says Wendy later that evening. 'Give the poor guy a chance.'

'But I haven't many weekends left here,' I remark, mobile clasped between my ear and shoulder as I blend eye shadow into my socket creases. 'And we haven't sorted out a date for *your* visit yet.'

'Don't make excuses,' comes the curt reply. 'We can visit Vienna any time with our staff tickets.

Besides, Céline gets tired easily these days, and I'm not sure a city break is the best thing in her condition.'

'And you?'

'Liam is short of volunteers at the riding school and I've kind of promised I'll support him on hacks whenever I'm free.'

'Liam's name has been cropping up a lot recently,' I say, ribbing her.

'I told you — he's the new stables manager,' she says evasively.

'And there's a smile in your voice whenever you mention him.'

Ignoring this last comment, she continues, 'Those kids so look forward ...'

'Yeah, yeah, yeah ...'

Joking apart, there's no doubt in my mind that Wendy's voluntary work at the riding school is a godsend. The reason? Because those horses, those disadvantaged children are helping *her* to heal. Catching a frisky pony in an open field or keeping a disabled child safe and happy requires the utmost concentration and doesn't allow your mind to stray elsewhere. Equine therapy, I believe it's called. All I'm suggesting is, where's the harm in her enjoying a little sexual therapy too?

'Don't change the subject,' continues Wendy after a pause. 'What's the matter with you, darling? Why are you dithering? You tell him yes right away, d'you hear me?'

'But ...'

'Ladies and gentlemen of the *On Golden Pond* Company, this is your Act One beginners' call. Act One beginners to the stage, please.'

'Wendy, you still there?' The phone clicks. 'Wendy?'

BA 0696 LONDON HEATHROW GELANDET

As I wait for Francesco to appear through the sliding doors of the arrivals hall, darts of doubt and insecurity stab at my brain. What will we talk about? Will Emily the actress be the same to him as Emily the waitress? Does he like the theatre? Will he find the play tedious? They're showing *La Bohème* at the opera house on Sunday, and I thought we could get a couple of tickets, but for all I know, maybe he hates the opera. Why didn't I book him a hotel? My idea that he'd enjoy a bit of Austrian hospitality courtesy of Anna's sister, Cristina, now seems a stupid idea. He's probably accustomed to staying in fancy hotels, and the last thing he wants to do is lodge with an old Austrian woman, who speaks very little English, let alone Italian.

No point fretting, because it's way too late; he is now standing before me, looking effortlessly stylish in faded leather aviator jacket, white shirt and cords, an expensive holdall bag swinging from his shoulder.

'*Ciao!*' He smiles his magical smile and kisses me on both cheeks.

'*Ciao!*' I smile nervously, dipping my head. We make our way down to the subway in silence. Oh dear, perhaps this really is a mistake.

'How was your journey?' I ask, attempting to fill the gap as the train clatters and jostles along the track.

'*Bene,*' he replies, shrugging his shoulders.

Oh God, next thing we'll be discussing the weather.

As we pull into Enkplatz, Francesco nudges my foot with his and points to a poster advertising the play. Our eyes meet. He traces his thumb back and forth across my hand, and the silence between us no longer feels awkward.

My performance that evening is not my best, as I find it hard to concentrate. In between my lines, when I'm normally listening to what the other characters are saying, I'm thinking about Francesco and wondering if he found his way to the theatre, did he pick up his ticket, and where should we eat afterwards? I am playing with fire. It therefore comes as no surprise that I miss one of my cues; serves me jolly well right. Oliver, ever the consummate performer, comes to the rescue, jumping in with his next line.

As soon as the curtain comes down for the interval, shamefacedly I flee the stage to the dressing room, slam the door shut and burst into tears.

Mags enters quietly, puts a mug of tea down in front of me and stroking my hair says soothingly, 'Listen, sweetheart, it happens to us all, and tonight, well tonight it was your turn. Not one member of that audience will have noticed you missed a line, believe me.'

'I wasn't concentrating. I was being totally unprofessional, and I've let everyone down,' I bleat through gasping sobs.

'Nonsense. Look, love, we all have our off nights,' she says putting a motherly arm around me. 'We're not superhuman. And promise me one thing: if Francesco, or anyone for that matter, congratulates you on your performance, you smile sweetly and simply say thank you, do you hear me?' she says firmly. 'Don't you *dare* draw attention to the fact you missed a line, or Mama Mags will be very cross with you, do you understand? Now dry your eyes and drink your tea before it goes cold,' she says, snatching a tissue from the box on the table.

As the curtain goes up on Act Two, I can feel the adrenaline pumping round my body. Five pages of dialogue until my next entrance. Can I put my silly goof-up behind me, or will I freeze and ruin it for everyone? Is this what they call stage fright?

Our doubts are traitors and make us lose ... Our doubts are traitors and make us lose ... rings Portia's voice in my head.

Despite my initial tentativeness, it goes without a hitch, and I am the complex Chelsea once more, at odds with her father and finally reconciled. The pent-up tears of earlier come in very handy during my emotional scene with Ethel, and then finally with Norman.

'*Bravissimo!*' enthuses Francesco, as I emerge from the stage door. 'It was *fantastico!*'

I give a modest smile and murmur, '*Grazie*'. The others file past, calling out their good nights. Mags turns and darts me a knowing wink.

Francesco takes my hand as we make our way along the Graben (one of the many posh, pedestrianised shopping areas), past the fountain and illuminated statue of Saint Leopold, up the alleyway, and through the stained glass doors of Annerls Beisl.

The waiter nods in recognition and guides us through the snugly arranged tables to a discreet, low-lit booth. As soon as we sit down, he brings over two glasses of complimentary champagne, lights a candle and hands out menus.

A pianist plays quietly unnoticed in the corner.

'*Allora, la mia cara attrice, come sta?*' asks Francesco, clinking glasses.

'*Bene,*' I reply. He looks at me expectantly. '*Bene, grazie.*' I swallow hard, shuffling in my seat. 'Erm, Vienna *è meravigliosa ... Che città fantastica!*'

'*E*-milee?' he says, with a seductively cocked eyebrow.

'*Che cosa?*' I say innocently from behind the menu, cheeks flushing.

'*E*-milee?'

'Okay, okay,' I say, raising my hands in submission. 'I haven't got past chapter three of *Italia Oggi*. Sorry, but come on, Italian and German are worlds apart. I mean, the other day, when I found myself ordering *G-nocchi* instead of *Knödel*, I realised my poor wee brain can't cope with learning two languages at the same time.'

'*Scusi?*' says Francesco, with his famous, whataya-talking-about-hand gesture.

'*G-nocchi*. You know, dumplings. *Knödel*, in German.'

'Aah!' he says, teasing me with a small smile. 'You mean *"gnocchi"*! My *cara imbecille*, the "g" is silent.' Leaning forward, he removes my glasses and plants a kiss on my nose. My heart gives a little jolt.

In between sips of bubbly and mouthfuls of dumpling, I tell him about Anna, Mags, Oliver, the play, the opera, the trip to the country. Francesco orders more wine, we eat, I talk some more, and because I'm a little bit squiffy, I divulge the Nigel saga (not, you'll be relieved to hear, in a bitter, all-men-are-bastards rant, but rather in a things-happen-for-the-best way). All the while he listens intently, shakes his head and smiles in all the right places.

'Hey, enough about me, Francesco,' I say, a voice in my head warning me my chattiness is verging on self-obsessed gabble. 'Tell me about the restaurant, Luigi, Nonna Maria ... I want to know everything.'

'Zio Luigi and Nonna Maria are well. They send *auguri* (good wishes). Every Friday and Saturday we now have *Serata di Opera* — how you say? — opera cabaret. Rosalba and Lucio, they perform opera, and the restaurant is so busy you must make a

314

reservation at least two weeks before. *Allora*, Zio Luigi is a *ver-ry* happy man.'

'And Sergio?' I ask as casually as I can.

'*Bene,*' he says, nodding. 'He will return to work very soon.'

'Aah,' I say, nervous of the answer to my next question. 'And what will you do then?'

'I will go back to my family in Napoli and continue to run our restaurant.'

'I see.'

Family? Does he mean parents, or wife and children? I don't want to press him, but my instinct is telling me to stop pussyfooting around, and before I know it, the following words escape from my mouth, 'I was wondering ... ' I venture, swallowing hard. 'In Naples, Torre ...?'

'Annunziata. Torre Annunziata,' he says, every syllable filled with warmth, pride — and just a hint of homesickness.

'Right. In Torre Annunziata, do you live in a house or ...'

'An apartment, right on the edge of the sea. We can see Capri from the balcony.'

We? Who's '*we*'? enquires my suspicious mind.

'That must be lovely ... and in this apartment, does anyone else ...?'

'*Mit* the compliments of the house,' says the waiter, delivering two Maria Theresien liqueur coffees. Francesco turns, raises his glass in thanks to the barman, then says, 'Look, *cara,* is your mother and father, over there.'

I lean forward, turn forty-five degrees, and sure enough, deep in conversation, oblivious to the world around them, are Oliver and Mags, the light from the candles lighting their faces. He takes a neatly pressed hankie from the top pocket of his jacket and gently

315

dabs her eyes. I bob my head back, pretending I haven't seen them.

'You don't say hello?' says Francesco.

'No ... don't wave,' I say, grabbing his arm in the nick of time. 'I don't say hello because ... well, it's complicated. But trust me, it's better they don't know we're here.'

'Aah,' he says with a sigh. '*Amore, cara,* is never simple — even when we are old.'

He then proceeds to tell me how his grandparents were married for sixty years, and at his grandfather's funeral, his mistress pitched up. It transpired their clandestine affair had been going on for over four decades. Francesco was only eight at the time, but remembers hiding under the altar table, hands clasped tightly over his ears to block out the caterwauling the arrival of the shameless *strega* (witch) brought to mass that day.

However, the two women eventually became friends and would meet in the piazza, where they would sip *limoncello* and compare notes about the old man's flaws and irritating habits. Both agreed they were better off without the old *bastardo*.

'Anna?' I enquire next morning.

'*Ja, liebling?*' she says, clearing away the breakfast things.

'I should have thought of this before, but do you know of anywhere that rents bicycles?'

'*Komm' mit mir,*' she says, wiping her hands on her apron, then leading me down to the basement. There, behind various old rusty garden tools, is an ancient bike with 'Schildberger und Sȍhne' painted in faded lettering along the crossbar.

'This bicycle belonged to my man ... in English, *husband, ja*? He worked for his father in the *Bäckerei*, the bakery,' she says, feeling the tyres. 'A little *Luft* (air), *dann ist alles in Ordnung.*'

I wiggle along the road, pushing both bikes, unwieldy as supermarket trolleys.

'*Buongiorno, principessa!*' calls Francesco from Cristina's balcony, as I weave unsteadily round the corner.

'*Buongiorno! Ho una bicicletta!*'

'*Madonna mia!*' He guffaws in disbelief, then smiles and gestures. 'Eh, whaddya think I am? *Il postino?* The postman?'

As we rattle across Herbert von Karajan Square towards the opera house, I can't help but think what Nigel would have said in Francesco's shoes: *Are you mad? There's no way I'm riding that heap of metal. We can afford a taxi. Why can't you be sophisticated? Just once?* Then we'd have an argument and he'd storm off. But he just didn't get it; you see, it has nothing to do with saving on taxi fares or worrying about how you look; it's about being a little bit wacky and not giving a damn if you might get oil on your designer jeans or mess up your neatly coiffed hair.

'*Eh, il postino! Attenzione prego!*' I yell. 'Stop here!'

We lean our bicycles against a lamppost and join the growing line of mainly American, Japanese and Spanish-speaking tourists waiting for the box office to open.

José Cura, the Argentinean tenor, is playing the role of Rodolfo at tonight's performance of *La Bohème*, and the couple in front of us has flown over especially from Buenos Aries to see him perform. (Pity his understudy.)

'Excuse me. Do you speak English?' comes an American drawl from behind.

I look over my shoulder, and before I have time to

respond, a large lady sporting a baseball cap and multicoloured poncho says, 'We were just wondering if you and your husband have ever seen *La Bohème,* and how it compares to *Les Misérables*? We saw that on Broadway and loved it.'

'Oh, um, we're not ...'

'My wife and I, we *love* this opera, don't we darling?' interjects Francesco, a cheeky grin creasing his chin. 'We come from England by bicycle to see it.'

'Really?' says the woman, mouth gaping to reveal a large piece of gum.

'*Sì*. And my great-grandfather, he write the music.'

'Omigod!'

'*Ja, bitte*?' calls the lady through the box office window.

'Two for tonight, *per favore,* in the upper circle. One for me — and one for my wife.'

'One hundred and forty euros, please,' she says with a knowing smile, as she passes the tickets through.

'We should be going,' I say, promptly dragging Francesco away by his sleeve, before our American friends have the chance to probe any further — and before I crack up.

We head out along the shady Augustinerstrasse, lined with rows of unchained bicycles (bike theft is non-existent here), past the antiquarian bookshops, quirky galleries, and a life-sized wooden figure of Pinocchio perched on a bench, and on towards St Michael's Gate. We stop by the church and go inside. The sweet smell of incense mixed with lilies hangs heavy in the air. Solitary figures sit in silent prayer. Who or what are they praying for, I wonder? For a sick parent, a pet, a premature baby, a son fighting in some foreign war, for a lotto win, or for success with

318

a job interview?

I look round to find Francesco lighting a candle, head bowed. I leave him to his private thoughts, and retreat on tiptoes to an empty side chapel.

I drop to my knees, close my eyes, and ask Steve to keep Wendy safe, to encourage her to pick up her paintbrushes again, and although no one will ever take his place, would it be all right for her to fall in love again someday?

Feeling a gentle hand on my shoulder, I tilt my head back and am met by Francesco's kind, watery eyes. He holds out his hand and pulls me to my feet, our fingers locking together. He kisses the crown of my head lightly, and as we walk along the red-carpeted aisle towards the exit, and out into the bright and busy square, I am reminded once more that silence can be filled with meaning; that you don't have to cram every void with inane chatter. I don't feel the need to impress Francesco with my wit or knowledge of Viennese rococo architecture, and am not embarrassed that he's already caught me crying.

Of all the places I have so far visited in Vienna, the little innocuous market just around the corner from Rudolfstrasse has to be one of my favourites. It's so … well, ALIVE. Sure, I appreciate the magnificence of the Opera House, the Spanish Riding School with its chandelier-lit paddock, the over-the-top, baroque, faded golden glory of Schönbrunn Palace, but they all have a LOOK-BUT-DON'T-TOUCH feel about them; whereas here, in this little market, I can see, feel, smell, listen to the Vienna of the here and now. I know I shouldn't compare, but Nigel would not have been impressed: *So what? It's just a market. All these historic buildings and you drag me here?*

'*Che bello!*' enthuses Francesco, disappearing into

its maze of colourful stalls: pyramids of blood-red, vine tomatoes, bunches of thin asparagus, reaching out like witches' fingers, rosemary, oregano and garlic bound up with raffia, swaying from metal hooks, roasted chestnuts, smoking in a coal-filled, metal drum, speckled eggs, nestled together in straw-filled baskets, row upon row of freshly baked Kaiser rolls, rye, wholegrain, sourdough and seeded artisan loaves that send your taste buds into overdrive, trays of sausages, cuts of meat in pools of pink blood, and trotters with sprigs of parsley stuffed between their piggy toes. Aaw. If I allow myself to think about those cute little porkers too much, I could turn vegetarian.

I seek refuge in the flower stall, where the air is perfumed with woodsy pine, cinnamon, eucalyptus and orchids. With Christmas just a few weeks away, it's like entering an ice white winter wonderland. Ladies in voluminous dirndls and boiled wool, fir-green jackets with rustic horn buttons and heavy-duty gloves deftly create advent crowns from aromatic spruce, holly, metallic frosted pine cones, red berries, cinnamon sticks, silver ribbons, garden twine and candles.

I return to the food section where I left Francesco. Through the rows of hanging, cheesecloth-wrapped salamis and hams, pretzels and dried chillies, I watch him as he zips from one stall to another, tasting olives, smelling herbs, feeling tomatoes and aubergines, checking they are ripe. He laughs and jokes with the amiable stall holders, cosied up against the cold in furry earflap hats and fingerless gloves, his hand vocabulary and humour bridging the language gap.

I'm learning that the Italian hand gesture can be used either to convey a meaning that it would take several words to express, or to simply emphasise a point — a kind of communication shorthand.

He's spied me and is gesturing for me to come over, so I shall now do my best to demonstrate this point:

'Eh, *cara,* I have an idea,' he says *(forefinger stabbing temple).* 'Call *(thumb to ear, little finger to mouth)* Anna and Cristina. Tell them tonight, before *(forefinger rotating backwards)* the opera, I prepare dinner.'*(fingers of right hand clasped together and indicating mouth.)*

'But you're on holiday.' I groan. 'You don't want to be cooking on your night off. There's a lovely taverna near ...'

'Punto e basta! Enough!' *(horizontal cross-over and swiping of both hands.)*

'But ...'

'I insist.' *(forefinger stabbing the palm of the other hand.)* 'Now, let's have an espresso.' *(forefinger and thumb touching, other fingers extended in drinking mime.)*

I sprinkle some of my precious Bad Aussee mix into the bath and slither down into the warm water, swishing my hand gently back and forth. I can almost feel the toxins draining out of my body.

Opening one eye, I lazily lift a pruney arm and grope around for my watch. 5.40. I haul myself out of my warm cocoon, slip into my LFMD (little flea-market dress), scoosh some mousse on my hair and scrunch it up, apply some lip-gloss and put on my shopping channel, diamante earrings. I grimace then grin as I relive that particular cringeworthy presentation ...

ME: *Notice the way they catch the light.*

VOICE IN EAR: *Twenty-five more seconds to fill. Keep talking.*

ME: Yes, the light catches them in a most alluring way — blinding even.
VOICE IN EAR: Twenty-two seconds.
ME: My mum has a pair like this ... and my friend.
VOICE IN EAR: Twenty seconds.
ME: And my aunty.
VOICE IN EAR: Okay, enough of the family-tree thing. Change tack. Eighteen seconds.
ME: In fact, Wills, if you're watching, I can guarantee Kate would love these and wouldn't be able to tell the difference between these and your granny's.
VOICE IN EAR: Cut!

'Ready, Anna?' I say, popping my head around the living room door.

'*Fertig*,' she says, buttoning up her dark green Lodenmantel and collecting her basket.

As we totter along the street arm in arm, she tells me that since Walter her beloved husband died, she rarely ventures out in the evening.

Her lovely warm face creases as she pats my hand and says out of the blue, 'Francesco is a good man, *liebling*. This I see in his eyes. *Und* good men are hard to find.'

'You can say that again,' I say, half laughing.

'So, you should marry this man, *ja?*'

'But we've only just ...'

'Life is short, and you are not so young,' she remarks squarely.

Had anyone else said this to me, I'd have thought, here we go. Give me a break — not all us single ladies of a certain age are on a quest to harness a husband.

Yet, old she may be, and like many Austrians, steeped in traditional values, but I know from our many discussions over coffee and strudel, Anna is a modern, forward-thinking woman, who juggled career and family life at a time before it was the norm. So, no offence taken this time — and maybe, just *maybe* she has a point ...

As we climb the winding staircase to Cristina's apartment, the mouth-watering, Mediterranean mix of sweet tomatoes, garlic and fresh herbs drifts down to meet us.

Anna depresses the brass handle of the solid dark wood door and beckons me to follow her inside.

'*Grüss Gott!*'

'*Guten Abend!*' replies Cristina, emerging from the gloom of the long, dark hallway, an antique rosary swaying from her waist. Her mouth breaks into an appreciative smile when I present her with the floral arrangement of trailing jasmine, paper-white narcissus and burnt orange roses I had created especially for her at the market.

She takes my arm and leads me into the front room.

While the sisters exchange some words in dialect, I look around. The apartment is very similar to Anna's: old-school Austrian, with high, ornate ceilings, weighty oak wood furniture, traditional double doors, lace mats and antimacassars, framed photographs and watercolour paintings depicting alpine scenes.

Francesco appears from the kitchen, the sleeves of his crisp, white shirt neatly rolled above the elbows, revealing a heart-shaped tattoo with the letters 'F' and 'A' intertwined.

'*Buona sera!*' he says, kissing each of us in turn. He cracks open a bottle of Sekt and Cristina takes four crystal glasses from the carved, antique cabinet.

'*Prost!*'

'*Salute!*'

'Cheers!'

We sit down to an *antipasto misto* of mixed Austrian meats followed by *Melanzane Aubergine Parmigiano*.

'*Mmm, das schmeckt*,' says Cristina, nodding her approval. '*Wie macht man dass?*'

'She says it's delicious, and wants to know how you make it,' I say to Francesco.

'*Allora ...*'

Cut the aubergine into medium, round slices and grill.
Prepare a tomato sauce of olive oil, chopped tomatoes and handful of fresh basil.
When aubergines are ready, place in a deep tray.
Cover with tomato sauce, mozzarella and ricotta.
Repeat the layering process until all the ingredients are used.
Top with fresh parmesan and fresh basil.
Bake in oven at a medium heat for 30 minutes until the cheese has melted and the top is slightly crispy and golden brown.

'The last time I went to the opera was in nineteen eighty-eight,' says Anna, putting down her knife and fork, and producing a sepia snapshot from her purse. 'This night it was also *La Bohème.*' She passes me the picture of a young man in military uniform. Her eyes mist over as she continues, 'Since many years, my Walter has wished with his whole heart to see this opera. I save my money to buy the tickets — to make his dream true. Three days after we see it, *Gott* has taken him from me.'

I return the picture to her and cover her hand with mine.

'Now,' she says, voice brightening, 'Francesco, it is my turn — today I make *schnell,* quickly, just for you, Austrian speciality.' She produces a foil-covered dinner plate from her basket. 'Apfelstrudel Anna.' We applaud the strudel, and Cristina shuffles off to the kitchen to heat up the vanilla sauce.

We make it to the opera house with fifteen minutes to spare, but arrive at our *seats* (luxury!) just as the lights go down.

The orchestra is tuning up. I steal a sideways glance at Francesco. He takes my hand in his. I look away quickly and try to focus on the story. That Mimi will die in the end is a given, but the circumstances leading up to this are doubtless complicated, and will require the utmost concentration, particularly as the dialogue is sung in Italian.

The interval arrives. Francesco goes to the bar while I nab a table. I put on my glasses and look at the programme. I need to know what the big deal was with Musetta's shoe at the end of Act Two. What the hell has a goddamn shoe got to do with anything? Why did she suddenly take it off and give it to the bearded man? It was like she wanted him to try it on, or something. It doesn't make sense. And I'd been doing so well up to that point.

All at once Francesco's mobile springs into life, buzzing and nudging its way across the table.

'Francesco! Your ...' I look for him, but he's lost in the crowd, queuing up for drinks. The phone has now worked its way to the edge, about to fall, so I grab it. My eyes flicker across the illuminated screen. A name flashes before me: ISABELLA ISABELLA ISABELLA. My heart does a nose-dive. Maybe Wendy's initial doubts had been well-founded. Perhaps he does have a wife and five *bambini* back in old Napoli. Poor woman — I can picture her now — hanging out the washing, screaming children pulling at her apron, pot of homemade pasta boiling over, while hubby is living it up at the opera in Vienna with his fancy woman. Now, hold your horses, retorts my practical, less paranoid side; Isabella could well be a sister, an aunt, a business partner. But the old insecure me is far from convinced and is pulling the emergency cord; telling me to get the hell out. He hasn't lied exactly, but he has hardly been very forthcoming with details of his private life, has he? Last night, when I was droning on about Nigel, he could have taken the opportunity to fill me in on *his* past. But he didn't. Why is that? (I know what you're thinking — poor chap couldn't get a word in edgeways.)

Oh, how much easier life would be if there were such a thing as a pre-dating questionnaire:

a) *Are you married/divorced/separated/single?*
b) *Are you looking for a serious/casual relationship?*
c) *Are there any significant exes one need know about?*
d) *Have you ever been attracted to someone of the same sex?*

I know this all sounds horribly neurotic and unromantic, but at least then you could make an informed decision whether or not to take things to the next level, thereby saving time and avoiding unnecessary heartache.

Madonna mia. He's coming back from the bar. What do I say? 'Is there something you want to tell me?' 'Is there something I should know?' 'Who's Isabella?' 'By the way, your wife rang?' I don't want a scene — not here, in this beautiful place; not tonight, when I'm having such a lovely time.

'*Salute, cara!*' says Francesco, handing me a glass

of Sekt and clinking glasses.

'*Salute!*' I reply with a big smile, blocking out all thoughts of potential wives and girlfriends, determined not to burst the magical bubble just yet. I promise myself that I will address the issue before he leaves — but not now. I'd rather spend the rest of our brief time together in blissful ignorance, rather than in an unhappy, disappointed, guilty, angry state of mind.

As Mimi lies dying, she and Rodolfo recall their past happiness, in the soul-stirring duet '*Sono Andati?*' A huge tear rolls down my cheek. I'm not just crying for Mimi and Rodolfo, but for Anna and Walter, who sat in this very place, listening to the same opera over twenty-five years ago, and who were to be parted forever just days later. Oh God, this is the second time I've cried in front of Francesco. He'll be thinking I'm a right drama queen.

The music rises to a crescendo. I feel his hand squeezing mine, then our fingers entwine. The space between us is electric. I close my eyes and let the music swallow me up. I don't want him to ever let go of my hand or for the music to stop. I wish I could hold onto this moment forever.

Placing his arm firmly around my shoulders, Francesco propels me across the cold, windy square.

'*Vai! Vai!*'

My hat blows off, and as he runs back to pick it up, I notice an attractive, middle-aged woman standing at the tram stop. She cuts a lone, forlorn figure, shoulders hunched against the rain, a Billa supermarket bag at her feet. She smiles wistfully then looks away. I am reminded of that night, waiting for Mags, eating a hotdog and enviously watching the loved-up couple dashing across the square. I wonder if the woman at the tram stop is going home to her partner, or to her one-bed flat and ready meal. Did someone break her heart? Is she trapped in a dead-end job or relationship, too afraid to make a change? If so, I'd like to say to her, *It's never too late. Life doesn't always go the way we plan, but some things happen for a reason. I had my heart badly broken and my world fell apart. But the life I have now is surprisingly better than the one before. I've learned to be stronger, to not put up with shitty behaviour and to just enjoy being in the here and now. So hang on in there.*

On the other hand, she's probably perfectly happy and wondering why there's a strange woman staring at her.

The Graben's opulent shop windows, a-shimmer with extravagant displays, cast their reflection onto the wet cobbles.

A violinist, wearing an old army coat, plays a waltz before the Pestsäule statue, undeterred by the downpour and lack of audience. Francesco tosses a handful of euros into the young man's instrument case, gives a little bow, and holds his hand out to me.

'What? Oh, no, Francesco, I can't dance. And anyway, it wouldn't feel right, dancing here, in front of a memorial dedicated to plague victims.'

'*Esatto!* We must celebrate the life, *cara — la dolce vita*,' he says. He takes my right hand, places it in his, wraps his arm tightly around my waist, and pulls me close to him. I freeze.

'*Uno, due, tre, uno, due, tre ...*' he whispers hypnotically, mouth grazing my ear as he gently rotates in time to the music.

'Francesco, please, I am not joking. I'll only tread on your toes ...'

'Uno, due, tre, uno, due, tre ...'

He pulls me closer, drawing me in with those magnetic eyes, his signature scent of Azzaro Pour Homme tapping into my female senses.

Slowly, tentatively, my brain gives my arms and legs the green light to loosen up, and I yield to the ebb and flow of the music, the rise and fall of my partner's body.

As we gather speed, I tilt my head back. Coloured lights flash across my eyes, buildings move, sounds are distorted, wind rushes in my ears. I am a child again; vulnerable, trusting, spinning, carefree, weightless, dizzy; like I'm back on the merry-go-round of my youth. Is this how it feels to be high on hallucinogenic drugs, I wonder?

How my view of Italian men has changed since that school trip to Rome when I was sixteen; I remember how my classmates and I watched gleefully gobsmacked from a street café during rush-hour, as overcrowded mopeds and cars mounted the pavement, while a group of cool Carabinieri posed in the doorway, smoking Camel cigarettes and flirting with pretty women, oblivious to the chaos all around them. I had grown up presuming all Italian *signori* to be loud, reckless, unpredictable, smooth-talking, fashion-addicted gigolos. Now I am learning that beyond the wild gestures and mad behaviour, these passionate people derive pleasure in the simplest of things: organic food, family, wine, debate, espresso, music, dancing — and it's contagious. Right now, I would rather be here, in this damp square, feet squelching, mascara running, nose dripping, than dressed up to the nines, sipping cocktails in some trendy nightclub in downtown Manhattan.

'My flight tomorrow is not until the evening, so we have some time together, *sì*?' says Francesco, turning me to face him as we turn into Rudolfstrasse.

'Sure,' I say in what I hope is a seductive tone, my head starting to swim with the giddy mix of Sekt, Strauss and *La Bohème*. He reaches out and removes a wet strand of hair from my eyes, then raises my freezing hand to his mouth. I feel the warmth of his breath on my skin as he says in a low voice, 'Aah, *cara*, today is *una bella giornata* — a beautiful day for me.'

I open my mouth to speak, but unusually for me, no words come, so I just grin. Long-lost emotions are starting to stir inside me. The passionate woman I used to be is coming back to life. I've missed feeling like this. I want to let myself melt into his arms ...

Geneviève: Remember le mystère.

Emily: But this is Vienna, the moon is full. I'm allowed to be a little bit crazy, n'est-ce pas?

Geneviève: Leave him wanting more.

Emily: He's so gorgeous, he smells so nice, and those lips, mmm ... so kissable.

Geneviève: And you are a little bit soûle, *how you say... teepsy.*

Emily: Come on, just one little kiss?

Geneviève: Absolument pas! You know where that can lead. Go inside, immédiatement. Le mystère, le mystère, le mystère ...'

Emily: OK, I'm going, I'm going ...

Before I have time to change my mind, I peck him hurriedly on the cheek, then pull away saying, 'Tomorrow — ten-thirty — Cristina's — okay?'

'*Sogni d'oro, bellissima!*' he calls as I disappear through the double doors.

Safe on the other side, I press my back against the cold stone wall and close my eyes, heart hammering in my chest, bosom heaving (I use the term loosely, but that's what they do in films, don't they?).

Geneviève, I am using all the strength I can muster to be the cool woman he can't quite reach, but to be honest, I don't think I can keep this up much longer.

The next morning as I arrive at Cristina's, Francesco's waiting for me in the square, astride his bicycle, raring to go.

'*Buongiorno!*' he says, kissing me on both cheeks. 'Today I get up very early to make some shopping. Now I am free until ... three-thirty,' he says, consulting his watch.

'I'm afraid I only woke up twenty minutes ago,' I say groggily, 'so the *Kaffeehaus* is the first stop for me.' (Truth is, I was awake until dawn, and then I had this horrible nightmare that Francesco and I were cycling through the sun-baked, back streets of Jeddah. He started to pedal really fast, and hard as I tried, I couldn't keep up. I called out for him to slow down, but he would only turn his head and laugh mockingly. I kept catching glimpses of him, but then he'd disappear again. I woke up, pillow on the floor, heart pounding, sheet wound tightly around my legs.)

'*Kaffee und Kipferln?*' says the waiter, taking a crisp, white tea towel from his long apron and flicking it across the table.

'*Natürlich. Zweimal, bitte.* Oh my God, Francesco, before you leave, you have *got* to taste *Kipferln* pastries — they are the best things EVER. Once you've tasted one of these ...'

'You are like we Italians,' says Francesco propping his chin in his hand and grinning roguishly. 'A good fork, no?'

'Sorry? A good what?'

'*Buona forchetta* — crazy for food — *passionate* about food.'

'Oh, yes, Francesco, I'm a very good fork,' I reply,

feeling a hot flush coming on.

Fuelled by coffee and pastries, we head south, towards another favourite place of mine, Belvedere Palace, which houses the world's largest Gustav Klimt collection. Now, I'm no art expert, but you can't be in Vienna and not notice the unmistakable metallic gold ink postcards, posters, key-rings and tea towels for sale in every *Tabak*, every gift shop, on every street corner. This makes Klimt sound like tasteless *kitsch*, but to stand here, before the real thing is … well, I defy anyone not to be bowled over by the glittering, sensual beauty of his paintings.

'*Mamma mia!*' exclaims Francesco (told you) as we enter the gallery.

This is the sort of modern art I like: not poncy, hurl-paint-at-a-canvas or nail-in-a-brick art, but simple, beautiful paintings I can understand and admire without having to think up some pretentious, symbolic, la-di-da nonsense as to what the artist is expressing through his work.

'For me, this is true, uncomplicated love,' says Francesco, rubbing his chin thoughtfully as he studies the painting entitled *The Kiss*. 'See the way the man protect the woman with his arm? And the woman, she feel safe with him. The love between them is equal. In many love affairs, there is imbalance, you understand?'

'Absolutely, Francesco, I know exactly what you mean,' I whisper, abruptly reminded that there may be an imbalance in *our* relationship; the imbalance being quite simply that I'm free to love him and he could be married/living with someone called Isabella. Drawing a wobbly breath, I open my mouth to speak...

'Look here, how she has one hand around his neck, the other on his hand,' he continues. 'This is no a casual relationship; this is about lasting love — there is *passion*, of course, but *this* love is about friendship, respect, trust — the kind of love maybe you find once in your life — two times, if you are very lucky.'

My gaze travels the length and breadth of him; his expressive, liquid dark eyes devouring every detail of the painting, his thin laughter lines creasing up, his strong hands emphasising every word — sorry guys, but when it comes to speaking the language of love (without sounding corny), nobody does it better than the Italians.

'Like Mimi and Rodolfo,' he continues.

'Like Posh and Becks,' I quip.

Francesco looks me at blankly. *'Chi?'*

Why must I always do that? Spoil magical moments by saying something flippant?

Ravenous once more (how nice to be with a man who doesn't calorie-count on my behalf), and with one eye on the clock, we leave Belvedere and head for the tranquillity of the Volksgarten, via the hot dog stand by the gates. As I'm a regular and speak English to the owner (he's a devout Anglophile), he always slaps two *Wurst* in my roll for the price of one.

'Good afternoon, *Fraulein*,' he says, switching off the radio.

'Good afternoon, Tobias,' I reply. 'This is Francesco, my Italian teacher.'

They shake hands. 'She is a good student, *signor*?'

'Eh, no bad,' says Francesco, turning to me with a smirk.

'If I did not have a wife, I will marry her,' says Tobias, scooping up four sausages with his tongs.

'*Would* marry her, Tobias. The future conditional is I *would* marry her,' I say with mock scorn.

'I *would* marry her,' he repeats, handing over my chubby hot dog. 'And you, *signor,* would you marry her?'

'*Allora ...*' replies Francesco, 'if ...'

'End of today's lesson,' I say quickly, darting Tobias a warning glare as I hand over my five-euro note. 'I'll see you tomorrow. You owe me an extra *Wurst*, mate.'

I lead Francesco to my favourite place to picnic, past the hibernating rose bushes to a secluded corner, where the gleaming white statue of the Empress Elizabeth, like an ethereal goddess, sits staring at the water fountain, lost in melancholy thought.

'Who is this *bella donna*?' enquires Francesco, spreading his scarf on the frosty grass before her, and beckoning for me to sit down. 'She look so sad.'

'Francesco, meet my friend Sisi, wife of the Kaiser, Franz Josef. I come and visit her whenever I'm passing. She and I have quite a lot in common.'

'*Cosa?*'

'We both used to travel a lot, and we both had our hearts badly broken.'

'The Kaiser, he was an *imbecille,* Sisi,' says Francesco, waggling his wrist at her.

'She's not too keen on Italians, I'm afraid.'

'*Perché?* Why? We are not all Romeos.'

'No?'

He looks at me, nonplussed.

'Maybe not, but she was murdered by one,' I continue.

'A dangerous race,' he says, solemnly shaking his head.

'Thanks for the warning, *il postino*,' I say through a mouthful of hot dog. 'Talking of Romeos and broken hearts,' I say, swallowing hard, 'I've been meaning to ask, in Torre Anun... Anun... in Naples, in your lovely apartment that overlooks Capri, does anyone else ...'

334

He sits, staring at the ground, saying nothing. I wait for the axe to fall.

I will be dignified and calm, and when I learn it's over, I WILL NOT: blub, shout, scream, flounce off or throw my *Wurst* in his face.

'I think you ask if someone live with me,' he says eventually, looking me straight in the eye.

I nod, scrutinising his face, watching for any flicker of guilt or awkwardness.

'Mr and Mrs Puccini!' comes a familiar transatlantic drawl behind us.

Jeez. It's them — our American friends.

'*Buongiorno!*' says Francesco, leaping to his feet and shaking their hands.

'Hi,' I murmur, giving a feeble wave.

'Did you enjoy the opera?' asks Francesco. (Oh, no, why did he just do that? He's only going to land us in deep water — again.)

'To be honest, and no offence to your great-grandfather, but we couldn't understand a word, could we, Bob?'

Bob opens his mouth to speak, but is cut off by his wife.

'And it was way too long,' she continues, pointing her camera at Sisi. 'Do you know anything about this statue?'

'*Allora* ...' begins Francesco.

'Darling, look at the time,' I say, in an attempt to rescue another potentially farcical situation. 'Plane to catch,' I say with a weak smile, hastily gathering up our stuff.

'Oh, we thought you said you came by bicycle ...'

* * *

Sono andati? Fingevo di dormire
Have they left us? I was not really sleeping
perché volli con te restare.
because I wanted to be alone with you.
Ho tante cose che ti voglio dire,
So many things remain for me to tell you,
o una sol, ma grande come il mare,
or just one, that is vaster than the ocean,
come il mare profondo ed infinito.
as the ocean so deep and infinite.
Sei il mio amore e tutta la mia vita!
You are my love and my whole life!

Tears spill freely down my cheeks as Mimi and Rodolfo's heartbreaking lament floats through the tiny speakers of my portable player. I read the words scrawled across the CD cover:

A la mia cara Wurst. Un caro abbraccio, Francesco.

('Sausage' is now his pet name for me.)

I will never forget last night — the opera, dancing in the square ... all over too quickly.

I glance at my watch and tell myself to stop daydreaming and concentrate on tonight's show. The prospect causes my tummy to flip over. It seems so long ago since Saturday's performance and my awful memory lapse. I must stay calm, not give in to stage fright and give a stellar performance.

I turn off the music and pick up my script. I know I'll feel better as soon as I've got that dreaded scene over with.

The loons have flown and so must we. The run has sadly reached its end. Goodbye, Vienna. Goodbye, Chelsea. Hello, London. Hello, Insecurity and Unemployment. Are you going to accompany me on my journey once more? I'm trying to think positively and visualise drowning in a sea of scripts, but I'm well aware that jobs are thin on the ground. Perhaps I've been living a little *too* much in the moment of late, splashing out on pastries, coffees, wine, the opera — and a need-it-now, winter coat by Viennese designer, Franz Blumauer. Oh *God* ... even if Luigi gives me my job back, how long can I survive on a waitress's wage? What about Francesco? I find myself thinking about him all the time now, and I realise my feelings for him have taken hold of me unawares. Even if there is no *bella donna* to welcome him back to Naples, how can we have a relationship one and a half thousand miles apart? Dare I allow myself to hope? Whilst it is good to know he will be waiting for me, I am trying so hard not to fall for him because in a couple of weeks' time he'll be gone. Why, oh why are things never straightforward?

Half asleep, I pull my bag off the carousel and head through the green channel towards the exit.

'Excuse me,' calls a customs officer. I turn my head towards him and mime, '*ME?*' He nods and beckons me over. 'Mind if I check your bag?'

It's the early hours of the morning, I've had about two hours' sleep, and there's a gorgeous man waiting for me on the other side of those doors, so of course I mind, but I somehow doubt Mr Customs Man would reply, 'No? That's okay, love. I'll try someone else. You have a nice day now.'

So with my best you're-barking-up-the-wrong-tree smile, I reply, 'Sure, go ahead.'

'Olly and I will wait for you outside,' says Mags reassuringly.

'Oh, don't worry about me,' I say airily. 'It's just a

formality.'

They throw me a dubious look.

'Really. I'll be fine. Your son will be waiting. Give me a call soon.'

We hug and they disappear.

I unlock my suitcase, and while the officer rifles through my toiletries and manky washing, I study the mixed bag of bleary-eyed passengers, sleep-walking their way to the chilly, outside world.

Snapping my bag shut, he says sternly, 'Come this way,' and I'm promptly ushered into a small interview room. As we enter, he slides the OCCUPIED sign across sharply and firmly closes the door.

'Passport, please.'

Hot-faced, I surrender it to him, hand jittering uncontrollably. He flicks through the pages in silence. Then looking at me with a weighty stare he says, 'Apart from Vienna, where else have you been travelling to?'

'Where ...? I ... nowhere,' I stammer, face reddening, doubtless giving the impression that I've got bags of heroin strapped to my thighs. I wiggle the loose button of my coat nervously. One eyebrow raised, he studies me for several seconds, a smug, disbelieving look on his face. I swear he's deriving some sort of twisted pleasure in watching me squirm.

He disappears, leaving me alone. I look around the stark white walls, my eyes coming to rest on the poster of a man behind bars. Underneath, in bold lettering are the following words ...

HM CUSTOMS AND EXCISE
DRUG SMUGGLING ZERO TOLERANCE

I scream inwardly. Ohmygod, ohmygod, ohmygod. I have absolutely no reason to feel guilty, so how come those words strike raw terror in me?

The flickering strip lighting is starting to make my head spin. Small beads of sweat are forming on my neck. I glug a cup of water from the machine.

Scenes from the film, *Bangkok Hilton* are flashing through my mind. You know the one, where Nicole Kidman's boyfriend hides heroin in his camera case and gives it to her to carry, then she's banged up abroad in a filthy jail until she eventually has to dig her way out? A knot of fear grips my throat.

The customs man reappears, accompanied by a formidable female (at least, I *think* she's female) officer, wearing latex gloves. She looks like she's been flown in especially from *Prisoner: Cell Block H*; not someone you'd like to bump into on a dark night, let alone be body-searched by.

The chairs screech harshly as they are pulled out from under the table.

Several plastic bags containing a white substance are shoved under my nose. Two sets of eyes glue themselves to my startled face.

'Can you explain to me what this is, and what it was doing in your suitcase?'

I look from one to the other in disbelief. 'I ... what ... erm ...' I bury my head in my hands. How idiotic of me. I should have left them behind. They were bound to cause suspicion.

Expelling a long breath, I look up and humbly confess. 'It's bath salts.'

The customs officer pauses for thought, brow furrowing. 'Bath salts? Hah! That's a good one.'

Reading the scepticism in his face, I do what I always do when I'm nervous or scared: PRATTLE. 'Really. It's salt, mined in the Austrian mountains. This guy, Gerhard, he's the director of the play I've just finished doing in Vienna, well, and oh, he's an

Elvis impersonator too, anyway, he makes all these spa remedies from purely natural things, and ... I've got loads. You'd be welcome to try ...'

He bursts the bag open and tentatively puts a little on his tongue, then passes some to Scary Mary.

Shaking his head, he pushes the bag and my passport towards me and deadpans, 'Thanks for the offer, but I'm more of a Radox man myself.'

With that they both stand up, indicating that it's okay for me to leave.

'Thank you,' I say, my voice diminished to a wobbly whisper. 'Sorry, I should have ... sorry.' I click my case shut and exit hastily through the sliding doors to freedom.

Francesco is pacing up and down by the barrier, looking overwrought and confused.

'*C'è un problema?* Your friends, they tell me you were stopped by customs ....'

'No, no problem.' I smile, wearily holding up a mollifying hand, then pecking his cheek. 'Just a silly misunderstanding. It's a long story. I'll tell you in the car.'

Hmm. Not quite the cinematic, running-towards-each-other-in-slow-motion reunion I've been dreaming of.

CHAPTER SIXTEEN
The Agony and the Ecstasy

WEAVING IN AND OUT of the early morning traffic on Francesco's 1950s' Vespa, I feel like Audrey Hepburn in *Roman Holiday.* Admittedly she sports a stylish headscarf, and I a helmet that makes me look like a Nazi, but in my mind I am her, hands clasped tightly around Gregory Peck.

One day. Just one precious day left, until Francesco returns to Naples.

There's an unspoken rule that prevents us from daring to utter those 'where-do-we-go-from-here?' words, otherwise a shadow will be cast over our remaining time together.

I tell myself that I am lucky he came into my life, even though he's destined to leave it again. I have learned so much from him; I don't just mean Italian, but he's taught me to let go of all the nonsense, that I'm okay just as I am, that I don't need to be rescued, and I don't have to be perfect for someone to love me. I will always be grateful to him for that.

I don't know what I'll do when he leaves. Luigi says he may be able to give me some shifts at the restaurant, but today I don't care. Today I am so happy I could burst. But then everything changes ...

We are on our way to Windsor. There's a low-lying mist floating over the frozen ground, the winter sun is peeking through the frosty trees. As we approach the Magna Carta Tea Shop in Runnymede, I signal for Francesco to stop.

After a full English breakfast (his first), we climb the paved path, stopping briefly at the temple, where I present a sketchy historical account of some document being signed by some king to prevent a civil war. We then ascend the granite steps to the JFK Monument and on, further uphill to the Air Forces Memorial, dedicated to over 20,000 airmen and women who were lost in the Second World War, and who have no known grave. I shiver. Francesco rests his chin on top of my head and wraps his arms tightly around my waist to keep me warm. We stand there, saying nothing, eyes drawn heavenwards. A steady stream of aircraft fly past on their journeys to and from Heathrow.

'What is this?' asks Francesco, lowering his gaze.

'What? Where?' I say, palming away a couple of errant tears.

He takes my mittened hand and points it in the direction of a huge arch in the distance.

'That must be Wembley football stadium,' I say, screwing up my watery eyes. 'About fifteen miles away.'

'Madonna mia! Twenty-three kilometres only,' he remarks with a low whistle. 'When I come back to visit, you will take me to a match at Wembley, *sì? Amo il calcio.* I *love* the football. '

'Really?' I say, making a face. I knew he was too good to be true.

My mobile rings. 'Hi, Faye! Hey, what's up? Faye,

slow down, I can't hear what you're saying.'

'Tariq ... school trip ... gone ...' she says through panting sobs.

Cold horror grips me to my core. 'What? How? Do you mean Sahir? But the court order. He's not allowed to take him out of the country.'

'You know Sahir. He thinks he's above the law — thinks money can buy his way out of anything. I *knew* this would happen sooner or later. It's karma because I took Tariq away from Dubai in the first place.'

How can I reassure Faye that everything will be all right when I know deep down that might not be true? 'What are the police doing?' I enquire. 'Are they setting up border checks at the airport?'

'I don't know. They keep asking me questions. I'm waiting for my solicitor to call.'

'We'll ring the British Embassy in Dubai and ... damn! Hold on ... I've got a call waiting.'

'Em, it's Nigel. I ...'

Good God! What the hell is he ringing me for? To invite me to be maid of honour at his wedding? Idiot! I hang up without a second thought.

'Faye? You still there?'

'I'm terrified, Em,' she gulps. 'Once they reach Middle Eastern soil, Sahir will be surrounded by a ring of protection — and I'll never see Tariq again.'

'Where are you?'

'Twickenham police station.'

'Hang on, love. I'm coming.'

I turn to Francesco, who's fixing me with a bewildered, concerned gaze.

'I'm so sorry,' I say, running my trembling hand through my hair. 'It's Faye. Something awful has happened and I have to go to Twickenham police station right away. I can't explain at the moment, as I don't have much time. Can we meet at Costa's at say, four, before your shift starts?'

He nods, asks no questions, grips my hand firmly in his and leads me swiftly downhill to the car park.

I tighten the straps of my helmet, flip down the visor, place my arms firmly around his waist, and we roar off, back along the A30.

As I wait at the police station for Faye's interview to end, my phone alerts me to two new voicemail messages:

1. Emily, my darling, it's Lionel. Call me as soon as you get this.

2. Em, Nigel. We got cut off. Listen, I haven't got long before I have to take this baby up into the air. I'm sitting on the tarmac, waiting for the remaining passengers to board before I push back for Abu Dhabi. I looked out of the window just now and I swear I saw Sahir, dragging a little boy up the aircraft steps. Must be Tariq. He seemed distressed. There's probably nothing to worry about, but just thought I'd check. If you get this message in the next ten minutes, call me, okay?

MESSAGE RECEIVED: 0910.
TIME NOW: 1100.

'He *definitely* said Abu Dhabi, Detective Chief Inspector,' I say, sliding my mobile across the table. 'Listen.'

'For your information, it's sergeant,' he says with a sniff, taking my phone and clasping it to his ear.

'Sorry. Been watching too many episodes of *Midsomer Murders*,' I say lamely.

'A-A-A-Abu Dhabi, eh?' he says, hanging up and leaning back in his chair. 'And yet Mr Haddad resides in Dubai, not A-A-*atishoo*-Abu Dhabi.'

'Yes, but don't you see?' I say, passing him a

Kleenex. 'He's not stupid. He'll know that the authorities will have been alerted. Flying to Abu Dhabi buys him more time. *Please*, they'll be landing in just over two hours. Can't you call the immigration people at Abu Dhabi airport?'

'Aah. It's not as simple as that, I'm afraid,' pipes up the solicitor. 'Now, if he'd taken him to a European country ...'

'But he hasn't!' I snap. She raises a strongly disapproving eyebrow. 'Sorry. I don't mean to be rude, but ...'

'It all depends on the parental rights of the country to where the child has been abducted,' she says, slowly removing her glasses. 'As far as I'm aware, the United Arab Emirates is not signed up to the Hague Convention ...'

'The what? Look, we're wasting precious time ...' My mobile rings.

'Didn't you get my message, darling? How fluent is your French?'

'What? I ... Lionel, so sorry, but now's *such* a bad time. I'll call you later — I promise.'

Faye returns, having collected a recent photo of Tariq and her wedding picture from home.

'Excellent,' says the sergeant, taking them from her. 'Please take a seat. Now I'd like you to complete this form ...'

My mobile rings again. 'Em, it's Drew.'

I excuse myself and exit to the corridor, shutting the interview room door firmly behind me.

'Drew! Everything all right?'

'Couldn't be better. Céline gave birth two hours ago — a bonnie wee girl!'

'But she's not due ... is ... is everything okay?'

'She's awfy wee apparently, but she's fine. They both are.'

'Congratulations. That's wonderful news.'

'She should have had her up here, as you know, but she took the train to London on Tuesday to do some last-minute baby shopping and her waters broke in Harrods, of all places. She's all on her own. I'm flying down tonight and her mum arrives from Paris tomorrow, but if you have the time, I know she'd love you girls to visit. She's in Saint Belinda's Hospital in ... somewhere in London. I'll text you the address and ward number.'

'Yes, yes, of course. I'll go this afternoon — and I'll let the others know.'

As I depress the door handle, I'm in a quandary whether or not to tell Faye the news.

'It wasn't Nigel, was it?' she says in a small voice, a tiny flicker of hope glimmering in her red eyes.

'No, my love, it wasn't,' I say gently. Sitting down next to her, I take her cold hand in mine. 'Just my silly agent.'

That afternoon, I'm at the maternity hospital, signing in, when my mobile rings. The receptionist glares at me and points to the *SWITCH OFF YOUR PHONE HERE* sign.

'Sorry, sorry,' I mumble, backing out through the revolving door.

'*Cara* is me, Francesco. Where are you?'

'Oh God, Francesco!' I exclaim aghast, checking my watch. 'I am *so* sorry. I completely forgot.'

'You forget me already?'

'Of course not. I'm now at a hospital in town.'

'*Madonna mia!* What happened?'

'I'm fine. My friend, Céline, you know the one who's pregnant? Well, she had the baby!'

'But she live in Scotland, no?'

'Yes, but ... I'll explain everything when I see you

346

tonight after you finish work. And if you're still speaking to me, tomorrow, at the airport, I'll buy you a double espresso as a peace offering before you leave.'

'Espresso? Espresso is no enough.'

'No? Okay, I'll throw in a croissant as well.'

'*Imbecille!* I want YOU, *cara.*'

Just in that instant, the last few hours are erased and I feel normal again: happy, excited, in love; but then little Tariq's face appears before me and the tension tightens its grip, reminding me that I have no right to be happy at the moment.

I make my way along the corridor to the ward, practising my over-the-moon face. This will be the biggest test of my acting skills to date: to appear ecstatic when inside I'm sick with worry, fear — and guilt. Yes, GUILT. I feel as guilty as if I'd stolen Tariq myself and personally handed him over to his father. I could have prevented this whole ghastly nightmare, had I only answered that call. And all those months ago, when I spied Sahir outside the school gates, why didn't I speak up then and warn the child protection people? Just when I thought I'd finally done with carrying guilt around with me, it comes knocking on my door once more. I will never forgive myself for this. Never.

Rachel and Wendy are already there, on either side of the bed, an 'It's a Girl!' helium balloon suspended from the white metal headboard. There, in the midst of them, is Céline, looking alabaster pale, yet beautiful, a tiny bundle cradled in the crook of her arm. As I enter, she pulls back the white shawl from the baby's doll-like, sleeping face.

'She's amazing,' I say, fighting back the tears.

'What a shame Faye isn't here,' says Céline with a sigh. 'Drew left her a message.' We glance at one another sideways.

'She wouldn't have missed this for the world,' I say feebly. 'She must have been called out on a night-stop or something ...'

It doesn't feel right, lying to her, but we all agreed that for the moment, it's best Céline doesn't know.

We sit clutching one another tight. There's an added intensity to those few minutes, in light of what's just happened. We take turns holding the baby. Her warm, silky head smells vanilla-sweet. I am transported back ten years to when Tariq was this size, his innocent, sleeping face wearing a hint of a smile, his long lashes brushing his wee olive cheeks; so tiny, so vulnerable. How do we keep our children safe from harm without stifling them? With the ever-present threat of Sahir one day taking his son, Faye was nervous of allowing Tariq to travel to London on that school trip to the Science Museum, but she knew she couldn't refuse. She had to put her trust in the school and in the universe.

In that moment I think that being childless is maybe not such a bad thing after all.

I catch Rachel's eye. Sliding my arm through hers, we slip quietly out through the French windows into the courtyard, and park ourselves on a freezing cold bench.

She turns to face me, and all at once her lovely face crumples as she dissolves into uncontrollable sobs. She buries her face in my shoulder. I comb my fingers through her hair and let her cry until there are no tears left. Catching her breath, she says mournfully, 'I know I shouldn't be thinking about me at a time like this, with Faye at her wit's end with worry and Céline so happy, but I'm jealous. There, I've said it. Why can't *I* have a child to hold, to worry about, to call me "Mummy"? It just doesn't seem fair ...'

'I understand, and it's not being selfish,' I say gently. 'What you're feeling is perfectly natural.'

'When the doctors told me I probably wouldn't have kids after the treatment, I was fine about it — thankful to be alive. I promised myself I would be eternally grateful for having been given a second chance, but ...'

'Rachel,' I say tentatively, 'tell me to mind my own business, but have you and Dave ever considered adopting? You'd make such wonderful parents.'

She shakes her head and sniffs. 'Dave won't hear of it. After the last round of IVF, he said if we can't have our own baby then he doesn't want one at all.'

'And what about you? How do you feel?'

'There's nothing I want more than to give a home to an unwanted child. Don't think I haven't tried talking him round, but we always end up arguing, so I've given up — for the sake of our marriage. Don't get me wrong — Dave's a lovely man, but he can be very stubborn at times, and there's no budging him on this. He says I must thank my lucky stars I'm still here after the cancer scare, and not yearn for what I can't have, but all the same I ...'

She looks away, her voice breaking again.

With a deep breath, she turns back to face me, and running a finger under each row of lower lashes, she smiles weakly and says, 'Come on, let's go back inside.'

How do people do this every day? Commute? Squashed between a large man who's obviously never heard of deodorant and a woman noisily tucking into chicken nuggets, I give up trying to read the *Evening Standard*, shut my eyes and allow my body to sway in time to the rhythmic clickety-clack of the train and my mind to drift ...

I awake with a jolt, realising my phone has been switched off since I arrived at the hospital a couple of hours ago. What if Faye has been trying to get through? Where do I tell her I've been? ONE NEW MESSAGE. Please, *please*, let it be good news ...

Emily, darling, it's Lionel. Where the hell are you? The office is about to close and you were supposed to call me back ages ago. Anyway, you'd better be free tomorrow morning, because I went ahead and put you up for the part of Louise, the French maid in Noël Coward's Private Lives *- a nice, comic, cameo role, and this is the best bit — it's a six-month run in the West End! Your audition is tomorrow at eleven at the Spotlight rehearsal rooms in Leicester Square. Ask for Nick. I e-mailed you the relevant pages of script. And I'm praying you didn't lie on your CV about having conversational French, because all your lines, all — seven of them, I think — are in French. Let me know how it goes. Break a leg.*

Talk about bad timing! With Francesco flying back to Italy tomorrow, he's whisking me away after work for our first 'proper' romantic night together (or should that be 'improper'? *Pardonnez-moi*, Geneviève) at The Parkway Hotel on Richmond Hill, complete with a river view room, balcony, Jacuzzi, champagne, breakfast hamper and everything. Now, instead of seductively sipping bubbly in my new, expensive, lace-trimmed, fuller-bust chemise, I have to don my specs, stick my head in a script, ensure I get a good night's sleep and no hangover. Ach well, at least Francesco can watch football highlights on the giant plasma TV.

No, no, forget all that. I just know I'm going to mess up this audition, so there's absolutely no point in going, is there?

350

Passion at The Parkway:

'But that's *fantastico, cara,*' says Francesco, stroking my damp hair as we sit snuggled up in super-soft bathrobes on a sofa big enough to accommodate The Waltons. 'Is your dream, no?'

'Yes, but ...'

'Punto e basta!' he says, covering my mouth, then pouring me another glass of champagne. 'Is your big chance.' He clinks his glass against mine. *'Buona fortuna!'*

How I hate to spoil this magical moment but I can't put this off any longer.

'Francesco, I need to ask you something before ... before we ...'

'Che cosa, cara?' he says, putting his glass down. I try not to drown in his stare.

'Who's Isabella?' I blurt out, voice shaky. He turns away from me. My heart starts to sink. 'I wasn't spying. It's just that when we were at the opera ...'

'Isabella is my daughter.'

'Oh. Why didn't you tell me? I don't mind that you're divorced.'

A cloud drifts across his face. 'Divorced? I am no divorced.'

So my gut instinct was right. Why didn't I pluck up the courage to confront him in Vienna?

'Alessandra, my wife,' he says in a low voice, 'and our second, unborn child were taken from me by a crazy motorcyclist driving too fast.'

I look at him in silence. Moments pass.

'God, Francesco, I am so sorry. I had no idea,' I whisper, squeezing his shoulder.

'Many years ago now,' he says, letting out a long sigh and laying his cheek on my hand. *'Allora, cara,* we must live every day like it is our last.'

'You're so right,' I say, humbled by his tragic story,

and ashamed for having thought him a love-rat.

'I want to tell you before, but is difficult for me ...'

His mouth then breaks into its customary playful grin as he says, 'Eh, you have some *caviale* ... how you say? ... caviar on your chin.'

As he wipes it off with his napkin, I feel the spark reignite. He tilts my face towards him and kisses me lingeringly.

But far from a last night together full of delicious naughtiness, we sit up in bed, just like Morecambe and Wise, reading the script aloud, me giving my Louise and him his Sybil, Victor and Elyot.

Don't ask me how I got the part. I thought the audition went *so* badly. The French dialogue wasn't the trickiest bit; when the director asked me to leave the room and mime staggering back in with a tray laden with coffee pot, milk jug, sugar bowl and basket of brioche, I had trouble controlling myself, as this ridiculous image of Julie Walters as the deaf, elderly waitress in the 'Two Soups' sketch immediately leapt into my brain — and refused to go away.

Obviously the Louise the director visualises is indeed a parody of the type of comedic character featured in many a Victoria Wood sketch. If it's a bumbling maid you're after, then apparently I'm your woman. Humph. A six-month contract in the West End, of course I'm pleased, but I'm still convinced there must be some mistake.

I swing around the corner into St Martin's Lane, collar pulled up against the driving rain. We have been previewing for two weeks now and tonight is press night, with critics, management and theatre angels (investors) invited. No pressure.

There's still a part of me that's convinced

whenever I arrive at The Belgrave Theatre, the stage doorman will say, 'Not you again. Look, love, I've told you before, you can't come in. This is a *professional* theatre for *professional* actors.'

I mean, my name's not up in lights with the others, is it? No, but if you happen to have a magnifying glass handy, at the foot of the poster you can just about decipher ...

Introducing Emily Forsyth as Louise

'Evening, Doug,' I say, ticking my name off.

'Evening,' he grunts, slithering down from his stool and taking my key from the hook.

'Don't suppose any of those are for me?' I ask longingly, indicating the array of first-night bouquets.

'Take a look,' he says with a shrug, eyes glued to *The One Show.*

Yesss! There, at the back, hidden by all the dramatic, OTT, beribboned floral arrangements, is a simple orchid with my name stapled to the cellophane.

Break a leg!
Best wishes from
all at Whiteley Productions.

Lovely of the management, I'm touched, but I can't help wishing they were from someone else.

I wend my way up two floors to my dressing room. It has a brass plaque on the door ...

EMILY FORSYTH PRIVATE LIVES

Sadly, the glamour stops there: step inside, and you will be struck by the faded, peeling Regency wallpaper, the grubby, threadbare carpet, the yellowish-brown stain on the ceiling, the one-armed chair with foam spilling from a rip in the seat, the dusty light bulbs (most of which have blown) around the cracked mirror, the rusty, Victorian radiator which doesn't radiate, and the resident mouse, whom I've christened Colin. And yet, I AM IN PARADISE.

Not long to go now until Act Three and my first entrance — oh *God*. I practise my breathing exercises and unwrap a Vocalzones lozenge. There is a faint tap at the door.

'Come in!'

'These just arrived for you,' wheezes Doug, one hand holding the door frame, the other a sheaf of deep red roses wrapped in green gauze.

'Thank you!' I say, leaping up and taking them from him.

He mumbles something under his breath and shuffles off down the corridor.

I tear open the envelope:

Buona fortuna!
Amore mio, ti voglio sposare.
~ Francesco.

How sweet! *Good luck! My love, I want to ? you. Francesco.*

Sposare? I haven't a clue what this verb means. *I want to ? you.* The random, wild translations that are teasing my imagination cause me to blush profusely. I grab my pocket Italian dictionary, sitting amongst my good luck cards, put on my glasses and flick through the pages:

sportivo
sporto

'Miss Forsyth, this is your call.'

sposa
sposalizio
sposare ~ to marry; to espouse.

The dictionary falls to the floor. I feel like all the air has been sucked out of my lungs. I catch sight of my reflection; face flushed under my beret, eyes the size of pizza pies.

'Miss Forsyth to the stage. Miss Forsyth to the stage, please.'

Jelly-legged, I make my way downstairs to prompt corner, dizzied by the crazy, jumbled up emotions spinning around my head. I collect my string bag of bread and lettuce from the props table, and take up position in the wings, waiting to make my first entrance, heart battering my rib cage. I love Francesco, of that I'm sure; I think about him constantly; he makes me feel alive, special, desired, respected, and I hate being parted from him; but if I marry him that would mean moving to Italy. Do I want to give up my dream just when I've been granted my first (biggish) break? All the hardships, the sacrifices I've made over the last few years, surely I owe it to myself to keep on this road and not allow my judgement to be clouded over by my emotional need to be loved, and my fear of this possibly being the last chance saloon.

But then again, have I invested *too* much hope, *too* much determination in my acting dream? Is it really the be-all and end-all? Do I want to end up a lonely old Miss Havisham with nothing but a scrapbook of yellowing newspaper reviews for company? And what about the girls? And Faye in particular? How can I abandon her? She needs the love and support of her close friends more than ever now. After all, I am Tariq's godmother and should be on hand to help

355

bring about his safe return. (Precisely *what* I can do I haven't the foggiest, but I'm working on it.) And Isabella? How would she feel to suddenly have to share her home and her father with a strange woman who can only speak a smattering of her language?

What lies ahead for me now depends on my response to Francesco's message.

From the darkness of prompt corner the stage manager mouths, 'Break a leg!' and points his thumb upwards.

I force my quivering lips into a smile.

I am so excited I almost forget to breathe. Mustn't miss my cue. Here I go … I inhale deeply and move towards the light …

♥

Marriage, Mafia & Mozzarella,
the sequel to *Learning To Fly*
will be published in 2018.

Follow me on Facebook
www.facebook.com/janelambertauthor
or Twitter
@janelambert22

21388614R00201

Printed in Great Britain
by Amazon